Praise for the Wereplanets series

"Crystal Jordan entrances and intrigues with...a series of intertwined novellas about a sensuous world of shape shifters and the mates that love them. Sit back, relax, and enjoy the world that is the Wereplanets." *-Talia, Joyfully Reviewed*

"This is the first book I read by Crystal Jordan and I could not put it down. So many emotions in this book longing, being lost, being found and being loved. Great supernatural romance with a strong male and female that find one another. 5 stars." *-Heather Gilmore*

"Full of surprises, this book is a fun, sweaty read! I'm looking forward to more from this author!" *-Zeek*

"This book will knock your socks off! I bought this book because I was intrigued by the stories (I love futuristics and shifter novels.) and am I sooo glad I did. Thank you, Crystal Jordan for writing this wonderful novel! It is on my keeper shelf for life!"

WEREPLANETS

COMPLETE SERIES

CRYSTAL JORDAN

CJ BOOKS

Wereplanets

Published by CJ Books

Book cover by GetCovers

Edits by Twin Tweaks Editing

First print edition 2017

CONTENTS

Dedication

First and foremost, this book is dedicated to Michal, best friend extraordinaire, the Mad Madam M, and the only girl I'd ever call my heterosexual life partner. Thanks for sticking by me even if this writing thing isn't something you always "get."

Much love and heartfelt thanks goes to my fellow smut peddlers without whom I might never have gotten up the nerve to submit a book for publication. They are Eden Bradley, Loribelle Hunt, R.G. Alexander, Dayna Hart, Jennifer McKenzie, Robin L. Rotham, Gemma Halliday, Gwen Hayes, and Lillian Feisty.

Finally, this one is for Grams. I love you for always believing in me and kicking me to write that first story.

~Crystal

In Ice

WEREPLANETS
BOOK 1

CRYSTAL JORDAN

CJ BOOKS

Chapter 1

"Help me! Please...somebody help."

Jain's teeth chattered as she scanned the foreign landscape. Snow covered the rocky ground in a thick layer, and massive trees surrounded the clearing on all sides, hemming her in so she couldn't get her bearings. Night began to fall, and the temperature dropped rapidly. Crossing her arms over her breasts, she rubbed her numb hands over her biceps to try to stimulate circulation. God, she was so cold. Ice bit into her legs, scraping the skin away and leaving her feet raw and bleeding.

She'd been wandering around naked since her ship crashed, and her personal pod had released her from cryogenic freeze. Had anyone else made it out? The ship had held a full crew and one other passenger besides her. It had exploded in a fiery array of reds, yellows, and oranges, but she'd seen no one else from the ship. The roiling smoke had spun through the towering trees and into the afternoon sky in twists of black soot. Since no rescue party had responded to the crash, she assumed she'd landed in an uninhabited area.

"Hellooooo!" Her voice echoed over the frozen landscape.

With each moment that passed, she felt her strength draining, her ability to reason slipping away. She struggled to collect her wandering thoughts, to plan how to save herself. Fading in and out of consciousness, she wondered how much longer she could last without shelter. She had no idea what planet she was on. She should have landed on Aquatilis, where her brother worked as a marine geneticist, but Aquatilis was almost completely covered in water, and she was in the middle of a mountain range. Something had gone seriously wrong. There weren't supposed to be any other inhabitable planets in this solar system, but she could breathe and the gravity was *almost* normal. Where the hell was she?

Kesuk had seen the fiery explosion in the distance and had come to investigate. His sentries fanned out to surround the clearing. The feud with the Grizzlies had just been settled, but it looked as though they wished to start again. He heaved a weary sigh, his paws crunching through the thick sheet of ice as he drew nearer the inferno. Would they never learn?

Their leaders smiled and bowed to his face while their warriors slaughtered his livestock and stole his women. He slid his tongue over his long fangs, enjoying the idea of catching them breaking the pact. His young daughter might enjoy a Grizzly slave. A low growl of pleasure rumbled through his chest at the thought. He hadn't started this feud, but he'd finish it.

Relishing the prospect of a good fight, he quickened his pace. Rolling his shoulders, he stretched into a lumbering run, his long strides eating the distance. Pricking his ears, he stayed alert for signs of an ambush.

"Help me."

The ragged cry sounded to his left, bringing him up short. His breath snorted clouds in the icy air as he waited to hear it again. Padding lightly, he crept between the trees, winding his way toward the origin of the noise.

A woman. A woman unlike any he'd ever seen. Naked, glorious, tiny, her short tufts of brown hair sleek against her skull. Her eyes drew him, greener than the leaves of a Sitka tree. He ran his tongue down a curved canine tooth, eyeing her softly curved form, the thatch of tight dark curls between her slim thighs. Perhaps it was not his daughter who would gain a slave this day. Her sudden appearance and odd coloring demanded he examine her more closely. His men would investigate the explosion and seek him out to report their findings. They knew their duty because he trained them well.

Foolish of her clan to allow her out alone. What was she doing in the borderlands? Her skin was too pale to be a Crescent or a Grizzly. He sighed in regret as he drew near. Perhaps she was addled; such birth defects or misfortunes were known to happen. She wandered through the snow, her broken gait and dazed expression making it obvious she would freeze to death. And soon. He raised his nose to the wind, trying to catch her scent. She wasn't of his clan, that much he knew, but she was on his land.

She belonged to him.

CHAPTER 2

She dreamed of a polar bear. Massive and frightening, it blurred and shifted, somehow turning into the most beautiful man she'd ever seen. Unfortunately, the man was also frightening. His white-blond hair glinted in the wavering sunlight while his coal-black eyes tracked her like a predator after prey. She squirmed under his gaze, uncertain how to proceed.

Neither of them wore any clothes, and they stood in a great green forest. He towered over her, forcing her to tilt her head back to maintain eye contact as he drew closer. Without warning, he thrust a huge hand into her hair and drew her forward, slanting his mouth over hers, muffling her weak protest against his lips. Hot excitement spun through her, dampening her pussy, making it clench with want. Her breath rushed out, panting against his lips as their kisses grew more urgent. His heavy masculine scent caressed her nose. She couldn't explain her fierce reaction, but she didn't want to, was content to follow his lead.

He forced her back into a snowbank, his big body heating her front as he came down on top of her. Her legs parted to accommodate him, and she gripped his shoulders to pull him closer. She wanted him. She wanted him now. Her fingers slid down his smooth chest, flicking over his flat nipples. He reciprocated by closing his mouth over the tip of her breast and drawing on it strongly. She moaned, sucking in frigid air as her body raged with unbearable heat. Her fingers tangled in his pale hair. The dense, silky texture was unlike anything she'd ever felt before.

Spreading wet kisses up her chest, he bit the side of her neck. She jumped at the sharp sensation, and then tilted her jaw to allow him greater access. The head of his cock rubbed against her pussy lips, probing for entrance. Lifting her hips, she forced him into her. Her slick sex stretched to admit his huge length, making her moan as he thrust deeper and harder, again and again. She wrapped her legs around him, moving with him, their combined body heat melting the cold snow. Hot pleasure came in rolling waves, building—

She jerked awake, still shivering with unspent desire. Panting for breath, she waited for her heart to stop pounding. The dream repeated in her mind. She frowned. She'd never fantasized anything like that before. Not ever. She'd always controlled the sexual encounters with her ex-husband, however unsatisfying those encounters had been for both of them.

Putting thoughts of her sad love life aside, she focused on her surroundings. Gray-striped pelts lined a massive bed, cocooning her in warmth. A fire crackled in a stone hearth, reflecting light in a round room. Leaning forward and twisting her head around, she saw the only entrance was an arched wooden door right next to her bed. The entire room looked like something out of a medieval holostory, except the walls were smooth and curved with laser precision. She squeezed her eyes shut, trying to blink away the remnants of her dream. Where was she now? Pinching herself hard, she winced. Definitely awake. Well, this was a far better scenario than the last time she'd been conscious, when she'd dropped into hypothermia. At least she was warm and sheltered. Lethargy weighed her limbs. She must have been given painkillers of some sort, because her feet ached a little, but not as much as they should. When she tried wiggling her toes, she found they were too swollen to move. Tugging the huge pelt up, she saw that someone had wrapped them in neat bandages.

The sweet, high-pitched sound of a child's giggle pierced the quiet as a little head poked up from the foot of her bed. Maybe six years old, the girl was paler than a moonbeam, her dark gaze dancing with merry laughter.

"You're awake." An odd accent spiced the child's voice, but she was speaking Earthan Standard. Curiouser and curiouser.

Jain decided to gather as much information as she could from the only human she'd seen since she landed on this planet. "Hello. Where am I?"

"Sea Den."

"Seaden?" She raked her memory for a city called Seaden. Nothing came to her.

"What's your name?"

"I'm Miki. Who are you?"

"Miki, that's a pretty name. My name is Jain Roberts."

"My brother's name is Nukilik."

"And how old is Nukilik?"

"We're both seven."

"Seven! That's very grown-up."

Miki nodded, sending her cloud of hair flying. Her smile showed an adorable gap in her front teeth.

Jain found herself smiling back. "And what about your parents? What are their names?"

"Mama's dead. And Papa's name is—"

"Lord Kesuk." A sub-bass voice boomed from the door. "That's enough, Miki. You know you're not supposed to be in here. Go find your nurse."

Miki's little face scrunched up in consternation. "I forgot, Papa."

"We'll discuss that later. Go on." Disapproval laced his deep tone.

Miki scurried away, pausing at the door to give Jain a jaunty little wave goodbye.

Jain tucked the furs under her armpits and attempted to sit up, not wanting to meet the man flat on her back. After a few moments, she admitted defeat. She didn't have the strength to rise. The bed dipped and a large hand settled between her shoulder blades, supporting her with ease, while another hand brought a cup of steaming liquid to her mouth. Her stomach growled, distracting her as she realized she was starving. She cupped her hands around the mug he offered and sipped at the hot liquid.

"Oooh, that's good." It tasted like some kind of spicy chicken stew. She turned to thank Miki's father and came nose-to-nose with the man from her dream. *Her very explicit dream.* Her heart skipped a beat before racing ahead at a gallop when she realized he was naked to the waist. He wore gray leather pants and laced moccasins, but his chest was bare and as smooth as she'd imagined. His hair was damp, but she'd bet when it dried it was the same silver-blond she recalled. Her mouth felt suddenly dry, and she drank more of the broth to stall a moment so she could collect herself before speaking. "Th-thank you."

"You are welcome." His gaze dropped to her lips as he spoke, his hand burning against the bare skin of her back.

She flushed under his scrutiny, smoothing her hand across the pelts, fully aware that she was naked. "What is this place?"

His eyes narrowed, assessing her. "You are not addled."

"Well, I may have hit my head in the crash, but I think I'm all right now." Had he just insinuated that she was stupid? Not knowing where she was made her geographically challenged, damn it, not moronic. It wasn't as though she'd crashed the spaceship. She was just a passenger, not the pilot. Who the hell was he to call her stupid? So, fine, he was huge and intimidating and gorgeous, but that didn't make him some kind of super-genius. She really didn't need to deal with some rude jackass today. Things were already bad enough without any help from him. She squelched her anger as she always did, pulling back from feeling too much. She pasted on a bright smile. "Were you the one who rescued me?"

"I did." Rising, he folded massive arms, triceps standing out in relief. He shifted, raised an eyebrow, and seemed to be waiting for something.

"Um...thank you?" She gritted her teeth over the sentence, hating even the slightest admission that she was incapable. She hated that she'd needed saving at all. She could take care of herself when things went according to her meticulous plans.

He grunted. "What clan are you, and how did you come to my land?"

"I don't understand."

"Don't toy with me, little bear." He stalked closer to the bed, looming over her.

She shrank back into the pillows. "I...I'm not from a *clan*. Am I in Scotland?" Relief sang through her. This explained everything. Her spacecraft had landed back on Earth. Someone could tell her why her ship had crashed and if anyone else had survived. Clans, indeed. "I was on my way to Aquatilis."

He snarled, his upper lip curling in disgust. "The fish people."

Assuming he must be one of the purists so adamant about not mixing human genes with animal, she sighed. This would be an ugly argument. She put on her best lecturing teacher face. "It's necessary for the survival of humanity to adapt to the conditions of other planets before the sun dies. Gene-splicing is the best way to make that happen."

Shock flashed across his face for a moment, followed by swift calculation. "You are Earthan?"

"Of course I'm Earthan. What else would I be?"

He leaned against the footboard, staring at her in complete disbelief. It was the most human expression she'd seen on his face since he'd walked in the door. "You left Earth before the sun died? That was a ship that exploded?"

"Yes, of course it—wait, what do you mean *before the sun died*? Scientists say it will be around for at least another hundred years." What the hell was going on here?

"No, our loremasters teach that the sun died too soon. All but the humans on the four experimental planets perished. That was nearly five hundred Turns ago." He watched her closely, waiting for her reaction, something akin to awe in his dark eyes.

Shock and doubt roared through her. Her ears buzzed, making her sway. "That isn't funny."

"It is not a jest, little bear."

"This is a joke. A horrible joke. It isn't funny! I don't know what kind of sick game you're playing, but I want my brother. Right now, do you hear me? *Right now.*"

He clamped his hands over her shoulders and shook her in short little jolts. Then he wrapped his fingers around her jaw, forcing her to meet his steady gaze. "Calm yourself."

"Five *hundred* years…no, that can't be. I'm supposed to meet my brother on Aquatilis. He works there. He…he's my only family. The only one I have left. Please…please, tell me it's a mistake." She tried to jerk from his grasp, but he was too strong. Hot tears flooded her eyes, and she choked to fight them back. She couldn't cry in front of this emotionless man who'd just ripped her whole life away with a single sentence.

He released her, stroking the skin along her jaw. "I'm not sure how it's possible, but it is true."

"It's not. I won't believe it." Irrational, unreasonable rage pounded through her, made her glare at him. She knew this wasn't his fault, but he was the only one here to blame. Everything was spinning out of control, and that couldn't happen. This was unacceptable.

A stoic sigh escaped his lips. He bent and gathered her furs tight around her and scooped her off the bed, lifting her as if she were a small child.

"What do you think you're doing? Don't touch me." She wriggled to get down.

"Be still," he snapped. "I'm hardly going to molest you. Invalids and simpletons do not arouse me."

"I am *not* a simpleton." She tugged her left arm free of the pelts and wrapped it around his neck.

"Then stop acting the part. We have a long way to walk, and you cannot travel the distance on your own."

She glowered at him but remained still. Where the hell was he taking her? Why couldn't he just *tell* her what was going on? She fisted her fingers in the furs. Anger simmered through her at one more thing slipping away from her control. She hated that he was right. She couldn't get far by herself, but she wouldn't give him the satisfaction of admitting it.

He chuckled. "Stubborn little bear."

"I'm not a bear. I'm full human."

With each of his strides, her left breast brushed against his chest. Though she wasn't cold, goose bumps shivered over her skin. The friction of each brush of her naked shoulder against his smooth chest seemed exaggerated. Excitement twisted through her, heating her blood until her heart pounded. Her nipples peaked and she was grateful for the camouflage of the thick furs. She tried to control her breathing, but his scent filtered in with every breath. She fought the urge to bury her nose against his neck and breathe deeply. Yeah, that would go over well. Actually, it might and that in itself could be a problem. He rolled his shoulder, and her arm slid across his skin. Oh, God. Just that small movement was enough to make her hyperaware of every inch of her body pressed against his hard muscles.

"Never think for a moment that I don't remember you are unique. You are nothing like my people."

Whispering erupted up and down the cave corridor as they walked through an intricate system of tunnels until she had no idea how far they'd gone. Pale-featured people with dark eyes stared at her from wide rooms and stone hallways. She shrank into Kesuk's chest, avoiding eye contact, feeling their gazes on her as they passed. Shafts of light pierced the gloom from small openings overhead no wider than her fist. Glass capped the holes and made the light reflect and spread.

A bend in the corridor showed an opening so narrow Kesuk had to turn sideways to get through it. The cold slammed into her like a wall of ice once they cleared the protection of the cave. She quickly pulled her arm back inside the pelts, snuggling up against him for warmth. How did he manage to go shirtless? He didn't even seem to notice the frigid wind buffeting them. A guard stood on either side of the entrance. They nodded to Kesuk but stared at her until he grunted at them; then they snapped to attention and resumed scanning the landscape.

"What are they looking for?"

"Predators and enemies." They crested a rise, and Kesuk spun them in a slow circle. "Look around you."

"Predators?" she squeaked. "What kind of predators?" This place got *worse*? She swiveled her head around, trying to see anything dangerous. Jagged mountain peaks covered in snow and a type of tree she'd never seen before soared toward the brilliant blue sky. These trees weren't firs or spruce or any other kind of evergreen she knew of, but they were a rich leafy green against the pure white snow. How was that even possible? It looked like something from an Amazonian rainforest. In the middle of Antarctica.

Nothing but a light breeze seemed to be moving, so she started to relax. They were safe.

Then Kesuk's whole body tensed, and his nostrils flared as he raised his nose to sniff the air. A quick glance back at the guards had them standing at alert on either side of Kesuk, spears in their hands.

"What's happening?" She turned back to look at Kesuk.

"An enemy."

"Who—"

"Shh."

She scanned the tree line in vain, searching for the enemy he spoke of. Straining her eyes, she still couldn't see anything but trees, rocks, and snow. Unease fluttered in her belly.

Suddenly, a large black figure broke through the underbrush. "It's a black bear!" she cried.

"Yes, he's from the Crescent Bear Clan." Kesuk's lips pulled back in a small snarl.

"Is he dangerous?" She flicked her gaze between Kesuk and the enormous bear lumbering toward them through the thick snowbanks. As he drew closer, she could see his muzzle was brown and a white crescent marked the otherwise black fur on his chest.

When the bear reared up on its hind legs and roared, she squeaked and tried to climb Kesuk. Her arm slid back around his neck in a stranglehold.

"Easy, little bear," he soothed, his gaze never leaving the bear.

A horrific sucking noise sounded as the bear seemed to shrink, his bones snapping and retracting, the hair disappearing from his legs until a huge, dark-haired man stood before them. *A very nude man.* She choked, still squeezing the life out of Kesuk, unable to believe what she'd just seen. A shape-shifting bear! There were only supposed to be fish-shifters on Aquatilis. No experiments had ever been conducted with large predators.

The stranger's black eyes gleamed with avarice as they swept over her, lingering on her bare arm and the upper curve of her breast. She retracted her limb into the pelts, trying to cover as much skin as possible. This man was dangerous, that much she knew, and Kesuk didn't seem to like him. He swaggered forward, his gaze never leaving her.

"That's far enough. What news from Meadow Den?" Kesuk's deep growl sounded even lower than usual.

"So the rumor is true, then? A *real* human."

"She crashed on *my* land."

"Does she have a name?"

"*Mine.*" Kesuk's voice was flat and brooked no argument.

The dark-haired man grinned, his fangs flashing as he took another step forward. One of his incisors was broken, the ragged tip impossibly sharper than its twin. His penis twitched and rose into a huge erection as he leered at her. "I'd offer an exchange. Three of yours for her."

An exchange? The man was trying to *buy* her? Three of Kesuk's what? What did they barter with here? Oh, God, he wouldn't give her to the disgusting man, would he? Her stomach executed a slow pitch and roll. After all, what did she know about her rescuer? Feeling light-headed, she started to gag a little, horrified by what the black bear might do to her. Rape at the very least. After he was done with her, would he pass her off to his men? She swallowed hard. If he had even half as many followers as she'd seen in the caves—she cut herself off, ruthlessly suppressing her panic. She couldn't even let herself think it.

Kesuk's arms tightened around her, and she turned into his shoulder, pressing her forehead against his collarbone, struggling to pull air into her dry throat. She was going to vomit, she just knew it.

"She is not for barter." Kesuk growled low, his chest vibrating with the sound. She looked up in time to see enormous fangs begin to slide out of his mouth. Kesuk was a bear, too? Realization hit her right between the eyes.

He was the polar bear in her dream.

Whipping her head around, she saw that the bear had come even closer. She froze, refusing to cower because she had nowhere to go.

"Five of your people for the little tasty."

An inhuman roar exploded from Kesuk, his fangs fully emerging, long, curved, and deadly. Clenching her teeth, she fisted her hands in the pelts to keep from screaming.

"Get off my land, Crescent. I have no more use for you."

Kesuk's guards raised their spears and began circling the man. He snorted at them but backed away, folding over onto all fours and shifting into his bear form as he ran. She shivered at the sickening noise the change made.

After the black bear left, Kesuk shifted her in his arms. "Believe me now, Jain Roberts? Is this the planet you knew? Is this the water world you intended to land on? Are we the advanced people you lived among all your life?" His questions hammered at her disbelief. She'd used his physical presence as a distraction before, but *this*...this she couldn't deny. This wasn't Earth. This wasn't Aquatilis, and she'd seen nothing so far to indicate the type of technology she was used to. And the black bear she'd just witnessed change shouldn't even exist. At least not yet, not in her time.

"Take me back to my room," she whispered, squeezing her eyes shut to block out the bright snowy-white day, so at odds with the black empty void yawning inside of her.

She held herself together during the interminable walk back to her round chamber, focusing on *not* thinking about what had happened to everyone she knew. How terrified they all must have been when the sun died too soon, the horrible deaths they'd faced. Kesuk deposited her in the wide bed, tucking the soft pelts around her. Everything that had happened since the crash hit her in one relentless wave after another. She couldn't take it all in, and the truth overwhelmed her. She twisted away from him. Jesus, she hated losing control in front of people. Burying her face in the furs, she tried to stifle the sobs she couldn't stop.

"I'm sorry." His hand cupped the back of her head, stroking her hair gently.

"Please, leave me alone for a while."

"I will return soon. We have much to discuss."

He moved away from the bed, leaving her cold and bereft. She didn't know what to do, what to think. Never intending to return to Earth, she'd left everything behind to join her brother on the Aquatilis colony. Pressure built in her chest, choking her. Tears leaked from her eyes, and she let herself sob into the blankets. Her brother, her only family, gone. All the people on board her ship, including her brother's colleague Sera Gibbons. She hadn't known any of them well, but they would have at least been with her now. And Sera, well, they might have become friends. A million possibilities spun away into nothingness. Everything and everyone she knew was dead, killed by nature and time. She was five hundred years from where she started. Loss and grief tore at her. She could cry forever and never be rid of it.

"I mnek." Kesuk nodded a greeting to the guard outside Jain's door as he passed, his stride eating the distance between him and the mouth of Sea Den.

The woman was a distraction he didn't need right now. Or ever. She attracted him too much. He'd come close to ripping the Crescent's throat out for daring to want her. She belonged to *him,* and no Crescent was going to take her from him. He shook his head. No. No, she was only here temporarily, so he couldn't get attached to her. She couldn't matter enough to make him lose control. He had his people to care for and protect. Losing control in front of an enemy was not a luxury he could afford.

He was master of himself and everything within Sea Den. She'd know that soon enough. She was a temporary distraction. Nothing more. A feral grin pulled at his lips. Perhaps she could serve as a very pleasurable temporary distraction. When she recovered her strength, he could think of many things to do with that pretty little body of hers. He had to keep in mind that she would only be here until he could hand the last Earthan over to the next trading vessel.

A *real* Earthan. Unaltered, unable to morph between human and animal form. Such a thing was unheard of on any of the four inhabited planets. Humans were extinct. He shook his head in astonishment, struggling to bend his mind around the explanation. Earth itself had faded almost into myth among his people. It wasn't until the weretigers' spaceship landed three Turns ago that they'd known settlements on other planets still existed. In fact, the weretiger king, Amir Varad, was scheduled to return before Thaw to exchange trade goods on his way to Aquatilis. That was only three weeks away. He respected Varad—perhaps the weretiger could offer some insight on how the woman could have been floating in space for centuries and be perfectly functioning after a crash landing.

A million questions raced through his mind as he calculated possibilities and probabilities. What had happened to make her ship go off course? Why had they never made it to Aquatilis? What was the likelihood that she'd land on the *one* planet in this solar system besides the fish world able to sustain life?

"Papa!"

Miki's small voice echoed along the corridor as she scurried after him, unable to keep up with his longer stride. An Arctic bear cub, Nukilik, trotted alongside her. Affection and pride squeezed his heart when he saw them. Miki puffed up beside him and collapsed against his legs with dramatic exhaustion.

Kesuk grinned down at her. "Yes?"

"Are you going sea swimming? Can we come? Please, Papa?" Miki's dark eyes widened, and she folded her hands together to plead with him. Nukilik nodded in agreement, bumping his shoulder up against Kesuk's other leg.

Please, Papa?

The cub's shaky telepathy was improving daily. Another fierce wave of pride hit Kesuk's chest, followed by an endless need to protect his young against all threats. He would not lose them to predators as he had lost their mother. Lingering pain echoed in his heart at the thought of Maruska. Their daughter looked so much like her. She would have loved to see their cubs grow.

"You can come, but stay near me at all times. Nukilik, go get four more guards to accompany us while Miki and I change."

Yes, my lord. The cub gave an exaggerated bow of his long neck before scurrying off.

"Scamp."

"Ready, Papa?" Miki tugged on his boot lacings.

He scooped her up and flipped her into the air, catching her over his shoulder while she squealed in delight. "Ready."

He set her down and watched while she changed into Arctic bear form, her little body stooping onto all fours, pulling in as white fur spread down her arms and legs. Her nose turned black and elongated into a snouted point. She bowed her head, her neck stretching in to the long slim line characteristic of his species. Tiny curved ears popped from the top of her widened skull. Though he'd done it himself countless times, the sound of changing forms had always bothered him, the strange suction and snapping pop of bone and cartilage as the body re-formed made his skin crawl.

She shook from head to claws, wagging her tuft of a tail so vigorously it shook her whole back end. Tumbling forward in a wild display of acrobatics, she landed with a splay-legged thump in front of him. He ruffled the fur on her head.

Let's go, Papa! Hurry, hurry.

"All right, youngling. Patience." In a moment, he'd assumed his own bear form, flexing his claws against the cave floor. His cub pranced on her paws ahead of him down the corridor, turning back to watch his progress every few steps, her black eyes shining with excitement. At the last fork in the tunnel to the sea entrance, they met with Nukilik and the four requested guards, two in human form and two in bear.

"My lord." The soldiers dipped their heads in salute.

He swung in next to the front guard, who glanced sideways several times before speaking.

Amir Varad comes soon.

Kesuk grunted. *The weretigers will land before Thaw, yes.*

The human would make an excellent bargaining chip.

Kesuk's hackles rose, and he had to rein himself in from snapping at the other bear. What was *wrong* with him today? The soldier was right, was he not? Isn't that what he should use her for? He'd saved her. She couldn't stay here. The weretigers would want her and would pay a great sum to have her. He snarled even thinking of it, stalking down the twisting tunnels until he reached the icy wading pool that opened out into the frozen ocean.

Several hunters passed them on their way in to the warm fires of the upper caverns, their fishing lines full of the day's catch. Miki plunged into the pool with her usual reckless enthusiasm while Nukilik preferred to wade in and test the water first. He'd worried for them since Maruska had died, but they'd adjusted well during the last two Turns. He was the one who'd struggled to move on. An unmated leader was looked upon unfavorably, a sign of instability in the clan.

A tilt of his muzzle signaled the two guards in human form to keep watch at the sea entrance while the two in bear form scouted out into the open water, wary of orcas. Shaking away his concerns, Kesuk slid in after his cubs, making sure they stayed above water, enjoying the rare time he had to devote to them.

Before he could stop himself, he wondered how the woman was faring. He licked his lips, anticipation building in his gut as he thought of seeing her again. The slim lines of her pale body were burned into his mind, and he wanted to stroke his hands over her, burying his cock inside of her again and again until they were both spent. He sighed. Unfortunately, there were a few things she needed to know before they could begin to explore the attraction between them. He doubted she would take it well when he explained the new position she had found for herself by crashing on his land.

Chapter 3

"I'm sorry I lost it earlier." Jain blurted out an apology to Kesuk as soon as he made it through the doorway, her cheeks flushing hotly. She had blubbered all over the man, and he hadn't even turned a hair, just tucked her in like a child. She was furious with herself for the lapse.

"What did you lose?"

Did she have to spell it out for him? Her face heated further. "I'm sorry I cried in front of you."

He raised a brow. "Are you sorry you cried or just that you cried in front of me?"

"Both." She glanced away, not meeting his eyes. "I'm just sorry. Can we talk about something else?"

"If you wish."

"What was that man going to trade me for? Five of something?"

"Five of my people they've taken as slaves."

"Slaves! That's awful. Barbaric."

He growled, his eyes narrowing. "Beware of passing judgment, little bear. Slavery is common practice here for those captured in raids or battles."

"You have slaves?" Something in his face made her swallow hard. Damn. She'd just insulted the big, scary man who'd saved her bacon and kept her from black bear rapists.

He returned a tight smile. "We need to discuss what to do with you now. I saved you, so your life is now mine, according to the customs of the Bear Clans."

Her eyes popped wide in shock. He thought he *owned* her? She bristled. No one, but *no one*, controlled her. "I don't live by those laws."

"You do now."

"So you saved me and I have to serve you forever?"

He shook his head. "No, slavery is not permanent. You work until your debt to me is paid."

"And who decides when my debt is paid?"

"I do."

She scoffed. "Oh, that's fair."

A deep growl rumbled up from his chest. His eyes flashed as he leaned close, getting right into her face, their noses almost touching. "You are not of the Bear, so I will forgive that insult. Once. Do not make the mistake again, and do not *ever* question my honor. You will be released when your debt is paid."

She bobbed her head in a nod, fear and adrenaline making her heart race. The man was enormous and he had fangs. He could kill her with both hands behind his back. She licked her parched lips and cleared her throat. "And where will I go then? As you said, I'm not a Bear. I have no clan to return to. From what I've experienced so far, I doubt I would survive on this planet without protection."

"There are far greater dangers than rival clans and the cold. We will negotiate your position here when the time comes, little bear. Rest now."

"Wait. Please. How will I work off my debt? I can't cook or sew or do anything domestic. We had machines to do that for us in my time. I taught history to children on Earth." She struggled upward again, and the furs slipped down, baring her breasts. Squeaking, she hauled the covers back up while he watched, his gaze lingering on the edge of the pelt. A hot blush flooded her cheeks again, but she set her jaw and ignored her embarrassment. After the incident with the black bear, she wasn't taking any chances. "I assume the work won't include *servicing* any of the men on this planet."

A dimple tucked into his cheek as his white teeth flashed. "That isn't work, little bear. That's pure pleasure."

Her mouth opened and closed, but no sound came out. Her mind replayed the dream she'd had of them together. Pleasure didn't even begin to describe it. She couldn't help but wonder if he was as good in real life as she imagined. Squeezing her legs together, she tried to quell the sudden ache between them. She'd just met him—how could he do this to her?

"Perhaps you need a demonstration."

His gaze heated and he leaned toward her, his lips touching hers. She caressed his jaw as her mouth moved under his. His hands caught hers, forcing them behind her back, holding them so she couldn't move. He tilted his head to deepen the kiss, sliding his tongue along her bottom lip.

"Open for me."

Obeying, she stroked his tongue with her own. Goose bumps erupted over her flesh, and her heart rate kicked into warp speed. Her skin felt too hot and too tight. Wetness flooded her sex, made her moan and press closer to him. She tugged at her arms, wanting to touch him, but he shifted her wrists into one big hand, using the other to thrust the furs down. His fingertips closed over her breast, his rough skin abrading her nipple.

"Oh, God." Her breath rushed in and out, but she still couldn't suck in enough oxygen to satisfy her lungs. She arched into his caress, pushing her breasts forward.

Nothing had ever felt this good. His steely hold almost made it better for her. *Sexier.* It was wrong to be so turned on by this, but she couldn't remember why just now. A low rumble sounded in his throat as he swooped down to capture her nipple in his teeth, worrying the peaked flesh. He flicked his tongue over the tip, exciting her further, making her cry out.

A light knock sounded on the door. "Lord Kesuk."

Kesuk jerked back, panting hard as he stood and tugged the cover up over her chest. He stalked to the door and flung it open to glare at the intruder. "Imnek."

A gangly young man stood beyond the threshold, his gaze darting from Kesuk's glower to Jain's flushed face and back again. Shifting nervously under Kesuk's glare, he cleared his throat.

"Speak, boy," Kesuk demanded.

Snapping his gaze away from Jain, Imnek focused on the hulking man in front of him. "M-my lord. The weretigers have landed and will visit High Den before traveling to Sea Den."

"Hmph. Leave us." Kesuk shut the door in the boy's face.

Jain cleared her throat, struggling to come to grips with what had just happened. No man had ever made her want so much, so quickly. Not even her husband. Just thinking about Kesuk made her body throb—having him near pushed her past anything she'd ever experienced. All the feelings rushing through her scared her to death. Feelings weren't logical, weren't controllable. She needed to step back and *think,* and she couldn't do that with him touching her and confusing her. When he swung to face her, his gaze hard with lust, she grasped at the first thing she could think of to distract him. "Um...weretigers?"

"Yes."

"They landed? They have a spaceship?"

Hope fluttered in her chest. There was technology somewhere. Not everywhere was like this, where they had slaves and bartered with human lives and kissed people without asking. She pressed her tingling lips together. The man had actually held her down to kiss her! Her sex clenched at the mere thought of what he'd done. She shook herself. She was not excited about some backwoods barbarian sticking his tongue down her throat. She *was not.*

"Yes."

"And...?" Could she have another word please? She wanted to know about the other wereanimals. Was he allowed to tell her more? Did he even know? Maybe the weretigers were better. Maybe she could go with them.

"And they will trade with the Grizzlies before they come here."

"Grizzlies? Not the Crescents?"

"No. Meadow Den is too remote; they will meet with the Crescents in the border-lands."

"I see." Only she didn't see. Grizzlies? Borderlands? "So, where do the weretigers live?"

"Vesperi."

"Is that a planet? Or is it a country on a planet?"

"A planet in a neighboring solar system."

"Are there any other people in *this* solar system?"

"Aquatilis."

Realization slapped her straight in the face. Oh, shit. She knew what planet she was on now. Icy dread slid down her spine. Only one other planet in Aquatilis's solar system could support human life, and she didn't even want to remember the stories about what happened to the humans who settled there—*here.* She shuddered, her stomach roiling because she had to ask and she really didn't want to. This should not have happened. She should be safe on Aquatilis five hundred years ago. Licking her lips, she forced the question out. "This...this is Alysius, isn't it?"

Please say no. Please say no. Please say no. For once, she actually wanted to be dead wrong.

"Yes."

Again with the one-word answers. She wanted to shake him. "Yes?"

His eyebrow hiked up. "Yes, this is Sea Den on Alysius. Home of the Arctic Bear Clan. I am Lord Kesuk, leader of the clan. Are there any more questions?"

She shook her head, mute. Entire settlements had been wiped out on this planet, the first ever to be colonized. Large animals had attacked and killed the unprepared settlers. When they'd founded the colony on Aquatilis, they'd abandoned the failed attempt on Alysius until they could develop a way to eradicate the animals without damaging the planet's ecosystem. Colonization had still been in its infancy when she left Earth. "In my time, scientists said adapting to Aquatilis and becoming merpeople would prove easier for humans than staying on this planet."

He sucked his teeth at the mention of merpeople. "It takes a predator to kill a predator. The first bear-shifters settled here just before the sun failed. We had to learn to survive with the means at our disposal. Or die with those who came before us."

"My brother said—"

"You journeyed to Aquatilis to join him, yes? What of the rest of your family?" He switched topics, turning the focus on her. She hated that. She didn't like to talk about herself or her past. Especially not her family.

"They were dead. After my divorce—"

He interrupted again. "What is *dee*-vorce?"

"My husband and I—"

"You are *mated*?" His eyes narrowed, his shoulders tensing.

A frisson of panic slipped up her spine, sweat breaking out on her forehead. It was the same look he'd worn before he mentioned his precious honor. What had she said? She raked her mind for what she might have done to piss him off now. "Divorce is when you get *un*mated."

"There is no unmating. Mating is for life."

She threw her hands up. "Fine, then. I'm a widow. He's been dead half a millennium. Oh, *darn*. Happy now?"

He growled but made no further response.

"Anyway. My husband and I divorced, and I was at loose ends, so I decided to stay with the one family member I had left. The Aquatilis colony was looking for teachers for the growing merchildren, and I hoped my brother and I would become closer if I moved near."

Now, why had she said that? He didn't need to know that "distant" was a good way to describe her relationship with her family. She'd been the misfit non-genius in her logical, rational, scientific family. She sighed, her mood darkening. Any opportunity she had to try developing a relationship with her brother was gone now, and she ached for the loss.

Her eyes smarted, but she resolutely pushed the tears away. There was nothing she could do about it. She shouldn't cry over something that never was.

"Your marriage was unhappy?"

"To put it mildly."

"He beat you?" Kesuk's fangs popped out, his face reddening.

"No!"

He relaxed a little, fangs retracting.

How could she say this in a nice way? "He just didn't want me."

"Fool. Who would not want you?" He snorted.

There was a loaded question. "Um. Well, he wanted other women."

And there came the fangs again. "He was unfaithful to you, *his mate*? Did the man have *no* honor?"

"Look, buddy. Honor wasn't a big deal back then. Neither was infidelity, really. I just got tired of dealing with it, so I bitched at him and he left me for his girlfriend. We divorced. End of story." And end of discussion. She didn't want to talk about this. Time to go back to her questions about Alysius.

His eyes lost focus for a moment, and his head cocked to the side as though he were listening to something. How powerful was a bear's hearing? She didn't know.

When his gaze sharpened and fixed on her, she shivered under his stare. If just a look did that to her, she didn't stand a chance if he touched her again. That terrified her. She controlled everything about her life, and he was not the kind of man to let her run things. That much she knew already. And he thought she was a *slave*. Nothing about him should turn her on. He was pushy, peremptory, and rude.

"I am needed elsewhere. I will return later."

She opened her mouth to ask another question, but he issued a sharp nod, then turned and left the room, leaving her mouth flapping over an outraged response.

"Well, I was just dismissed, huh?" She stuck her tongue out at the now-closed door.

Yep. Definitely rude, crude, and socially unacceptable. At least in her society. So why had she stared at his tight ass in those leather pants while he walked away from her?

She sighed, wondering where he'd needed to go. Whether she liked it or not, she was bored and lonely without him.

Chapter 4

Jain's eyes narrowed as she lay in that big bed of hers. Her pretty mouth tightened into a scowl of annoyance. Tension stiffened Kesuk's shoulders. He'd had enough to deal with in the two days since he'd seen her without coaxing her out of an ill humor. He considered her for a moment before deciding she needed a reminder of who was in charge here.

"Would you like to see more of your new home, slave?" He asked it just to tease her. He couldn't help himself. His little bear reacted so well. Remembering the indignant look on her face when he'd left to handle an altercation between two soldiers had made him laugh, and he resisted the smile that pulled at his lips now. Preparing for the weretigers' arrival had consumed his every waking moment the last few days, but he'd found himself thinking of her far too much. So, here he was, taking the first opportunity he had to come to her.

"Can I have some clothes first?" She shifted, tucking the covers tight to her chest.

"You have no clothes?"

She smacked a hand down on the fur pelts. "Nope. Completely naked here."

"Are you, now?" A slow grin spread over his face, and he let his gaze slide down the soft curves of her body outlined by the pelts.

His cock twitched as he recalled the first sight of her naked in the snow. It was all he could do not to slide his hand to his leathers to readjust the uncomfortable fit. Her breath caught as her eyes locked with his. She felt this, too, he knew it.

Blushing, she looked away and licked her lips. He cut off a groan. Surely she knew what that did to a man. He wanted that little pink tongue caressing his cock.

Her gaze flicked back to him. "Don't look at me like that."

"Like what?" He let his desire for her show, so there was no mistake, just to see how she'd respond. It was only a matter of time until he had her. It had been a very long time since any woman presented any challenge. For the duration of her stay here, she would be his.

"Like *that*."

His grin widened, and he ran his tongue down his canine tooth.

"Like you want to undress me."

"You are already undressed."

"That's entirely beside the point."

He approached the bed and watched her breathing speed up as he neared. Her gaze flicked over him, cheeks flushed. Good, he made her nervous. An excellent place to start. As he reached out to touch her, her pupils expanded, staring at his hard dick straining the fastenings of his pants.

"If you wish me to stop looking at you as though I want you naked, then do not look as though you want me to undress you."

"I'm not." Her voice was breathless, her gaze riveted on his cock.

"Stop."

"What?" She looked up at him, naked hunger on her face.

"We go." He bent and scooped her up before he talked himself into burying himself between her legs and staying for a full Turn. She was well enough to suffer from boredom, but not well enough to walk. If she couldn't walk, she was too weak for the hard sex he had in mind. He schooled himself to patience, knowing he would have her slim legs wrapped around his waist soon enough. Or around his face. He banished that thought before he made it impossible to walk correctly.

Her small form fitted against his chest, her cheek on his shoulder, her short dark hair tickling his skin. The sweet smell of her filled his nose. He breathed in, enjoying the experience of being this close to her.

"Where are we going?" Her arm slid around his neck.

Eyes closed for a moment, he savored the feel of her fingers splayed across his shoulder, her other hand pressed to his chest, stroking over his nipple. His breath hissed out. She would drive him to madness. His cock rode the seam of his leathers as he walked out of her chamber and into the main corridor.

"Is everyone here usually naked?" Her wide green eyes followed the progress of a soldier who'd obviously just assumed his human form.

Kesuk growled to hurry the guard on his way, not liking the way his little bear stared at the other man.

Glancing down at her, he answered her question with a shrug. "No, but our clothing does not come with us when we shift."

She blushed, glancing into a side cave at an equally nude woman before turning away. "We had laws in my time about indecent exposure."

"Indecent? Nudity is a natural thing, little bear." He frowned. The advanced past had been so provincial?

"Ooooh." Her grip tightened around his neck when she spied what lay beyond the end of the tunnel. He gritted his teeth as her breasts moved against his chest, nothing but the edge of a fur keeping her soft flesh from pressing against his.

Dripstone rose from the floor and spiked down from the ceiling, creating a circular stone paddock. Only his ancestors had been able to carve with such precision. They'd lost so much in the centuries since settlement. The little one in his arms brought that home to him more forcefully than anything had since the weretigers landed on Alysius.

"Stalactites and stalagmites. I saw them in the Carlsbad Caverns when I was a child. These are huge compared to those."

"Dripstone. It is created by dripping water." He jerked his chin to indicate the droplets of water falling from the tips of the stone.

"What is this place? And why are some of the areas laser cut and the rest natural?" Her wave encompassed the cavern and the dripstone.

"Whatever was expedient. This area needed to be large for the herds."

"Herds?"

They cleared the upper tunnel, and noise from the paddock rose to an overwhelming cacophony. From this position, they overlooked the wide valley of stone separated into paddocks by carved barriers. Loud bawling of cattle and sheep in large grassy fields echoed around them. Sunlight streamed through thousands of covered light shafts in the cavern roof. Men and women roamed the herds, checking the health of young calves, rounding up the sheep for shearing.

Jain leaned forward as he backed away from the precipice, trying to look at everything at once. A sweet smile spread over her lips when she got a better view of the herdsmen. When she stopped trying to keep a stranglehold on every detail, she let herself enjoy life. He could help her in that area. She might even thank him.

"Where are we going next?"

She turned that wondrous smile on him, and he almost missed a step. The woman was beautiful. All the women on this planet had dark eyes and were tall with sleek muscular bodies. Not Jain. Perhaps it was her childlike size that made him feel protective. Even that excuse sounded flimsy to him, because he'd never thought of her as a child. Since the moment he'd seen her, he'd wanted her, and he always got what he wanted.

"We go to sup in the main cavern."

He wound his way through the twisting tunnels with an ease born of long practice, the smells of cooking food calling to him.

She sighed. "I'll never find my way back."

He grinned. "Reach into my back pocket."

Her eyes widened, snapping up to his face. "What?"

"My back pocket, little bear. The left one."

Her hand slipped from his shoulder down his back, smoothed over his bare skin, bumped the top of his leathers before curling into his pocket. His breath hissed out as her fingers moved over his ass, rubbing against him as she searched the pocket.

Keeping his tone innocent, he shrugged. "Oh, did I say left? I meant right. Try the other pocket."

"You did that on purpose!" She slapped his chest.

"Perhaps. The right pocket, little bear. Go on." Teasing her meant teasing himself, and he wanted to take her against the tunnel wall. Right now. He usually had more control than this when dealing with women. Frowning, he shook himself. He was no randy boy intent on mating with anything that moved.

Dipping her hand down, she tugged a folded sheet of parchment from his leathers. She smoothed it out against his shoulder. "It's a map."

"Yes."

Her smile was back and was the first thing his people saw as they walked into the wide cavern. All noise fizzled to a slow stop. She tensed, going rigid in his arms when she noticed they were the center of attention. She looked up at him in distress.

"Shh, little bear. They are simply curious about you. It will fade the more you are around them."

Her lips tightened and she said nothing, her chin jerking down in a small nod. She tugged up the furs self-consciously. He hadn't the heart to tell her they'd all seen her naked the day he brought her in from the snow. It had taken many people many hours to get her warm again, to save her fingers and toes from frostbite.

"Jain!" Miki waved from the head table, bouncing in her chair, a huge smile splitting her face. Her nurse saved her cup from tipping over as Miki's waving got a bit too enthusiastic.

Jain smiled back at Kesuk's daughter and returned a small wiggle of her fingers.

"Where is Nukilik?" Kesuk directed his question at the nurse as he settled Jain into the chair to the left of his.

"He decided to break his fast with the guards in the lower caverns."

"Ah." He smiled, remembering he had done the same as a boy, eager to learn the ways of warriors.

"Have you met Nukilik?" The nurse turned a kind smile on Jain, and Kesuk blessed her for her open warmth. He had chosen well when he made her caretaker for his cubs.

"I've only met Miki and Kesuk. Oh, and my guard, Imnek, when I tried to leave my room." Jain turned an accusing glare on Kesuk.

"It was for your own protection."

"Sure it was, but then I am a *slave* here, aren't I?" Anger made Jain's brilliant green eyes almost incandescent.

He leaned close to speak in her ear. "Yes, and as such, you are under my protection. The caves can be dangerous, little bear. Your insistence on independence does not erase the need for caution."

She wrinkled her pert nose at him and turned away to speak to Miki's nurse.

He chuckled, sorry he'd missed young Imnek trying to keep her in her room as Kesuk had ordered. As he'd said, it was for her own protection. She wasn't yet well, and even with his map, she could easily become lost in the caverns. Some of the caves were no longer in use, and it would take a while to track her, especially if she fell and hurt herself. Refocusing on the women at his table, he caught a lively conversation about Earthan versus Bear Clan politics.

"It's too much." Jain folded her arms and glared at the stubborn man across from her. As usual, Kesuk remained cool and collected. It made her want to kick him. Why couldn't she ever hold on to her calm when he was around? He'd invited himself into her room again, and Imnek had just let him in. This was why messing with the boss was never a good plan—they did whatever they wanted and didn't ask for permission.

"What is?"

"What? This! All this." Her hands flapped to encompass the room, which was now overburdened with more clothes than she could ever wear.

Kesuk shrugged. "You said you needed clothing."

"I just wanted an outfit."

"You have been outfitted."

She sighed, knowing she wouldn't win this one. Settling back into the padding of her large chair, she toyed with the cord that belted her leather pants. Kesuk leaned back into the cushions of the matching chair that sat opposite hers. A crackling fire lit the handsome planes of his face. "Thank you. It's more than I need."

"If you need anything else, ask in the kitchens and they will give you whatever you require."

"I'm used to providing for myself. Working for what I have." She shifted under his stare. Why had she even admitted that?

"You are not yet well enough to work. Give yourself some time. You nearly died, little bear. You look lovely in that."

Pleasure warmed her, and she brought herself up short. His approval shouldn't matter this much to her. She shouldn't care about this man. He was dangerous to her peace of mind, her hard-won calm. When the weretigers came, she was leaving. She needed to remember that. She shrugged, brushing a negligent hand down her bottle-green wool tunic. It matched her eyes. "Thanks."

He casually waved in a serving woman who brought a tray of food. The woman smiled at Jain and she grinned back. Her name was...Bel? "Thank you for bringing me dinner."

"Supper," Bel corrected gently. "We call it supper here."

"Supper." Jain nodded in acknowledgment. She noticed the tray Bel set down held more food than she could eat in a week. She raised her eyebrow, meeting Kesuk's gaze as Bel left the room. "Inviting yourself to dinner?"

He lounged in his chair, handing her a mug of mulled ale, serving up plates for both of them. "You don't really want to dine alone."

She didn't, but it irritated her that he said it. "You know me so well."

"I wish to."

Something about the position of his body or the hot, hard expression on his face made her recall her dream. "Kesuk, the day we met..."

"Yes?"

Hot blood singed her cheeks, and she knew her face had gone bright red. Smooth, Jain.

Very smooth. "Did we...did you...what exactly happened after you found me?"

"You don't remember, Jain?" A wicked grin spread over his face, belying the innocent tone.

A shiver slid up her spine at the sound of her name on his lips. "I was naked—"

"Indeed." The grin grew wider, his eyes twinkling at her.

"—and freezing to death. I don't remember much of anything." Unless the dream was real, and then she remembered too much.

His tongue slid down a canine tooth, a sign that she already knew meant he intended to tease her. Here it came.

"It was such a deeply moving experience for both of us, little bear. I'm crushed." Clapping his hands over his heart, he actually batted his eyes at her.

"Oh, brother." She rolled her eyes.

"I'm *not* your brother."

No kidding. As if she'd have those kinds of fantasies about her brother. "I just...tell me what happened. Please?"

He tilted his head and considered her for a moment, sipping from his mug. "My guards and I saw the explosion and came to investigate. I found you naked and freezing in the snow. When I changed, you fainted."

"You were in your bear form?"

"Yes."

"I saw you change?"

He shrugged. "I believe so. You were not coherent, little bear. A bit longer out there and you would have died."

So it had been a dream. A very *lusty* dream. She flushed, recalling how vivid the texture of his skin and hair had felt.

His gaze swept her face, and his voice became silky. "Why do you ask?"

She cleared her throat, blushing so hard her face tingled. "No reason."

"Come now, you don't expect me to believe that, do you?"

"I had a dream," she mumbled into her cup while she took a quick sip.

His eyes gleamed. "A sexy dream?"

"Maybe." She stared at her lap, not daring to look up.

"Tell me."

"I can't do that!"

"You can. Tell me, little bear. Did it make you moan?" His eyes locked with hers, heated, a little smile playing over his lips.

"Yes," she whispered.

"Was I inside you?"

Nodding, she squeezed her eyes tightly shut, as the fantasy played out in her mind. Her thighs clenched together as she tried to contain the wet heat building between them.

A small choking sound came from Kesuk, and she opened her eyes to find the fire in his gaze matched the flames in her body.

"Come here." His voice was low, demanding. Its rough edge slid over her skin like velvet.

She stood, her cup falling from her numb fingers. She walked to him as if it was the most natural thing in the world. No thought, nothing. Just reaction to this man, this moment. When she reached his chair, his hands rose to her waist. He pulled her into his lap, and her legs straddled his thighs. The muscles in his legs flexed, spreading her farther, pressing her against his straining erection. She gasped, rolling her hips to increase the contact. Sweet pleasure arced through her body. Nothing had ever felt this amazing. And he wasn't even inside her yet.

His lips touched hers, a gentle brush. She opened her mouth on his, darting her tongue out to slide over his lower lip. He tightened his grip on her waist, pulling her against his cock, grinding their pelvises together.

She moaned into his mouth, the sound waking her from her daze. She pulled back, panting. "Kesuk."

"I love my name on your lips, little bear."

"We shouldn't." Her fingers gripped the arms of his chair, her hips moving backward. "It's too soon. We just met. We have to be rational."

His hand stayed her motion, not letting her escape, but not forcing her closer, either. "Passion and reason don't often mix, Jain. And this is passion."

Taking her fingers, he guided them to his hard cock, cupping them to stroke his length. She closed her fingers around him, taking over the motion, fondling his dick through his leather pants.

He groaned, dropping his head back against the chair as he pressed himself into her caress. "Little bear, the things you do to me."

She wanted more, needed it. Throwing a lifetime of caution aside, she traced her hand over the lacings of his pants, using nimble fingers to untie them. His cock sprang free into her hand, the head glistening with pre-cum.

"Stroke me, little bear. I love your hands on me."

"You do?" Her gaze flicked to his handsome face.

"Oh, yes."

"Touch me, too."

"Where did I touch you in your fantasy, Jain?" His eyes were hard, glittering with unmasked lust.

Could she tell him? Maybe if she started small. "My hair."

"Like this?" His strong fingers slipped into her hair, massaging her scalp, sending tingles over her skin.

"Yes."

"Where else?"

"Everywhere," she whispered.

Sliding his hand down from her hair, he circled her nipple through her tunic. "Here?"

She froze at the sensation of his hand on her, hot pleasure storming through her. Nodding, she leaned forward, her nipples peaking into tight crests.

"Where else?"

Blood rushed to her face, her breath panting out. "B-between my legs." Just the thought of him touching her there made her thighs quiver.

"I like this dream." His other hand slipped low, cupping her sex, moving against her tight leather pants.

"I do, too."

She caught her lower lip between her teeth and arched forward to meet his stroking, still fondling his cock. Her hand slid up the shaft and then curved over the head as she rotated her palm over the bulbous crest. She wanted to put her mouth on him, feel the slide of his long shaft between her lips as she sucked him. She licked her lips, staring at his cock. Anticipation rolled through her in waves as his hands teased her pussy and nipple.

A soft growl sounded from his chest. "Keep looking at me like that and our night will be over far too quickly."

"I want to suck you." She looked him in the eye.

He groaned and laughed at the same time. "Little bear, you're killing me."

"Please."

"Later, I promise. Later."

She nodded, scraping a nail over the tiny opening of his cock. He pulled in a sharp breath, arching into her hand. He clamped his fingers around her wrist, removing himself from her grasp.

"Take your tunic off," he ordered.

Arms crossing over her body, she grasped the edges of her top and pulled it over her head in one swift motion, baring her small breasts to him. He dipped forward, catching a nipple in his mouth and sucking hard while his fingers tugged at the laces on her pants. She jerked back, standing to shove her pants off. She couldn't wait, didn't want to wait. Her sex clenched tight. She wanted that thick cock moving inside of her, wanted him more than she'd ever wanted any man in her life.

"Ah, Jain. Come here." While she stood, he jerked his shirt off, tearing his pants completely open.

Stepping forward, she swung her leg over his lap and mounted him in one smooth motion. He pulled her in, his hands guiding her hips forward until her wet pussy hovered directly over the head of his dick. Then he pushed down, forcing her to take him deep. She balanced her hands on his shoulders and sank down on him, feeling him embed so deep he touched her womb. God, he was big. She squirmed, just to enjoy the friction.

"You're so deep."

"Yes." He grunted, beginning to work her on his cock, lifting, lowering.

She squeezed her knees into his flanks, rising to ride him. Their plunging dance moved faster and faster, skin slapping together loudly.

It felt so good, so amazing, so *right* that for a moment it scared her. Her movements faltered as she tried to focus on something else, to not have this white-hot pleasure matter so much. He shouldn't be able to do this to her—she shouldn't *let* him do it to her. Staring at the chair behind his head, she concentrated on history lessons she used to teach her classes on Earth. Yes, now the pleasure was not so close, so deep. Now she could think.

He froze, pulling her tight against his pelvis, stilling their movements.

She blinked, focused on his eyes. "Why did you stop?"

"Why did you? One moment you were with me, the next you were gone."

A guilty blush washed into her cheeks. "Gone? You're still inside of me."

Cocking an eyebrow, he didn't bother to contradict her. "Do you want me to stop?"

Did she? Would it make it easier? "No," she whispered. "Don't stop."

"Kiss me."

Leaning forward, she pressed her lips to his, light caresses of warm flesh. His tongue swept out to lick her bottom lip before pressing into her mouth.

"Mmmm." She leaned closer until her breasts brushed his chest, rubbing her nipples back and forth over his skin. The feel of his flesh against hers was amazing, and she sank again into the intense visceral pleasure of his touch. His hands stroked up her back, tugged on her hair. She tilted her head back, and he nipped at her throat. Winding her fingers through his thick hair, she pressed him close.

Shoving her away, he knelt on the plush fur rug, lowering her and spreading her legs wide, a hand pressing each thigh to the floor. She flushed, her hands lifting to cover her exposed breasts.

"That's right, little bear. Fondle them for me."

"Kesuk…"

He smiled, his hot dark gaze sliding over her body, focusing between her legs. Bracing his forearms on either side of her hips, he lowered his shoulders between her spread thighs. His tongue parted the lips of her pussy, slipping over her labia before flicking her clit.

"Kesuk!" She fought to keep her fingers from burying themselves in his hair, from tugging him closer.

Do you know how good you taste, Jain?

She pressed her hand to her forehead, gasping as his voice echoed in her mind. "What? How?"

His tongue circled her clit with deliberate slowness before he drew it between his lips, suckling her wet flesh.

One of the many benefits your generation left behind. Don't you like it?

"Yes."

Play with your nipples for me. Show me what you like.

Panting, she relaxed her hands to cup her breasts, lifting them high before letting them bounce back. She circled her fingertips around the areolas, made them pucker into tight nubs.

This is a great deal of sweetness, little bear. Do you think it rational? Using that wicked tongue, he lapped at her juices, sucking her swollen lips between his teeth.

"Kesuk."

Perhaps if I made it easier for you, more controlled.

"What do you mean?" Her hips strained toward his mouth, pushing her toward orgasm, not caring what answer he gave. Her eyes squeezed closed. She was so close. Any moment now she would—

He pulled back and her eyes popped open. "Hey…"

One hand reached for the slim cord that had belted her pants closed. He turned back to her, licking her cream from his lips with obvious relish. She blushed, glancing away. He clasped her wrists in his right hand and with a quick twist, tied the cord around them. "Hey!"

"Relax, little bear. You will enjoy this."

She jerked at her wrists as he tied the other end of the cord around the heavy leg of her chair. "I don't—"

"Have you not enjoyed everything else I have shown you?"

"Yes, but—"

Then you will love this. He maneuvered back between her thighs, his broad shoulders forcing her legs wide as he resumed the ministrations of his mouth and tongue on her hot flesh, sucking hard on her clit.

Her back bowed at the abrupt change in sensation, wrists pulling hard on the cord as she struggled to move against him. "Kesuk, I want—"

Shh...let go.

She whimpered, tugging at her hands. "I can't let go of anything. I'm tied up."

Her pussy flooded with more moisture from saying the words out loud. She shouldn't like this so much. Tears pressed against her lashes as her thighs burned and her sex pulsed with want.

You don't have to control anything, to be rational or reasonable. Just feel how good this is.

It *was* good. The panic from before reared again, but she couldn't back away from it this time—she was bound. And free to do nothing but feel. Oh, God, it was so good, so hot. She twisted against the bindings, chafing her wrists, the heat building higher, hotter than ever. Spiraling down into intense need again, she couldn't fight it this time, didn't want to. She gave herself over to it. Tingles washed over her skin. She *felt.* She felt the softness of his hair brushing the insides of her thighs, the bite of his fingers into her flesh as he held her open for his mouth, the sharp nip of his teeth on her clitoris, the wetness of his tongue deep in her pussy. She screamed, jerking on the cord, needing this, *him,* right here, right now. Loving what he was doing to her, for her. It had never been this good before.

Yes, Jain. Let go for me.

He growled against her pussy, the vibrations making her sob. She was so close she could feel herself teetering on the edge of orgasm. "*Please,* Kesuk."

Lunging up, he braced his arms on either side of her torso, holding himself above her as he buried his huge cock into her quivering pussy. She wanted to rub her hands over the flexing muscles of his chest, feel the sinew shift under her fingers, but the bindings held fast when she pulled. His hard thrusts pushed her forward, the soft fur rug sliding against her back as they moved. The feel of the fur and his silky hot flesh pushed her closer, higher. She arched her back, rubbing herself against his chest and the rug.

"Kiss me," she demanded. Her hand met with the chair leg she was bound to, and she curled her fingers around the wood, the sharp carvings biting into her palms. The slight pain was just one more sensation piling on top of all the others.

He slanted his lips hard over hers, his kiss almost punishing. His dick worked inside her, shoving deep. Her body bowed under the building waves of pleasure washing through her. It felt so amazing, so hot. They were wild, biting at each other's lips. His fingers clenched hard around her thighs, jerking her farther open so she couldn't control the depth of his thrusts. The slapping sound of flesh on flesh turned her on. He manipulated her clit with his fingertips, flicking it in time with his pounding thrusts.

"Kesuk!"

It was more than enough to push her over into orgasm. Her pussy tightened on his cock as she came. Their eyes locked, and she gasped as the midnight irises of his eyes bled all the way to the corners, turning the entire orb coal black. His back bowed hard, hunching forward as he rammed into her, then froze. He threw his head back, his fangs sliding out as he roared his orgasm, his hips pounding forward in short jerking thrusts.

He collapsed onto his elbows, careful not to crush her. His forehead rested against hers as they panted hard. The *snap* and *pop* of the roaring fire sounded loud to her ears, and she noticed they'd crashed into the table, spilling their drinks onto the fur rug. That was a mess she didn't want to explain to Bel. Shoving himself up to balance on his hands, Kesuk pulled out from her pussy. The slide of his cock made her moan. Tugging her wrists free from the cord, he rubbed the circulation back into her fingers. His arms slipped beneath her shoulders, and he lifted her against his chest. Her head fell into the crook of his shoulder and her eyes drifted shut. He dumped her on the bed, and she bounced, her eyes popping wide. Spinning away, he walked stark naked to her door.

She crossed her arms over her bare breasts. What the hell had happened? Hadn't he enjoyed it as much as her? He was leaving, so apparently not. Humiliation crawled over her skin. "Kesuk?"

She hated that her voice wobbled on his name. Just when she thought she had a handle on the situation, he did something to confuse her again.

He paused, the open door in his hand.

"Is everything okay?"

Why was she even asking? She shouldn't care. She didn't even like him. Did she? No. Of course not. Then why had she slept with him? Everything was confusing and out of control again, so she hugged herself tighter and tried to pull back, shutting down the emotions, trying to remain calm and logical like her parents and husband had always insisted. Ten deep breaths and she'd forced herself back to cool composure.

"Everything is fine."

"Okay. Sure. Thanks for having dinner with me."

Dinner, right. They hadn't even eaten. She told herself it didn't hurt at all that he never looked back, shutting the door behind him with a final *thunk*. Crawling under the coverlet, she tugged it up to her chin, curled into a tight ball, and escaped into tear-stained sleep.

Chapter 5

After leaving Jain, Kesuk plunged into the icy sea to cool his blood. He sucked in a breath as the freezing water met with his semi-erect cock. The water swirled around his chest as he walked deeper, hoping the frigid temperature would cool his ardor. He couldn't believe he'd lost control over the woman and almost shifted while still inside her. He hadn't lost control during sex since...ever.

What would have happened if he had changed inside of her? Such a thing was not practiced among his people. Jain was a tiny woman—hurting her would be too easy. A good lover, a good man, a good *leader* should be able to maintain control at all times. Tonight he had failed in that.

He still wanted her. The woman was addicting. Her smooth, soft skin and Sitka-green eyes drove him mad. Touching her had been a bad idea. He needed to stay away from her until the weretigers took her off his hands.

He rolled his shoulders, trying to work out the tension.

My lord?

Flaring his nostrils, he caught the scent of Jain's young guard as his large white bulk maneuvered down the tunnel and into the sea entrance. "Imnek."

My rotation is complete, my lord. You wished for my nightly report on the Earthan. The Arctic bear dipped his head in salute, not meeting his eyes. Imnek had been standing outside Jain's door all night—the young guard knew what had happened. Kesuk's respect for the boy increased that he would do his duty even though he'd have to deal with his lord's sour disposition.

He returned the nod. "Report."

She is bored and needs stimulus. We need to set her to a task.

"She tried to escape you, I've heard."

The bear shifted from paw to paw. *She...may have tried, but I handled the situation, my lord.*

"When I ask you to report on her activities, I expect a complete report. Am I understood?" Irritation whipped through him, and he knew he spoke unfairly to the boy, but his reaction to the human had him rattled. He attempted to rein in his ill humor without much success.

Yes, my lord.

"Is there anything else you'd like to tell me?"

A long pause ensued while the young guard obviously raked his mind for any small detail he'd missed. *She is beautiful, and all the clansmen stare at her.*

Kesuk growled, slapped the surface of the water, his jaw clenching. They would dare to ogle her?

Imnek hurried on. *I believe she is unaccustomed to and uncomfortable with male attention. Or nudity.*

Impressed with the boy's sense of observation, Kesuk found himself nodding in approval. "Well done. Report again tomorrow."

The young bear straightened, snapped a crisp nod, and turned in the direction he had come.

"But Imnek? I expect to be apprised of *all* her movements."

Very good, my lord. Bowing again, Imnek left, his claws scraping against the stone floor as he went.

Digging his toes in the soft sandy bottom of the pool, Kesuk considered the situation. He couldn't let anyone else deal with her. She was his problem, and he wouldn't push her off onto anyone else. Especially any of his men. They might get ideas about sampling her sweetness, and he had to protect her.

Tonight was a mistake he wouldn't repeat. He simply had to maintain control and do his duty. Touching her again was not an option.

But now that he'd thrust inside her, not even the cold water could dull his lust for her slim body. His cock twitched in fevered memory and he groaned. This did not bode well.

"I can walk by myself." Jain's irritated voice echoed down the long corridor. Kesuk had insisted on continuing her tour of the caves, but she didn't have to be nice about it.

She hated being carried and not having any say about where she went or how fast she got there. After what had happened the last time she'd been helpless in his arms, she didn't want to repeat the experience.

Or maybe she did, but without the part where he dumped her into bed and ran like hell. Her luck with men was holding strong. Damn.

Heaving a long suffering sigh, Kesuk set her down and steadied her until she gained her balance. Her feet were encased in supple leather boots, double-layered in fur for cushioning. Her long dress fluttered down to cover her legs. The gown was almost medieval in cut and style, with a tight bodice and belled sleeves, only it was made from butter-soft leather and lined in the same gray-striped fur that covered her bed.

"This is the main entrance of Sea Den."

The tunnel twisted down at a sharp angle to a wide mouth. It overlooked a breathtaking view of a frozen ocean. Sentries stood on either side of the entrance, and she nodded to them in greeting. They stared at her for a moment before nodding back. She walked quickly to escape their stare and nearly stepped off the edge of a cliff. Kesuk reached out and caught her before she went over.

"Oh, my God!" She clung to the arm he wrapped around her waist, her heart pounding. Her limbs started to shake from the close call, and she slumped back against him.

"Careful, little bear. It's dangerous."

"Why is the main entrance so hard to get to?"

"To keep out enemies and predators."

A huge black and white whale leaped from the ocean beyond the ice shelf. She gasped. "A killer whale!"

"An orca."

"Oh, that's what we called them on Earth, too. How did they get here?" She turned and grinned up at him.

"Our ancestors brought them. Sea life is abundant here, and the water makes them safe from the predators. The land animals have had a harder time surviving. As have we."

"Why didn't they have merpeople here, then?"

"They may have intended to. The sun failed before anything more than the basic settlements were in place." He shrugged, his shoulder moving against her back.

She shivered as an icy blast of wind scoured the sea cliff. Glancing up, she noticed a narrow path winding far up the rock face. Snow spun in whirling gusts from the sheared-off edge of the mountain. He lifted the edges of his cloak and drew them around her. She snuggled back into his warmth.

"Is the entire planet covered in ice?"

"No, but the high reaches are the areas least inhabited by predators, so the clans settled here. The original Earthans were in the southern hemisphere. Dangerous there."

"How many other dens are there?"

"Two. One for the Grizzlies—High Den—and one for the Crescents—Meadow Den."

"Are they near here?"

"The Arctic lands form a large triangle. The Grizzly lands border us to the south, the Crescents to the north. Their lands extend beyond ours into the mountains and eventually meet."

"Do they like each other?"

"No more than we like them. The Grizzlies don't coexist well with anyone, and the Crescents are thieves and scavengers who'd pick the bones of their dead."

"That's disgusting."

"Indeed."

An icy blast of wind whipped the cloak around them. "Well, are there seasons in the high reaches or is it always cold?"

"Cold? This is warm. Thaw is only a few weeks away."

"Warmer weather. Oh, thank God."

"Thaw is when the predators venture north to hunt."

She didn't want to ask. "Hunt what?"

"Us."

"There's always a catch." She sighed.

His chest rumbled in a quiet laugh.

"How do you survive?"

"Hibernation begins at Thaw and lasts during the summer. We stay in the den until the first snowfall."

"We can't leave at all?"

"Hunting-and-gathering parties go out to collect food stores, but no one else. It is too dangerous."

Then she should put in her request before Thaw came. "Where'd my ship crash?"

"Southwest of here." He tensed against her back.

She twisted to look him in the eye. "I want to see it."

He sighed. "Jain."

"Please, Kesuk."

"It's nothing but a charred hull. You were the only survivor."

"I know, but—"

"My warriors scouted the area thoroughly after I returned with you. No one could be found."

"I believe you, but I need some closure. It's important to me. I...I didn't know anyone on board really well, but they were the last humans like me." She laid a hand along his jaw.

He sighed, his dark eyes showing resigned affection. "As you wish."

"Thank you." She placed a soft kiss on his lips.

He went rigid against her for a moment, then groaned and tilted his jaw down to deepen their contact. She sucked his tongue as it pushed past her lips.

Thank me properly, slave. His growl echoed in her mind.

Spinning quickly, he swept her into his arm, fingers quickly working her long skirt up around her hips. The cold air hit her naked skin, and she shivered as he cupped the backs of her thighs and drew her legs around his waist. He freed himself from his pants in a few seconds. Her back hit the cliff wall as he shoved his hard cock deep inside her.

"Yes!" The abruptness of his thrust made her back bow at the intense pleasure-pain, her pussy stretching to the limit. She dug her nails into his shoulders as she wrapped her legs tight around him, clamping her knees on his flanks to ride him. Needing to touch his skin, she slid her hands under his shirt, splaying her fingers on the flexing muscles of his back.

You dreamed of us in the snow, did you not?

He scooped a handful of snow from the rocks beside them, rubbing it against the back of her thigh. She gasped and arched in shock, the cold making her hotter for him, her moisture coating his cock with each push. He rotated his hips as he plunged into her, deepening his thrust, changing his rhythm. She stayed with him, their mouths fused, tongues dueling. She sucked his bottom lip into her mouth, bit down, and scraped the soft flesh as she pulled back. He groaned and dipped his tongue back into her mouth. The coppery taste of his blood excited her more, spurring her on. Her nails bit into his back, raking over his flesh. He grunted, his hips slamming harder into hers. His hand pulled back and slapped her thigh. She peaked into orgasm, fisting hard around his cock, milking him.

He filled his hands with her ass, pulling the cheeks apart. He stimulated her anus with a finger before pushing in.

She drew in a sharp breath. "Kesuk!"

Chuckling, he buried his finger in her ass again and again, rocking her on his cock. He worked in a second finger, and the sensation was more than she could take. She was so full, so hot. Grinding against his dick and fingers, her pussy clenched tight before she shuddered again, coming hard and fast.

He pulled his cock from her soaking pussy, lifting her higher on the wall. His fingers spread her ass cheeks farther.

"Oh, God." She moaned into his mouth as the head of his penis pressed against her hole.

He sank in deeply, one slow inch at a time. She gasped, her ass flexing around him. Too full. It was too much. She wanted more. Using his shoulders for leverage, she lifted off his cock, letting gravity sink him back in. He groaned, burying his face in her neck.

He thrust deep and hard, moving them at a punishing speed, their ragged breath and slap of skin on skin echoing off the cliffs. He slid a hand over her hip and between them, working her clit with a finger. She cried out, the sensation more than she could take. When he sank his teeth into her neck, she convulsed into hot orgasm again. Moments later, he groaned his own completion, pumping hot fluid inside of her.

She panted, her forehead resting against his shoulder as she came down from the high. The pleasured fog that settled over her mind gradually receded as her heartbeat slowed and her muscles relaxed. What had he done to her? She had *never* had sex in public before. Embarrassed heat raced through her when she remembered the way she'd cried out. Then a horrifying thought occurred to her.

"What about the guards?"

"Hmm?" He licked a lazy line from her neck along her collarbone, making her shiver as the cold touched her wet skin.

"The guards. They must have heard us. I'm so humiliated."

"I told them to withdraw when we first came out. Did you not notice them leave?" He pulled back to frown at her.

"No. Telling them to leave is just as bad. They're going to know what we did."

"Would you have preferred they stayed nearby and heard us? I prefer my sex a bit more private than that. If you have other ideas..." A wicked grin spread over his handsome face.

"No! Jesus, Kesuk. That's gross."

He shook his head. "Half of the time, I don't understand the way your mind works, and the other half I am certain I don't want to. Why are we talking about my soldiers?"

"Let me down. I can walk on my own."

He snorted. "Where have I heard that before?"

"I have no idea. You must have a nasty habit of hauling people around."

She moaned at the slow slide of his flesh inside of hers as he pulled his cock out. God, he still had a semi. She gave serious consideration to shoving him up against the mountain and going at it again, but then she really might not be able to walk on her own. Wouldn't that just give him all kinds of ammunition for carrying her around everywhere? Nope, not happening.

She turned toward the cave, ignoring the throb of want in her wet pussy and the sight of his cock disappearing inside his pants as he fastened the fly.

Chapter 6

A week after Jain arrived, Miki came to fetch her for her first day of "slave" duty. She blushed at the thought of what had happened the last time Kesuk called her that.

Kesuk confused her. Her violent reaction to him was completely out of character, and being with him made her do things she shouldn't. Like have sex on the side of a mountain. Wanting him this much made no sense. It was too intense for her to control, and it wasn't logical at all.

"Here we are." A flourish of Miki's tiny hand ushered her into a large room filled with children of all ages, half of them naked.

She shook her head. She'd never get used to this comfort with nudity, though Kesuk did his level best to keep her naked as often as possible. Sighing, she pushed thoughts of him aside.

"Where are we?"

"The lesson room."

"Lesson room?"

"Yes." Miki nodded, a smile creasing her lips. "Papa says you're our new loremistress. Our old one died last Thaw."

"Loremistress? I'm your new teacher?"

Miki bobbed her little head as she leaned in to whisper, "Don't tell, but I think you're much nicer than her. Or the loremaster before her. They were both *old*."

Compressing her lips to keep the smile from breaking through, Jain wagged a finger at the girl. "Now, Miki, that's not nice."

"But it is true." A young male voice spoke from near her elbow. She glanced down and found a smaller version of Kesuk looking up at her, complete with serious expression.

"You must be Nukilik."

"Yes. Miki and I are to help you settle in today."

"Well, lead on, kind sir."

Nukilik's forehead wrinkled as though he wasn't sure if she was teasing or not. Then he stepped forward and introduced her to the rest of the rambunctious group. The class immediately fired off a wild cacophony of questions about Earth. They wanted to know where she had lived and what were *mi-cro-waves* and how old she was. The day slipped away in organized chaos as she finally assumed a role she knew—teacher.

The next day, five adults attended her class. Then ten. Then twelve. Soon she had a constant audience slipping silently in and out of the back of the lesson room. The adults' endless curiosity about her matched the children's. They surrounded her at mealtimes and in hallways. These were the kind of eager students she'd have given her left arm for on Earth.

Miki and Nukilik were her constant companions, followed by Imnek, who she'd already surmised Kesuk had sent to watch her. Even when he wasn't there, he controlled her. It wasn't as annoying as it used to be. Maybe *half* as annoying. And a little endearing that he cared. Even though it was obvious he didn't *want* to care. She kept that little bit of knowledge to herself, glad she wasn't the only one struggling with whatever was happening between them.

The days and nights slid by. Though she would never admit it to Kesuk, she was adjusting to this new lifestyle with greater ease than she could ever have imagined. She hoped the weretigers were as welcoming as the Arctic Bear Clan. Over a week after her first class, she was at dinner, surrounded by the usual motley crew of adults with questions, when Miki tugged on her sleeve.

"Yes?" Jain asked, grinning down at the girl.

"I have something for you." Miki smiled shyly, an expression Jain had never seen on her face.

"That's so sweet. I love presents." Please, God, don't let it be anything live or slimy.

Miki tugged Jain's hand into her lap and dumped a small pile of something into her palm. Jain lifted her hand and found a dozen tiny round shells. They looked like a cross between a tiny conch shell and a sand dollar from Earth. All of them were perfect.

"Oh, Miki. They're so pretty. The best present *ever*." And they were. Jain didn't remember the last time anyone had given her an unpractical, just-because present. Her family had thought holidays too foolish and sentimental, and her husband hadn't cared enough to bother. She hugged Miki tight and started to tear up, but she managed to blink back the emotion, burying the happiness along with the hurt the way she always did. Tucking the shells into her pocket, she cleared her throat and straightened, resuming her meal.

After dinner, Jain and Kesuk returned to her room. She expected him to pull her into his arms and make her scream for hours. She shivered, a little grin playing over her lips. He made just as much noise as she did when they had sex.

Instead, he sat down on the bed, his fingers splayed on his spread knees. His expression was unusually serious. "Since you came here, you act as though you're living someone else's life. As though all this is temporary and you intend to wake up soon. You pull back when circumstances become too real, when you feel too much. You did it when we loved the first time and again tonight with Miki."

Crap. He'd noticed that? She sighed. "That's how I was raised, Kesuk."

"Hiding from life won't make it stop moving forward without you."

"Like time did."

He snorted. "An unfortunate comparison, but yes."

His hands curved around her waist, lifting her astride his lap. The position brought her eye to eye with him, and nothing had ever felt this intimate. This *right*.

She jerked back, denying herself and him. "I shouldn't want you this much. Ever since I came here, everything's been jumbled up and confused. I didn't used to be like this. I never doubted who I was or what my purpose was. Everything was clear—what I should do, who I should be with, where I should go. It was all planned, all logical. My life made *sense*."

"That was the way of your world, your people. Everything ordered and in its place. Life is not about planning every moment. Joy comes in the spontaneity of life, Jain. It doesn't have to make sense. Sometimes people die when they shouldn't. They also love where they shouldn't. Those are things you cannot decide."

"I enjoyed my life before," she insisted.

"Such rigidity is not a good thing in one as young as you."

"I'm over five hundred years older than you."

He cocked a thick blond brow and folded his arms.

"All right, fine. I'm still not that young. And I'm not rigid—I'm logical."

"No, your family was logical, perhaps. Your mate. But not you. You pretend to be logical, because you think you should, because it's safer to believe you're in control. Deny yourself all you want, but I see the passionate woman in you. I've held that woman in my arms, clawing my back, screaming my name in ecstasy."

She squeezed her eyes closed, shutting out the image he painted. He was right. She always pulled back when emotions got too deep. Her family had been scientists, eminently logical. Nothing emotional was acceptable. Since her husband left her for another woman and her parents had died, her emotions had been locked in ice, frozen and untouchable. Was that who she really was? Who she really wanted to be?

She sighed. "I'm sorry, Kesuk."

"Do not be sorry. Be here."

"I want to be." And she did, so much. She wanted to be where she mattered, where she was safe to *feel*.

"If you want it, then you'll do it." He pulled her tighter to his pelvis until she felt his hard cock.

"That simple, huh?" Arching an eyebrow, she smirked down at him.

"Some things are. Like this." He slipped a hand between her legs, rubbing her through her leather pants.

Pleasure swirled through her, but she twisted her leg to avoid the touch. If he wanted to bring up personal issues, she had a thing or two to say to him as well. Maybe they should just get this all out in the open. She wasn't the only one here with flaws.

"And then there's *you*."

"M e? I have done nothing." He cocked an eyebrow, wary of what she might say. Women were unpredictable. A man never knew what strange things ran through their minds or what would pop out of their mouths.

"Ha! You're Mr. Fix-It. You have to fix everyone and everything. Let's forget about me and my control issues for a second. You also keep your soldiers from fighting *and* insist on handling every last detail of the preparations for the weretigers' arrival. You need to try delegating some things. Let the rest of us work it out for ourselves. Trust your people. Trust me. We won't end up killed by predators."

Her hands planted on her hips, which still straddled his thighs. They should be loving now. How had his evening's plans gone so awry?

He narrowed his eyes. "You would prefer I'd left you dying in the snow?"

She snorted at him. "Don't be deliberately dense. I'm not saying we don't need you or your help *at all*. I'm saying we can do some of it ourselves. You don't have to be all things to all people, Kesuk. You have advisers and soldiers. Let them do their jobs. They're competent, or you wouldn't have put them in those positions in the first place. Am I right?"

"Yes." He didn't like the direction of her questioning.

"I'm guessing this micromanagement started after your wife died. You used to listen to your councilors, used to let your lieutenants make some executive decisions about their men."

"I was younger then." Why was he defending himself? She *wasn't* right. Was she?

"And now you know everything and don't need anyone?"

"I did not say that."

"But that's what your actions say to your people every day."

"That—"

"Everyone else is allowed to be human, Kesuk. Me, your family, your men, but not you. You have to be perfect. Why is that?"

He slid his tongue over his teeth. Perhaps now was a good time for a distraction. "It was a human between your legs last night, was it not?"

She ignored him. "You see your wife's death as your failure. Now you keep everyone at arm's length so you never get hurt again. Miki and Nukilik are your only exceptions."

Anger flashed through him. "Are you finished pretending you know me?"

She flinched. "I didn't realize I was pretending."

"You've known me only a few weeks, yet you've uncovered everything that's wrong with me. How miraculous."

Face flaming, her eyes sparked with anger and challenge. "And you're any better? You constantly tell me how wrong I am, how I need to let go and feel. Sometimes it takes an outside opinion to see what's really going on."

He snarled, his fingers tightening on her hips. He did not wish to consider this. "You have no idea what you are talking about."

"If I'm wrong, I'm wrong. It wouldn't be the first time I misjudged a man. Don't dismiss what I said because it's uncomfortable to think about. Deep down, you know I'm right." She poked a finger into his chest.

A knock on the door interrupted his retort. He growled. Typical.

"Come," he snapped, holding Jain still when she tried getting up from his lap.

Imnek opened the door, glancing at them once before fixing his eyes on the far wall.

"My lord, the weretigers have crossed the border into our land."

Jain's lips tightened. She thought he'd run off to fetch the weretigers himself. And she'd be right. He sucked his teeth in self-disgust.

"Take a contingent of guards and escort our guests to Sea Den."

"Me, my lord?" The boy's eyes popped wide, his voice rising an octave.

"You are qualified, are you not?"

He snapped upright. "Yes, my lord!"

"Go, then." He turned back to Jain, smirking. "There, you see? Delegation."

She lifted her chin and folded her arms, which plumped her breasts. His hand twitched as he fought to keep from peeling away her clothes and filling his palms with her soft flesh. "Uh-huh. Make a habit of it."

Growling, he gave in to impulse and pulled her closer to him, crushing her lips under his, ending the argument the best way he knew how. He closed a hand over her breast, making her moan into his mouth. She responded to him every time. He loved that about her. His cock hardened to painful stiffness, and his free hand cupped her ass, lifting her so he could rub himself against the juncture of her thighs.

"Papa?" Miki's wavery voice sounded from outside the room.

"Every time. Every *single* time." He groaned and laid his forehead against hers.

"I seem to recall at least one time on the side of a mountain..." Those exotic green eyes tilted up at the corners as she grinned.

She licked her lips, her eyes dropping to his mouth. He stroked the breast he still held, plucked at the nipple. Gasping, she leaned into him.

"Jain?" The door latch rattled as Miki struggled to get in. "Please, let me in."

The ragged edge of Miki's little voice alerted him. A nightmare. She hadn't had one in over a Turn. He set Jain on the bed and opened the door, stooping to gather Miki up to his chest. She buried her head in his shoulder, already sobbing, her thin arms clinging to his neck.

"Sweetie, what's wrong?" Jain rose and reached over to smooth Miki's hair, obviously distressed by his daughter's tears.

"I h-had a bad dream. Can I s-stay here with y-you, Jain?"

"Of course."

Kesuk groaned, mourning the loss of a night in Jain's bed. A father's duty was never done. Miki leaned away from him and held out her arms for Jain. His eyebrows rose. That was new. Miki never sought out anyone but him when she had a night terror.

His surprise was echoed by the look on Jain's face as she tucked Miki into her arms. She rocked the girl, swaying from side to side with each step as she walked to the bed. Tucking Miki under the furs, Jain crawled in next to her, snuggling close. He shifted, feeling awkward and unnecessary. Jain looked up, patting the bed in invitation. Walking across the room, he banked the fire until the room was lit in a soft glow and joined them.

Jain hugged Miki closer, resting her chin on top of the girl's head. "What was your nightmare about?"

"Mama."

"Oh?"

"About when she left."

"It's all right to miss her."

"Papa says we don't need to because we'll see her in the next life."

Jain seemed to consider that, to consider his beliefs before answering. "Remembering the way you loved her in this life isn't bad. Even if you get to see her again."

He smiled down at his daughter, propping himself up on an elbow. "You will see her again, Miki. Don't ever doubt it."

"I won't, Papa."

"Go to sleep now." He tucked the covers under her chin, and she closed her eyes.

"I love you."

"I love you, too." Kissing her forehead, he petted her hair until her chest rose and fell in slow, even rhythm.

"She's not allowed to grieve?" Jain asked.

He turned the question on her because he knew his response would only make her bring up his need to control everything. "Do you allow yourself to grieve? Truly?"

She didn't speak for a long moment, and when she did, she changed the topic rather than answer him. "How did your wife die?"

Her soft words washed over him in the darkness, and he closed his eyes against the ugly memory, the guilt of his failure. The woman was right about that, the failure, the guilt. "There was a raid."

"And she was taken as a slave?"

"No." He couldn't speak of this to anyone. He never had before.

A small hand cupped the side of his face, stroked his cheek. "Tell me."

"The Crescents overran a hunting party. It was normal—it happens all the time. We attack them, they attack us. Slaves are the commodity of choice. Trading them is how we get the things we need. Deer and bison stay to higher elevations, and fish are in the sea. We use the exchange of people to get goods. Simple. Easy."

"But not that time."

He swallowed hard. "No. Not that time."

"What went wrong?"

"During the raid, predators attacked, too. My mate was with the hunters and she…she was taken by the predators."

The memories washed over him in relentless waves. After his warriors told him Maruska was gone, he'd hunted for her for hours, tracking the pack of predators until he finally found her body. She'd been mangled and half-sunk in an icy stream, her blood making the water run pink. He'd roared out his grief, the pain more than he could contain. Then he'd taken her in his arms and rocked her, knowing he was too late to protect her. She was gone.

His breath shuddered out as he allowed himself to recall his failure. He couldn't bear to suffer such loss again. He would never leave himself or his clan so vulnerable. Hunting parties now went out with an entire contingent of guards. No women or children ventured out alone. Ever. He accompanied as many expeditions as he could manage. It was his duty to protect his people. He would not fail again.

Jain's soft hand stroked over his cheek, pulling him from his reverie. He shook away his gloom, turning to face her. She withdrew her hand, settled her chin in her upturned palm. "Hi. Where did you go?"

I'm right here.

"You loved her."

Fierce guilt hit him again, threatened to strangle him. "I did."

"I'm so sorry, Kesuk."

"Yes." He made his voice abrupt, hoping she would let this subject go. He did not wish to speak of it.

"What was she like?"

He sighed. Maruska. What had she been like? He was ashamed to admit he could no longer see her face in his mind, but he remembered the life they'd shared. He summed it up as succinctly as possible. "She was the exact opposite of you."

Jain gasped, a small sound of pain. "I understand. Good night."

She slid down to curve around Miki, closing her eyes. He winced, realizing how what he'd said would be taken by his current lover. Foolish.

Our marriage was arranged by my father. We were raised together, respected each other's strengths. Love grew from that respect, slowly and over time. She was...boisterous and wild.

"Nothing like me."

"Don't assume that is a bad thing. My mate is dead. I don't wish to replace her with a pale imitation." He reached out to slip his fingers through Jain's hair, the dark silken length sliding between his fingers. She tilted her cheek to lean into his palm, opening her eyes to meet his gaze.

You are a beautiful woman, Jain.

She huffed a laugh, looking away. "Right."

"What's this? Look at me, little bear." He frowned when she didn't comply, tilting her chin so he could see her expression.

Her jaw flexed in his hand, but she didn't try to pull away. "You don't have to say those things to me, Kesuk. I know what I look like. You don't have to lie."

He swallowed his anger at that, stroked his thumb along her jaw. "Questioning my honor again, Jain?"

"No!" She glanced down at the sleeping Miki and whispered, "No."

"Why would I bother to lie?"

She shrugged, looking anywhere but at him. "I don't know."

Something deeper lay here. "Who made you doubt?"

"I'm just not pretty, okay? I've always known it. Besides, beauty is not as important as intelligence."

He heard the echo of someone else in her voice. "Hmm...your family told you this? Or your mate?"

"Both. He, my husband, and I grew up together. He was part of my family."

He suspected her husband had been far more a part of her family than she had. "They were proud of you?"

"No, I..." She shook her head. "They were very busy. We didn't spend much time together. They worked on projects and experiments."

"They sound frigid."

"Their work was very important." Her voice came out stiff, controlled.

"Did they not love you? Tell you they approved of your accomplishments?"

She scoffed. "I'm just a teacher. My brother and husband were the scientists."

This explained so much about her—her need to control everything in a world that wasn't safe. Anger burned in his gut, the muscles ticking in his clenched jaw. He wanted to go back in time and pummel the unfeeling parents who had abandoned the vulnerable young Jain. He growled at the mere thought of her mate, a man who should have made up for a lifetime of no love. Made her see she was beautiful and wanted. He would never permit Miki to mate with such a man.

"Here we have no scientists. Loremasters are valued. They carry our history into the future."

"Things here are backward of what I know."

"Different is not bad, Jain. You will adjust." What was he saying? She was leaving when the weretigers arrived. He sighed, pushing that knowledge away. Best not to deal with it tonight.

"Do I have a choice? Everything here happens to me. I have no say in it."

"Controlling everything is not the answer, either, Jain."

"Controlling nothing is irresponsible. I'm going to sleep now. Good night, Kesuk." Her voice was prim and antagonizing.

Sighing, he fought the urge to throttle the stubborn wench. Yes, entirely the opposite of his easygoing mate. Too bad he'd developed a soft spot for recalcitrant women.

He dipped his head to meet her gaze. *You are beautiful, Jain. I would not say it if I did not mean it.*

"I know." She shook her head and closed her eyes again, sighing.

In time, she would come to see he was right. Unfortunately, with the arrival of the weretigers, their time together would soon draw to a close. He hated to miss seeing her passionate nature come full bloom. He didn't allow himself to consider that some other man might get to enjoy her after she left Alysius. She deserved what happiness she could find. Chest tight with an emotion he had no business feeling, he reached out to slide a tender hand down her soft midnight hair, reveling in the silky feel of her soft cheek. He lay for a long while, watching her chest rise and fall in sleep before he tucked the furs tighter around her and his daughter. The two most precious females in his life.

Chapter 7

At sunrise the next morning, Miki dragged her along on a hunting-and-gathering party. She was curious to see more of the planet. With her clothes on this time. They bundled in warm cloaks and slung gray-striped leather satchels across their shoulders. Everything was striped here. She made a mental note to ask Kesuk why at dinner this evening.

That thought brought her up short. This outing was also a convenient way to escape Kesuk. He hadn't been in bed when she woke up this morning, and he hadn't bothered to leave a note about where he'd gone so early. She didn't really want to see him after they'd shredded each other last night. She'd said more than she should have about her family history. Her heart gave a painful squeeze. What an awful mess.

Miki thrust her hand into Jain's and pulled her as fast as her little legs could go. "Jain! Come on, we must keep up."

"All right, I'm coming. Hold your horses." At least spending time with Miki was guaranteed to lift her dark mood.

"We need to stay with the guards. There are predators at Thaw."

"Have you ever seen one of the predators?" She swallowed, glancing around, grateful for the full contingent of Kesuk's huge guards.

"Yes, but I've never seen a horse. What is it? Why do you have to hold it?"

Squeezing the girl's hand, Jain laughed. "It's an expression that means *don't be impatient.*"

Miki wrinkled her pert little nose. "I don't think I like horses."

Soon they were spread out in a small clearing, chattering, laughing, Miki showing Jain how to pick fresh berries.

"This one. It's the very best one this Turn." Miki held up a tiny plum-colored berry between her fingers before popping it into her mouth and chewing with exaggerated delight. She'd declared the same thing about almost every fruit she'd picked.

"If you don't stop eating the very best ones, how will anyone know you found any at all?"

Miki grinned. "I'll tell them. Oh, but *this* one. It's the very b—"

A high-pitched scream of animal pain rent the air, raising chills down Jain's arms. Her head whipped around to see one of the guards go down in a spray of crimson blood and gore on the white snow. A huge gray tiger-striped animal pounced on his chest, fangs bared. It was vaguely the shape of an Earthan wolf but nearly the same size as Kesuk in his bear form.

Jain gasped. "Oh, God."

"Come, Jain, back to the caves. They hunt in packs!" Again, Miki grasped Jain's hand tight, pulling hard.

Women and children ran and screamed, dumping their satchels and changing into bear form to run faster.

"Go, Miki!" Jain ran behind the girl, making sure she kept up as they followed the line of Arctic bears. Adrenaline sang in her veins. Her heart pounded as her arms and legs pumped hard, kicking up snow behind her. Roaring sounded from the clearing they'd left behind.

They skidded through loose gravel alongside the steep ravine that led to the back entrance of Sea Den. Suddenly, Miki lost her footing and dropped over the side.

"Miki!" Jain dove for the girl, catching her hand and keeping her from falling to the rocks below. Miki's wide, frightened eyes locked with hers as her desperate grip tightened. Her dark irises disappeared as the black spread to touch the corners of her eyes.

"Don't let go!" Miki's nose turned black and started to elongate, her breath panting out. She grew heavier by the second as she started to shift forms.

"I won't, honey. But I can't hold you if you change into a bear, okay? I've got you. It's okay," she soothed.

Miki whimpered, but her nose resumed its human shape. "Okay. Okay. Can you pull me up?"

"Yeah." Jain grunted and shimmied backward over the gravel. Small rocks scraped the skin on her stomach as her short tunic rode up. She wrapped her free hand around a protruding rock, ignoring the bite into her bare flesh, because it kept her from sliding into the ravine. Miki hefted her torso over the lip of the crevice, and then curled up her knee to hoist herself the rest of the way. She flopped over on her back, panting.

"Come on, sweetie. We need to hurry." Jain pushed onto her knees, intending to pull the two of them to their feet.

Miki sat up, sniffing the air before her gaze focused over Jain's shoulder. "*Get down.*"

Jain hit the ground, hunching over Miki as a hulking dark shape flew over their heads and down the side of the ravine. The predator scrabbled for purchase, growling and leaping for the top. Its loud baying would bring more if they hunted together. Where the hell were all their guards?

Jain hauled Miki into her arms, sprinting for the nearest tree with low limbs. It was a young sapling, but it looked like it could hold them. If the predators were like the wolves on Earth, they wouldn't be able to climb a tree. She hoped.

The predator topped the edge of the ravine and hurtled toward them at astonishing speed. Oh, God.

She shoved Miki onto the lowest branch. "Climb up!"

After Miki hefted herself up to the next branch, Jain jumped to catch her elbows over the branch. She'd always been awful at chin-ups in school. Her booted toes kicked into the tree trunk, giving her purchase so she could haul her left knee up. Something snapped around her right ankle, yanking her back, her chin scraping on the bark. She caught the branch with her hands, and it bowed under the combined weight of her and the predator.

"Jain!" Miki shrieked.

Jain screamed, panicking as the predator's teeth bit into the tough leather of her boot with crushing force. She swung wildly, fighting to hold on to the branch. Looking over her shoulder, she could see the evil thing's yellow eyes. Drawing her free foot back, she aimed for the tip of its snout. She connected, hard.

The predator yowled and dropped her foot, shaking its head madly. Adrenaline pumped through her veins as she hauled herself back up onto the branch. She sobbed for air, bouncing on her good foot and forcing herself to climb up and up, away from the predator.

"K-keep going, Miki. High as you can."

"Are you all right?"

"Yes. Just c-climb, sweetie." Jain pulled herself as high as she could before the slim branches began bowing under her weight. That put her only about thirty feet above the ground, and the little tree shook as the predator hurled itself at the base. She straddled a branch and tugged Miki down in front of her, wrapping her arms around the trunk to secure them in place. Bark bit into her fingers, and the branch chafed her inner thighs. The pungent aroma of tree sap filled the air as leaves and twigs broke away.

A second predator joined the first, circling the tree, baying eerily. The hairs stood up on the back of Jain's neck, and she prayed harder than she ever had before. *Please, let the guards be all right and on their way to help. Please let Kesuk come.* Her ankle throbbed, and she squeezed her eyes shut, not wanting to watch as the predators hurled their combined weight against the slender trunk. The budding leaves shivered at each impact.

A deep roar sounded in the distance. More must be coming. What the hell was she *doing* here? She didn't want to be mauled and eaten by some freakish wolf-tiger beastie. She bit back a sob, pulling air in through her nose to calm her erratic breathing, coughing as she sucked pollen into her airway.

"Make them go away, Jain." Miki whimpered, her tiny fingers forming claws to dig into the tree. Jain couldn't think of a single comforting thing to say, so she just hugged her close and held on for dear life. They weren't getting her out of this tree until they knocked the damn thing over.

The roaring came closer, almost upon them. She turned her head in the direction of the clearing, watching to see how many predators would come. Instead, a massive Arctic bear broke through the line of trees, followed by four more. It let out a bellowing roar, leaping forward with claws extended and fangs bared, galloping for the nearest predator. The two met with a loud crunch of bone and sinew, two huge animals locked in combat.

"Kesuk," Jain breathed. The two rolled away, and she strained to see what was going on, careful not to lose her balance.

Terrifying growls, squeals, and grunts exploded from the two fighters. They reared back on hind legs to slash at each other with tooth and claw. The predator slammed Kesuk over, and they spun sideways through the snow before crashing into the base of the tree. Jain squashed Miki against the tree as the wild swaying started to crack the trunk. The whole tree began to give way as half of the roots tore from the ground. The two hit the slim tree again and again, the impact of fangs on flesh audible as they ripped into each other.

As quickly as it had begun, it stopped. Everything was silent.

"Papa!" Miki tried to dive down, but Jain held her still.

Groaning, Kesuk heaved away from the still predator. Blood matted his white fur. He shook hard from head to tail before approaching the foot of the tree. The predator's fleeing pack mate was easily overtaken by the other bears and dragged to the ground. Jain looked away—she didn't want to see anymore.

Come down now. It's safe. Kesuk's thoughts echoed in her mind.

She eased her cramped grip on the trunk and scooted back to let a straining Miki down first. The girl made short work of the climb down, landing on her father's back and chattering about how she hadn't been scared and how exciting it was and how Jain had saved her from the big, bad predators.

Jain followed more slowly, the ache in her ankle becoming more pronounced. Adrenaline still pumped through her system, making her hands and legs shake. She reached the lowest branch and bent to grasp it, lowering herself to dangle a foot from the ground. Bracing herself for the pain, she dropped down. Gasping as her ankle nearly buckled, she stumbled back against the trunk.

Jain?

"I'm fine." She straightened, laying a hand on the dense fur on Kesuk's back while his now human and very naked warriors gathered their silver-and-black striped kill. Well, at least she knew now why almost everything they wore was striped.

Shaking that inane thought away, she turned toward Sea Den and began the long, slow walk back, careful to pick her way through the rocks and gravel so she didn't worsen her ankle by twisting it. A large young bear pulled alongside her, nudging her hand with his nose until she used his shoulder for balance. She suspected it was Imnek but couldn't be sure and didn't ask, because she was so focused on getting back in one piece. Miki, now in her bear form, gamboled ahead of them, pouncing into snowdrifts.

Steam rose from the large tub, the heated water lapping around Jain's thighs and buttocks as she lowered herself into her bath. A low moan slid from her lips at the sensuous delight of the water on her skin. The stiffness eased from her calf and ankle, and she flexed the joint. Sighing, she leaned back against the rim and tried to relax.

The fear she'd felt this afternoon was not something she'd soon forget. How had these people survived so long with those *things* hunting them? Why had they settled this planet if they hadn't been able to eradicate such a threat? Back on Earth, she'd heard reports of whole settlements being wiped away without a trace. Now she understood why.

She tapped restlessly against the sides of the tub, water sloshing as she shifted. Sighing, she gave up trying to relax and attempted to leverage herself out of the tub. She was still too keyed up from the adrenaline rush. She was still half in, half out of the water when the door slammed back against the wall, making her jump.

Kesuk stood there naked, having just shifted. His eyes were still black from corner to corner, and something wild and dangerous lurked in his gaze. Her stomach fluttered, breath speeding with anticipation. Sharp desire rushed through her, peaking her nipples, dampening her pussy, readying her for penetration.

He kicked the door shut behind him with one foot as he advanced across the room. "I won't be gentle."

"I don't want you to be." No, she wanted him fast and hard, to burn off the terror she'd experienced today. Knowing what he needed, what she needed, she lifted her arms in invitation.

Never hesitating, he scooped her out of the tub, dripping water all over the floor. She ignored the mess, thrusting her fingers into his hair, pulling his lips to hers. They bit and nipped at each other, and she dragged her teeth hard over his bottom lip.

Setting her on the edge of her side table, he lifted her knees, pushing between her thighs. "Lean back," he rasped.

She reclined on her hands, widened her legs for him, arching hard as he jerked her pussy lips apart to thrust into her. He started a fast, deep rhythm, pumping into her hot channel.

They fell on each other with a desperation she'd never expected. Beads of bathwater rolled down her arms and legs, making her slide on the table. Her head rested against the wall, her neck tensing as she moved with his thrusts. Tears gathered at the corners of her eyes, slipped unchecked down her cheeks, the emotions of the day pushing forward until she couldn't contain them anymore.

He was hitting her just right, and she was screaming, the sound too loud to her ears, but she didn't care anymore. Her fingers wrapped around the edge of the polished wood table, and she pressed her pelvis up to meet his hard thrusts. He pulled her knees higher on his hips, pistoning deep, faster and faster.

"I'm coming!" Her hips froze midair, legs tensing as her pussy spasmed once around his cock. His thrusts became deep and wild as they raced each other to orgasm, their eyes locked, riding the storm together.

She imploded, her sex milking the length of his dick in rhythmic pulses. His fangs slid out and he roared as he came, his head thrown back, the muscles on his neck and shoulder tensing. His hands clamped on her ass, pulling her closer, pressing his cock as deep inside her as she could handle. Then he sighed, relaxing, his forehead dropping to rest on her chest.

The drag of his hot flesh in hers as he slid out of her made her pussy clench on his dick.

He groaned, thrust against her cervix hard and pushed her into an aftershock of climax. She shuddered, clinging to his shoulders. Backing away, he slid an arm under her legs, lifting her against his chest. A few steps and he laid her across the bed, settling beside her.

He feathered his fingers down her legs, making her shiver at the light touch. She eased her thighs apart a little, hoping to encourage further exploration. His fingers circled her injured ankle, and she flinched from the touch. She could walk on it, but it was bruised.

"Did I hurt you before?" Concern creased his forehead as he examined her leg.

"No. It's just sore. Really." He wasn't going to stop for the night, was he? He'd never stopped at one orgasm before. She felt cheated.

"Hmm...I think you need to keep this ankle elevated." He flashed a wicked little grin, and her heart turned over. God, she adored being around him. Just in these small moments between them. How he teased her and made her laugh. Maybe even when he made her mad. Even when she wanted to kick his ass, she knew he cared. Her problems mattered to him. She had a very short list of people in her life she could say that about. Plus, sex with him was the best she'd ever had. She smiled back at him. Nope, she couldn't forget the great sex.

Still grinning, he propped her legs on his shoulders and kissed his way down her good leg to swirl his tongue under her knee. She moaned, surprised that was such a sensitive area. He nipped the soft flesh, and an echoing fire flashed between her legs. As always, she was hot for him within two seconds. She didn't think she'd ever get used to it.

"Put your hands above your head."

"Yes, *master.*" She smirked, but stretched her arms up, locking one hand over her opposite wrist.

"I see you're learning your place here."

She opened her mouth to argue, but when he shifted suddenly, pressing his cock deep into her wet pussy, all that emerged from her throat was a low moan.

He grasped her thighs, controlling her movements, pumping so slowly she wanted to scream. The angle was amazing. It was so tight. Rolling his hips, he increased the friction, slipping one hand down to flit over her swollen clitoris.

She strained upward, her hand tight on her wrist. "Please let me touch you, Kesuk. Please, I want—"

Begging, little bear? I like that. Do it again.

"Please." Her hips bucked, but his hand moved from her clit to press down on her belly, staying her movements, making her sob in frustration. "Go faster, deeper, *something.*"

Chuckling, he resumed his lazy circling of her wet flesh, pushing into her, pulling away. She clamped her pussy on his cock, squeezing tight with each thrust until he groaned. Grinning, she watched his control slip. His breath hissed and his fangs slid out.

"Jain," he growled.

"Yes?" She kept her tone as sweet and innocent as she could, but she knew her wide grin gave her away.

His next thrust slapped against her and she gasped. Hot pleasure rolled through her. Her legs flexed to meet his next push. He slapped the fleshy part of her upper thigh, the shock thrusting her into orgasm.

"Kesuk!"

But he wasn't listening. He'd lost all control. His eyes were solid black, and he pounded roughly into her, consumed by his own needs. He threw back his head and roared his finish, filling her with his hot seed.

He collapsed beside her, panting. He turned her on her side and then buried his face in her hair, each breath fluttering the short strands. His arms tightened around her, pulling her back against his chest, cradling her to him.

She fought the sudden tears pressing against her lids because she felt...safe. Right here on this barbaric, backward planet with this uncivilized man.

"I thought I'd lost you. That I failed you." His harsh whisper seemed to echo in the chamber. "You and Miki. I thought..." He swallowed, shook his head, and stopped speaking.

"You didn't." She turned to face him, laid a hand on his cheek, smoothing her fingers over his strong jaw.

"I could have. In a few more moments—" He leaned his forehead against hers, shuddering, his breathing ragged.

Stroking his shoulder, she tried to comfort him. "It didn't happen. You can't control everything, remember?"

He chuckled. "My own words used against me."

"Used *for* you. You were right." Her fingers slipped into his hair.

"Truly? Say it again, little bear. My ears must be deceiving me."

"Shut up!" She laughed, bucking away from him.

Planting his palm in the middle of her back, he arched her torso toward him, dipping to suck her nipple.

"Ah!" Clenching her fingers in his hair, she pulled him closer.

He bit and released her nipple, just rough enough to make her moan, pulling as much of her small breast into his mouth as he could. His stubble scraped at the soft underside. She hooked her leg over his thigh, opening herself to his thick cock.

A crisp knock interrupted them, and they both groaned.

"If it's one of my soldiers, he'll be on night duty for a full Turn." Kesuk reared up, his still-hard cock bouncing in the air.

A sleek man with dramatic black-striped auburn hair walked in without waiting for permission. His kohl-rimmed gaze took in the entire situation, including Jain's blushing cheeks. Everything about the man was golden, including his skin, his eyes, and the thick loop in his ear. What appeared to be faded henna tattoos curved in stripes over his forearms.

Kesuk gave a warning growl before jerking the pelts over Jain. "You have a great deal of nerve coming in here, cat king."

"The correct term is *Amir,* and felines are known for their arrogance. I am no exception." The golden man favored her with a charming smile. His pupils were slitted like a cat's. Fascinating.

Forgetting to be embarrassed, she held out her hand. "Hello. I'm Jain."

"So you're the lovely woman who's caused such a fuss. I am the Amir Varad Mohan." Ignoring Kesuk, he swept her hand to his lips.

"Are you really a cat king? They were just considering gene-splicing experiments with Siberian tigers when I left Earth."

"Yes, tigers were successfully spliced. The king of the jungle, as it were."

"That was lions."

"I don't see any lions left. They abandoned the throne." His golden eyes twinkled in good humor, and she liked him immediately.

F ive minutes later, Kesuk padded naked to his own room with Varad on his heels.

"My apologies for interrupting, Lord Kesuk. I wished to warn you—"

He glanced back. "Warn me? Of what?"

The weretiger's hands spread. "The Aquatilian ambassador accompanied me on this voyage. He awaits us in your main hall."

A growl rose in Kesuk's throat. "He should have remained on the ship. He has no business here."

"He wants to collect the humans."

He frowned, shooting a quick glance at the other man. "The humans? There is only one."

"No, there is a second. She was at High Den."

"What did you have to trade to get her?" Grizzlies were notorious in their wily dealings, so much so that he was amazed they had parted with the other human at all. Especially if she was as attractive as Jain.

"Nothing. They thanked me for taking her. She is not as...amiable as your human."

"Mine?" He missed a step, the blow hitting him hard. *Jain.* He braced an arm against the wall, trying to catch his breath. A hard hand closed over his shoulder.

"I am sorry, my friend."

Kesuk shook Varad off. "I'm fine. I knew this day would come. I planned to send her with you when you came."

"Not everything goes according to plan. Keep her if you wish. Unless my instincts deceive me, the lady would remain if you ask."

"No. She is not suited for this world." If he said the words enough, he would believe them. He had to. It was his duty to do what was best for those under his protection. Look how close he had come to losing her this day. He shook his head. He couldn't keep her, and she would be safer hidden under the oceans of Aquatilis.

"Kesuk—"

"I will join you shortly. I must dress."

Chapter 8

Jain pulled the soft dove-gray tunic over her head. It fluttered around her thighs, almost brushing her knee-high charcoal boots. Wanting to look good for Kesuk and his guests, she forked her fingers through her short hair. The side slits on her tunic exposed tight striped leather pants with every step she took. She hurried to the main hall, limping a little on her stiff ankle.

Before she'd even entered the room, a loud feminine voice demanded, "I don't want to be patient. I want to see her now. I want to make sure she hasn't been mistreated."

She knew that voice. Breaking into an uneven jog, she rounded the last corner.

"She has not been mistreated." Anger laced Kesuk's deep voice, his prickly honor at question.

"Dr. Gibbons? *Sera?*" Jain asked, stunned to see someone from her ship.

"Jain!" A huge smile lit the young scientist's face.

"Where did you...*how* did you...the ship exploded. No one else got out but me. I waited and waited and no one else was there."

"My cryogenic pod was thrown from the ship. The ship probably started breaking up when we entered the atmosphere. I was thrown clear of the crash somewhere in the mountains and ended up with a bunch of smelly bear-shifters... You're hurt." Sera abruptly changed topics as her gaze took in Jain's limp. She turned an accusing glare on Kesuk. He growled in return, his irritation plain.

"I had an accident, Sera. It wasn't Kesuk's fault. He saved me from hypothermia." No need to mention the predators.

Jain stepped up onto the dais that held the main table and Kesuk's large chair. She stood next to him, placing a hand on his shoulder. Bare-chested, he wore tight leather breeches and a long, sleeveless leather cape with a huge fur collar, making him appear even more massive than he already was. A hammered silver circlet hugged his muscled bicep. Some symbol of his rank in the clan? She'd never seen him wear it before. He lounged in the chair, his leg hooked negligently over the arm, chin propped in his hand. She fought a grin as she realized he was playing the barbarian they thought him to be.

Sera sniffed, scanning the large hall with obvious distaste. Jain stiffened, wanting to defend this place. She loved it here. She loved the people—exuberant Miki, contained Nukilik, controlled Kesuk. *Kesuk.* She tried to be rational, to see Sea Den through Sera's eyes. Large, scrubbed bare stone floors, decorated skins on the walls, trestle tables. It lacked the technology she was used to, but the roaring fire and groups of chatting people made it homey and welcoming.

She wanted to stay.

"You're coming with us, Jain."

Sera's voice broke through Jain's reverie. "What?"

"We'll be on Aquatilis in three weeks. They came to get us."

"They?" She swiveled around, seeing Varad and another man behind him. The stranger's pale skin set off the sheet of inky hair that hung straight to the middle of his back. Almost as pale as Kesuk, he had deep turquoise eyes and a high forehead. He also had an air of perpetual blasé boredom.

The man had a small flat nose, and his nostrils flared in obvious distaste as he took in the main hall of Sea Den. Then he turned to Jain and executed a neat bow. "Ambassador Hahn of Aquatilis at your service, Dr…"

"Oh, I'm not a scientist. My brother was. I'm a schoolteacher. And, please, call me Jain."

Disappointment flashed in his turquoise eyes, but he recovered quickly. "How charming. You may call me Bretton, of course."

Memory kicked in and her history knowledge popped up. "Sirius Hahn was the founder of the Aquatilian colony. Is he your ancestor?"

"The very same." A wide genuine smile curved his lips. Bretton was a handsome man when he wasn't wearing a condescending look. "Aquatilis will embrace a woman with so fine a knowledge of our past. I'm sure we can arrange for more…comfortable lodging than the Alysians offered you."

"I somehow doubt Aquatilis could compare." Jain grinned, remembering the feel of soft pelts under her back as Kesuk pounded inside her. A private smile lit Kesuk's face as he glanced up at her, letting his gaze slide down her body.

Bretton's lip curled. "Unlike the barbarians, we still have use of most of the technology from your time. It will be much more to your liking."

Kesuk's gaze flashed with resentment. When he smiled, he let his fangs show. "It is unfortunate that our calls for aid from your *advanced* people resulted in nothing. Our loremasters teach that while we were struggling to survive, your *technology* was worthless because you never came. How un-neighborly."

The ambassador flushed, taking a small step back. "Yes, well. We had our own problems when no supplies were delivered from Earth. Our life-support systems were failing, and half our population was still made up of unaltered humans. You understand our dilemma."

"Oh, yes. I understand perfectly."

A cold silence settled over the group as old bitterness played out between Kesuk and Bretton. Jain took a breath. "As far as I can tell, every one of the colonized planets has done what they must to survive. For Aquatilis, that meant preserving the technology that runs your life-support systems in the underwater city. For Alysians, it meant learning to cope with being hunted by predators." Flexing her sore ankle, she shivered at the ugly memory.

Varad stepped forward. "An excellent assessment. I'm sure you would be fascinated to know about the adaptation the weredragons have made on their desert world."

"*Dragons?*" Sera and Jain echoed together.

Sera's brow furrowed. "That's not feasible. All the other shifter species were created from splicing human genes with known animals. Dragons are a myth."

"These are not." Varad shrugged.

"I want to see." Academic zeal lit Sera's eyes. This was the kind of puzzle the woman lived for.

"We have several Harenan diplomats stationed on Aquatilis. You'll see them soon." Bretton's nasal accent cut across their conversation. He smiled at Sera, and she all but melted in a puddle at his feet. Oh, dear. Sera was the youngest scientist to be recruited to Aquatilis, and only then because of her precocious genius. She had no social skills or experience with men. How unfortunate that her first crush would be on such a techno-snob.

Jain rolled her eyes and sighed. She probably fawned just as much when Kesuk smiled at her.

Kesuk rose from his chair and bent to Jain's ear. "We must speak, little bear." He held out his hand, and she placed her fingers in his proffered palm. He drew her away from the group as they discussed the vagaries of dragons and led her down the hall to her chamber.

She knew what this was about. What he was going to say. Panic exploded in her belly. No. Please, no.

His big hands closed over her shoulders, and she leaned back into his warmth. His forehead rested against the back of her head.

"I don't want to go." The words burst from her.

Tears pressed against her lids. How could she leave this place now? She loved it here. They needed her for what she could teach them. She was valued, free to be herself as she never had been before. No expectation of rigid logic. If Bretton was anything to go by, she doubted that would be the case on Aquatilis.

"You cannot stay." Kesuk's hands tightened on her shoulders.

She closed her eyes over the pain. Her voice grew softer. "Why?"

"It is not safe here."

"It's not safe anywhere. Even technology malfunctions. How else did I end up here? Now?"

He sighed, his breath tickling the back of her neck. "Jain—"

"Safety isn't a good enough reason. What else do you have?"

"I don't want you here. This is my Den. You must go."

He didn't want her to stay? Pain hit her square in the chest, squeezed her heart in an iron grip. She searched for something, *anything* to change his mind. "But...but, my debt isn't paid. I'm still your sla—"

"You risked your life to save my cub. Your debt is repaid. I release you."

She turned to face him, pulling out of his arms. "I only did what anyone would have done."

"That is not so. Anyone not in my clan would have left her for dead."

"That's horrible and barbar—" She cut herself off, the look on his face freezing her blood. "Oh, Kesuk, that's not what I—"

"No. Perhaps you are right. You will be more suited to the *civility* of Aquatilis." He spun on a heel and strode from the room, never once looking back.

Her breath choked on a sob. "Kesuk."

Light-headed, she leaned against the bed, her body tingling with shock. She felt as though a part of her had been ripped away. He wanted her gone.

Well, she sure as hell didn't want to stay where she wasn't wanted. She began to pack, stuffing her clothes and belongings randomly into a satchel. Her hands shook so badly, Miki's shells slipped through her fingers and scattered across the floor.

"Damn."

She gathered up the shells, crawling halfway under the bed to retrieve a few strays. The only man to ever make her feel didn't even want to be on the same planet with her. Her breath rattled past parched lips as she tried to swallow the huge lump in her throat. She pressed her forehead against the cool stone floor, trying to push away her emotions like she used to. She tried to make it matter as little as her husband leaving her. She couldn't.

Someone knocked on the door. "Jain?"

"I'll be out in a minute, Sera."

"What are you doing under there?" Footsteps tapped across the floor.

"I dropped Miki's shells." Where were they? She searched, frantic to find them all. She couldn't leave them. She just couldn't. They were her present. Her breath sobbed out, stirring the dust.

"There are plenty of shells out here. Just leave them."

"No! I have to bring them all. I *have* to." Tears burned her lids, and she clamped a desperate hand over her mouth to stifle her sudden sobs.

"Okay...okay...I'll help you." Sera's usually impatient voice was kind and soothing.

"I can do it myself. I can—" They were her *present.* The only connection she'd have to Kesuk and his family after she left. Her hand closed over the last tiny shell. She sighed, an inordinate amount of relief singing through her. A tear leaked down her cheek. "I have it now."

She swiped at her eyes, sniffling as she shimmied out from under the bed, dragging a few stray dust bunnies with her. Standing, she brushed off her clothes and turned to slide the shells into her bag, avoiding eye contact with the other woman.

"It's better that we're leaving, Jain. We were supposed to go to Aquatilis in the first place."

"I know." She cleared her throat. She'd dealt with difficult situations before. She could handle this. She didn't have a choice. If Kesuk didn't want her to stay, then that was it. End of story.

The big bed was empty without Kesuk. Cold. Jain squeezed her eyes shut, willing sleep to come. Wavering dawn sunshine filtered through the small light shafts in her ceiling. He hadn't come to her. She swung her legs over the side of the bed, standing. If he wouldn't come to her, then she would go to him. She deserved one more time in his arms, damn it.

She realized she was stark naked and had no idea where his room was. He had always stayed with her. Stumped, she sat back down. Looking around, she tried to remember where she'd put the map he'd given her when she'd first arrived. Maybe his chambers were labeled. On her knees, she rummaged through her pack, trying to find something that felt like parchment.

Her door swung open.

She froze. She didn't even need to look to know it was him. "Kesuk."

He didn't say a word. In two strides he was on her, scooping her into his arms. She clung to his neck, wrapping her legs around his waist. Thank God he was already naked. She could definitely develop a distinct liking for nudity. If only she had more time. She shoved the thought away, focused on enjoying this time with Kesuk. Her last time.

Stroking his hands over her back, he seemed to relish the feel of her skin, burying his face in her neck to breathe deeply. Surprised that he wanted to go slow, she tightened her legs to press closer to him.

"Kesuk, I—"

The time for words has passed, little bear. Be with me tonight.

"Yes." The answer was simple, plain. She'd take what she could get before she had to leave. One night. One time. One moment. If that was all there was, she'd let go and enjoy it. He'd broken down all her barriers, and she was done pretending he hadn't. She wanted him.

His mouth covered hers, his tongue twining with hers in a slow, deep kiss. Walking blindly, he lowered her to the bed. The furs felt soft against her back as he settled on top of her. The tip of his dick rubbed against her wet pussy lips. Arching up, she waited for the hard thrust that would bury his cock deep within her. It didn't come. Instead, he moved backward, spreading soft kisses over her jaw and neck. She gasped when he nipped her earlobe, the sting causing hot moisture to pool between her spread thighs.

"Please."

Shh.

He pressed his lips to the base of her neck, and his teeth raked over her collarbone. She buried her fingers into his dense, silky hair, loving the texture of it, tugging sharply to speed his progress. Not wanting to wait, she wriggled her hips, pushed the head of his cock into her sex. He sucked her nipple deep into his mouth, drawing hard on the tip.

Frantic, she bucked against him, her heart pounding hard. She couldn't wait. She needed him now. She clamped her legs tight around his hips, pulling him down as she arched up. He groaned, his cock sinking into her, setting a slow, steady, maddening rhythm. Twisting beneath him, she tried to urge him on.

"Kesuk, *please.*" She cupped his cheeks between her hands, forced him to look at her. "I want you. No one can make me feel the way you do. Only you. Now, *hurry up.*"

Surprise flashed across his face and he laughed, a cocky grin playing over his lips. *Like this?*

Three quick hard strokes filled her to the limit. "Yes."

Her hands closed over his ass, pulling him closer, deeper. He quickened his pace, taking her hard, just like she liked it. His masculine scent filled her nose as she sobbed for breath. She clung to him as he rode her, locked together, driving toward orgasm. A few more moments and she would go over, but she held it off, fighting to draw the pleasure out.

He froze, his eyes going all black, then his hips jerked in fast, plunging strokes as he came inside of her. Groaning into her mouth, he sucked her lower lip between his teeth.

Jain. I...Jain.

His thought echoed in her mind, connecting her to him as she shuddered hard, pussy clenching around his dick, her nails biting into his back, her legs tight around his waist.

"Kesuk," she whispered.

Dawn broke and lit the small skylights in her room, the beams gilding his pale skin in a golden glow as they held each other tight, not wanting this last moment to pass. He pressed his forehead to hers, his unsteady breath caressing her face.

Then he rolled off her, taking his warmth with him. He rose gracefully from the bed, his large body beautiful in the morning light. "I will leave you to your final preparations."

She swallowed and crossed her arms over her breasts. "You're not even going to see me off?"

His long fingers clenched on the wood doorframe. His voice grated out. "No. I...can't. Imnek will escort you."

Hot tears flooded her eyes, and she tilted her head back, trying to hold them in. "Okay," she whispered. What else could she say? It was over. Finished.

"I'm sorry, little bear."

A soft laugh caught on a sob at his use of her nickname. God, she would miss that.

He finally looked at her, glancing back over his shoulder, a sad smile playing on his lips. "You wanted me to delegate."

"Just...go." She made herself watch the door close behind him.

Chapter 9

A thin layer of ice crunched under Jain's heavy boots. She walked with Sera, Bretton, and Varad toward the weretiger ship. A huge number of Kesuk's guards accompanied them. He seemed to have emptied out the entire Den for their escort. After her last jaunt outside, she wasn't complaining, but it seemed overkill to send this many to protect them. Her steps dragged. They'd been walking for hours, but it seemed the shortest journey of her life. Everything inside of her wanted to turn around and run back, but instead she pressed forward.

"I have some theories."

Jain sucked her cheeks in to stifle a laugh. How many times had she heard that phrase when Sera was working with her brother? Her heart squeezed at the bittersweet memory of her emotionally distant brother. It hurt so much that even the possibility of growing closer had died with him.

Jain gave Sera a sad smile. "Theories about what?"

"About why we never made it to Aquatilis, of course." Sera rolled her eyes as though she couldn't believe Jain wasn't keeping up with her line of thought.

"Tell me." Jain wasn't sure she'd understand half of what Sera said, but she'd listen. *Anything* to help her not think of Kesuk.

"I would like to hear this as well." Bretton walked a few paces behind them, his hands clasped behind his back.

Sera blushed and swallowed hard. "Um...well, it's simple really...we, um, we...it's possible the hyperdrive failed when we were down-jumping, and my postulation is that we came out of lightspeed too quickly and actually ended up in the neighboring solar system, still traveling toward our destination, but slowly. Then we were caught in the orbit of Alysius for centuries, those on board sustained by the life-support systems in our individual cryogenic pods."

"Why wasn't the crew alert to the problem?" Varad matched stride with Jain on the right.

"Our ship was strictly a supply berth. Jain and I were the only passengers. On supply ships, it was procedure for the crew to enter cryogenic freeze shortly after the jump to lightspeed, and the system would automatically wake them at the end of the standard jump. Ours was not standard, so the crew never woke up. However, it *is* possible—"

"So, why did we crash? Why didn't we remain in orbit forever?" Jain interrupted Sera's academic rambling.

A frown puckered the other woman's face. "Well...I don't know exactly."

"You're here now. That's all that matters." Bretton smiled at Sera.

Jain actually thought the good doctor might swoon. She fought her fifth eye roll of the day. Her gaze met Varad's, and he coughed into his palm to hide his laugh.

"What's Aquatilis like?" Sera grinned back at the ambassador.

"It's wonderful, much better than this. Atlantis is a beacon of lights you can see for miles. We have acres of botanical gardens inside the city proper with dozens of shops to choose from. Saltwater silk would look phenomenal with your lovely hair, Doctor." Bretton's nose wrinkled at the thick fur cape Sera wore now. *Jain's* cape.

Jain's hands balled into fists as she tried to rein in her anger. Bretton had been here only a few weeks. He didn't know anything about these people. She brushed aside the fact that she'd been on Alysius only a few days longer than he had. It had been, what? Three weeks? That was all? It felt like forever. And yet, it had passed far too quickly.

Sera smiled. "I can't wait. I hate it here. It's like something out of a backward caveman holostory."

"Not everyone here is like the Grizzlies." Jain bit her tongue. Damn, she should learn to keep her mouth shut.

Their guards grunted in agreement.

"Look at this place." Bretton waved his elegant hand to indicate their uninhabited surroundings.

"It's beautiful. Just because it's not like *your* planet doesn't mean there's anything wrong with it. You're awfully rude for someone who's supposed to be a representative of your people, *Ambassador* Hahn." Jain didn't bother hiding her disdain.

Bretton flushed, whether from anger or embarrassment, Jain didn't know or care. The snob could go sleep with a predator for all she cared. They'd be the perfect match, and she didn't give a damn that she was being unfair to the Aquatilian.

"If you like it here so much, why are you leaving?" Varad's casual question knocked the wind out of her anger.

"Kesuk...doesn't want me." Jain's voice sounded stilted, even to her own ears.

God, it hurt to even say it, let alone feel it. He didn't *want* her.

Varad folded his hands behind his back. "Huh...that's funny."

"I'm not amused." She shot him a dirty look. Had she thought Varad was the polite one? Well, chalk that one up to another wrong assessment of a male.

"I meant, Lady Jain, that your Lord Kesuk—"

"He's not mine." She clamped her eyes closed, determined not to cry. Not now, not in front of all these people. Striving for her old calm, she opened eyes that were still misty with tears. Damn Kesuk for making her feel and then throwing her away.

"As I was saying, Lord Kesuk did not act like a man who didn't want you."

"That *is* funny because he's the one making me leave. So what did he act like, hmm?" Her voice was so sweet it was acidic.

"Like a man doing his duty and cutting his heart out in the process. Like a *good* man with the misfortune to be in love." Varad's mouth kicked up in a memory only he could see.

"You speak like someone with experience." Jain's mind raced. Could it be true? Kesuk was making her leave as a duty? He loved her?

"I am mated."

She blinked, paying only half a mind to the conversation. Her heart fluttered wildly in her chest. Kesuk *loved* her. Stupid man. Stupid, wonderful man with his stupid, ridiculous honor. She smiled at Varad, a huge blinding smile.

Varad blinked, looked away, and muttered again, "I am mated."

The spaceship came into view, a huge monolithic silver blemish on the pristine forest landscape. Seeing it, Jain made an immediate decision, no thinking, no planning.

"I'm staying."

"Excuse me?" Bretton looked stunned.

"You can't be serious," Sera exclaimed.

Jain took a deep breath, and the heavy weight that had been crushing her chest lifted. "I'm staying. I hope you all have a nice trip."

Varad threw back his head and laughed, the rich sound bouncing off the surrounding mountains. He caught her hands in his. "Oh, my lady. Remember the look on his face when he first sees you. You must describe it for me in detail when I come back next Turn."

"Only if you bring your mate with you so I can meet her."

"Done." Varad kissed each of her hands.

"My lord would not appreciate your actions," Imnek growled. Surprised, Jain glanced at the guard who'd stayed within three steps of her the whole journey.

At first she thought Imnek meant encouraging her to stay, but he didn't even look at her. Instead he stared pointedly at Jain's hands tucked in Varad's grip. Varad stepped away from her, bowing to Imnek. "I trust you will see her safely back to Sea Den."

"Her protection is *my* duty." He glared at the weretiger.

Jain didn't even want to figure out what kind of manly undercurrents were going on here. She was just glad no one was going to make her get on the ship.

"You should come with me. You'll be living in the Dark Ages here." Sera frowned at Jain from the bottom of the pallet loaded with all the trade goods. As the men started loading supplies onto the Vesperi ship, Jain crawled on top and pilfered through the bags until she found hers.

Jain hefted her pack, stepping down into the slushy Thaw snow. The men were growing impatient, watching them work it out. "I love him."

"You could love someone on Aquatilis. That's where we were supposed to go in the first place. And even Varad says it's not as backward as here."

She arched a brow. "That doesn't sound like Varad."

"Not in so many words, but that's basically what he said." Sera folded her arms and jutted her jaw.

Jain sighed. "Things have changed."

"No kidding."

"I meant things have changed with me. Maybe you can walk away from love and find something else that will make you happy. Maybe all you need is your work and your machines, but I need Kesuk and I'm staying."

Sera's eyebrows rose until they almost met her hairline. "You are different."

"I just said that."

"Yes, but you would *never* have said anything like that before. Or told off Bretton. It was always yes, Dad, yes, Brother, yes, Husband."

"*Yes, Sera.*"

Sera snorted, then sobered. "You're sure you'll be okay?"

"As sure as I can be."

"Good luck." Sera leaned in and offered a tentative hug, awkward with affection.

Jain squeezed her tight, popping a kiss on her cheek. "You, too."

"We'll see each other again," Sera whispered in her ear. Then she bolted up the ramp and into the ship.

Waving until the door sealed closed, Jain turned to Imnek, grinning. "Ready?"

"Lord Kesuk is going to kill me."

She looped her hand through his arm. "Well, he wanted you to make more executive decisions. Congratulations, you've succeeded."

Imnek just groaned in response.

It was for the best. It was for her own good. Kesuk stalked to her room, flung the door open, and stomped inside. His gaze swept the room. He could still smell her. Smell the lingering scent of their sex. He dragged in a deep breath, knowing he'd need to remember every detail in the future, when the pain had subsided. It had been that way with Maruska. Someday, he would cherish his time with Jain. Someday the pain would fade. Now he felt as though a dull blade had ripped his heart out.

He'd been so careful. Not to need her. Not to get attached to her. Not to love her. He wasn't strong enough to lose two women he loved in one lifetime. Nothing had ever hit him as hard as Jain had. Feelings had developed gradually with his mate. But with Jain? His world had tilted on its axis when she crashed into it. Going back to the cold man he had been before her wasn't appealing. Duty was a poor substitute, he knew that now. He'd had Jain to point it out. Passion he could handle, control. But love? He sighed, laid a hand on the untidy furs, imagining he could still feel the warmth of her body on them. The warmth of her smile, her touch.

"Papa?"

He straightened, turning toward the small voice. Miki and Nukilik stood in the doorway, tears streaking their faces. "Yes?"

He waved them forward and they ran in to hug his legs. "Where did Jain go?"

"She left for Aquatilis. Did she not say farewell?" Surely Jain would never have done such a thing. She adored his cubs, of that he had no doubt.

"She said she had to leave. When will she be back? Next Turn with Amir Varad?" Nukilik's steady eyes gazed up at him, waiting for him to say the right thing. He wished he knew the answers for them.

"That's a very long time to wait, Papa. We'll be so much older then. What if she doesn't recognize us?"

"She's not coming back."

"Not coming back? Why not?" Nukilik's forehead furrowed.

Miki dug her fingers into the top of Kesuk's boot. "She'll miss us very much. She loves us. She said so before she left. She said we weren't to forget."

"Then you're not to forget." He stroked back Miki's soft hair. He took a deep breath, sat on the edge of Jain's bed, and pulled a child onto each leg. "Jain was supposed to go to Aquatilis. She needs to be there."

"She didn't like Ambassador Hahn. I could tell. She likes us, so she should have stayed here." Nukilik nodded at that logic. Simple. Reasonable. Fair. The boy would grow into an excellent clan leader someday.

"She has to come back. We love her and she loves us," Miki sobbed, her fingers clenching in the laces on his shirt. He hugged her close, knowing nothing but time would ease her grief.

The distant roar of the weretigers' spaceship flying over Sea Den shook the ground under his feet. The dull ache in his chest intensified to a sharp, blinding pain. He closed his eyes, swallowing. Jain was gone. It was well and truly over now. He felt...empty.

Jain found Kesuk lying in her bed, the covers still mussed from their lovemaking, his arms folded behind his head, staring at the curved ceiling.

"I couldn't do it."

Jerking upright, he twisted to stare at her. He blinked, his expression blank for a moment. "You're supposed to be on the ship."

"I couldn't leave. I was there, ready to board and do what you wanted, what you thought was best. Hell, what was *logical,* but I just...couldn't do it." Spreading her hands, she shrugged.

"I told you I didn't want you here."

"You lied."

He blinked. "What?"

"You lied. I understand—you were trying to do the right thing. I really do get it."

He rolled to the edge of the bed, his booted feet landing on the fur rug. "You won't be able to leave for another Turn."

"Yes, that ship has sailed." She grinned, starting to enjoy his confusion. It was about damn time she had the upper hand in something.

"Jain…" He trailed off, at an obvious loss for words.

"I'm staying. I already decided and there's nothing you can do about it. Be angry if you want, but I'm still here. You won't stay mad long, though. You want to know why?"

"Why?"

"Because you love me."

He choked.

"That's right, you love me. It took me a while to figure it out, but now it all makes sense. You try to make me happier with myself, more comfortable in my own skin. You worry about me all the time. You sent a whole legion of soldiers to guard me today. Did you really think we needed that many? You saved me from the snow, treat me with respect even when you're being a bossy jerk, and you get angry when people try to hurt me."

"I would do the same for anyone under my protection."

"Maybe, but you didn't have to bring me under your protection in the first place. The Crescents wanted to buy me, so you could have gotten rid of me if you wanted to. You didn't want to. You wanted to keep me."

"Crescents are scavengers. I wouldn't—"

"We can argue about this all night long if you want, because I'm here for another year, so we have plenty of time. Or we can occupy ourselves with something more entertaining." She smiled at him and unbuttoned her heavy fur-lined jacket. Her tunic quickly followed, and his gaze locked on her bare breasts. She bounced on her toes a little to make them jiggle for him, their tips peaking tight.

He sucked in a hissing breath. "Jain—"

"Touch me." She leaned forward so he could do what she wanted.

His hand lifted to stroke down the slope of her breast, fingers plucking at her nipples. Using his other palm to cup her ass, he pulled her forward and buried his face between her breasts. He breathed deeply, nudged her soft flesh with his nose, and slid his tongue up to swirl around the crest before sucking it deep into his mouth, pulling back to worry the very tip of her hard nipple between his teeth.

She caught her breath, rising on tiptoe to get closer to that wicked mouth. She moaned deeply, fisting her hands in his hair. She loved the silky feel of it.

He sucked a deep breath, let go of her nipple, and rested his chin on her chest. "I did the right thing."

"You did. So did I." She stroked his hair, tears gathering in her eyes.

"Kiss me."

A wicked grin played over her lips, and she dropped to her knees between his spread thighs. She slid a fingernail up the seam of his pants toward his cock. It strained against the leather as she traced the lacings to the top and tugged the strings open. "As you wish. You didn't get to have me as your slave very long. Maybe I should make it up to you?"

"Ah, little bear. I do love how your mind works."

His heavy dick slipped free, and she wrapped her fingers tight around the base and stroked to the tip. Rotating her hand around the head of his cock, she licked a bead of pre-cum from the tip. She sucked the whole head in, her lips slipping down to the shaft as her hands worked his flesh up and down, slow at first, then faster and faster.

He groaned, his fingers slipping into her short hair, using his grip to pump her mouth as if it were a pussy. His cock touched the back of her throat. "Hmmm," she hummed around his dick, looking into his eyes so she knew he saw her envelope his cock in her mouth.

"Jain!" Panting hard, his hands slid under her arms, lifting her off the floor and away from his cock. He rolled them onto the bed and jerked at the lacings on her pants, which tangled tight.

She laughed. "Hey, I wasn't finished yet."

"I very nearly was."

"That was kind of the point."

He growled in frustration, ripping her pants open, the tough leather snapping under his strength. "Lift your ass."

She obeyed, leveraging her hips up to help him slide her pants down, trusting him to take her where she needed to go. He had her naked in a few seconds and rolled her to her hands and knees. He slid his fingers between her pussy lips, stroking her clit. She moaned, pushing back into his hand. He pressed down on the small of her back, arching her ass up.

The head of his cock pushed at her opening and then slid hard and deep into her pussy. She dropped down, pressing her face to the covers, gasping at his deep penetration. His hand reached around to stroke her clit in time with his slapping thrusts.

"I can't—"

"You can." He rotated his hips, grinding her in a different rhythm.

"Kesuk…"

"Straighten up," he ordered. His hands pulled up on her ribcage until her back pressed to his chest.

One of his hands resumed stroking her clit. The other fondled her breasts.

She reached back to tug on his hair, twisting her head around to pull his mouth to hers. His lips captured hers, stroking his tongue into her mouth. Their tongues rubbed, stroked, dueled as their bodies moved together in hard, pounding rhythm.

Blood sang through her veins, pumping her heart fast. She rubbed her ass against his pelvis, bouncing on his hard cock. He broke from her mouth, his teeth moving to her shoulder and biting down.

"Kesuk." She clawed his strong thighs, which flexed to pump his cock into her hot pussy.

He pressed down on her clit, rode her on it with his thrusts, pinching her nipple hard.

"I'm coming! Kesuk, I'm coming!" She twisted under the lash of pleasure, her pussy spasming hard. Her heart pounded so hard she could feel the beats just under her skin, her whole body flushing. Oh, God.

"Yes." He pounded with short, jerky strokes, his breath harsh against her neck. Stiffening, he froze, shuddering his orgasm.

Gasping hard, they collapsed onto their sides. He wrapped his arms around her, cradling her back against his chest, burying his nose in her hair, breathing deeply.

She rubbed her hand over his forearms in lazy circles. "I was right. That was definitely more fun than arguing."

He grunted, his arms tightening. "You had your chance to go. I let you. Now you're mine."

"And you're mine. Forever." She sighed, snuggling back against him, content.

"Forever."

"I love you, Kesuk."

"I know."

"*I know*? That's all I get?" She clawed his arm in retaliation.

He chuckled. "I love you, too. Now kiss me."

His cock rose between the cleft of her ass, and she gasped in surprise, pushing her hips against his hardening flesh.

"Again?"

"Forever."

IN HEAT

WEREPLANETS
BOOK 2

CRYSTAL JORDAN

CJ BOOKS

Chapter 1

The snow tigress was in heat.

His nostrils flared. He could smell her desire from across the ballroom. Her scent called to him, tempting him to cast off the veneer of civility and take her in any way he could.

Mahlia Najla Mohan.

His mate.

Longing warred with sadness at the thought of her. Of their lost child. Pain exploded in his chest, choking him. *No.* He would not think of that. He could not. The agony would drive him to his knees.

"Amir Varad." His manservant's voice pulled him back to the present. Varad pasted a charming smile on his face, appearing the besotted male who would soon have his mate begging him for the surcease only he could grant her. And possibly conceiving an heir to the Vesperi throne. A new heir.

"Welcome back, my brother." Taymullah's hand clapped on his shoulder.

Varad quirked a brow at the shorter man. And he was a man—the boy he'd left behind six months ago had grown into someone Varad hardly recognized. The last half Turn had been a difficult time for all of his family.

Taymullah's face settled into serious lines as he turned to look over at his brother's mate, Mahlia. "You have a great deal of work before you, Varad."

"I know."

Varad swallowed, his gaze tracking her movement. Mating on Vesperi was a complicated affair, only lasting from a woman's heat cycle to the next. Because Varad was here, no one would touch his woman. Had he not returned in time, it would have been a different tale. However, she could always choose to mate away from him. His gut clenched. *No.* Mahlia was *his.* Had been his since the moment he'd looked into her ice-blue eyes, so rare among his people. His treasure. She would have no other for as long as they both lived. Whatever tragedy they shared could not destroy the depth of emotion that had always pulled them together.

Gods, he was tired. Six months on a spacecraft for the trade run was more than he cared for, but he doubted the werebears on the planet Alysius would trade with anyone except him personally. Lord Kesuk was not a trusting man.

A genuine smile tugged at Varad's lips as he thought of the Arctic Bear Clan leader. He wondered how the enormous man had fared after Varad had encouraged the tiny human woman to return to the werebear's caves. The man hadn't stood a chance. Lady Jain would have seen to it. Varad's grin widened. Mahlia would like Jain immensely.

And Kesuk would try to kill him when Varad returned next Turn, no matter how happy the werebear lord was with his lady. It would be an interesting fight. Varad flicked a barely visible piece of lint from his sleeve as he wondered who might be the winner. A tiger versus a bear. Yes, interesting.

He shook his head, marveling again that a spaceship could have drifted among the stars since before the Earthan sun had died. Two unaltered humans, Lady Jain and a young scientist, Sera, had survived a crash landing on the werebear planet. Humans were extinct now, having had no way to survive the harsh environments of the four colonized planets. Only gene-splicing with different animal species had made it possible for humans to survive at all.

He wondered how the two women would fare. Lady Jain had her new Bear Clan to contend with, but Sera had insisted on journeying to Aquatilis, the planet that maintained the greatest level of technology from old Earth. He suspected her choice had more to do with her fascination for a certain merman ambassador than her need for machines.

"Amir, your guests await you." Varad's valet bared his teeth a bit at the word *guests.* Varad chuckled as he descended the curving staircase from the wide balcony. Unlike Taymullah, one of the few who had supported Varad's expeditions, his manservant disapproved of the trade relations with Alysius.

"Well, we shouldn't disappoint our *valued* visitors." A warning was in Varad's tone. He was the king here, the Amir, and his wishes would be obeyed by all. If he bore the responsibility of leadership, he demanded the respect that came with the position.

"Yes, my Amir." His servant bowed and backed away.

Trade had always been maintained between Vesperi and the Harenan weredragons, but many had thought Varad mad when he set out to find the other two planets. It had been a risk, he admitted. But what was life without risk? None could deny that the new flood of goods from the werebears and merpeople were good for all four planets. No matter how much his doubters might like to protest. He tried to cover his laugh in a discreet cough.

He sobered abruptly, the grin falling away from his face. Many of his people agreed that trading with the seemingly barbaric werebears was a mistake. They were a rough people, but he'd grown to respect them, especially Lord Kesuk. He sighed, the weight of his responsibilities riding heavily on his shoulders. He shrugged as if to shift the burden, but nothing could ease his troubles.

A sweet laugh rippled across the ballroom, and he wasn't the only one who turned to smile at the source. Mahlia. Another challenge to face. Whether it pleased either of them or not, he would soon have her.

The room gleamed with white marble and wildly colored swaths of fabric—all the ostentation a feline could need. He worked his way across the vast ballroom to her side, nodding to his guests, noting the flashing scales of the Harenan weredragons, the imposing bulk of the first Alysian werebear ambassador, the violently colored hair of the Aquatilian merpeople. An interplanetary gathering, just as he had hoped. Excellent. When he reached Mahlia, she was entertaining a merman and the werebear ambassador with a story about her inability to master the waltz as a child.

"Amira Mahlia." Varad's hand stroked down the length of her bare arm, tracing the tan stripes on her creamy skin with a fingertip. He savored the feel of her, enjoying the way her servant had gathered her long cream-and-bronze-striped hair on her head, leaving her shoulders bared in a laced black corset. One of her legs was exposed by the filmy deep-blue skirt slit to her waist. His cock hardened, the need to have her fisting his gut. A deep breath dragged her scent to him yet again. Only because he was so focused on her did he hear the soft catch in her breath before she turned icy blue eyes on him. The natural black lining that surrounded all weretiger eyes made hers stunning.

"Amir Varad." She attempted to curtsy before him, but he quickly squeezed her elbow to keep her upright. Even after a Turn, she was not accustomed to her role in society. Or perhaps she was still uncomfortable with him. It mattered not. His mate would not bow to him. She was his equal—the only true partner he had in his world. He inclined his head to her, and after the briefest of pauses, she followed suit.

"Your Amira was just telling us an amusing story, Amir." The sub-bass rumble of the werebear split the silence, and a white smile flashed in his dark face. The hammered metal circlet welded around his massive bicep, a mark of his standing among the Bear Clans, glinted in the light from the glowlight chandeliers.

"Yes, the Aquatilians wish you all felicity in your return." The merman's nasal tone and sophisticated speech demonstrated the difference between the merman's culture and that of the werebear. Only Mahlia could have charmed the two into maintaining a peaceful conversation for more than a few minutes.

"Welcome home, Amir." He turned to see Ketryn, his mate's closest friend, approaching their group. Her dark hair rippled to her hips, and her golden skin was set off in a stunning white gown reminiscent of an ancient Grecian toga. The weredragon was beautiful, but the first thing one noticed about her was the purple scaling that crept from her wrists to her biceps.

Still, no other woman had ever called to him as Mahlia had. Anticipation tensed his muscles. Soon. Soon he would have her. Would have her legs about him as they rode each other, her slick heat tight on his thrusting cock. He bit back a groan and traced a finger down the lacings of her corset. Her breath panted as her scent increased, surrounding him, commanding him.

The hunt would begin soon.

T he hunt would begin soon.

Heat spun through Mahlia's body, a force she could not control. Need made her hands tremble and her legs shake. She turned her desperate gaze to Ketryn, but her friend just shrugged. Mahlia closed her eyes. No. No one could save her from this. She could not even save herself. Sweat beaded on her upper lip. When she breathed, it was only to pull in Varad's scent. Desire slammed into her, dampening her pussy.

The endless, relentless need of her breeding time tightened her core until she bit back a scream. Her breath panted between her lips. She didn't want this. She did not want another child. Ever. Losing her young was more than she could bear.

Her physiology did not care what she wanted.

Varad's hand splayed across her back, easing up over the naked skin of her shoulders. She didn't look at him, but she knew he craved her. The heat rose, tearing into her with the fierce claws of the tiger within her. A low snarl pulled from her throat, and her fangs bared as her head tilted back against her mate's shoulder. His gaze clashed with hers, the slitted pupils in his golden eyes expanding wide, his nostrils flaring.

He could smell her need. His fingers moved to spread over her lower belly, pressing her backside to the rigid line of his cock. It burned through the thin material of their clothing. They locked together in that moment, the animals buried just beneath the surface rising to strip them of anything but the instinct to breed.

Her control spun away, and it began. A tiger scream ripped from her, and she jerked away from Varad. The whole ballroom turned to look at her, most of the tigers' lips curving into knowing smiles. She was beyond caring, beyond embarrassment, beyond anything but the driving need to have her mate buried deep inside her. Her eyes darted to the nearest exit. Yes. There. Run. Make him catch her.

She leaped forward, her legs burning as she pushed herself to get a head start on Varad. His roar sounded behind her, the crowd parting to allow them through. She slid through the arched doorway, the rich tapestries lining the walls blurring into a rainbow of deep color as she sped past. His pounding footsteps echoed behind her, gaining on her. Where could she go? She needed to go *faster*.

The dune-racers. She could get away on one of them. Where was the corridor that led to the dune-racer bay? Lust clouded her thoughts, made her want to run without a plan. Straight and fast and long until she was caught. The end of this game was inevitable. She knew it, but she could prolong the anticipation. Adrenaline pumped through her system, and the freedom of the hunt made her laugh. She broke left, rushing headlong toward the open racer bay.

Hearing the sucking *pop* of bones reforming behind her told her that Varad had changed into a tiger. One glance over her shoulder confirmed it. The auburn-and-black-striped hair spread down from Varad's head to cover his body. Claws bit into the white marble floor as his paws hit the ground. The hard, possessive golden eyes locked on her as the graceful cat's muscles bunched and flowed, racing after her. Her womb contracted, juice pooling between her thighs. She hissed, facing ahead once more, pushing herself to greater speed. Faster. Faster. Don't stop.

"Ha!"

She'd made it to the bay. Now she needed a dune-racer. There, the blue glow of exhaust rolled from one of the racers. Her boot heels rang against the hard floor, and her legs burned, but she couldn't stop—he was getting closer, almost upon her. Sweat poured down her face, slipping down her chest and beading between her breasts. The corset bit into her flesh as she sobbed for air and her breasts almost spilled from the top with each deep breath she dragged into her lungs.

Flinging herself at the racer, the slit in her skirt allowed her to swing a leg over the side. Her hands grasped the handlebars, and she twisted the left grip to accelerate. The bottom dropped out of her stomach as the racer shot straight up into the air and then roared forward, heading right for the open bay doors. Varad's cat shriek of frustration echoed through the immense bay, drowning out even the racer's engine. She was almost free of the palace proper. The doors came closer and closer with every nanosecond.

Metal rang as a huge tiger's weight slammed down on top of a large hovercraft, his paws stretched forward in a leap. Her breath caught as she watched Varad change in midair back to his human form. He was nude, the golden sinew of his muscles rippling as the fur retracted to reveal the subtle stripes on his skin. She screamed as he flipped neatly behind her onto the racer. It dipped under the added poundage, and she fought to control the machine so they didn't crash.

The Dead Sea curved to her right, a wide swath of underground water and the lifeblood of Vesperi. Excitement spun through her as the amazing speed of the racer shot them out and across the open white sand dunes. The wind whipped at her hair, ripping it from its bindings to wave behind her.

"Mahlia." His smooth, cultured voice was a guttural growl in her ear, and a lightning flash of pleasure zinged to her pussy.

One of Varad's hands slid against her scalp, making gooseflesh erupt down her arms. She could feel the sharp points of his claws on her skin. He was almost feral. She had pushed him that far. Just the thought made her sex clench. His lips pressed to her shoulder, tongue laving the flesh. Then he bit her. Hard.

She sucked in a shocked breath and shoved her hips back to rub against his thick cock. All that separated her from him was the thin film of her garments—the bulbous crest of his dick teased her. Liquid heat rolled over her in waves. The claws of his other hand raked up her thigh, and he fisted his fingers in her skirt to rip it away, letting it spin off into the wind. She gasped at the slight pain and the coolness on her naked flesh. His hands fitted to her waist, shoving her up to lean over the handlebars of the dune-racer. The machine wavered as she overcorrected. Gods, she couldn't crash them, couldn't die without knowing the feel of him pounding within her once more.

The blunt tip of his cock brushed against the lips of her pussy as he slid beneath her raised hips. Then he forced her down to the base of his shaft in one brutal thrust. She screamed as her inner muscles stretched and convulsed around his dick. She wanted more, harder, faster. Her hands clamped on the racer's handles, fighting to hold on to her sanity as pleasure slammed into her.

"*Yes*, Varad. Please." She breathed the words, doubting he could hear her over the racer's engine and the wind. He set a hard, driving rhythm, hammering into her wet pussy. Her cat senses could smell the musk of their combined sexes over the rush of wind. Her heart pounded loudly as exhilaration twisted inside her.

I always please you, Mahlia.

His telepathic words stroked over her mind just as his hands jerked hard on the lacings of her corset, pulling it down until her breasts sprang free of the restraint. Cold wind puckered the tips, and she arched as his hands rose to cup them, his fingers grinding her nipples, pinching them, pulling them hard. Her body bowed under the harsh lash of pleasure. She wanted it hard, swift, and rough. The heat inside her built, screaming for all he could give her.

More, Varad. More!

Yes. His voice dropped to a silken purr in her mind, the calm before a dangerous storm.

His fingers dropped to wrap tightly in the corset laces, and he used the leverage to pull her against him as he shoved his thick cock deeper into her. Her clit rode the cold metal of the racer as his hot flesh slammed into her from behind. She wanted to close her eyes and revel in the sensations exploding through her, but she had to focus on controlling their skimming flight over the dunes. The dangerous thrill of it made the sex better for her, made her want him more, made the pleasure writhe like an untamed thing through her.

Varad, I'm going to—

Come for me. Be wild for me.

He roared as he ground against her pussy, his fingers jerking her down. Harder and harder. Faster and faster until he froze behind her, shuddering as his seed spurted inside her.

Yes.

She threw her head back and screamed out her orgasm, her tiger's roar resonating against the dunes.

"Mahlia!" Varad's arms wrapped around her, and he leaped, pulling both of them away from the racer seconds before it exploded into the side of a massive sand dune.

He rolled them over and over, away from the smoking fire. His body settled over hers to surround her, shelter her. He buried her face in his shoulder, his big hand splayed against the base of her skull.

"Are you all right?" He pulled back, straddling her as his fingers brushed over her body, looking for injury.

"Yes," she gasped. The heat burning within her returned full force. She needed him again. *Craved* him.

She arched beneath him, lifting her hands to stroke over the stripes on his chest. His skin gleamed in the light of Vesperi's three moons. He was such a beautiful man. His auburn-and-black-striped hair brushed his shoulders, and a thick loop earring studded his left ear. Unexpected in a civilized king. Dangerous. Sexy. Even in the night, her cat's eyes could see the details of every slope and plane of his muscled body. Her fingers brushed over his flat nipples, and they hardened under her touch. She swallowed, lust spinning wild in her, clouding her thoughts, bringing her world down to one thing, one need. To mate.

Varad, I need...

She couldn't finish the thought, her mind an incoherent babble of begging, desperate want. Her hips twisted against the sand, and she snarled low in her throat, daring him to deny her, to claim her.

He extended the claws on one hand, slashing her corset to ribbons. Retracting his talons, he fisted his fingers in the tattered remains and ripped it from her body, baring her to his eyes. All she wore now were her long black boots. His gaze swept over her flesh in a heated caress before locking with hers. The gold of his irises bled to the corners of his eyes, his pupils expanding to see all of her.

He bent to suck her nipples into his mouth. She tangled her fingers in his soft hair, sifting through the bi-colored locks, pulling him closer. His teeth nipped at the swollen crests, making pleasure again flood her pussy with moisture. Cool air brushed over her damp nipples as he trailed his tongue down her ribcage, circling her navel. Her breath sped up in anticipation, and she parted her legs to allow him access to her core. He bit the soft swell of her belly, and she gasped. Settling between her thighs, his hard fingers shoved her legs wider for him.

A slow lick teased her dewy lips and clitoris. She panted, pushing closer to his mouth, needing satisfaction. He chuckled, flicking his tongue over her clit but not giving her the hard, insistent contact she craved.

Her fingers flexed in his hair, tugging hard.

"Varad!"

Your taste is lush on my tongue, Mahlia. Tell me you want my fingers within you.

"Touch me," she begged, sobbing hard. "Please, Varad."

He purred against her pussy, and her heels dug into the sand, shoving her hips up as her torso bowed. Her pussy clenched tight on his invading tongue. His fingers pressed into her wet depths, stroking hard and fast, giving her just the kind of friction she needed. Her thighs shook as she rode the high edge of orgasm, and tears gathered at the corners of her eyes to slip down her cheeks. Excitement flashed through her, tingling over her flesh. She was so close she could taste the sweet bliss of it. He sucked her clit, and she screamed as pleasure hit her in a rush, orgasm fisting her pussy in rhythmic waves.

Oh, Gods. Oh, Gods.

It wasn't enough. Her mating heat pressed in on her. She needed his cock moving deep inside her. Now. Her fingers dragged at his hair, pulling him on top of her.

Come inside me.

Oh, I will, my Amira.

He lunged up, covering her with his long, muscled length. She gasped at the hot press of his flesh against hers. It had been so long since she'd felt this—six excruciating months. His chest slid against her breasts, and he shifted to guide his cock to her opening. Her breath seized at the slow, hot glide of him within her. He ground his hips lightly to stimulate her clit. She closed her eyes, hooking her booted feet under his buttocks to keep him tight to her.

He grunted as he sank deeper in her, but he stopped moving. Her palms pressed to his back, fingers curling over his shoulder from behind. His head dipped to sip the skin of her throat just where she liked it. She purred in pleasure, but wild craving bit into her. Heat swamped her, made her hiss and arch beneath him, thrashing in the harsh grains of sand.

I can't wait, Varad. Don't tease.

"Tease?" He pulled back, a charming grin curving his lips. His pupils contracted into thin points when she stared up at him. She knew her own eyes would have no white around the irises. The pale blue would reach from corner to corner. Her claws bared, and she raked them slowly down his back. His breath hissed out as his hips bucked against her.

Yesssss.

Her eyes closed as the heat slid over her consciousness, instinct taking over. Her legs tightened on him, her pelvis rocking against his hard, thrusting cock. He was so big it almost hurt to have him inside her even now. She loved it. She wanted it. They moved together, slick skin slapping against slick skin as a fine sheen of sweat sealed their flesh with each quick thrust. She could smell the spice of his skin mixed with their sex. His lips pressed to the side of her neck, and he bit her again. She could feel the soft prick of his fangs as he scraped gently. It was enough to shove her over the edge.

"Varad!" Her scream carried across the sand dunes.

His head bowed back, and his fangs glistened in the moonlight. He roared his orgasm, riding his cock into her soft, welcoming flesh. His warmth pumped into her, and her sex contracted to keep his seed inside.

And finally she relaxed, spent. Panting, she waited for the high to crash, for her heart to stop pounding. She pushed against his shoulders until he rolled off her. Pulling her knees to her chest, she arched into a nimble leap, landing on the balls of her feet, the heels of her boots sinking into the soft sand. She turned away from Varad and faced the direction they had come from. She couldn't see the bulbous points of the palace. It was designed to look like the old Earthan Taj Mahal—the building rose high into the sky, a beacon for travelers, as the rest of the city was buried beneath the ground. They had gone much too far if she could not see its impressive heights. Her stomach churned in uneasy fear.

Are you certain you are well, Mahlia?

She jerked her head to the side, ignoring the concern in his tone. "I am fine."

More than fine, she was now in control of herself again as the overwhelming waves of mating heat receded in the cold reality of near death. Gods, she was such a fool. What had she been thinking to ignore the dangers involved in handling a dune-racer? And now they were countless miles from the capital, with no way back. The sun would rise soon. She squeezed her eyes closed. Stupid, stupid, stupid.

And she was, in all likelihood, pregnant. Her stomach pitched at the thought. She would know soon enough. If she hadn't conceived, the heat would continue until she did. It was the nature of a weretiger. Then she would have the four short months of tiger gestation to brace herself for the terror of being a mother again. Tears stung her eyes. She couldn't do it again. Her breath escaped in ragged puffs. Gods, she wasn't strong enough to watch the life drain bit by bit from a tiny being who'd captured her heart. To see the genetic disorder so rare among the weretigers eat her child from inside out. She remembered the silky feel of Jeevan's skin, the milky breath as he'd cuddled against her. Nausea rolled over her, and she swallowed hard to push it back.

"How long do we have to get back before the sun rises?"

"A few hours."

"We'll never make it back in time."

"We must try. Rescue is not coming."

A bitter laugh squeezed past her tight throat. "No, you're right. No one will be looking for us. They'll assume we're holed up somewhere fucking each other senseless in our quest to beget them a living heir."

"Mahlia—"

She slashed a hand through the air. "No. I don't wish to speak of this. Let's shift into tiger form. We'll move faster that way."

"As you desire, *my Amira*." His jaw clenched as his head dipped in a sharp nod.

Chapter 2

She was so lovely in the moonlight, but it couldn't stop the anger that licked at him for her insistence that they ignore Jeevan's death. By ignoring it, she let it grow like a wide gulf between them. His gaze followed her pale body, his cock twitching to life once more. He groaned. He should not want her again so soon, but it had always been so with them. No other woman could compare.

He growled, stooping to change into a tiger. The suction of bone and sinew popping into a new shape sounded loud in the quiet stillness of the desert. The sound was mimicked by Mahlia's change into her snow tiger form. Her long boots lay discarded beside her as they faced each other.

Watching her, he considered. He could obey her wishes and not speak of their lost son, or he could use the time she was trapped with him to his advantage. He dragged his tongue down a long fang and then stopped himself. He'd picked up the habit from Kesuk over the past three Turns. He shook the thought away, focusing on his mate.

It was not your fault he died, Mahlia. Or mine.

Incandescent rage burned in her blue eyes as her tail lashed behind her. She pivoted on her haunches to run for the capital city, her long white-and-brown-striped body gliding over the brilliant white sand. He pulled even with her shoulder but did not pass her. He did not want her to fall behind. Her safety was precious to him, and he would not lose her to the scorching heat of the sun. If not for the near constant twilight the moons provided by blocking the sun, Vesperi would be far too hot to inhabit. It was too close to the sun. No human could survive under its blistering heat for more than a few minutes. They would be incinerated.

I know that.

Her telepathic voice was a tight, furious cadence in his mind.

Yet you are angry with me.

You left me! You left me here to cope alone.

You told me to leave.

The pain of that still reverberated through him, but he'd had six months without her to know that he had no desire to live that way. Her quiet strength was a balm for him, and he'd craved her every day he'd spent alone.

You wanted to go. You wanted to run away, and I wasn't going to beg you to stay.

He snorted. *Beg me? You never acted as though you wanted to have anything to do with me. How was I to know, Mahlia? I am a king, not a mind reader.*

You didn't ask me to come with you.

Space travel is dangerous, Mahlia. I won't—

And your worry is greater than mine? You think I don't fear that you'll never return when you leave for half of each Turn?

He continued as if she hadn't interrupted. *I won't risk your life. I won't lose someone else it is my responsibility to protect.*

Her stride faltered for a moment before she picked up her speed, stretching into a sprint. *Don't you see that you're losing me anyway?*

His breath caught. *Mahlia—*

She shook her head, pointed ears twitching. *What of this child? If we've made a—*

We have. And if not, we will try again.

Maybe we shouldn't. It is not unheard of for an Amir to have multiple mates throughout his life.

His roar sounded over the sand. *Never!*

Varad—

He leaped in front of her, whipping around so they stood face-to-face, noses nearly touching. His eyes locked with hers, awareness spinning between them as it always did. He wanted her still, again. Always. He made his thoughts low, coaxing, seductive. *Could any man please you as I do, Mahlia?*

She paused, her gaze sliding away. *No.*

The bare whisper met his mind, but he was satisfied. She could not consider leaving him. Pain banded his chest. He shook his head. He would not stand for it. Ever. Stepping aside, he jerked his chin in the direction of the palace, indicating that she continue.

She pressed forward, and he fell in behind her, the fast rhythm of her smooth stride a pleasure to behold. *You will see our babe for barely a month, and then off you'll go, disappearing into the ether for the Gods know how long.*

I do what I must for our people. Trade keeps us prosperous.

You also need to do what you must for our mating. For our family.

You think I neglect you?

I am not a mind reader either, Varad. I think you don't care for my company enough to see me for more than a few stolen moments to roll in bed. I am merely a convenient bedmate. Even then, it is for but half the Turn. What tigress would be satisfied with that?

He snorted. *You think this is* convenient? *If I wanted a bedmate, I could have anyone I desired.*

She hissed at him, but said nothing more. She was jealous. Good. It meant she cared, no matter what she pretended. He spoke nothing less than the truth. Sex was an easy thing, but mating? That was another issue altogether. Did she not know he would do anything for her? Anything except let her leave him.

Still, she had not discussed Jeevan with him. For both their sakes, they needed to talk about this. Silence stretched between them while they ran as fast as their legs would carry them. Their breath grew labored, and his muscles screamed with pain. Every part of him ached, and with each step agony slammed into him, racing up from his paws to the base of his skull. He knew not how many miles they had traveled. The distance before them stretched interminably. The dunes gave way to hard-packed white dirt, and he breathed a momentary sigh of relief. They were getting close. Pointed spires rose into the sky, the golden tips coated to catch the solar heat and power the capital. The sky began to lighten with the ominous beginnings of sunrise.

His gut tightened. Gods, they might not make it. No. They were too close to fail.

Hurry, Mahlia. He sent the command and picked up his pace until he drew even with her. Her pale blue eyes were dull with exhaustion when she looked at him. Her head dipped low with each stride, labored breath whistling out. *We are almost there.*

Just...go...

Her telepathy was barely above a whisper, and his heart stuttered at how weak she sounded. He prayed as he had not since his son lay dying that there was a miracle for them. Go on without her? He snorted. Foolish thought.

I will not leave you.

Then...you will die.

I have faith.

I do...not.

Go, Mahlia. He whipped his tail at the back of her legs. She hissed at him but did not slow, racing for the gates of the city. Good.

Oh, Gods. The gates. He narrowed his eyes and saw that the massive metal gates were swinging closed as they did at every dawn. Fear hammered at his heart. No. He would not let his mate die. Not another life so precious to him. Never again.

Open the gates!

He shoved the telepathic command as wide as it would go. Surely someone would hear him and obey their king. The gates shuddered, creaking to a slow stop, only a hairbreadth of an opening between them. Would the guards be able to reverse the mechanisms in time? Varad's breath bellowed out as he ran, his legs shaking with fatigue, no longer landing solidly beneath him. He willed the gates to part with all his might. They groaned and began to swing open again. Yes!

Run, Mahlia! For Gods' blessing, run!

He had no idea how it was possible, but her paws dug deeper into the ground, and she sprinted even faster. The glow of sunlight began to lighten the horizon, and they had but moments before it would kiss them with its deadly rays.

The gates loomed closer, and they were almost upon them. A few more strides would take them through. The scorching burn of the sun hit the backs of his legs, and he yowled at the pain.

Varad!

He shifted to his human form, his bones popping back into place. Leaping forward, he wrapped his arms around Mahlia and lunged through the opening. They rolled, tumbling until his back slid against a solid stone wall. He groaned as Mahlia collapsed beside him, her white fur matted and filthy. His chest burned with every breath he pulled past his parched lips.

"We...made it. I told you...we would."

She growled but did not so much as twitch the tip of her tail. He reached out to stroke his hand down her back. A low, soft purr vibrated her body.

A resounding crash closed out the light in the tunnel between the gates and the city. Covered walkways with tiny skyholes would let in enough light to see by but not enough to burn. The rest of the city was lit with solar-powered glowlights.

"Amir! Amira! Are you well?"

Two guards erupted from a side door. They knelt beside Varad, helping him to his feet.

He hissed at the sting to the backs of his calves. He tipped and leaned on the wall, his forehead pressed on his forearm.

"Varad?"

Mahlia heaved to her feet. She turned to the guards, lifted her chin, and they nodded, turning to run for the palace.

"What...was that?" Varad asked her.

I...sent them for a healer. You're hurt.

He sighed, too weary to argue. Turning, he rested his back against the rough wall and slid down to sit, crooking his legs so the burns would not touch the stone ground. He tilted his head up and closed his eyes, another deep breath escaping.

A triumphant smile curved his lips. Gods, they'd made it.

I *won't lose someone else it is my responsibility to protect.* Responsibility. A bitter laugh slipped past Mahlia's throat as she shifted into her human form. Just what she'd never wanted to be. Her father had passed his duty for her protection on to Varad. And happily so. What minor pride lord wouldn't want his daughter mated to the Amir of Vesperi? All her sisters had mated well because of her match.

She slumped down in the open hovercraft that carried Varad and her to the palace. Her head lolled on her neck as she watched the passing buildings. People stood in clumps, bartering, haggling, just as they would any other day. Some were naked, having obviously just shifted from their animal form. She yawned and turned away. She was so tired she could sleep for a full Turn.

Varad lay with his back to her, a cloth slung across his hips while a healer bent over his scorched legs. Guilt swamped her that he suffered for having saved her. Her heart squeezed. Varad was a good man. She should be content with that, but she just...wasn't. It wasn't his fault. It was hers.

She'd never expected to love him or to be so crushed that he thought of her as a duty. He had mated to a naive girl a Turn ago, but so much had happened since then that the cocoon of security she had always known was now ripped away. Nothing could have prepared her for her role as Amira. Weretiger prides were political to an extreme degree.

Who sat beside whom at meals, who spoke to whom and in what order. What she wore, how she spoke. Everything was scrutinized and criticized or emulated. The only friend she could keep was Ketryn. As a weredragon, she was separated from pride politics. Ketryn's ambassador father negotiated with Varad and no one else.

The healer knelt beside her. "Amira?"

"Yes, how is Var—the Amir?" Straightening her shoulders, she struggled to sit properly, as befitted an Amira. The healer laid a gentle hand on her shoulder, forcing her back down.

"The Amir will be fine in a few days. His legs look worse than they are and will likely not scar. He was quite fortunate."

"Yes. Fortunate." She sighed.

"Are you well, Amira?"

She nodded, serving up a wan smile. "Just tired. It was a long night."

Her eyes never left Varad, and she considered her situation. He made it clear he wanted her, of that she'd never had any doubt. But could she live forever on the scraps of his attention? Half of each Turn alone, ruling the planet by herself? Bombarded with questions and demands, never permitted a moment to relax? Was it worth it? If Varad returned her love, she'd have no doubts. If she had someone to count on, to depend on when everything fell to pieces, she would gladly make the sacrifices.

After last Turn, after Jeevan had died, Varad had abandoned her, leaving her with no one to share her grief. Varad had gone, and she'd been left to be the brave Amira her people needed. Her personal loss was Vesperi's public tragedy. Her hand rested low on her belly. Gods, why did it have to be so hard? Love shouldn't hurt this much. Shouldn't be coupled with so much crippling despair.

Varad leaned up on an elbow, glancing over his shoulder at her. She tried to smile but failed. He winced a little as he shifted position.

How do you feel?

Better than I look, no doubt. He winked.

Claw marks scored his back in wide swaths. She had done that, just as he had left behind bruises and wheals on her breasts and thighs. Mating was not a gentle process, and she stretched her sore muscles, promising herself a long bath when she returned to her chambers.

The healer squatted before her. "I can examine you when we return to the palace, Amira."

"I said I was fine."

"Of course, Amira. I meant to confirm that you are with child."

Her heart jolted. Dear Gods. How had this happened? Not again. She snorted. She knew how this had happened. How Varad had happened. Now that the healer had said the words, it wasn't something that was just between her and her mate. It seemed so much more real now. So many expectations rode on this pregnancy. She couldn't just "be pregnant," couldn't have her fears about the child's health, future, and happiness without discussing it with advisers and making a public decree.

As she licked her parched lips, her mind scrambled for a way to escape this. To run away from her reality. She cut off the thoughts. No. No turning back. This was her life. She was with child, she was mated. Acceptance was her only option. Her shoulders flexed, already feeling the weight of her responsibilities settling, a cage closing around her. If she listened closely, she could swear she heard the lock snap into place. Trapped.

The hovercraft jerked, throwing her forward. Her muscles groaned in protest at the sudden movement. She hissed out a sharp breath, squeezing her eyes closed.

"Mahlia?" Varad turned to face her.

She lifted a hand to ward him off. "Don't."

Don't pretend you care now. Don't pay attention to me for a few moments and then ignore me when your duty calls you away. Don't be concerned while you're with me and expect everything to be as you left it when you return. Just don't. But she kept the words back. It wouldn't help, and he didn't deserve her discontent. He was just being...an Amir.

Pulling herself over to the side, she slipped off the hovercraft and stood naked in front of the palace. The craft was swarmed with servants who wanted to help her and Varad. They wanted to coddle them, but if either she or Varad allowed it, it would be looked down upon as a weakness. It didn't matter. She wanted to be left alone. She rolled her eyes at the double standard, but a small smile quirked her lips. Tigers were a peculiar lot, and they were her lot.

Varad's manservant moved to his lord's side, an ever-present frown in place. Taymullah watched this and then snorted and walked up to stand beside Mahlia, his hand grasping her elbow in support. "Stodgy old bugger."

She glanced up at Varad's younger brother. He looked so much like her mate, slighter perhaps, but with the same deep amber eyes, full lips, golden skin, and auburn and black hair. Why couldn't she have loved him instead? He was easy, uncomplicated...and she felt nothing but friendship for him. He had been the first to make her laugh after Jeevan had died. After Varad had left. Without Taymullah's knowledge of the inner workings of palace politics, she never would have survived. Varad would have returned to a revolution.

Taymullah grinned down at her. "So...interesting evening?"

Nudging him with her shoulder, she grinned. "Hold your tongue."

"I could, but I'd look ridiculous."

She giggled, lifting her hand to cover it with a cough. People would think her callous to laugh when her mate was injured. Lifting her chin, she walked inside the gleaming white building. Varad would return to his chambers and sleep. She was not needed, and she craved a few hours of blissful slumber herself. And a bath. A long, hot bath.

Taymullah spoke to her as a low aside. "Do you need any assistance?"

"No. Your brother might."

"I suspect you'll see him sooner than I will." His wicked chuckle spoke volumes, and if they weren't in public, she would have boxed his princely ears.

"Haven't you anything better to discuss than your brother's mating habits?"

"Certainly not. The whole planet is abuzz with rumors of a new heir."

Her stiff fingers folded over her belly, pain zinging through her at the thought of palace gossipmongers. "It could be a female."

"A female can grow old enough to breed a proper heir."

She snorted. "*Proper* indeed."

"I say only what is true, Amira."

"How is it that you are such a tease and so very practical all at once?"

He released a great sigh, his boots rapping a staccato beat on the marble floors. "A talent I learned at my elder brother's knee."

"A truer statement has never been uttered."

"Taymullah the Truthful. Shall I have a statue carved in my honor?"

"And where shall we put this statue, brother?"

They both jerked as Varad's low tone sounded behind them. Taymullah stepped aside, bowing slightly, a hand over his heart. "Why, in the nude gardens, of course. So that my likeness could watch over the lovely ladies who were so educational to me as a child."

"A fitting place, I think." Varad's gaze danced with mirth.

Mahlia choked, biting her lip to keep from laughing. She recalled how her eyes had popped wide the first time she had seen the white marble statues of women frolicking naked in the lower gardens. Varad had followed her outside that evening, and they'd made love for the first time at the foot of a voluptuous goddess.

Meeting Varad's gaze, she saw that he remembered as well. His pupils expanded, and he stared at her lips, her breasts, and the thatch of hair between her thighs. Heat followed in the wake of his gaze, sliding over her skin. Her nipples hardened into tight crests, jutting toward him. Wetness flooded her pussy. Adrenaline hummed through her body, made the exhaustion fall away into nothingness. Gods, she wanted him.

Taymullah coughed into his fist. "Well, I believe the two of you have some...catching up to do. I'll see you at the first moonrise meal."

A small smile pulled at Varad's lips as he stalked forward, his smooth stride backing her into the wall. The gold of his irises bled out to the corners of his eyes.

"I—I should get some rest."

He bent his head to her throat, inhaling her scent. "Yes, bed is an excellent place for you."

"You should sleep, too. You're hurt."

"Will you kiss it and make it better, Mahlia?" The wicked promise in his voice made it clear that he meant for her to kiss something besides his injuries. Her breath caught at the thought, and her head tilted back. The slight roughness of his tongue flicked across the pounding pulse at her throat. She moaned, falling back against tapestries that lined the walls.

"Varad."

Yesssss?

He dragged the word out, a seductive stroke on her mind. Her hand lifted to slide down his smooth chest, the tips of her fingers tracing the light stripes that crossed his skin. She dragged her nails over his flat nipples, and they beaded at the rough contact. He hissed out a breath, leaning into her. The jut of his cock pressed to her belly, and liquid heat pooled between her thighs. Anticipation thrummed through her body.

His lips dipped to caress her collarbone. She tilted her chin up to give him better access. Her hands slipped around to press against his shoulder blades. A low purr soughed from his throat. He opened his lips to bite her lightly. She moaned, and he swallowed the sound in his mouth as he moved to kiss her. His tongue thrust in, hard and demanding. She met it with her own, her lips shifting beneath his. Her fingers curled into claws, raking down his back. His hips jerked, slamming into hers.

Yes. Please.

I love when you beg, my Amira.

He suckled her tongue, drawing her into his mouth. Lifting his hands, he cupped her breasts and tweaked the tips until they stood in hard points. Oh, Gods. She couldn't take it. Desire made her body throb.

Drawing back, he lightened the kiss. Teased her. Toyed with her. Broke away to spread kisses along her jaw, down her throat.

Her head fell back against the wall as she gasped for breath. "I'm dirty."

"And thank the Gods for that."

She grinned, shifting her torso to rub her nipples against his chest, loving the friction of his rougher skin on her sensitive flesh. "I *meant* that I spent the night running through the sand, and I'm filthy. I can't go to sleep this way. I need a bath."

A dark chuckle slid from his throat. "Then we should make certain your needs are...satisfied."

But he stepped back, left her barren of his touch. She arched toward him, wanting. Just wanting.

After you, Amira. He grinned and tipped an easy bow before her.

She huffed out a laugh. *Tease.*

"And you like it."

Yes, she did. Pushing away from the wall, she walked to her door on legs that shook beneath her. Every step brushed her thighs together, stimulating her pussy. It was all she could do to hold back a moan. Her mating heat had ended, but the aching, relentless want still rode her. She was afraid that where Varad was concerned she would always feel this way.

The carved wooden door of her chambers loomed before her. She grasped the slick metal handle in her hand and pushed the door open. While glowlights illuminated the corridor, her servants had pulled the shutters on her windows to block the sun and left the room in darkness. She stepped into the gloom, her cat eyes quick to adjust to the lower lighting. Varad followed close behind.

"I want—"

"A bath? Yes, you said."

Flicking a finger over a panel on the wall, Varad cued hot water to pour into the immense pool that was sunk into her bathing chamber. Steam rose in lazy curls within a few moments. Sitting on the edge of the tub, she pushed forward to slip into the hip-deep water. She hummed in pleasure as it lapped over her flesh. It would rise to just under her breasts in a few moments. She loved to bathe, loved the caress of warm water against her skin. Like most of her kind, she liked to swim in her tiger form as well.

She rolled onto her back and started with lazy strokes across the tub. Bobbing upright at the opposite side, she turned to see where her mate was. Varad sat on the ledge and dipped his feet in but made no move to join her.

She swam back toward him until she could lay a hand on each of his knees. His eyes heated to the color of molten gold, zooming in on her floating breasts.

Her heart pounded until she could feel each thrumming beat throughout her body. "Aren't you going to join me?"

"I think I'll enjoy the view for a while." He leaned back on his hands, casual, cool, calm. But his body betrayed him. His cock curved in a hard upward arc, the veins coursing blue beneath the thin skin.

She quirked a brow, grinning. "So long as you don't mind me doing the same."

"It's only polite."

"Mmm...polite. We should always be polite." She licked her lips, staring at his long dick. He had the most beautiful cock she'd ever seen. She wanted it inside her. Her hands rubbed over his muscled thighs.

"You wanted a bath."

"I am in the bath." Each kick of her legs sent a stream of hot water to caress her already overheated pussy. If he didn't get in here with her soon, she was going to scream.

"So I see. Do you feel clean yet?"

A slow, hot smile pulled at her lips. "I'm not certain. Perhaps you should come see if I missed any important areas."

"Like where, for instance?"

"Well, my back."

"Your back?"

She nodded and slid backward in the water, paddling her arms to stay afloat. He arched his hips and dipped into the pool after her. Thank the Gods.

"I do think I see somewhere you missed."

"Do you?"

He laid his arms along the edge of the tub, resting against the side. "Yes, come here so I can reach it."

Diving beneath the surface, she flitted over until she reached the side and exploded up to twine her arms around his neck. He laughed and pulled her in, his hands cupping her buttocks. Her breasts crushed to his chest. She closed her eyes for a moment, just to enjoy the feel of him.

"I thought you were going to see if I missed something."

"Ah, yes. Duty calls." Reaching back, he dipped his hand into a bag of cleansing sand. He offered her a handful and then took one for himself. He rubbed his thumb over his fingers to work up a lather. Then he stroked over the long strands of her hair, massaging her scalp. Gooseflesh shivered over her skin. She followed suit and buried her fingers in his striped hair. It felt like Aquatilian saltwater silk against her palms.

His hands dropped to slip down her back, the sand a sweet roughness on her skin. Would he...? Yes. His fingers dipped between her ass cheeks to tease at her anus. She gasped, pushing back against him. She squirmed as the grainy sand pushed into her ass along with his finger. He stroked her until the sand dissolved into a slick lubricant. Closing her eyes, she moaned, pleasure lancing through her.

"Very dirty."

"Please, Varad. I need..." Her head fell back on her neck as her hips worked against his fingers. A hot thrill made her pussy tighten, clenching on nothing. Tension spun through her, and she panted. Oh, Gods. Oh. Gods.

"Yes? You need what?" He added a second finger, thrusting as deep as he could within her.

She didn't answer but buried her face in his neck. Her ass bucked backward. She was going to...going to... Her breath caught as orgasm slammed into her and her body arched while hot pleasure lashed at her. He drove his fingers in her, drawing the sensation out for her until she shuddered and moaned.

He spun her in the water until she leaned back against the edge of the pool, his hands lifting to bracket her shoulders and grasp the ledge. His knee rose to nudge her legs apart. Moving forward, he stroked his cock over her pussy lips. She gasped, tilting her hips to open herself wider for him.

"My turn."

She wrapped her legs tight around his lean hips, her heels pressed to the backs of his calves to pull him closer. He hissed, and she froze, heart pounding. "Did I hurt you? Your legs?"

He shook his head and hitched her higher against the side of the pool, lifting her legs until her knees pressed to the small of his back. She pressed herself to him, the water sealing their bodies together. His cock probed at her swollen entrance, and her eyes slid closed, enjoying the feel of his skin on hers. He thrust into her, hard, fast, deep. She gasped. The angle was incredible. He moved, and the water lapped around her, feeling like a thousand fingers caressing her flesh.

Each stroke hit her in just the right spot. Her nails dug into his shoulders as she held on tight. Her hips arched to meet his, to bring him deeper.

"Oh, Gods."

"Not a god, just a king." His low chuckle rumbled from his throat and sounded through the wide room.

Her head bowed back on her neck, and her pussy contracted around his cock with each thrust. "Don't stop. Please. Don't...stop."

He groaned, and his arms corded as his fingers tightened on the ledge. "I couldn't."

Twisting her hips, she felt her orgasm gather. Sweat and steam dampened her skin, and droplets slid down her body. The added sensation increased her pleasure, driving her on. Her claws extended to score his shoulders. She was so close.

Her pussy clenched tighter and tighter, and every thrust of his cock made it better for her. And then the sensation broke. She sobbed as light exploded behind her lids. Her pussy flexed over and over around his dick. He tensed, going rigid against her. His hips slammed forward in a last jolting push before he groaned and shuddered.

She pulled him nearer as he dropped his head to rest in the crook of her neck. Both of them were gasping for breath. Every ounce of tension leeched from her muscles, and she purred as he kissed her throat softly.

"We should get out." His voice hummed against her skin.

"I'm comfortable here."

He chuckled and pulled away. In one graceful move, he rose from the tub. Bending, he lifted her from the water, cradling her limp form against his chest. She sighed. Feline lassitude pulled at her, and she sank into a dreamy state of consciousness. He deposited her on her soft, wide bed and crawled in with her. It felt unusual to have anyone in bed with her. She'd almost forgotten what it was like to share her private space.

Varad lay between her legs, his chin resting against her belly. Desire for him filled her. Warm fingers stroked over her body. His hair tickled her thighs. He dipped to kiss the swell of her stomach. Fine, saltwater silk sheets caressed her back, and she stretched her arms over her head.

"We need to talk about Jeevan, Mahlia."

His words sent an arrow of pain straight to her heart. "Why? It won't help anything. He's *dead*, Varad. My son is dead." Her voice faded to an agonized whisper as she spoke. Her body tensed as the pleasured fog cleared from her mind.

"*Our* son."

She hissed at him, anger flashing hot through her. Why could he not let this rest? They had achieved some semblance of peace, and he kept pressing on a sore spot. "Fine. We should move on and just...heal."

"Have you?" The gold of his eyes expanded to the very corners. His fangs slipped past his lips.

"What?" Her voice was defensive, rude. And she didn't care. She jerked up and back, pressing herself against the headboard.

He sat up. "Moved on? Healed? Have you managed to do so? Because I cannot see the evidence of it."

Acceptance. She breathed deep. She had to accept. Wasn't that what she had decided? And he was determined to ruin it for her. To force her to talk about... *No.* "Get out."

"Excuse me?" His brow lifted, incredulity flashing across his face.

"This is my chamber, and I wish to rest. You've gotten what you wanted. I'm pregnant. So...leave. It's what you do best." Her face flushed, and her voice shook. Her hands clenched and unclenched. Gods, she was so close to breaking. How did he do this to her? Only he could. She loved it. She hated it.

He stared at her for a moment, assessing. Anger flashed in his eyes, but he mastered it. His pupils contracted into thin lines, irises solidifying to round human orbs, the tiger within him firmly leashed. He blinked, and she couldn't read anything on his face. His usually smooth movements were jerky as he stood and walked toward the door. Before he walked out, he turned to her once more, his body rigid. His long fingers clamped so tightly on the door handle she heard the metal squeak.

"This isn't finished, Mahlia...but I have time, don't I?" Dark promise laced his low tone.

Gods help her. She curled onto her side, tucking her knees under her chin. Wrapping her arms around her legs, she closed her eyes and forced herself to think of nothing. To remember nothing. To let the exhaustion of this endless night take over. Pulling in a slow, shaky breath, she let herself fall into a deep, dreamless sleep.

Chapter 3

Varad's bare feet slapped an angry rhythm against the cold marble floor. His fists bunched at his sides. Woe to anyone who tried to speak to him just then. He slammed into his chamber. The wooden door shuddered in its frame as it crashed closed.

He paced across the wide room, frustration making it impossible to relax. Damn her. *Damn* her. Was this how she wanted their life to be? Never working to overcome problems? Temper boiled in his veins. And damn her for making him lose control this way. He made logical decisions in his personal and public life, ruled an entire *planet* with a fair, even hand. Then he encountered her and went insane.

He snarled just thinking about it. Pain that was ignored festered, never healed. Who but he would understand her loss? Who but he would want her no matter what? Who but he would crave her for all the days of his life? He thrust a hand through his hair, gripping the still damp strands. He could smell her sweet scent on his skin.

A knock sounded on his door, and he hissed. Who was disturbing him in the middle of the day? Did no one tell them that cats were *nocturnal*? They should be abed. Like his mate was. Without him. He sucked his teeth in disgust, not at all surprised to find his fangs fully extended. His nostrils flared, catching the scent of his unwelcome guest.

Taymullah.

Care for a walk, brother? I can feel your rage through the door.

Why are you even awake?

It's a sad day when you even need to ask. Amused satisfaction filled his brother's telepathic voice.

Varad's lip curled. He did not want company—he wanted to stew in his own discontent. His breath huffed out. Insane *and* foolish. He could lay both at Mahlia's feet today.

His brother's voice turned cajoling. *Come along. We have seen none of each other since your return. A walk will clear your head.*

He jerked a saltwater silk robe from his bureau, tightening the belt as he wrenched open the door. Pulling back when he came face-to-fist with Taymullah's upraised hand, he swatted at his brother's arm. "Fine. I will come."

Taymullah grinned. "I'm so very glad of your sweet-tempered company."

Varad growled and said nothing as he stalked past. Taymullah clasped his hands behind his back, matching his older brother's stride. Varad could smell the sex on him. *Three tigresses?* He rolled his eyes.

"Where shall we go? The nude gardens?"

And recall the feel of the first time he'd slid hard and fast within Mahlia, her moans kissing his ear, her nails clawing his back as she screamed his name and came apart in his arms? He thought not. "The market will be fine."

"As you wish."

They walked in silence. The wide stairs of the main doors led to a sloping path down to the market. The underground walkways kept out the sun, even at midday, but the heat enveloped them, and they were sweating within a few moments. A few industrious merchants were setting up for the first moonrise market. Colorful carpets littered the paths. Baubles from Vesperi and their trade worlds mingled on sale carts. The smell of the Dead Sea and sand dunes wafted on the hot desert breeze, along with cooking meats.

Taymullah cleared his throat, glancing at his brother several times. "Nice day."

Varad snorted, in no mood for idle chatter. "You have a purpose for this walk, brother. Speak your mind and be done with it."

The younger man sighed. "I adore your mate."

Snarling, Varad whipped around to slam Taymullah against a wall, bits of stone raining down on them. His fingers fisted in his brother's shirt. "Careful, Taymullah."

"*As a sister.* I must say she does not look as happy as she should to see her mate."

Varad hissed, angered even further that anyone could see things were not right between them. What could he say? Nothing. That he couldn't fix the problem, couldn't find a way around or over it without some cooperation from Mahlia, made frustration tear at him with a tiger's claws.

"She has never dealt with Jeevan's death. This Turn was rough for her."

A bitter laugh threatened to choke Varad. "I know it. She refuses to speak of it."

"You haven't dealt with it either, brother."

His shoulders went rigid, his fingers tightening on his brother's clothing. "I am *trying*."

"Try harder." Taymullah shook off the harsh grip, straightening from the wall.

Varad rubbed at the back of his neck, attempting to ease the tension. Looking for a neutral topic, he thought of the upcoming evening and the work that awaited him. "I need to speak to the werebear ambassador about—"

"Done." His brother flicked negligent fingers through the air.

Varad blinked. "And the weredragon ambassador—"

"I'm speaking to him at second moonrise."

"And how will you deal with him?" His brows rose. When had Taymullah learned to negotiate with dragons?

"With a firm hand and a great helping of patience for a people whose behavior makes little sense and who don't care to explain." Meeting his brother's eyes, Taymullah shrugged. "I may have assisted your mate this past Turn. As I thought you would have wanted."

"Trying to take my kingdom, brother?" He was only half joking. It had happened before, and Varad knew that his absence would make it an easy thing. His heart contracted at what that might mean for Mahlia and their child. He hated to ask his brother, even in jest, but he had to know.

The shorter man stopped dead, turning to face him, a more serious expression on his face than Varad had ever seen. His brother dropped to his knee before Varad, a hand placed over his heart. "Never. I wish you, your mate, and any kits you may sire a long, healthy life and prosperous reign."

Varad swallowed, shamed for what he had accused his brother of. But he would do whatever it took to protect his mate. "I see."

"There are two people on this planet you can trust without question, brother. I am one of them. Your mate is the other, though she may not know it." His brother smoothly regained his feet and turned to continue their walk.

Varad cleared his tight throat. "Thank you."

His brother glanced back when Varad did not immediately follow. An easy grin split the younger man's features, made his amber eyes dance. "I have no desire to be an Amir, but I will do what I must in your stead to ensure you have a throne to return to."

"Taymullah the Wise." He chuckled, falling into step beside his brother.

"That would be a statue for a different garden, I think. Though, if my likeness is to populate the planet, I would prefer it to be in the form of wee kits to frolic at my feet."

"Is there a mate you have in mind to bear these children for you?" Mahlia would love to meet the woman who claimed a permanent place in his mischievous brother's affections.

"Mmm...no. But I will keep testing them until I find just the right one. Don't worry, brother. I take my duties seriously."

Varad laughed, clapping Taymullah on the shoulder.

T here was a purple dragon wrapped around one of the pillars that supported the silken canopy over Mahlia's bed. Its great black eyes stared into Mahlia's when she awoke. She sucked in a shocked breath as she bolted upright, her heart racing.

"Gods, Ketryn! Are you trying to kill me?" Her hand pressed to her chest.

No, but since you don't have your mate in here with you, I thought you could use some company. She unwound her long body from the bedpost and slid with reptilian grace to the floor.

"You're supposed to ask permission before entering."

The dragon snorted, stretching onto the windowsill. The shutters were wide open to let in the moonlight. The second moon already hung heavy on the horizon. The dragon twisted, popping and reforming into Ketryn's human form. Her smooth cinnamon skin contrasted with her ebony hair. The purple scaling on her arms and thighs glinted in the mellow lighting.

"I did ask, Amira, but you were not coherent enough to answer."

"How did you know Varad wasn't here?"

"I saw him leaving the palace with Prince Taymullah near first moonrise."

"Oh."

"Yes, oh." She lifted her delicate nose to sniff the air. "He was here but not in your bed. *Tsk, tsk.* Waste of a perfectly good bed, in my humble opinion."

"Humble, ha." Mahlia hugged her knees to her chest, propping her chin on the bony plateau.

Ketryn's long hair shifted to pool in her lap as she looked out the window. Her voice was deliberately casual. "You always supported his decision to trade with all the colonized planets."

"That was before—"

Ketryn's dark eyes flashed as she turned back to face her. "Before you had to take some part in what that meant for your planet?"

"So it's my fault?" Mahlia's shoulders tensed, waiting for her friend's response.

Ketryn huffed an impatient breath. "Why are you so eager to blame anyone?"

"Can we talk about something else?" Desperation sounded in Mahlia's voice, and she didn't care. She couldn't do this now. Or ever. It was enough that she was dealing with her *current* pregnancy.

"As you wish, Amira. But if you'll take a small piece of advice from someone who loves you and wants what's best for you: talk to Varad. He needs you as much as you need him."

She shifted, uncomfortable. "Does he? I'm not so sure."

"I am. I would give half my scales for a man to look at me the way he looks at you. And that is all I will say on the matter."

Relief flooded Mahlia, and she released a huge sigh.

A coy smile curled Ketryn's full lips as she turned back. "So, tell me... How was the mating ritual?"

Mahlia laughed and then sobered to put on her primmest Amira voice. "I do not reveal the details of the Amir's sex life."

"Oh, come now. Let me live vicariously. Is he as good as his reputation says? It takes at least twice to be a true judge of these things. So..."

"Ketryn!"

The weredragon opened her mouth to respond when she froze, her head cocking to listen. Mahlia lifted her sensitive nose to sniff the air, straining to hear as well. Varad. Her heart seized at the thought.

The door pushed open as an enormous tiger stepped in. He flicked a glance at Ketryn. She stood, bowed, and padded on silent feet out the door, closing it behind her.

Mahlia lifted her chin. "I was talking to her."

You'll be talking to me. His voice went silky, dangerous in her mind.

The great tiger stalked forward, its golden gaze locked on her, and she swallowed. He ran his tongue down a long fang, fierce passion in his eyes. The smooth, feline grace couldn't cover the barely leashed violence. His claws bit into the silk sheets as he leaped onto the end of her bed. His eyes never left her as he moved, forcing her to lie back as he stood over her. Her fingers rose to sink into the warm fur at his neck. His head tilted back, and he began to change. Within moments a naked Varad lay nestled between her spread thighs. Her fingers buried in the soft hair at the nape of his neck.

Her body reacted, dampening, loosening as she arched beneath him. Her knees rose to clasp his hips through the saltwater silk sheets. His buttocks flexed, pushing his erection against her heated pussy. Desire roared like a greedy wildfire through her, burning everything in its path.

He rolled away, leaving her barren, cold, aching for more. She curled to her side, squeezing her thighs together in a desperate attempt to ease the relentless need that throbbed there. He sat on the side of the bed, propping his forearms on his thighs.

He twisted to glare at her, his pupils thin slits of anger. "I will not be distracted. We have yet to finish our discussion from earlier."

Discussion? The words struggled to register in her lust-filled mind. *Jeevan.* He wanted to talk about their son's death. Nausea pitched in her stomach, and she felt as if she couldn't breathe.

Make it stop. Make the pain stop. Please, Gods. That's all she'd done for the past Turn. One day at a time. One breath. One moment. Anything but confront the fact that her son, her sweet child, had been ripped away from her life by an accident of fate. Her hands fisted at her sides, nails biting into her palms.

She closed her eyes, agony rolling over her in a suffocating wave. "I can't...I'll just start yelling at you again."

"So yell, scream...just do *something* but remain angry. It won't help you to hold it all in."

"*No.*"

A low, snarling hiss issued from his throat, and she swallowed, scooting back against the headboard. His hand whipped out, caught her wrist in an iron grip. His eyes were full gold, the tiger stalking her. She panted, excitement and fear sliding through her.

Varad?

"You know what happens to those who don't please their Amir?"

She licked her lips, her blood pounding hot and wild in her veins. He pulled her to him, easy strength overpowering her. Digging her heels into the mattress, she tried to resist, but it was a halfhearted effort. Her pussy was on fire, cream flooding her core. Her body screamed for him to take her. Swift and hard and *now.*

Oh, Gods. What would he do to her? She'd never seen him this angry. Never pushed him this far.

"I—I..."

"You refuse to speak to me, Mahlia. This I cannot tolerate." A sharp tug flipped her facedown on his lap, her hair brushing the floor beside the bed. Her wrists were caught in his firm grip at the small of her back. Blood rushed to her head, and she felt a giddy anticipation balloon in her chest. His palm stroked over her backside, and she moaned.

"Oh, Gods," she whispered, her body tensing against his legs.

A sharp slap echoed through the massive chamber. She jumped as flames licked over her skin. His palm landed hard against her ass, alternating cheeks, falling in an unpredictable rhythm. Just when she relaxed, another slap would fall. Her sex clenched, aching to be filled. She arched up into his hand, a dark pleasure she couldn't define exploding through her.

Then it stopped, and she was left shuddering, confused. Wanting more.

"Do you like this, Mahlia?"

Her breath sobbed between her lips. "*Yes.*"

His fingertip skimmed over her sore skin, making her gasp as the sensations skittered over her hot flesh. He dipped between her buttocks, and she froze, waiting. One finger swirled around her anus.

Yes. Please, Varad.

He lifted her, tossing her onto the bed with careless ease. His weight pressed her deep into the mattress as he settled on top of her, behind her. His cock nudged her ass, and she arched beneath him, spreading her legs wide. Shameless abandon ripped through her.

"*Please, Varad,*" his voice mocked her as his breath caressed her ear. He slid a hand around her stomach, lifting her hips to dip his finger between her legs. He parted her pussy lips with rough fingers, flicking the tips against her rock-hard clit. His fingers swirled in her depths. A low purr dragged from her throat.

His cock thrust into her anus, a slow push that stretched her past bearing. Pleasure-pain lashed at her, her ass too tight on his driving cock. Her fingernails extended into claws, tearing into the expensive sheets. She pressed back against him, wanting more, *needing* all he could give her. He moved in smooth, hard strokes, burying his dick deep within her ass again and again and again. His fingers matched his cock thrust for thrust until she was screaming. She was so full, so desperate for more. Sweat slid down her face, and her arms shook as they tried to support her.

The muscled ridges of his stomach spanked against her hot backside, the slap of his flesh meeting hers loud to her sensitive ears. She loved it. Moaning, she writhed beneath him. Fire licked through her, drew her muscles tight.

Then he stopped. She sobbed in protest, shaking with her need.

His smooth, wicked voice sounded in her ear. "Do you want more? Would you beg for it?"

"Yes, anything, Varad. *Yes.*" Her breath shuddered out as she gasped for breath.

His cock pulled out and slammed deep. His fingers flicked over her clitoris. The dark magic of his tone seduced her as surely as the pleasure twisting through her.

"Do I please you as no other?"

"Yes." She closed her eyes, orgasm gathering in her pussy. A few more strokes, and she'd go over. Oh, Gods, *yes*.

"Say you'll talk to me."

Her tongue barely wrapped around the words. Anything to make him keep from stopping, to make him move. She would die if he stopped again. "Yes."

"Are you not my Amira, my queen, the jewel of my kingdom?"

"Yes. Yes. *Yes.*" Starbursts exploded behind her eyes, her muscles locking as she came.

A tiger's roar sounded behind her, echoed by her own high-pitched, animalistic scream. She threw her head back, fangs fully extended as the tiger within her sprang free. She shuddered over and over, Varad pumping within her, dragging out her orgasm until the world went black and she collapsed, spent.

Chapter 4

Varad loved this view. The rapidly cooling air caressed his bare skin, and he stood with a forearm braced against the open window, watching the last fading rays of the sun being swallowed behind the moons. A great sigh slid past his lips. Gods, he was tired. And no closer to resolving his problems with his mate than he had been the day before.

She still lay on the bed sleeping. Her pregnancy would sap much of her strength over the next few months. He could hear her slow, deep breaths and smell the fragrance of her soft skin mingled with the lingering scent of their vigorous sex from the night before.

Hopeless exhaustion pulled at him. He wanted to give up, give in. Closing his eyes, he dropped his chin to his chest. He was so tired of fighting her, fighting to preserve their mating. It would pass, he knew. The endless longing he had for her was too deep-seated, too essential to his being for him to ever let go. He shook his head.

"Mmm...Varad?" Mahlia's sleepy voice pulled him from his weary thoughts. He turned to see her push herself upright, sweeping her hair out of her eyes. She slipped to the side of the bed and gathered the sheet around her, tugging it over her breasts. The silk pooled at her hips, exposing the sweet curve of her backside as she stood. Waiting, he watched her walk to him, the sheet parting to reveal her long, slim legs with each step. He purred at the sight, desire kicking him in the gut. His cock hardened, throbbing.

She yawned as he folded her into his arms, her cheek lying on his shoulder. His hand swept up the soft, soft skin of her back. She dropped the sheet to let it pool around her hips. Her palm cupped his bicep as he pulled her other arm over his shoulder, slipping his finger down the silky underside of her arm.

"Mahlia."

When she tensed against him, he knew she waited for him to push. Again. The sadness of this moment spun between them, and for once she didn't fight. She swallowed. "I know I promised, but..."

"Are you angry that he died, Mahlia? Or angry that I left?"

"Neither. Both. Stop it, Varad." She shook her head and tried to pull away.

He tightened his arms. This was it. Now or never. He'd reached the end of his endurance. "I cannot."

Her fingers bit into his shoulder. "Why? *Why*? I did everything I was supposed to do, Varad. Isn't that enough?"

"No." Both of their breaths sped as agitation rippled through them.

"I hate you!"

He flinched back, pain ripping through him. "That is unfortunate, my mate."

"Stop reminding me." Her hands crossed to clench the opposite arm.

"I cannot help what you are to me, Mahlia."

Her voice broke. "You can! You're the *Amir*. You can do anything."

"Except cut out my own heart, my love." Agony exploded deep within him, and each breath was a painful rasp of air.

Her head shook, making her striped hair fly wild around her shoulders. "I am not your love. You don't...you *can't*. You left us like we were nothing to you. Don't pretend, now that it's convenient for you."

Grief settled cold and heavy on his chest, forced the air from his lungs. "I never left Jeevan, Mahlia. I was here through all of it, by your side, and his. Every. Single. Moment."

Her arms folded around herself, and she swayed on her feet. "I know. I wanted to hold him so much. I couldn't...I couldn't."

The memory sliced through Varad, flaying his heart, his soul. He groaned, closing his eyes. He remembered. Gods, he remembered everything. At the last, even the lightest touch had made Jeevan scream in pain. So they had stood on opposite sides of his tiny bed and watched as their babe had drawn his last shuddering breath. A low keen of pain had erupted from Mahlia's throat as she'd hit her knees, curling into herself and rocking. Varad had stared for a moment, but it was too much for any father...for any man. He had turned and walked away, his steps picking up speed until he was running as fast as his legs could carry him, the scream of a tiger's roar echoing down the corridor as he went.

Nothing had drawn them together since.

He turned to her, closing his hands around her arms. She jerked back, tears swimming in her beautiful blue eyes. Her lips shook and compressed into a soft line. Then her face crumpled, and she broke, the tears finally falling. She collapsed against him.

Sobs racked her body as she pounded her fists on his chest. "You just l-left us. You didn't care. His b-body wasn't even cold yet when you f-flew away without a backward glance."

Shock slammed into him, exploding in his mind. His hands bit into her arms. "You truly believe that? *I loved him, too.* I miss him every single day. There's a hole in my heart where Jeevan should be."

She let go, crying so hard she gagged. No more hiding her anguish, no more pretending to carry on in stoic silence for her people. She screamed with her grief, and it tore at him. He pulled her tight against his chest as emotion so deep it threatened to swallow him ripped through him. Salty moisture filled his eyes, and he held his mate to him, needing her soft body and sweet strength.

Spent, she lay limp against him, hiccupping sobs shaking her slim frame. "I can't do it again, Varad. What if—what if it's our genetics that don't combine and this child has the same defect? What if it was no accident of nature?"

His hands brushed through the long strands of her hair. "We will do it because we must. If this babe has the same defect, we will love him or her for the time we have together. It is that simple and that difficult."

"Such cold logic." She huffed.

He snorted. "Love has no logic. Love is insanity."

"Love, *ha*."

Could he say it? Outright, no subterfuge? Yes. She needed the words, and he needed to say them. Still, his throat constricted. "I *love* you. I always have. I always will."

Her jaw jutted stubbornly. "Varad—"

Sighing, he tipped up her chin and forced her to look at him. "Perhaps you should see it from my point of view. Did you never think to ask? I left you to do what must be done because I trusted no one else to do it. I had to leave. To do my duty. I *trusted* you to do the same. There is no one else I would as easily trust my people to, my throne to, my heart to. Only you."

Her eyes widened, wary surprise flashing through their pale blue depths. She said nothing, just stared up at him.

He swallowed, forced out the words. "I died every day without you, knowing the one person who could understand, who would feel as I did, could not be with me. If it makes me cold, calculating, then I confess to it. I never meant to hurt you, Mahlia. If you believe nothing else, believe that."

She glanced away, another tear slipping down her pale cheek. Her eyes clenched closed, and she whispered, "I believe you."

The tight band around his chest snapped as relief rushed through him. Finally. Finally something to give him...hope. That they could make it through this. He loved her so much it was a physical pain at times. A life without her would be no life at all.

Thank the merciful, benevolent Gods.

He cupped her jaw in his palms, stroking his thumbs down her cheeks to wipe away the moisture. She leaned into his touch, pressing her hands to his chest. Her fingers idly circled his nipple, and he sucked in a breath, desire punching him. His dick hardened at even the simplest touch from her, no matter how serious the moment. An ironic smile twisted his lips.

She stared at his chest, watching her fingers move as she toyed with him. "I—I'm scared, Varad."

"So am I."

Tilting her head, she glanced up at him from the corner of her eye. "You are?"

"Of course." What sane man wouldn't be? Only a fool would remain unruffled when all that mattered to him hung in the balance. Would she accept that they belonged together regardless of the pain they might experience? Had he convinced her? Baring his soul to this woman was a trivial thing if it worked.

S he wasn't alone.

The thought, inane as it was, ran through Mahlia's mind over and over.

She wasn't alone. Varad was scared, too. Somehow that made it...easier to admit. To face. To get through this new pregnancy and pray to all the Gods for a happier outcome. Pulling in a deep breath, she felt as if she were surfacing from a deep swim in the Dead Sea. As if the heavy water had closed her in darkness and someone had reached out and caught her before the tides had ripped her away.

Varad. Her eyes closed. Gods, she loved him. And...he loved her, too. Sweetness bubbled up within her, and a smile burst over her lips. He *loved* her.

He grieved for their babe, too, suffering in solitude as she had. Smiling through the rage and pain as she had.

No more. No more of that for either of them ever. She squared her shoulders. It was right that they have each other. No one would ever know what they had been through, how they had survived. They were good for each other. They needed each other. The rest would take care of itself.

His hands stroked up and down her back, comforting her. Even that light touch was enough to make her shiver. Glancing up, his golden eyes swirled with the carnal heat that spun between them. Her sex tightened, drenching with moisture, and she gasped. She splayed her fingers wide over his chest, and he leaned closer, a rumbling purr vibrating under her fingers.

I crave your touch, Mahlia.

"You crave my touch?" Sliding her hand between them, she wrapped her fingers around his cock. Squeezing, she worked up to the flared crest and rotated her palm over the head. His eyes drifted closed, and his face flushed with pleasure.

"Yes. Touch me."

Dropping to her knees before him, she continued to pump his dick in her fingers. She wanted to taste him, to suck him. She licked her lips, a teasing grin playing over her face as she looked up at him. *What about my tongue, Amir? Do you crave that as well?*

He sucked in a harsh breath, his pupils expanding as he watched her. He cupped her jaw while the other hand toyed with her hair.

Locking her gaze with his, she started to change, knew the color in her eyes bled out to a solid blue. She focused the shift, let her tongue become rough and textured, stroked it lightly from the base of his cock to the tip, swirling it around to dip into the tiny hole. The salty tang of his juices slipped over her tongue.

"Mahlia," he gritted out her name, a warning, a plea.

His fingers fisted in her hair, and his hips bucked, thrusting his cock to the back of her throat. He snarled, hovering on the edge of feral. Her thighs tensed. Seeing how she could push him to the limit made her so wet. Heat fizzed in her veins, made her heart pound. She loved it. She wanted more.

"Mmm..." She hummed around his shaft and purred deep in her throat.

Gods, Mahlia. His groan reverberated through her mind.

Come for me.

Moving with the lightning-fast reflexes of his tiger side, he flipped her over onto her back. "Come for you? Not just yet."

She gasped, arching beneath him. His hot flesh burned her front as the cold marble floor seared her back. Shuddering at the exquisite contrast, she lifted her legs to wrap them tight around his hips. "I want you, Varad."

"Say you love me. I want to hear it." His fingers threaded through her hair, his eyes meeting hers straight on.

She swallowed, and her heart stilled as she met his gaze. Tears welled in her eyes, and her lips shook as she tried to smile at him. Her voice came out a soft whisper. "I love you, Varad."

His breath hitched, and he closed his eyes as though savoring the sound of her words. She lifted her palm to stroke his strong jaw. *I love you, Varad.*

Tightening her muscles, she tucked her ankles under his ass. He dipped his head, his lips caressing hers in a slow, soft kiss. He licked his way into her mouth, tongue stroking hers. Her pussy spasmed, empty, aching, wanting. She moaned into his mouth, excitement simmering through her. Her heart raced, sweat beading on her skin. Suckling his tongue, she bit down lightly. He groaned, his fingers tugging on her hair, brushing over the back of her neck. She shivered at the contact as chills spread down her arms.

His cock probed at her damp pussy, entering just a little and then retreating. Teasing her. She slipped her fingers into his silken hair, loving the texture against her palms. His scent filled her nostrils. Varad. She immersed herself in him: the feel of his skin on hers, the taste of him in her mouth, the hot, masculine smell of his body. She craved it the way he craved her.

Look at me, Mahlia.

Her gaze met his, blue on gold. Her breath caught. The molten fire in his eyes was hot enough to burn. He entered her in one long, unhurried push. Her pussy stretched to accommodate his length. He pumped into her, slow and hard. The moment spun between them, passion rising higher and higher until her muscles screamed at the leisurely pace he set.

"Please, Varad. Faster, harder, something. *Anything.*"

"Anything?"

"I need—"

His dick slammed into her, and she arched to meet him thrust for thrust, their gazes still locked, still together as they rode the storm. Together, yes, perfect. Yes. Her orgasm gathered slowly, rising like a tide within her. Heat sizzled, burned, and then roared through her until she bucked against him. She was so close she shook with it, need exploding deep in her belly. Sliding her hands to cup his shoulders, her fingers clenched, nails biting into his flesh as her excitement expanded. He reached down, fondling her clitoris, flicking over the sensitive nub until she cried out. Tingles raced over her skin as she flashed over into orgasm, coming in a rush so hot she thought her body couldn't contain it.

Varad.

"Mahlia."

She watched his eyes lose focus, turn inward as he came, his hips jerking as he shuddered over her, in her. Her pussy clenched again in a small orgasm, and she flushed, moaning. She panted, her muscles relaxing one by one until she lay limp beneath him.

She sighed as he pulled away. Stretching catlike, she purred as her muscles bunched and flexed. His arms enveloped her, lifting her as he carried her to the bed. She drifted in a dreamlike state for a long while, feline satisfaction coiling through her.

She lay curled against his side, her cheek pressed to his chest. She could hear his heartbeat, steady and strong, just like him. His hand splayed over her lower belly, and she felt the familiar flutter of fear. Her eyes closed, but she confronted it. Yes, she was afraid. Yes, she didn't know what would happen next. But Varad was here with her, and together they would face whatever might come.

She was strong enough for this.

And she would soon welcome a child into the world. A smile curved her lips, the first shimmer of joy spreading through her.

"Thank you," she whispered.

"For what?"

"For this. For not giving up on me."

"Never."

She opened her eyes and traced an idle finger over the stripes on his chest. "I'll miss you when you leave."

He lifted her hand to his lips. "It will be difficult to miss me when we're closed up in a flying canister of metal. I suspect we might try to kill each other. Won't that be fun?"

Jerking back, she sat up to stare down at him. Shock flickered through her. "Wha—"

His arms folded behind his head, a smug grin curving his mouth. "Taymullah is old enough to reign as regent while we're gone. And fully capable of assuming command. I'll speak to Lord Kesuk and try to convince him to trade with Taymullah in my stead next Turn. I think my brother would enjoy Bear Clan women. They are...buxom."

"You had best not know anything about their sexual prowess from personal experience."

"I was trading for several Turns before we met, my love." He held up his hands, innocence wreathing his handsome face.

She hissed at him. Innocent, ha. Not her Varad.

He heaved a long-suffering sigh. "As I was saying…if anyone would understand the need to protect a mate and young, Kesuk would."

"So would you." She laid her palm on his cheek. "You don't have to do this. I—I know why you have to leave, and I support you in this. I can stay."

"But I want you with me. I want to see my child grow. I don't want to miss any of it. Not one more moment with you or my heir." His fingertip brushed over her stomach before trailing up to swirl around her nipple. Her breath caught as he tormented her, a tiny smile pulling at his sensuous lips.

She swallowed. "I love you."

His serious amber eyes met hers, all teasing gone. "And I love you. If…if our genetics don't mix, and we cannot have a healthy child together, then I will declare Taymullah our official heir."

"Varad." He would do that? Give up the possibility of any child, for her? Emotion banded tight around her chest, squeezing her throat closed.

"You are my heart and soul. I will have no other."

She cupped his jaw. "Nor I."

"Then come back down here." He crooked a finger at her, the playful smile back in full force.

Wrinkling her nose at him, she grinned. "Lead on, *my Amir.*"

"Yours. I like the sound of that. Of course, that means you have me for the rest of your life."

"I think I can handle that."

"Yes, we are well matched, are we not?" He laughed, rolling her beneath him.

Her arms slid around his neck, sweet contentment wrapped around her heart. "So you keep telling me."

"And, of course, I was right all along."

"Show me how well we fit, Amir." She mated her sex to his, lifting her hips to rub against him.

An arrogant, feline smile curled his lips. "My pleasure."

"And mine."

In Smoke

WEREPLANETS
BOOK 3

CRYSTAL JORDAN

CJ BOOKS

Chapter 1

So that's Harena.

Ketryn tried to dredge up some excitement. It was her first visit to her home world, after all. Even if she hadn't been there since she was a small child, she should feel some connection to it, shouldn't she? But no. She had no desire to be here. Now that her ambassador father was dead, her family intended to marry her off as a member of some man's *harim*. Would that make her his third wife or his fifth? She had no idea. She only knew his name was Lord Nadir. The rest was a complete mystery. What she knew about her own kind could fit onto the tip of her smallest finger, with room left to spare. Weredragons weren't known to give away the secrets of their society, and Ketryn hadn't grown up among them, so she felt the keen lack of knowledge more now than ever before.

Gods. She'd traveled for six standard months just to get to this sunburnt rock in the back end of space. The thought didn't please her. As low as her expectations were, the planet below was worse than she'd imagined. No blue of ocean broke the landscape of endless red sand. If it looked this bad from here, she wasn't certain she wanted to get much closer. As if she had a choice now. She sighed and rested her head against the curved window of the observation lounge.

Ketryn wrinkled her nose at her wavy reflection in the glass, noticing the thin layer of purple scaling that reached from the middle of her hands to her biceps. The barest touch against her scales could elicit an intense sexual reaction. Dragons were very proud of their markings, or so her father had once mentioned to her. It was one of the few things he'd ever told her about her race before he'd died. She only knew she was entirely different from the weretigers she'd grown up with on Vesperi.

She was concentrating on the window so hard she didn't notice her best friend, Mahlia, walk up behind her until she spoke. "Look, Ketryn! Isn't it amazing?"

"Yes, Mahlia, that is exactly what I was thinking." Ketryn made a derisive noise in the back of her throat, but it erupted as a reptilian hiss. She'd spent too many Turns picking up the conversational habits of tigers.

Mahlia raised her eyebrows and lifted her baby, Crown Prince Razak, against her shoulder to pat his back. "Such enthusiasm. This is an important trade relationship to maintain between our planets...and in order to trade, we're finally getting off this spaceship. Thank the Gods. Besides, it could be fun."

"Says the happily mated woman with new twin cubs." She smiled to take the bite out of her words. If anyone deserved the joy they'd found, it was Mahlia and Varad. The two weretiger monarchs had lost their first child to a rare genetic defect, and the agonizing loss had nearly dissolved their mating. Ketryn longed for that kind of mating, a bond that could survive anything, no matter how tragic. But being raised among those unlike her, and returning to a planet where she knew nothing of the culture, she was unlikely to find that kind of acceptance, the sense of belonging she had always craved. Always apart. That was her fate. She sighed and leaned against the window.

"Now, now, Ketryn, you just can't judge a tiger by its stripes." Ketryn groaned as Mahlia fluffed her cream-and-bronze-striped hair. "And they are throwing us a welcoming party when we get to the landing site."

"Yes, so the men can club us and drag us back to their sand pits." Ketryn arched an innocent brow.

"Well, I guess that makes us the cat's meow."

"Mah-lia, the cat jokes are so trite."

"Here, kitty, kitty, kitty," Mahlia singsonged.

Ketryn laughed so hard she had to wrap her arms around her belly. Trust Mahlia to make this easier for her, to make her laugh about it. Her friend knew how upset she was about the arranged mating, about the lack of a single mate. Tigers might have many mates throughout their lives, but only one at a time. That she was now to be just another woman in a dragon's *harim* made her stomach churn in disquiet. "Just wait until you see the dragon-skinned boys down there. Then we'll see how funny it is."

Mahlia straightened at the reference to ancient Earthans' practice of gene-splicing humans with sea dragons to make shape-shifting dragons. Unlike the three other shape-shifting races—werebears, weretigers, and merpeople—weredragons were the only ones that had been created from a non-Earthan animal. The desert climate created by the binary suns of Harena called for a wereanimal that could withstand a harsh, drought-prone environment. When, for unknown reasons, gene-splicing with Earthan reptiles had failed to take, scientists had turned to the sea dragons found on the water world of Aquatilis, home planet of the merpeople. Mahlia tilted her head. "I've never been with a weredragon, only tigers. Are our hosts really scaled all over?"

"Not all over, but I'll let you guess exactly which parts are." Ketryn leered, but she didn't know the true answer. She'd never had sex with a dragon either. The only other weredragon on Vesperi had been her father. She shuddered. No, she'd definitely never been with another dragon.

Mahlia gasped, her eyes rounding with horrified fascination. The slitted cat's pupils in her crystal-blue snow tiger eyes expanded. "Really? Down there?"

Ketryn chortled, flicking imaginary dust specks off her purple scales. "You don't want to play snake charmer, Amira?"

"It might be interesting to find out what that feels like. You shouldn't limit yourself, Ketryn."

"Yes, and she's the only one of you who might find that out." A low growl sounded from the doorway. Varad padded in with his daughter cradled to his chest. He bent to press a gentle kiss on his mate's lips. The twins reached for each other, patting their hands together and gurgling. The tiny girl, Princess Varana, had her father's golden eyes and auburn-and-black-striped hair, whereas Razak had his mother's paler snow tiger coloring. They were both the most beautiful babies Ketryn had ever seen. She sighed, allowing herself a moment of pure, self-indulgent envy. She wished her future looked half as bright as Mahlia's, but it did not. Her heart twisted. She'd never have love, never know the sweet, hot lust for a mate that she saw so often in her friend's gaze. No, Ketryn's life would be the same one she'd always known, no matter which planet she lived on. She never belonged anywhere or to anyone.

Everything will change soon.

The telepathic voice of Nadir's mate filled his head. A harsh, desperate edge colored Tarkesh's tone. Nadir slipped his fingers over the band of silver scales that formed a rough crown on his mate's forehead and then buried them in the other man's long hair before he answered.

Then we must take advantage of the time we have now.

Tarkesh ran his hands down the wide, muscled planes of Nadir's chest. His breath hissed out as Tarkesh's fingers danced over the black scales that trailed down the centerline of his torso. His hips jerked forward at even the light contact. Nothing felt better than his mate's hands on him.

"Don't tease me, Tark. I'm in no mood for it." His hand snapped out and caught the slimmer man around the waist to draw him forward. Their cocks stroked against each other, and they both groaned at the contact.

"Nor am I. I need..." Tarkesh chuckled at Nadir's usual rough impatience, so Nadir scraped his nails down the silver scales on Tarkesh's arm. A draconic shriek ripped from his throat. Goddess, but he loved that reaction in his mate.

"I know. Bend for me, my mate."

A cheeky grin spread over Tarkesh's sculpted features. Leaning sideways, he hooked a finger around a bottle of spiced oil from the bedside table. He handed it to Nadir. His dark eyes flashed with heat and anticipation. "I live to please you, my mate."

"Now." Nadir could tell his mate needed it rough and fast this night. No niceties, no subtlety, no playing. Just hard, deep fucking. The silver dragon wanted to forget the changes they faced as a mated pair. And he would give that to him. Gladly.

Nadir fisted his fingers in his mate's long hair, jerking his head back to nip at his throat. He felt Tarkesh's breath brush against his temple, felt his pulse pounding beneath his lips. Lust clenched in his gut. No more. He couldn't wait. Using his free hand, he shoved Tarkesh backward onto the wide bed. Smooth, black saltwater silk sheets from Aquatilis felt slick under his knees as he climbed up. He flicked the cork from the blue glass bottle and poured oil into his palm.

"Open for me." He didn't wait and shoved his mate's legs high and wide. Working his fingers against the tight hole of Tarkesh's anus, he eased the oil into his mate's ass. Tarkesh groaned, his hips arching off the bed. Ah, yes. This oil had spices designed to elevate passion, to burn. He wrapped his other hand around Tarkesh's cock to slip up and down the long, hard shaft. Tarkesh swallowed audibly, his eyes pinching closed as he arched into Nadir's stroking fingers. Nadir rubbed his thumb over the tiny opening at the crest, smearing the glistening drop of cum around the tip. He let a wicked smile curve his lips. *You want this, don't you, Tarkesh?*

Tarkesh's dark eyes flashed open, clashed with Nadir's. They blazed with anger and uncertainty. *Yes, fuck me now.*

I'll fuck you hard. I know how you like it. Nadir knew Tarkesh needed to forget, to be pushed past the worry that consumed him. That he would enjoy the pushing was an additional boon. He did what he must to please his mate. A harsh laugh rumbled his chest. A man's duty was never done. He smiled and firmed his hold on Tarkesh's thick cock. *After I've made you come, I'll slide my cock inside your ass and ride you hard. You love that, don't you?*

"Yes. Nadir."

He watched a muscle tick in Tarkesh's jaw and his breath choke out. A hiss erupted from the silver dragon's throat. His eyes glazed, unfocused. His cock slid faster and faster through the tight grip of Nadir's fingers. Tarkesh's hips jerked, slamming upward as Nadir's hands worked downward. Nadir smiled as he watched his mate's face flush with hot lust, watched as orgasm dragged him under. He froze, and his pelvis lifted. As he came, his juices erupted over Nadir and the bed. "Nadir."

Leaning forward, Nadir braced his hands on either side of his mate's shoulders. Tarkesh wrapped his fingers over the back of his neck, pulling him down for a kiss. Their lips fused, and he thrust his tongue into Tarkesh's mouth. He shuddered as his mate's hands ran over his scales. Lust clouded his mind, his control ripping loose. He thrust his cock between Tarkesh's legs. He didn't pause—he needed more and needed it now. Dragging his mate's legs up to wrap around his waist, he slid into the oiled pucker of his anus. Tarkesh groaned, lifting his hips into the thrust. Nadir worked the full length of his cock inside the other man, his strokes building in speed and force. His breath hissed out at the hot, tight fit of his mate closing around his dick.

Orgasm fisted in his gut, building higher, pushing him past the edge of his endurance. His heart slammed in his chest, his head bent back, and he roared out. His cum jetted inside his mate. "Tarkesh."

Intense carnal feeling, twisting with hot emotion, banded his chest. Goddess, but he craved this man. More than his next breath. Nothing could compare to what he felt when Tarkesh was near. Slamming his eyes closed, Nadir let the feeling take him. Only with Tarkesh had he ever let go of the control he held onto so tightly. Only the silver dragon could match him for ferocity, for passion. Never would he let him go—he would do whatever it took to keep his mate.

Sliding from Tarkesh's anus made them both groan at the drag of flesh on flesh. Nadir collapsed beside his mate, panting. He kissed the silver scales that trailed down the slimmer man's shoulder, curving an arm around his waist. Tarkesh remained quiet, still, a sure sign that he was thinking deeply. Nadir sighed and shifted to settle against the pile of pillows, hugging Tarkesh to him. Long experience told him he would have no peace until his mate talked through whatever troubled him. "You are worried."

"When will she be here?"

Ah. So that was the way of it. He blew out a breath and waited for the same discussion they'd had a hundred times before. "Soon. A few days. This upsets you?"

"Do you truly believe that adding her to our bond won't change things between us?" Impatience rang from Tarkesh's voice. It seemed as if they'd both had more than their share of this subject.

Nadir stroked his hand down the sensitive silver scales covering his mate's spine, eliciting a small shudder. "We have no choice. You know this. Mating with her will cement our position in the matriarchies. We have to be a breeding partnership."

"I know." Tarkesh relaxed against him, sighing. "It is simply that..."

Nadir forced his voice to remain calm, soothing. "You fear change. A *harim* is not a bad change, Tarkesh. You don't know that we won't love her, and she, us."

The saltwater silk rustled as Tarkesh flopped over with a low growl. "You don't know that we will. She could make things difficult with us, with her foreign weretiger ways."

"She is a dragon in the most powerful matriarchy on Harena, regardless of where she was raised. We agreed her lack of experience with dragons would only be for the good. Mating with her will benefit all our families and will give us the legitimacy that both of us desire." Nadir shrugged as he stated what he saw as obvious.

Tarkesh sucked in a breath through his teeth. "I understand all this. Goddess knows we've discussed it a thousand times. That doesn't change the situation."

"I can't give you any guarantees." Frustration clawed at Nadir's gut. This was the *only* option open to Harenan pairs of the same gender. Matings that could not produce the rare dragon child were compelled to take a third mate of the opposite sex, to form a *harim*. Most saw it as a convenient arrangement, but he knew Tarkesh wanted more than that from *any* mate.

"And I'm not asking for any."

Nadir shrugged again, at a loss about how to make this better, easier for his mate. "What would you have me do?"

Tarkesh tensed beside him, and he heard him drag in a deep breath. "Allow me to meet her at the shuttle landing and accompany her to the capital myself. Alone."

Nadir chuckled, propping his hands behind his head. This was a request he hadn't anticipated. "Afraid I'll scare her, Tark?"

Tarkesh propped himself up on an elbow to look down at him, his forehead furrowing with worry. A sudden, sly grin spread across his features, and he shoved his long hair out of his face. "No woman has been man enough to satisfy you before. I was the one who happily switched back and forth before mating with you."

Nadir laughed outright at that, wrapping an arm around his own belly. He stroked his fingers down his short goatee to try to hide a grin. "It isn't that women aren't appealing. It's simply that my tastes are too rough for most of them. Delicate little desert blossoms."

And it was the truth. Women were attractive, arousing, but many shied away from his rougher tastes. He knew himself, his preferences. Only Tarkesh had ever matched him for his demanding pleasure.

"Don't let a matriarch hear you say that."

"I wouldn't." Nadir reached out to slide his fingers through his mate's hair, cupping the back of his head. "Would it ease your fears to meet her before the binding ceremony?"

"Yes." Tarkesh leaned into him.

"Then go, with my blessing." He let a grin tug his lips up. "And be certain to test her skills at bed play. I wouldn't want to terrify the blossom. Break her in gently."

Tarkesh chuckled, his fingers wrapping around Nadir's cock to stroke him back to full arousal. Nadir groaned through gritted teeth. Tark mused aloud, "Perhaps. For now, my mate, I have no desire for gentle."

Nadir rolled Tarkesh onto his belly, pulling his hips up. He slid his hands down to cup his mate's ass and parted the globes to rub the tip of his cock against the tight anus. "I live to please you. My mate."

Chapter 2

The metal floor rattled beneath Ketryn's feet. Her stomach pitched as the space shuttle dropped through Harena's atmosphere. Her knuckles turned white as her fingers bit into the safety straps that held her in place. She wished the nausea churning in her belly was just the unfamiliar change in pressure that made her ears pop, but it wasn't. This was it. There was no escape for her now. Her fate was sealed. She swallowed a lump that threatened to strangle her.

She squeezed her eyes shut and struggled to control her breathing. The spaceship shuddered hard, and she bounced in her seat. She moaned, leaning into the harness. Praying that this landing would be over soon would only bring her mating that much closer.

The ship seemed to jolt sideways and knocked the wind out of her as they bounced on the ground. Metal ground against metal. Were they landing on sand or something man-made? She hadn't bothered to ask where they would land or how the weight of the ship wouldn't sink them into the loose sand—she'd been more concerned with what would happen to her after they touched down.

"That was...exciting." Mahlia's voice broke the silence, and Ketryn opened her eyes to see a gamine grin spreading across her friend's face. It was so good to see her blue eyes clear of the crippling pain of Jeevan's loss. The sadness still lurked there, and Ketryn suspected it always would, but Mahlia smiled now, and it shone in her eyes. Her friend was happy. Ketryn tried to imprint this moment on her memory. This might be the last time she saw her, and that knowledge cut deep. She had so few true friends, so few people she trusted. Mahlia and Varad would hand the trade run over to Varad's younger brother, Taymullah, when they returned to Vesperi this Turn. One ship made one run each Turn to all four colonized planets. So much of the Earthan technology had been lost. Only Aquatilis maintained any level of technology in order to generate the life-support systems in their underwater cities.

Ketryn sighed. "I'm ready to have my feet on solid ground."

"I confess that I would like that as well." Mahlia leaned over to unbuckle her son from his carrier. He swung his arms in clumsy circles, kicking his feet and cooing.

"I'll hold him." Ketryn flicked off the harness straps and scooped up Razak. "It will be the last time."

"You don't know that. You can never tell what the future holds, bitter or sweet."

Tears pressed against Ketryn's eyelids, and she spun toward the door, cradling the baby against her breast. "Then it will be the last time I see him so small."

"That is the truth. They gain flesh with every day that passes. Soon I won't be able to carry them." Mahlia straightened her ceremonial robe, running her hands down the royal-blue saltwater silk. Ketryn shrugged to resettle her own lavender robe. It was sleeveless to leave her scales bare. They had all changed into their finery before preparing for landing. A trading party would meet them, goods would be exchanged over several weeks' time, and then Varad and Mahlia would fly away and leave her behind. What happened to her after that, no one knew. No one knew anything about Harena or the weredragons who populated the world. No one even knew why they kept so much to themselves.

The muscles in Ketryn's shoulders drew into a rigid line. Her breath grew overloud in her ears, her heart thumping in slow throbs. She swallowed hard. Dread knotted in her belly. Her every footstep clanged against the metal flooring, ringing like a death knell. Her ears popped again as wind sucked around the lowering ramp. She squinted against the harsh sunshine that flooded the airlock. Razak fussed against her, and she jiggled him. His rosy lips formed a moue. Sweet affection wrapped around her heart, and she smiled down at him. She wished she could see her friend's children grow up. Mahlia was as close to family as she had ever really known. Her father had never spared more than a moment for her. And now she was to be left with a planet full of people like her father, married to another man like her father. She ran her finger down Razak's silky cheek. "We're here, little prince. Let's go see, shall we?"

She glanced up and met the intense, dark gaze of a tall, exotic-looking man. Her heart jolted. A weredragon. Her nostrils flared to catch his scent. Hot and masculine. His scales glinted silver in the sun, but it was his eyes that caught her. Something possessive danced in their midnight depths. She took a step toward him, drawn in. Something about the man called to her. She wanted to speak to him, know him. The need shook her to the core. She drew in his scent again. How she knew the scent belonged to him, she didn't know.

"Ketryn?"

Jolted from her reverie, she turned to see Mahlia standing with Varad and a slender woman. The woman's scent was unusual, though there was something vaguely familiar about it. Ketryn's nose twitched.

"I'd like you to meet Elia Iden, the Aquatilian ambassador on Harena. We'll be taking her back to her home world and bringing her replacement back next Turn." Mahlia wore her Amira smile, polite and somehow warm and distant at the same time.

Ketryn let a welcoming grin tilt her lips. That explained the familiar scent—this woman smelled similar to the handful of mermen Ketryn had met. "Lady Elia. It is a pleasure to meet you."

"It's 'Ambassador.' Aquatilis is a democratic republic—we don't have lords and ladies. Please, call me Elia." She tilted her head to the side, and a sheet of flaming orange hair streaked with gold and tipped with red swirled around her shoulders. Ketryn had never seen a mermaid. Only the mermen came as ambassadors to Vesperi, but women didn't have much power among the weretigers. Only through their husbands could they become leaders—like Mahlia, who'd ruled the planet while Varad went on the trade run last Turn. Ketryn was uncertain of the practices on other planets. Harenans kept to themselves, and contact with the other planets was so new that there was little anyone knew other than who traded in what. Amir Varad and Ambassador Bretton Hahn of Aquatilis were the only two people to have ever visited all four colonized planets.

Ketryn sighed. Adventure had never been one of her longings. Mahlia wanted that. Ketryn simply wanted to belong somewhere, to someone. To fit. To be needed.

"I've never met a mermaid before."

"Yes, well. After his first Turn here, Ambassador Hahn believed a woman representative would...achieve better results."

What was that supposed to mean? She opened her mouth to ask, when the mermaid turned to speak quietly to Varad. Her dragon senses allowed her to hear Elia anyway. "I am anxious to return to Aquatilis, Amir Varad. How long will..."

Then the weredragon's scent came to her again, closer. She whipped around and found herself staring at the most beautiful male chest she'd ever seen. He wore no shirt, simply a robe that draped from his shoulders. Tight muscles formed ridges over his abdomen and tapered to narrow hips. A wide belt hugged a pair of loose pants to his waist. A silver band of scales stretched across his forehead, and his dark hair fell in a smooth sheet to his shoulders. She'd never been so intensely aware of any man in her life. And she had lain with her fair share of them. This was different, though. Perhaps it was that he was her kind, that he was a dragon. She didn't know, but she wanted to find out. Desperately.

"Who are you?"

"I am Lord Tarkesh. I am to escort you to the capital. To Lord Nadir."

To the end of life as she knew it. Depression made her shoulders droop, and she turned away. She walked down the ramp to see what she could of her world. It was late afternoon here, the binary suns dipping toward the horizon. Deep red sand dunes stretched as far as her vision could strain. And she had the enhanced senses of a dragon, so her sight far exceeded those of her human ancestors. The harsh beauty of the land pulled at something deep within her. Some small tug of familiarity settled in her bones. She dragged in a deep breath. The desert wind didn't have the salty tang of the Dead Sea on Vesperi. It was the clean, dry scent of pure sand. No moisture. In fact, her nose didn't catch the scent of any bodies of water. That confirmed what she'd seen of the planet from space.

That begged the question: how did dragons survive without water? She sighed. Just one more thing she didn't know about a world that was supposed to be her *home*. She choked back a bitter laugh. Home. Of course. She had all manner of experience with that, right?

To her left lay a small town of lavish tents. They spread around the massive landing platform that the ship rested on. Several dragons stood around the platform, and they glanced at her curiously before returning to the work of unloading the goods from the cargo holds. The wild colors of their scales flashed in the sun as they worked. They were beautiful. A strange emotion twisted within her. These people were her kind. She wished more than anything that this place felt like home, that she could be welcomed among weredragons. But she was a stranger, apart.

"Look, little one. Isn't it gorgeous?" She lifted Razak so he faced the landscape. He gurgled and squealed in delight, his arms windmilling. She laughed, cuddling him close.

"Yes, it is." Tarkesh's smooth voice sent a hot shiver down her spine, snapping her back to the present.

She turned around to face him, settling Razak against her shoulder. Clearing her throat, she met his gaze. Her heart seized again, and a flood of moisture gathered in her pussy. She clenched her thighs together and tried to keep her voice calm, even. "So, how far are we from the capital? Is that where Lord Nadir lives with his *harim*?"

She tried to keep the displeasure from her voice, but some of it must have slipped through, for Lord Tarkesh's brows arched in surprise. His tone went flat, emotionless. "You are upset by a match with the son of a powerful family?"

"I am not happy to have no say in the man I must mate to."

"I see." His face showed no expression, and he folded his hands behind his back. "It is five days to the capital. We travel by Gila caravan with dune-racer outriders as guards."

"We need guards?" Her stomach dipped.

"I was informed that your father died in a dune-racer accident, and I'm sorry if it upsets you, but the guards are necessary. There are renegade bands that would attack a trade caravan. Especially one as richly stocked as ours will be."

"I see." Now it was her turn to keep her face clear of expression. She was the daughter of a politician. Whether she wished it or not, she knew how to hold her tongue and give little away. Her preference was to confront life head-on, but the tigers didn't care for that kind of bluntness. She very much doubted dragons would be different in that respect. Any people that could keep its secrets so tightly guarded probably preferred subterfuge and guile. Sighing, she sought a more pleasant subject. She waved a hand at the hundred or more tents. "Will everyone accompany us to the capital? And who is Gila, Lord Tarkesh?"

His white teeth flashed against the swarthy complexion common to all weredragons. Dark hair, tanned skin, dark eyes. The only thing that seemed to make weredragons each uniquely colored was their scales. "Call me Tarkesh. Please."

"And you must call me Ketryn." She offered up a tentative smile.

"Come with me, and I will introduce you to a Gila." He started down the ramp that led to the landing platform. When she didn't immediately follow, he turned back with an expectant expression on his face.

"I must ask Amira Mahlia if—"

His eyebrows contracted in a frown. "You do not answer to the weretigers."

"No, but she is my closest friend, and I am holding her son. It would be rude to walk away without a word." Her voice cracked a little. She'd soon be walking away from her only friend forever. Blinking rapidly, she tried to keep tears from her eyes. She would save her weeping for when she was alone. Breaking down in front of these strange men who shared her race was not how she wanted to make a first impression.

A quiet sympathy warmed his dark gaze, and he nodded his understanding. "Go then. I await you."

"Thank you, Lor—Tarkesh. Thank you, Tarkesh." She swept a small bow, holding Razak firm to her shoulder.

"I'll take him, if you like." She turned to see Varad standing behind her. A tiny smile creased his handsome face, and his gold eyes twinkled down at her. Then concern flashed in his gaze as he glanced between her and Tarkesh. He pitched his voice low. "You are attracted to him."

She nodded, not speaking.

"Have a care. I would hate to see you hurt."

"I can enjoy my last moments of freedom, can't I? My choices have been taken away from me about whom I shall mate with, but this time I have left is mine."

He sighed. "Yours is too kind a heart to be broken."

Tears welled again, but she blinked them back. "I shall miss you, Varad. Take care of Mahlia."

"I swear it." He bent and lifted Razak from her arms. He kissed Ketryn's cheek. "Thank you. For being there for Mahlia last Turn when she needed support. You and my brother saved her when I could not be there. I will never forget that."

"She would have done the same for me."

"Yes. She loves you dearly."

Her throat closed tight. "I love her, too. I—I need to go."

He nodded and stepped back. "Go."

She spun around and scurried down the ramp to Tarkesh. He looked over her shoulder to meet Varad's gaze. Something passed between the two men. Perhaps they spoke telepathically. She didn't know, but they nodded to each other, and Varad turned away to rejoin his mate and Elia. Then Ketryn faced Tarkesh and tried to smile. "Shall we go? I would like to see this *Gila*."

Chapter 3

"Are you well?" Tarkesh didn't lead her away from the spacecraft. Instead he lifted his hand and brushed a lock of Ketryn's hair away from her face. The attraction that had rolled over her the moment her gaze met his rose to the surface. No matter what she'd said to Varad, it would be unwise to engage in an affair with this man when she would soon be mated to another. She had no idea how conservative the weredragon culture was, and she didn't want to upset the family she had never met by her ignorance of her own race. Tarkesh cupped her cheek, and she allowed herself to savor the liquid fire his touch lit within her, spreading to heat her sex. Gooseflesh broke out down her arms, and she forced herself to step away from him, away from the pleasure of his skin on hers.

"I am fine. Please do not concern yourself with me. May we go?"

"Yes. Gila. This way." He smiled gently, and it warmed her. Had she ever received kindness from her own father? She couldn't recall any. She realized she'd expected all dragon males to be like her sire. Cold, distant, unfeeling. Ketryn had simply been a hostess for the Harenan Embassy, just one more person to serve her father's whims. But Tarkesh seemed...different. And so appealing. It was a shame she had to mate with this Nadir instead.

Tarkesh's hand settled hot and solid against the small of her back. His touch burned her through the saltwater silk of her gown. She shuddered as longing washed over her, and she swallowed back a soft moan. He guided her around the corner of the landing site and through the maze of sand-colored tents. "Are we very far?"

"Not far. Just there." He pointed to an enormous animal a short distance away.

Ketryn's mouth flapped open and closed several times before she could speak. No animal that large lived on Vesperi. She'd never even heard of such things. The huge reptile had four widely spaced legs that barely held its belly off the sand, a long tail, a wide, fat head, and tiny eyes. The coloring was unique, though. It was intricately patterned in black with uneven stripes of orange, pink, and peach. Its scales looked like large, rough bumps. "*That* is a Gila?"

"Yes, it's a Gila beast. They are used as riding and pack animals."

"Are they native to Harena?"

He frowned. "Yes, though I do believe they got their name because they resemble an ancient Earth creature."

"Earth had reptiles so large?"

"I don't think anyone on Harena can answer that question. Certainly not I." His eyes gleamed. "Though I would love to speak to the new human women who crash-landed in the werebears' laps."

She laughed. "Varad has met them. You could ask him about them."

"Perhaps I will." His fingers stroked sensuous circles on her back as he looked down at her. Heat warmed his dark gaze. She leaned into him instinctively, tilting her face toward him. Yes. Something about this man was intoxicating. Irresistible temptation. She wanted to know more, to touch him. She shouldn't give in to this desire, this unexpected passion for a man she'd only just met. Something inside her pulled toward him, this man who could never be hers. Longing twisted deep within her, and her pussy clenched.

His hand lifted to the back of her neck, threading his fingers through her hair. "Ketryn."

"Yes." She closed her eyes, reveling in the feeling his simple touch elicited in her. No one had affected her this way before. His fingers on her skin were soft and gentle. Goose bumps rippled down her arms. She laid her hands on his bare chest, stroking her fingertips over his smooth skin.

He groaned and brought his palms up to cup her hands. "I need to..."

He leaned closer, and his lips brushed over hers, still soft, still gentle. She moaned into his mouth, her nipples beading tight as she pressed her breasts to his warm, wide chest. He swept his tongue out to lick her bottom lip. Shuddering, she opened for him. His mouth meshed with hers. Slow fire built within her. Seducing her. His fingers slid down her long hair and then cupped her hips to move her against his erection. She rubbed herself on him, desire whipping through her body.

Someone behind them cleared his throat, and they jolted apart. She fought a moan as the heat of Tarkesh's body abandoned her. The man who'd interrupted them shifted uncomfortably. "Lord Tarkesh, I am sorry—"

Tarkesh straightened the robe he wore, and offered up a calm smile. "No, it's fine, Lord Baleel. Please, I'd like you to meet Lady Ketryn. Ketryn, this is a good friend of mine, Baleel."

He stood as tall as Tarkesh but had a wider build. A midnight-blue robe covered pants and a shirt in the same color. Brilliant gold scaling peeked out from his sleeves and collar. Unlike Tarkesh, he wore his hair cropped close to his head.

"Hello." She stepped forward and offered her hand. He engulfed it in his large palm and gave her an easy smile before releasing her hand. Her breath whooshed out in relief as she realized he didn't seem to be upset about her kissing Tarkesh. Perhaps dragons were as open about their sexuality as tigers were. She hoped so.

Tarkesh's hand settled on her lower back, and she fought the urge to arch into his touch. "I was just showing Ketryn the Gila beasts."

Baleel's smile widened, his eyes curious as they looked her over. "You've not seen one?"

"No. Never. May I touch them?" They fascinated her with their enormity and complete foreignness. She wondered what their scales would feel like under her fingertips. Silky and smooth like dragon scales? Or hard and rough?

"Yes, they are quite tame." Baleel gestured for her to precede him.

The Gila beasts didn't seem to be caged in any way. They wandered close to the tents in a large pack. There were between twenty and thirty of them. She approached the closest one with caution. Tame or not, it was a huge animal that could hurt her without meaning to. She lifted her palm and laid it against the Gila's side. This one was black with peach markings. The scales rose in high bumps that fit her hand. They were coarse and hard but warm to the touch. "How do you ride one? The scaling would make it uncomfortable."

"If you were to ride them bareback, yes. But we have padding that we strap around their belly. Just there." Baleel pointed to an area midway down the Gila's back. Their bodies seemed to hinge in that area, their forelegs leading in one direction, their hind legs following on a disjointed parallel. She could understand that to sit too far forward or back might give the rider motion sickness from the swaying their movements would create. Every move seemed slow and cumbersome.

The Gila she was petting made a sound between a wheezing groan and a grunt. She jerked her hand back, and both men chuckled.

She flicked a glance over her shoulder at them. "I'd like to see how well either of you would react to the native flora and fauna of Vesperi."

Baleel bowed low before her with a small grin. "Such a tart tongue. That settles it—it is truly genetics."

"What nonsense is this?"

"I speak of your cousin, Adriyana. She has…strong opinions about everything."

"And that is an undesirable trait in a dragon woman? Are women not allowed to speak their minds?" What a horrifying thought. Women on Vesperi could not inherit wealth or title, so they sought their power and influence through the men in their lives. However, there were many tigresses who were powerful, and none were forbidden to express an opinion.

Both men blinked at her. Tarkesh glanced at Baleel, and the man nodded and faded away into the herd of Gila. Tarkesh spoke quietly. "I…mean no disrespect when I ask this, but…you do realize that weredragons have a matriarchal government, do you not? Women own all property, and family loyalties run through the female line."

She blinked. "I—I didn't know. I don't know much about dragons."

"Your father was a weredragon. He told you nothing?" His dark gaze pinned her in place, searched her eyes for the truth, and invited her to tell him everything. And she wanted to. It surprised her. She wasn't one to share too much or too soon.

She shifted, uncomfortable with how *comfortable* she felt with him less than an hour after meeting him. "No. My mother died within a Turn of my father's appointment to Harena. He…I never knew anything but weretigers. They raised me, taught me, befriended me. Father and I were the only dragons. Who else was I to associate with?"

A kind smile slid over his lips. "If you have any questions on our journey, I would be happy to answer them."

"You won't—you won't think me foolish? I feel ignorant for knowing nothing about my people. Shouldn't I know these things?" How could her father have kept this from her? Why hadn't he told her? If women were so powerful, so needed, why was she—a woman—so unimportant to him? Despair wrapped around her. A tiny part of her longed for some warmth from her father. To belong to something more powerful than just herself—a unit, a family. No tenderness or kindness had ever been forthcoming. She straightened her spine. She didn't need to contemplate that. It wouldn't help anything. She didn't miss her father; she hadn't spent enough time around him to miss him. She missed the possibility of the connection with another being, a person connected to her by blood or love. The only people she had like that were Mahlia or Varad, and they were flying away into space in a matter of weeks. Her heart twisted. "When will we be leaving for the capital?"

His mouth had opened to answer her first question, and then it closed. He arched his eyebrows at the change of subject. "Tomorrow morning, my lady."

Icy fear slipped down her spine, and all her dread at the mating roiled inside her. She felt the blood drain from her face, and she swayed on her feet. "So soon?"

"Yes, my lady. The bonding ceremony takes place in six days' time, the day after we arrive in the capital." His hands snapped out to catch her shoulders, and he pulled her close to his chest. His fingers smoothed down her hair. She leaned into him, craving the comfort his embrace seemed to give. Had she ever felt so at ease with someone so quickly? She didn't think so, but she couldn't force herself to step back, to step away, to give it up for the short time she had him with her. Five days. That was all she had. She would savor this small moment with him before she mated with a stranger. She pushed away the dread that welled up in her and burrowed her nose into his throat, inhaling the warm, spicy scent of his skin.

She flicked out her tongue to taste him, and his hand dropped to cup her ass. He tugged her hips forward so he could ride against her pussy. He spun them around and backed her against something hard. A Gila. It shifted, and the roughness of its scales abraded her through the thin saltwater silk of her robes. His hard chest pressed to her front, his skin smooth beneath her fingertips as she lifted her hands to touch him. His lips brushed against hers, tentative, questioning. Sweet. Intoxicating.

Sighing, she leaned into the caress of his mouth. Slow fire built in her belly, and she wanted more. Her sex fisted on emptiness, the need to be filled more than she could bear at the moment. Stroking her fingers up his chest, she buried them in his long, silken hair. She shivered as the texture of it slid against the scaling that drew to points on the backs of her hands. Lust slammed into her, deep, uncontrollable. Always this happened when her scales were touched. Always she craved more.

Yes. Please, Tarkesh.

His answering groan reverberated in her mind, vibrated on her lips. She shuddered at the double contact. Arching against him, she rubbed her hardened nipples against his chest. Passion coursed hot and heavy through her, pooling between her legs. She wanted more. She needed—

"Ketryn!" Mahlia's call in the distance reached her ears, and she moaned a protest at the second interruption to her pleasure. Did no one wish her to enjoy her last moments of freedom? She frowned, her mouth setting in a line. Her muscles grew tense with frustrated lust. A hiss bubbled up in her throat.

A low chuckle slipped from Tarkesh. "You sounded very much the dragon just then, my lady. I am a good influence on you."

Rolling her eyes, she let a reluctant laugh straggle out. "I refuse to incriminate myself by answering that, my lord."

"Tarkesh."

"Tarkesh." She nodded and smiled up at him, stroking a single finger down the centerline of his chest before withdrawing. His dark gaze flashed hot, but he stepped away just as Mahlia broke through the line of tents.

"There you are." A brilliant smile graced her feline features. "I was beginning to worry. You've been gone a very long time."

"Have I? I hadn't noticed." And she hadn't. Perhaps because all thoughts of time fled her mind when Tarkesh put his hands on her. How unusual for her. She pursed her lips. It wasn't something she was willing to examine too closely. That way lay heartache. Tarkesh was here to take her to the man she was going to mate with—another man, she reminded herself with ruthless force. She could not get attached to him, no matter how attractive she found him.

"How could you not—"

"Look, Mahlia. These are Gila beasts. Harenans ride them." Ketryn flashed a smile at her friend and stepped aside so she got a full view of the enormous lizard. Mahlia's blue eyes lit with interest, and she stepped forward.

Mahlia's gaze landed on Tarkesh, and Ketryn watched her fascination with the new creature war with her monarchal duty. Ketryn bit the inside of her cheek when duty obviously won. Then her friend froze, her nose lifting to sniff the air delicately. She cut her gaze to Ketryn, and she spoke telepathically as she dropped a graceful curtsy. *I can smell you on him, Ketryn. Did I interrupt anything interesting?* Her blue eyes sparkled with suppressed mischief. When she spoke aloud, she addressed Tarkesh. "Hello, I am Amira Mahlia. And you are?"

He bowed before the weretigress. "Amira, I am Lord Tarkesh."

"It is a pleasure." She nodded to him and glided forward over the sand to lay a hand on the Gila. Ketryn grinned. Even her duty wasn't going to prevent Mahlia from exploring. "This is a beautiful land with beautiful creatures, my lord."

"My thanks, Amira. We are honored you are enjoying your stay with us."

Ketryn's grin widened at the formality they used with each other. Neither used those tones with her. For a moment, she wondered at Tarkesh's automatic casualness with her. Was it because she was a dragon, or was it something else? Did he feel this strange *connection* between them? Part of her hoped so, and the more sensible part knew it would be easier to be mated to another if he did not. She reached out to lay her palm on her friend's shoulder. "Mahlia...I am leaving in the morning."

"Wh—what? But we will be here for several more weeks trading." Her blue eyes went wide and filled with tears. Her lips trembled, and she compressed them into a flat line. "I don't see why you must go so soon."

"Tarkesh will escort me to the capital. For my mating ceremony. In six days." If Ketryn said it enough, perhaps it would feel real.

Mahlia turned accusing eyes on Tarkesh. "Then, if I will be here for the ceremony, I will go with you to the capital to witness it."

"No." Tarkesh shook his head, his gaze hard. "Foreigners are not permitted to leave the landing site. Not ever. Ambassadors and traders remain *here*." His wave indicated the city of tents.

"I am her best friend."

His brows arched, but his voice remained adamant. "Then, as her best friend, you will respect the customs of her people."

She snorted and turned away. "Fine, but I do not have to be happy about it."

"Of course not." He bowed to her, and she swept past to disappear into the maze of tents. He sighed and turned back to Ketryn. "I don't believe I made a very favorable impression with your friend, but it is the law. I am sorry."

"*Why* is it the law?" That was what confused her.

"You have met people from all the colonized planets, yes?"

"Yes. My father was an ambassador. I met people from everywhere. It was my duty to serve as hostess to all of them. What does this have to do with weredragon law?"

He flashed a grin, and a sweet feeling clenched her belly at the sight. He was a beautiful man. His hand snapped out to catch her wrist and draw her against him again. His lips brushed over the sensitive flesh where her neck met her shoulder. She shivered. "I'm getting to that. All these other people—what kinds of government do they have?"

She struggled to focus as his tongue flicked over her skin, tasting her. Her hands lifted to clench his strong shoulders. "Ah...the tigers have a monarchy, the merpeople have a republic, and the bears have a feudal lord system. I believe that's all correct. Why?"

"Well." His wide palms slipped down her back to cup her hips. "In all those cultures, do not the *men* have a majority of the power? Even in the supposedly equal mer republic?" He bit down on the corded muscles of her neck.

"Yes." Her voice erupted as a squeak. This was the most erotic lesson in politics she'd ever received. Her body pulsed with need, reminding her exactly how long it had been since she'd bedded a man. Too long.

His rough voice scraped over her nerves as he continued the story. She struggled to comprehend, to learn, when she wanted nothing more than to drag him into the nearest tent and quench the need building deep within her. "When dragons came to Harena, we barely survived as a people. It was a woman who stepped forward to take control of the chaos that ensued. A woman who created laws that governed the people, a woman who established the first trade with Vesperi. Her name was Kelyn, and she found the tigers unwilling to deal with her because she was a woman, because women cannot have true power among the tigers. Thus the laws. No foreigners can leave the landing site for fear that they will contaminate our society, the balance that keeps us all alive. Weredragon men are warriors and traders—we go out and conduct whatever relations there are with the other weredragon bands and with the other planets. Women stay on their lands. They control all property; they produce the children and therefore ensure our future. The most powerful women have properties in and around the capital."

"That's why the mermaid ambassador is the only female I have seen since landing?" She'd only just realized this was true. No women in the tent city. Not one. Then he slid his fingertip down the scales on her arm, and all thought fled her mind. Her breath tangled in her throat. She leaned forward to bite his collarbone and sooth the sting with her tongue.

He groaned, his palm moving to cup her breast and rub his thumb over her hard nipple. "Yes. Your family is descendant of Kelyn, the most powerful matriarchy on Harena. I—"

Standing on tiptoe, she pressed a light kiss to his jaw, his chin. Her fingers gripped his inky hair to drag him down to her mouth. "Tarkesh. Be silent and kiss me."

Dropping his forehead to hers, he gave a strained laugh. "I cannot."

"Why not?"

"Because the evening meal is upon us, and if we are late Baleel and the Amira will come chasing after us. I prefer to savor my pleasure. For hours." She shuddered as he whispered in her ear before sucking her lobe between his teeth. He nipped at her flesh, and her pussy spasmed hard. Gods, she wanted that, too. Savor. Hours. With him. Inside her. *Yes.*

As though Tarkesh had conjured him to prove his point, Baleel stepped out from behind the Gila. "My lord. The caravan is prepared for the morrow. The dune-racers have been checked, the Gila beastmasters will have them packed or saddled by dawn."

"Excellent." Tarkesh nodded to indicate they begin walking toward the tents, and they fell into step with him.

The sunlight seemed to have winked out in an instant, without much fanfare. Twilight lasted for hours on Vesperi, and it was one more reminder that she was out of her element.

An enormous fire danced in the middle of the tent city, with what looked like a Gila beast roasting on a spit. Mahlia and Varad stood on the far side talking to the mermaid ambassador and a rotund dragon with pink scales. The man looked...odd in that color. Ketryn bit the inside of her lip to keep from giggling. He laughed, and his jowls shook, the movement making his scales twinkle in the firelight.

"He's very proud of his scales. As are all dragons." Tarkesh's breath brushed against her ear as he bent to speak softly to her.

"I'd heard that somewhere." She shuddered as his fingers drifted down the scales on her arm. Clenching her teeth, she tried to fight the rising passion that slicked her sex. Gods, help.

She jolted when his hand closed around her elbow, her body arching at the harder contact with her sensitive flesh. Tarkesh gave her an innocent look as he guided her over to her friends. She returned a skeptical glance and snorted.

The evening passed in a blur of feasting and dancing under foreign stars to wild music that tickled her memory. She spun in Tarkesh's arms until she was breathless with laughter. Sweet, tender emotions wrapped through her that she could do nothing to stop. He passed her to Varad, to Baleel, and even to the pink dragon. Her feet ached, and her mind whirled with too much wine when she collapsed into her bunk onboard the weretiger ship.

Chapter 4

The next morning came too soon, and Ketryn had barely closed her eyes when Mahlia shook her awake.

"Noo," Ketryn moaned and curled into a ball. Tears flooded her eyes to streak down her cheeks, everything she'd been holding back for months exploding from deep within her.

"Shh, shh. We will see each other again someday. I have faith." Mahlia crawled in next to her in bed, wrapping her arms around her. Ketryn laid her forehead against her friend's shoulder and sobbed until her throat was raw. Mahlia shook with her own crying, and they held tight to each other.

"I don't want to go. I don't want to do this." Ketryn met her friend's blue gaze and balled her fists in her royal-blue gown.

"I know." Mahlia's lips twisted, and she stroked Ketryn's hip-length black hair away from her face. "I wish I could—"

Shaking her head, Ketryn closed her eyes for a moment before sitting up. Her head pounded from all the alcohol the previous night. *Gods' blessing.* She swiped at the tears on her cheeks. "You can't...you can't save me from this. It would ruin the trade relations between our worlds, and I'm not worth that."

"Sad but true." Mahlia's eyes had the same hard truth in them that Ketryn knew. One person's happiness was not worth the prosperity of many.

Resignation filled Ketryn's chest, hollowing her out. "It's time." She sighed. "I have to dress. Baleel had them load my things on the Gila beasts, so...it's just me that needs to get ready."

Mahlia slid out of bed, shoving her blond-and-brown-striped hair back. "I know."

Bending to the floor, Ketryn scooped up her traveling clothes. She had no idea how they'd gotten down there. They had been folded neatly on her bed the day before, ready for her to wear them. She tugged on her pants, tucked the bottoms into heavy leather boots, and shrugged a layered, filmy tunic over her head. When she looked up, Mahlia stood in the open doorway holding her travel pack for her. They walked in silence to the ramp that led down to the landing site, their hands clasped tightly together. After the initial storm of tears had passed, Ketryn felt numb. This was it. There was no going back, no hope of escape. Unlike her friend, she had little faith that they would ever meet again. From what Tarkesh had said, Ketryn would never be allowed to leave the capital again, and Mahlia would never be allowed to leave the landing site even if she ever made the trade run again, which wasn't likely. No. There was no hope for it. She would never see her friend after today. A band of emotion cinched around her chest, cutting off her breath. Each footstep echoed in her mind, a death toll on her closest relationship.

She glanced over and saw silent tears streaking down Mahlia's cheek. She squeezed the other woman's hand. Varad awaited them at the bottom of the ramp with Tarkesh and a saddled Gila beast. When they reached the men, Ketryn wrapped her arms around her friend. She whispered in her ear, "I love you."

"I love you, too."

Pulling back, Ketryn turned to Varad. He engulfed her in his strong arms, lifting her off the floor to squeeze her tight.

"Take good care of her," Ketryn said.

The big weretiger nodded against her temple, stroking a hand down her hair before he stepped back. Mahlia leaned against him for support, and his arm curled around her shoulders.

Tarkesh climbed aboard the Gila and twisted to offer her a hand up. She scrabbled up to land in front of him. His thighs flexed, and the Gila rocked to a start. Ketryn leaned to the side, looking back at Mahlia and Varad to wave until they were no more than a speck on the horizon.

They merged into the middle of the long caravan, dune-racers buzzing up and down the column of Gila beasts. The sand they kicked up made her sneeze, and Tarkesh tugged a wrap up to cover her mouth and nose. Tears made tracks down her face, and her chest shook as she suppressed her sobs. He said nothing, just cradled her against his chest while she cried.

The twin suns blazed down hot and fierce upon them, and her mouth felt dry and sticky. She laid her cheek on Tarkesh's shoulder and tried not to allow her stomach to heave at the constant rocking motion of the Gila beast. After what felt like centuries, she fell asleep in his arms.

So responsive, so fiery and passionate. Ketryn held nothing back. She loved fiercely and openly, had a deep loyalty to those she cared for. Tarkesh admired that, and in so short a time, he already respected her steady resilience. No protestations—she just tucked her chin down and faced a painful loss without flinching. His gut clenched at the thought of her tears. He'd wanted to comfort her, to make it right for her, but he could do nothing. To let her go would mean losing her himself, and he couldn't do that. Her family would never allow it, and she was just what they needed. He could feel it in his bones. Perfect. Nadir would adore her. His cock hardened at the thought of his mate. At the thought of watching his mate make her scream with pleasure. He'd assumed she would compete with him for Nadir's attentions, but now that he'd met her, tasted her himself, he no longer feared this.

"Tarkesh."

He nodded a greeting to Baleel as the other man reined in his Gila beside them. Ketryn still slept in his arms. He checked the scarves over her mouth to make certain she didn't inhale the sand.

"The dune-racers have located a good place to camp tonight."

"Good." They could never camp in the same place twice or take quite the same route from the landing site to the capital. To do so would leave them too open and vulnerable to renegade bands of outcast dragons. The inconvenience of new routes was worth the safety it offered them.

Baleel's gaze fell to the woman sitting before Tarkesh. "Lord Nadir will approve of her, I think. But that is why you came along, is it not? To get the measure of her first?"

"More or less." He *had* wanted to get the measure of her, had he not? He'd worried about whether her presence in their bond would drive a wedge between Nadir and him. If she could be trusted, if she could *love* them both. Nadir was a man of practicality, of duty, but Tarkesh knew that wouldn't be enough for him. If Tarkesh had wanted mating to be easy, he would have mated to a woman and been done with it. Instead he'd mated to Nadir—a rough nobleman who challenged everything Tarkesh believed in. *Nothing* was easy with Nadir. He chuckled. Watching his mate clash with the passionate, independent

Ketryn would be...entertaining. He could already tell she was a woman often left to her own devices, with no matriarchs to guide her or make demands of her. If her father had neglected her to the point that she knew nothing about her heritage, her home world, then he assumed most of her decisions had been made without consulting anyone else. Life among the matriarchs would be a shock for her. Nadir and he would be there to help her where they could, but men and women had little influence in each other's affairs. He sighed, worry for her well-being nagging at him. He stroked a hand down the length of her silken hair. It slid like water through his fingers. It would wrap around both him and Nadir as they fucked her from both sides. Had she ever been with two men at once? A woman as responsive as she would enjoy the experience, he was certain.

As if echoing his earlier thoughts, Baleel spoke up. "She...seems to know very little of her own people. You can have some influence there, but her family may want to take her in hand."

"True. Though she doesn't seem the kind to be easily *taken in hand*." He frowned. She seemed to think she was mating only with Nadir. He was unsure how to tell her that wasn't the case. Did she even know what a *harim* was? He didn't know. How much should he reveal, and how quickly? He feared that giving her too much information would scare her. And her feelings had become vitally important to him. Something deep within him had shifted when he'd met her. Mate. She would be his. His and Nadir's. He wanted to slide his cock into her wet heat and thrust until she fisted tight around him. The possibilities with all three of them were...exhilarating. He couldn't wait.

Baleel's saddle creaked as he shifted. "Adriyana will love her."

"Adriyana is an easy woman to love, isn't that so?" Tarkesh slanted a glance at the other man, who harrumphed and remained silent. Tarkesh grinned but said nothing more. Everyone knew Baleel had been courting Adriyana for months with little success. A part of him felt sorry for the man, and another part was simply grateful he didn't have to deal with such a complicated courtship. He had Nadir, and now Ketryn would be theirs soon enough. He heaved a sigh of relief.

She stirred in his embrace, and he fought a groan as her sweet little ass rubbed against his cock. Dear Goddess, if he had to endure her lush curves rocking against him for the next five days, he might explode. No matter what Nadir had said, he had no intention of bedding her until after his mate had met her and they were bound together for the rest of their lives. Ah, but he could kiss her, stroke her, tease her. He couldn't resist how quick she was to react to his touch, how hot she became in his arms. He shuddered, slipping his fingers under her tunic to rub the taut skin of her belly.

Shivering, she straightened. Her breath caught, and her fingers clamped over his. "Tarkesh," she whispered.

"You were expecting someone else, my lady?" He nuzzled the back of her neck, flicking his tongue out to taste her flesh. She moaned softly, her fingers biting into his forearm, but her head arched back on his shoulder to afford him freer access. Moving his mouth up the length of her neck, he caught her earlobe between his teeth and tugged.

Tarkesh, she moaned in his mind. He dipped his fingers over the fabric of her pants to rub between her thighs. Her legs parted subtly to admit him. She flicked a frantic glance around. He met Baleel's gaze and jerked his chin down. Baleel nodded and reigned in his Gila, slowing to allow them to pass before he turned to ride back down the column of the caravan. Tarkesh tugged his cape around them both so his hands could roam freely. Her hips squirmed, her ass moving against his stiff cock. She froze when she came into contact with his hard flesh.

He could feel the heat of her through her pants, and he groaned. "So hot, so sweet. If I slipped inside you, you'd be tight around my cock, wouldn't you?"

Oh, Gods. Her hand closed over his, guiding him deeper between her legs. He stroked one finger down the seam in her pants. She rocked against his fingers.

Goddess. Dragons worship the female form. Like this. His other palm lifted to cup her breast. Her hard nipple stabbed into his hand. He pinched her through the silken layers of her tunic, and she arched and twisted in his arms. He rubbed his finger against her pants, stroking over her clitoris. Low keening dragged from her throat, and his cock throbbed at the sensual sound. He rocked with the rhythm of the Gila, lifting his hips to rub himself deeper into the soft curve of her buttocks.

"Gods. Goddess. Please. I'm...I'm going to..."

"Come? Oh, yes." A dark chuckle dragged from his throat. "I'm going to make you scream but not today. We wouldn't want everyone in the caravan to know how hot and sweet you are, would we?"

"No. Yes. I don't—I need... Please, Tarkesh." She shook her head on his shoulder, and her silky hair brushed against his skin. Her light fragrance caressed his nose. He drew in the sweet scent, so exotic, different from the heavier oils worn by the women of his world. It made his blood burn to have her in his arms. Everything about her brought out the possessive dragon within him. That, more than anything, made him believe this bonding between the three of them would work. None had ever elicited this reaction from him, save Nadir. The thought of both of them made his cock jerk in his pants. Heat slammed into him, made his skin feel too tight, as if he would explode from its confines. He squeezed his eyes closed, surprised that orgasm fisted tight in his gut. He'd meant to push her, but he had pushed himself, too. He couldn't detach himself at all—her passion called to him, dragged him under.

"I know what you need. I'll give it to you. Now." He ground himself into her from behind, pressed down on her clit and stroked fast, and twisted her nipple hard. He froze, his muscles locking as he shuddered and came. Her breath caught, and her body bowed, arching into his harsh caresses as she came as well. She twisted in his arms, her hips jerking. He lifted one palm and clamped it over her mouth, working his other hand against her soft pussy. Her wetness had leeched through to dampen the fabric of her pants. She moaned and whimpered behind his hand, her breath panting through her nose. A tear leaked from the corner of her eye to slide down his fingers.

She collapsed in his arms, and he cradled her against his chest. Shivers racked her body. He smoothed his hand down her hair. This couldn't happen again, not until they reached the capital. He reversed his earlier decision to toy with her until then. Goddess, she lit him on fire. If he was going to keep his promise to himself to wait until he and Nadir were mated to her, he couldn't risk touching her again. And he had four more days of her rocking up against him on the Gila beast. He bit back a groan.

She stiffened in his embrace, drawing as far away from him as she could, which wasn't far, because the rolling stride of the Gila pressed her back to him. She twisted around to meet his gaze. "This can't happen again, Tarkesh."

He frowned. What had brought on this abrupt change? "Why not?"

She hissed impatiently, the fire that always simmered beneath the surface flaring to life. *Isn't it obvious? We aren't mated, and we barely know one another. This cannot happen again, Lord Tarkesh.*

Confusion and anger whipped through him. She wanted to deny this connection that had formed between them? What did it matter how little they knew of each other, that they weren't yet mated? He ignored the fact that he'd just made the decision not to touch her. It rankled that she wished to refuse him. He ground his teeth together, trying to rein in the dragon within him that wanted to mark her, claim her as he and Nadir had claimed each other. This wasn't like him, this kind of impatience. He let his hands fall away from her, leaning back. He shoved his temper away, forcing himself to some semblance of his normal calm. Nadir would be highly amused to see him so disgruntled about being denied by a woman when he *agreed* with her about the need for abstinence. He snorted an ironic laugh at his own expense.

"If that is your wish." He nodded down at her, forced an easy grin to his face. Of the two of them, Nadir was never the diplomatic one. That was Tarkesh's place. So, what was wrong with him now? Ketryn. She was the problem, and he wasn't certain there was a cure. Or if he even wanted one.

A tentative smile graced her full lips, and it was a punch straight to his heart. Goddess on fire, he was in so much trouble here. They needed to get to the capital fast—now wasn't too soon. She was a temptation he wasn't certain he could resist. She cleared her throat and turned to let her gaze scan the endless sea of rolling sand dunes. "Well, we'll be riding this beast for a long while. What shall we talk about?"

He chuckled. There was only one thing he craved knowledge of right now. "You."

Chapter 5

The days passed, and Ketryn rode before Tarkesh on the Gila. The journey that should have been endless and monotonous, with spurts of panic over her impending nuptials, was instead fascinating because of Tarkesh. They talked about everything. Her family, his family, his interests, his place in dragon society, her unique position in the weretiger political structure.

She couldn't keep a wistful note from her tone when she spoke of Vesperi. She spoke to him of things she'd never told another soul, not even Mahlia. Something in her reached out to him, *trusted* him to guide her in this foreign world that was now her home.

She stared into the fire that danced before her. They'd made camp for the fourth day. Tomorrow they would be in the capital. Fear skittered down her spine. What would she do when she mated to another man? Would she be allowed to keep male friends? She didn't know. Even with all Tarkesh had told her about the planet and culture, she still knew so little.

A small, bitter sigh slid from her. Damn her father for keeping this from her, for never bothering to spare a moment of his time for her. Would she ever belong here? Would she ever get beyond the fact that she was raised in another culture among a people that were not her own? She'd do her best—that was all she *could* do. Despite her assurances to herself, she couldn't quiet the unease that rippled over her skin. She hated the uncertainty of it. So many variables she didn't know. At least in the intricate dance that made up weretiger politics, she knew the steps. Here she was off balance, tentative. She clenched her jaw, frowning. Her temper was on edge this evening, and she didn't want to speak to anyone, didn't trust herself not to lash out.

She shook herself from her dark thoughts when she heard footsteps crunch against the soft sand. The camp looked like a smaller version of the tent city at the landing site, the sides of the fabric tents snapping in the wind.

"We'll be in the capital at midday tomorrow." Baleel approached to kneel on the other side of the fire. He reached out his hands to warm them in the heat. Like Vesperi, night on Harena brought chilly temperatures. Tonight was especially frigid, the stiff breeze lashing through her clothing. She shivered and sank deeper into the folds of her cloak.

"Fine. I'm heartily sick of the great monster I have to ride. I'm sure it will serve as a stringy meal for some poor caravan soon enough." She winced at the tart bite in her voice. She really shouldn't associate with anyone this evening in this kind of temper, but she couldn't bring herself to close herself in with her own thoughts in her tent.

"You remind me of Adriyana more every day. Not just your features, which bear a distinct family resemblance, but your bearing, your attitude."

"She is hardheaded then?" A grudging smile tugged at her lips. Baleel had kept her company almost as much as Tarkesh these last few days. He was a calm, quiet man, but she found she liked him. She could easily see why he and Tarkesh would be friends. And at this point, it was more than obvious how much she liked Tarkesh. Another reason for her ill humor. He had kept his hands to himself since that first day. She was grateful and frustrated about it at the same time. She wanted him. Learning more about him in the last days had only increased her attraction, and she knew she shouldn't give in to it again. She could so easily lose her heart to him, and she might never recover from it. She owed it to herself to give her mating to Lord Nadir her best effort, and loving Tarkesh would help no one.

Baleel laughed, returning her attention to their conversation. "Yes, but in the best way."

"You are close to her? Do you know my...family well?" Just using the word *family* was enough to make her belly cramp. Hope pushed hard against her breast. Perhaps she wouldn't have the happiest of marriages. Perhaps she would never have what Mahlia had, but she might know her family. She might grow to love them, become a part of them. Belong. As much as losing Mahlia hurt, as much as mating with a stranger stung, she refused to give in to despair. There *had* to be something good that came of returning to her home world. Her family might be it.

"I am working to convince Adriyana that she should mate with me. And your family? Yes. They are allied to mine, but a mating between our matriarchies would benefit every-one."

"She doesn't want to be mated?" Or maybe she didn't want to mate to Baleel. A pity, really. He seemed a good man.

"She will be mine. Have no doubt. She can fight forever, and I still will not relent in this." His eyes flashed anger, hurt, steely determination. Something deeper lay between her cousin and this man than what was apparent at first glance. She didn't want to pry, but he was upset, and she didn't want to ignore what was so obvious.

Reaching out, she laid a hand over his for a moment. "Don't relent. I don't know her, but my dearest friend has a mate like that—one who would never give up on her, even when she had given up on herself. They needed each other. I—I don't know why I'm telling you this, but I hope she deserves your devotion as much as my friend deserved her husband's."

"She does. Her life of late has not been kind to her. A man." His fists clenched until the knuckles shown white against his dark skin. "A man who is fortunate he has never crossed paths with me."

"I believe you." She wanted to ask who the man was and what he had done to Adriyana, but she didn't. It wasn't her place. And if she'd learned anything among the gossipmongers in the Vesperi court, it was to keep her own counsel and to guard her privacy with ferocious zealotry. Opening up to Tarkesh had been wonderful and frightening all at once. Speaking of Mahlia's private matters was completely out of character for Ketryn, but Baleel had looked so...lost and upset. She sighed. He reminded her of Varad after his son had died. Sad, hurting, but refusing to give in to the pain. Ketryn missed her friends. She was so homesick for Vesperi it made her heart ache at times. The smell of the Dead Sea, the cool gardens in the lower caverns, the white sands, and marble halls...it was all she had ever known, and she found herself longing for the familiarity of it.

Baleel straightened and flicked a glance over her shoulder. Her nostrils flared to catch whoever approached her from behind. A guard. She didn't know his name. He approached her to stand directly behind her, invading her personal space. She shifted, uncomfortable, but he didn't move, so she stood to face him. He flashed a friendly smile before sliding his hands up the scales on her arms. She shuddered at the unwilling pleasure that arced through her system at the contact. Rage at his arrogance slammed into her. How dare he make sexual advances on her? Jerking back, she hissed an angry warning, her hot temper from earlier resurfacing with a vengeance.

"What do you think you're doing?" She felt her control spinning away, and her scales rippled up her shoulders to spread over her body. Her mouth opened to shriek in draconic fury. The man paled beneath his dark tan and scrambled back, his hands raised in placation. Her emotions boiled up, untamable, unstoppable. Change was upon her.

Tarkesh appeared from nowhere, and his hands closed over her shoulders to hug her against his wide chest. "Shh...Ketryn. Calm down. He meant no offense. It's often a greeting, a bonding between dragons to touch scales."

"Well, I was not raised among dragons, and I do not care to be touched unless I *ask*." She jerked away, rejecting his touch. He flinched.

"After that reaction, I'm certain it will not happen again."

She shook her head, unfocused terror and blind rage coursing through her as she backed away, shaking her head wildly. "I'm not trying to be difficult...I'm just not accustomed—"

"To dragon customs? I know. You are unique. Lovely. It's all right, Ketryn. Everything is going to be all right." Tarkesh reached for her again, and she hissed, backing away.

"Don't touch me."

He dropped his hands to his sides, his eyebrows winging up. "Ketryn, please. Be—"

"No. Just leave me be." She knew her words and actions were unreasonable, but she couldn't help it, couldn't stop now. Her fists balled at her sides, a sign of her anger at all the things she couldn't control in her life now. Of all the things she was ignorant of, all the things she should know and didn't. Spinning away, she ran as fast as her legs would carry her. She needed to escape, to be alone. Her chest felt tight, her control stripping down to nothing but animalistic urges. She dropped to her hands and knees in the sand, gasping in ragged breaths. Moaning, she fumbled with her robes, stripping them away until she lay naked on the grainy earth. Her back arched in reflex, the smooth purple scales glinting in the moonlight as they spread over her entire body. She closed her eyes, twisting in the ecstasy of change. Sucking pops sounded overloud in the quiet of the night. Her bones retracted, reformed her body into the reptilian shape of her dragon side. She hissed, her voice clicking as the breath slipped passed her throat.

Digging her toes into the sand, she moved with great speed over the terrain. Her body was built to thrive in desert conditions. Away, *away*. She wanted away from everyone and everything. She didn't even want to smell the faintest trace of them on the wind. Her emotions were too raw, too painful. Tonight showed so clearly how ill prepared she was to live among dragons. Embarrassment and dread burned through her. What would they all think of her? What would they say about her actions tonight? Tigers were acutely aware of their peers and the opinions of others. Judging, jostling for position, everything counted for or against something. One wrong move could destroy a reputation forever.

And she'd no doubt failed tonight. Failed as a dragon, failed as a woman, failed to keep control. Failed. She didn't want to return, didn't want to face how poorly they would think of her.

Her breath sobbed out, and still she fled from all of them, from herself. She crested a dune and collapsed, panting. She curled into herself, wrapping her tail around her body. She missed her friends, missed a world she understood. People she understood. Would she ever fit here? Could she? Doubts flooded her mind and pressed down on her chest until she couldn't breathe. Burrowing into the sand, she let the pleasant feel of it scraping over her scales distract her from her misery. She wished she could reach out to someone, connect with someone. Who would understand? She was alone, apart. Just as she'd always been. She sighed, rolling her eyes at the self-pity she was wallowing in. It wasn't like her, but how the dragons in her caravan would react to her social misstep was one more thing she didn't know. Would they gossip about it with other dragons when they reached the capital? Or would this be nothing to them, and her reaction now was simply an overreaction based on what she knew of the weretiger culture? Again, she didn't know. An impatient hiss slid past her throat. Lying there would not make it easier for her to return.

She unfurled herself from the sand, stretched, and began the long walk back. Her haste had taken her a long way from the caravan. Bending her nose close to the ground, she followed her own scent back the way she had come. It was slow going. The desert wind tried to confuse her. She had to backtrack twice before she caught the smell of the caravan—and Tarkesh. His scent called to her, and for once she followed her instincts, her heart. She had already humiliated herself publicly, and she was through worrying what they would think of her. The constant strain of it weighed on her chest. For tonight, she would be free.

Following Tarkesh's enticing scent to his tent, she slipped through the delicate folds of saltwater silk at the doorway. He lay with his hands propped behind his head on a soft pile of furs and silk. His eyes were closed, and his chest rose and fell in the slow rhythm of sleep. She shuddered at the sight of his beautiful form. He was naked, all well-defined muscles and smooth dragon scales.

Tarkesh.

He jerked upright. His nostrils flared as he sucked in a deep breath. His eyes snapped to her, wildness in their depths. The dark irises bled out to the corners of his eyes. His lip lifted to bare his fangs. Then he blinked. His gaze dropped to her, his irises reformed.

Ketryn?

Twisting, he moved to sit on the side of the bedding. She moved forward and, with each step, shifted back into her human shape. She stretched her arms above her head, settling into the new form. His eyes widened as he took in her naked body, sliding down to focus on her breasts, the thatch of hair between her legs, the glint of scales that lined her thighs. Her nipples beaded under his perusal, lust flooding her system. Heat built between her legs, and her pussy grew slick with juices. She cupped her hands around her breasts, tweaking the tight nipples. A groan slid from his throat, and she watched as his cock rose long and hard from the nest of dark curls between his thighs. She wanted him, wanted to feel that cock thrusting in her sex. His eyes dropped to half-mast as her fingers slipped between her thighs to stroke the heated cream that coated her pussy lips.

He gazed up at her, awareness and passion lighting his eyes. She arched toward him, letting her feet carry her to him.

"Ketryn—"

She lifted her hand to his lips to stop him. "No. Touch me. I want to feel your hands on me, Tarkesh. My choice. One last time."

His tongue flicked out to suck her fingers into his mouth, licking the juices from her hands. She shivered at the feel of his soft lips closing over her fingertips. When she leaned in to kiss him, he pulled back to meet her gaze. "Ketryn, before we do this, you need to know—"

She cut him off; she didn't want to know. Didn't want any excuses, any deterrents. She just wanted this with him. Now. Her lips pressed to his, and she thrust her tongue into his mouth. They came together in a hot clash of lips and teeth and tongue. He tried to lean away, so she slid her hands down the cool smoothness of his scales. He went rigid, jerking under her touch. He groaned, his strong arms snapping around her to yank her onto his lap. She smiled against his mouth, knowing she had won. Her legs straddled the lean musculature of his thighs. The head of his cock nestled against the heat of her sex. She arched, rubbing her wetness over his hard flesh. His hands dropped to her hips, drawing her closer.

He shuddered and lay back to stretch out beneath her. His hips lifted to rub the bulbous head of his cock along her slit. *Ketryn, I think—*

Love me tonight, Tarkesh. That's all I need. I don't want words. Please.

Indecision showed in his eyes. Eyes that glazed with hot, hard lust. She watched his struggle to focus as she rotated her pelvis to increase the friction of his flesh on hers. *But—*

An impatient hiss bubbled up in her throat. Why could he not just do what she begged of him? Desperation raced through her. She didn't want to talk about this, didn't want logic or reason, or she would stop. And she needed this, needed to *feel*. Her heart squeezed, and desperation twisted tight within her. She shoved it away. *No. Don't think, don't stop, just don't.*

Thrusting her hips forward, she seated herself fully on his cock. They both groaned. He closed his eyes and arched beneath her, a deep flush running under his dark tan. He groaned deep in his chest, and his hands settled on her thighs. She sucked in a sharp breath as his fingers grazed the scales that ran diagonally from the outside of her thighs to the insides of her knees. Freezing in place, she waited to see what he would do with her sensitive flesh.

"Tarkesh," she whispered.

"Yesssss?" He drew out the word in a low hiss. His eyes opened to meet hers, a wicked glint in their depths. His claws extended from his fingers, and he raked them lightly down her thighs. "Is something wrong?" he teased.

"Yes. Harder, faster. Please, Tarkesh." She shuddered, wrapping her arms around herself to slip her hands up and down the scales on her arms. Tarkesh pressed against the scales on her thighs, caressing her flesh. One hand moved around to slip between her buttocks. He moved against her wet pussy lips, stroking her with his cock and his fingers. Her breath caught as he pulled back to press a finger against her anus. He swirled her own moisture over the tight ring of muscle. She shuddered as he pushed in, thrusting deep. His finger pressed against the head of his cock through the thin wall of flesh that separated them. She ground her hips down, exploding over the edge of orgasm.

"Ketryn." He gritted her name between clenched teeth. Throwing his head back, his fangs bared, and his eyes bled to black. A draconic roar ripped from him, and she echoed the sound as another hot wave of pleasure slammed into her, dragged her under with its force.

Her heart beat hard and fast, emotion she couldn't name banding her chest. Goddess above, this was perfection. She craved this feeling, wanted it to never end. How could she go to a loveless, lifeless marriage after knowing how sweet it could be with a man she cared about so deeply? Pain and gratitude warred for dominance within. She was so lucky to have ever known something so good, so sweet, but the pain of losing something—something she'd never imagined having—so quickly after finding it was past bearing. The unfairness of it threatened to strangle her of breath. Life wasn't fair. She'd learned that at a tender age when her mother had died and her father had treated her as an inconvenience. No, life was never fair, and it never would be. Duty and passion didn't often coincide, and they certainly weren't about to begin now.

Something in the way she reacted to Tarkesh was unique, special. Sweet. She needed it, needed him, needed the way he made her feel. She wanted that intense emotion forever. Her heart stuttered, realization slamming into her. She *loved* him. How had it happened so fast? How had he become so necessary to her? This was a disaster. She was to be mated in a matter of hours to another man. Goddess help her. She squeezed her eyes closed over a flood of tears. How could this have happened? All the men she had known, all the Turns she had been having sex, no one had ever touched her so deeply. Why him? Why now? Why couldn't he be Lord Nadir?

Anger at herself, at her rebellious heart, at Tarkesh for being so wonderful, slammed into her. Tears welled in her eyes. Helpless, hopeless. She rolled herself away from him and curled into a ball, letting bitter words trip from her lips. "Tell me, am I to be the fourth wife or fifth in Nadir's *harim*?"

He jolted and sat up to lean over her, but she refused to look at him. "Neither. Lady Ketryn, I think you are under a misconception of what a *harim* is."

She sniffed. "Isn't it a man who is mated to many women?"

"It *can* be—"

"Ha. You see?" She flashed him a triumphant look, but she found no pleasure in being right.

He chuckled, stroking a single finger along the very edge of her scaling so that half of his touch moved on her skin and half on her scales. She shivered. "It can be a man with two wives, or it can be a woman with two husbands."

"But only three people? Never more?" She shifted on the blankets and finally faced him.

He shook his head. "No. The point of a *harim* is to ensure a mating that can produce offspring. Dragon children are rare."

"I didn't know that." She was quiet for a long moment. "So, I am joining Lord Nadir and his current mate in a *harim*. And if he needs me to be able to breed, then he must be mated to another male or mated to a sterile female. Would I...would I be expected to bed the wife as well?"

He sucked in his cheeks, a dimple tucking into the left one. "You don't care for women?"

"I am not attracted to women, no. Only men." She folded her arms, and his gaze landed on her plumped breasts.

He cleared his throat, the smile dropping from his face as heat filtered into his dark eyes. "That is fortunate, then. Nadir is mated to a male dragon."

"And do they...do they *like* women, or are they just mating with me because they have to?" She arched under his gaze, no longer caring what the answers to her questions were. She had no choice in any of this, but she had choices tonight. And she wanted Tarkesh again, now.

He dipped his head to lick along the edge of her arm and over the curve of her breasts. The wet stroke touched both scales and sensitive flesh. Hot pleasure flooded her pussy. She closed her eyes and enjoyed the sweetness of his touch. "I do not pretend to know all of Nadir's thoughts, but I do know he is physically attracted to women, though he has never—"

"Tarkesh." A cool, rough voice sounded from outside the tent. Ketryn had her mouth open to ask a question, but Tarkesh lifted a hand to still her words.

"Yes, Baleel?"

"I am sorry to interrupt, but a missive has arrived from Nadir."

Tarkesh groaned and rolled to his feet to fetch whatever message her soon-to-be mate had sent. Cold fingers of reality stroked over her skin. Her mate. With whom she would bond tomorrow. And she was in the bed of another man. Guilt and shame rolled over her in a suffocating wave. Goddess help her. While Tarkesh spoke to Baleel, she jerked to her feet and forced herself to exit the tent from the rear. She shivered as the chill wind hit her naked flesh. It was common for wereanimals to be nude in public—they couldn't take their clothes with them when they shifted—but she hurried along just the same, afraid one look at her would tell anyone what they needed to know. She was betrothed to one man and in love with another. A sob caught in her throat as she threw herself into her own pallet on the floor of her tent and buried her face in the saltwater silk coverings.

She was in love, and she'd never been more miserable in her entire life.

Chapter 6

Nadir paced the length of the balcony that overlooked the main thoroughfare of the capital. The whole city lay deep within the red rock canyons that made up the western plains of Harena. Every dwelling had been carved into the stone by their ancestors' ancient tools. Those tools, along with most of the old Earth technology, had been long lost. The canyons provided some shelter from the constant wind that moved the sands.

He forced himself to stop and folded his hands behind his back. They would be here soon. Tarkesh and their new mate. This female with whom they had to breed. His gaze swept the winding canyon that led to the main square of the capital. How would it look to a woman raised on another world? He had never known another place, another planet. What was Vesperi like? And the icy bear world? The water world? He'd never viewed a body of water so large he couldn't see across it, but Aquatilis was supposed to be completely covered in liquid. And ice? It didn't snow on Harena. Not with the two suns to evaporate the little rain that did fall. Water was a scarce commodity that bloody, centuries-long wars had been waged over.

He scrubbed a hand over his hair, his gaze following the road to its end at the main square and the Goddess's temple where he and Tarkesh would mate with Lady Ketryn. Dragon figures served as pillars in the reliefs that were carved into the deep red stone on the cliff wall. It was modeled after an ancient Earthan temple in Jordan. Petra, he thought it was called, but history had never been his best subject. He preferred to focus on the present and plan for the future. He wasn't a man to look back. He assessed a situation, made the best choices he could, and did whatever it took to execute his decisions. Tarkesh was the one who thought a situation through deeply before he made a change.

Nadir was distracting himself from worry. He knew it and made himself continue. His worries wouldn't abate if he let himself dwell upon them. He focused on the temple. The main road leading through the canyons opened up into the square and took up one side. Making up the other sides of the square were the residences of the descendants of the first matriarch, Kelyn, and the massive council building where the matriarchs met to deliberate on politics.

Impatience slid through him. He wanted them here now. What had Tarkesh discovered? Would Tarkesh be satisfied with the new mate? They had no choice. The mating would go through whether Tarkesh approved or not, but Nadir wished to know how difficult this would be for them until they came to a workable relationship with the woman. She needed only to breed with them—she didn't need to love them. He didn't need an emotional connection with her. He had Tarkesh for that. The woman was a means to an end. It was a political boon that Ketryn happened to belong to the most powerful matriarchy on Harena.

But Tarkesh was not one to settle on necessity, and Nadir's gut knotted. His shoulders drew in a tense line. The waiting wasn't something he enjoyed. He leaned forward to brace his hands on the red stone balcony railing. Where were they? He shoved away a tiny thread of worry. They were supposed to have arrived at midday, and it was nearly evening. The last rays of the binary suns kissed the top of the high stone canyon walls. Torches would soon flicker to life up and down the main road. Nadir straightened and resumed his pacing. Many things could delay a caravan. They were, by their very nature, a slow-moving procession. But...renegades could also bring a caravan to a stop. A full punch of worry hit him, and he clenched his fingers into fists. They were not yet late enough to be anxious. They would be fine.

"My lord, can I get you something for your evening repast?" A servant approached him from the balcony doors.

"No. I'm not hungry." Nadir didn't allow himself the luxury of snapping at the intruder, though he would have given much to vent his anger at someone. He looked back over his shoulder at a pale yellow weredragon.

The small man shifted where he stood. "You've been out here most of the day, Lord Nadir."

"And I will be out here for as long as it takes. Thank you." Nadir refocused on the main road, dismissing the servant.

"Very good, my lord."

Nadir heard the man back away and leave him alone. He breathed deep and caught a new scent. Tarkesh. He knew his mate's smell anywhere. He narrowed his eyes and waited. They would be here soon. He could also smell the heavy musk of Gila beasts, many of them. A cloud of dust rose from the far end of the canyon as they approached. Dozens of Gila stretched in a line that filed toward the main square. He braced his hands on the railing before him and waited for his mate to pass beneath him. There. Toward the end of the procession. Tarkesh's eyes caught his, and there was something troubled in their depths. Nadir's eyebrows rose. Interesting. His mate's attention was called away by Lord Baleel. Nadir's eyes narrowed on the woman mounted before Tarkesh.

She was lovely. Her inky hair rippled to her hips, and the scarves used to cover the face during open desert travel lay draped around her neck. Slim and elegant, her arms showed a purple scaling covered in a light film of travel dust. He would enjoy watching her bathe.

The thought took him by surprise. She turned then to look up at him, and he was caught. Her dark gaze showed pain and sorrow, and something within him wanted to ease it for her. She licked her full lips, an unconsciously sensual act. His fingers clenched around the ledge of stone before him, and his cock doubled, hardened to the point of pain. Just to look at her was a dual kick to the groin and chest. Something about the way she looked, held herself, smelled—yes, he caught a unique scent on the wind—was not quite dragon. And yet she was one of the most beautiful dragon women he'd ever seen. Unusual, exotic, unexpected. Her eyes narrowed at his continued stare, her brows lifting to reprove him.

Welcome, my lady. He dipped his head and let his gaze run down her figure, taking in the swell of her breasts, the smooth length of her legs. He could not wait to see more. Anticipation hummed in his blood.

Shock flashed across her face at his insolence. She did not yet know who he was. He smiled tightly, possession gripping him. His. The woman would soon be his. His and Tarkesh's. Excellent.

She twisted in Tarkesh's embrace to keep Nadir within sight as their Gila carried them toward the main square. His smile stretched wider, and he let the hot desire he'd experienced when he'd first seen her show in his expression. With her enhanced dragon senses, she would see him even from the widening distance between them. He liked the look of her already, and he wanted to know more. He also wanted to know what his mate thought. The upset on Tarkesh's face bothered him. Well, he would find out what that was about. Now.

Spinning on a heel, Nadir strode through his matriarchy's manor and down the stairs.

His residence here was temporary. When he and Tarkesh mated with Ketryn, they would move into her matriarchy's manor. Any child Ketryn bore them would belong to her family, any trade agreements Nadir or Tarkesh arranged with other matriarchies would now go to benefit her matriarchy. And they were very good at negotiations. Nadir applied pressure where it was needed, pushed hard when necessary, and Tarkesh made giving in look easy, simple. Together, they'd been very convincing on a number of occasions, which made it rewarding for the most powerful matriarchy on the planet to arrange a mating between them and one of its daughters. Goddess, he hoped Tarkesh approved of the woman. Politically, it would be suicidal to consider balking at the mating ceremony now. Tarkesh knew that, and he would do as he ought to, but Nadir disliked uncertainty.

Nadir wound through the Gila beasts until Tarkesh and Ketryn were in sight. A group of women swept in and surrounded Ketryn, separating her from Tarkesh. His mate stepped forward to catch her hand, but she was quickly jerked away. Tarkesh's face shadowed with a look of...guilt? Nadir arched his brow. Interesting. The woman affected his mate. That could be either good or bad.

"Welcome home, my mate." Nadir settled a hand on the shorter man's shoulder.

Tarkesh whipped around to face him. His fingers snapped out to fist in Nadir's shirt and hauled him forward. Their lips met in a harsh, desperate kiss. Nadir lifted his hand to grip his mate's long hair. His heart pounded in his chest, and he could feel his mate's dick hard and urgent through his pants. Their tongues slid together, battling for control of the kiss. Knowing his mate's body intimately, he dragged his nails down Tarkesh's back where his scales lay beneath his travel robes. The silver dragon hissed and bit him, drawing blood from his lip. Nadir groaned, enjoying the sting with his pleasure. His cock was still semi-erect from his brief encounter with Ketryn, and now it hardened again. Lust burned in his veins, the dragon within him shrieking for him to claim his mate. Again. Forever. Always.

As quickly as it had begun, it ended. Tarkesh jerked back, his breath bellowing out. "Nadir, I..."

Nadir studied the silver dragon closely but could read nothing except a troubled countenance. He tilted his head back toward his matriarchy's manor. "Walk with me."

"I...should oversee unloading the caravan."

"Baleel will take care of it. He wants to watch Adriyana fawn over Ketryn, and this will afford him the best vantage point." Nadir met Baleel's gaze, and the man made a rude gesture with his hand before turning to speak to the Gila beastmasters.

Nadir started for the manor, Tarkesh falling into step beside him. He could feel the stress that radiated from his mate, drew his body into taut lines. It was unlike Tarkesh to show his upset in public. Something had changed in the past days, and Nadir intended to find out what as soon as they reached the privacy of their chambers.

The silver dragon ran a hand through his long hair and snarled a curse when his fingers caught in the windblown locks. Nadir's eyebrows rose in surprise. Yes, something was very wrong with his mate. Tarkesh flung himself into a chair when they reached their apartments. Most of their belongings were packed in crates for the move to Ketryn's matriarchy tomorrow. Only a scattered chair or two and the bed were left out. Tarkesh scowled at him.

"Alysian ice wine?" Nadir hefted a decanter of sweet red wine from the werebear world.

"Fine."

"Would you like to talk about it?" An interesting role reversal. Usually it was Tarkesh coaxing him out of a foul, impatient mood.

"There's nothing to tell."

Nadir made a low, derisive noise in his throat as he handed over a large glass of wine. He still held the decanter in his hand, waiting for his mate to speak.

"There isn't!" Tarkesh's dark eyes flashed angry fire, a warning not to press, but Nadir had never been one to obey warnings like that. He pushed anyway.

"Perhaps you can start with how you took me up on my offer and slept with our new mate." He locked his gaze on Tarkesh's face, waiting for even the most nuanced response to that. There was no denying the claim—he could smell sex and the woman's exotic fragrance all over his mate.

Tarkesh paled beneath his tan. Torment raged in his midnight gaze. "I—I did not intend for it to happen. I—she—it was an accident...mistake...I wasn't going to touch her until we were mated to her. I swear it. But she needed...and I couldn't—" He cut himself off and dropped his forehead into his hand, scrubbing his palm down his face. "Goddess, Nadir. I don't know what I'm doing."

He was in love with her. It was obvious. Perhaps not yet to Tarkesh, but he was. And so quickly. Nadir knew better than anyone that it could take only a single look for a man to lose his soul to someone. It had been that way with him when he had seen Tarkesh. Nadir examined his feelings on the matter. His mate loved another. Was he jealous of the new woman? No. Relief wound through him. No, he wasn't jealous. Some *harims* became a constant battle between the three members when they claimed to love each other. He would not allow that to happen with them. It was good that Tarkesh loved her. It could only benefit them. He wondered if Ketryn shared Tarkesh's feelings.

"I told you to sample her. Are you satisfied?" Nadir set the decanter on the sideboard, settled back against it, and folded his arms.

"I...don't know. She doesn't know she's mating to both of us. Just to you. Apparently, the weretigers think a *harim* is a man with dozens of wives. I explained that they were three-way matings, but—well, our conversation was interrupted, and I didn't have a chance to tell her after that. I spent the day on a dune-racer trying to keep the caravan moving after an older Gila went down. We had to redistribute the load to the other Gila. I only rode with Ketryn the last hour, and she was speaking to Baleel about her family the whole time. And...I didn't get a chance to tell her that she'd be mating to *me* tomorrow." His words tripped over themselves in his need to justify his actions. Unusual for something to happen that Tarkesh did not intend. Even more unusual for him not to have three contingency plans to correct the problem.

Nadir snorted at the foolishness of tigers, but better for them to make assumptions than to impose their beliefs on the dragon culture. "Did her father not explain *harims* to her?"

Tarkesh's voice grew guttural with anger. "No. Her father told her nothing. She is ignorant of all things dragon. It's criminal, his neglect of her."

"Then we will teach her what she needs to know, and the members of her matriarch will teach her the rest. You approve of her, I take it?" He had no doubt of the answer—the little desert blossom had rattled his normally unflappable mate. It would be amusing if this situation didn't have such high stakes.

Tarkesh folded his arms and sat back. "Who wouldn't approve? She's lovely. Intelligent. Passionate."

"Excellent. I'm sure she'll be a wonderful mate." And if she wasn't, he would keep it to himself for Tarkesh's sake. This mating had just become a great deal more complicated than a political arrangement.

A small woman with blood-red scales that formed a delicate ridge on her forehead engulfed Ketryn in a tight hug. Stunned at the exuberant welcome, she stood still for a moment before wrapping her arms around the woman. Her mind was still on the heated encounter with the man on the balcony who had looked at her as if he wanted to lay her out for his evening meal. She shivered at the image of what his mouth might feel like on her flesh, how his short goatee might tickle her in very interesting places. What was the matter with her? Was it not enough that she'd bedded Tarkesh, that she loved Tarkesh? Now she had to lust after some man who'd done no more than look her over?

"Hello, cousin." The woman before her flashed a smile, drawing her out of her dour thoughts. "Welcome home."

Warmth spread in Ketryn's belly, thawing some of the icy fear that had ridden her all day. Home. Goddess, she wanted to be home. She twisted around to try to see Tarkesh, but he was nowhere in sight. Baleel directed the unloading of the Gila beasts. He caught her gaze, dipped his head, and spoke to her telepathically. *He went home to his matriarchy. You will see him on the morrow at your bonding ceremony.*

My thanks. She nodded in return, but his dark eyes had locked on the red dragon in front of her. Ketryn swallowed hard. Her heart clenched at the thought of being mated to Nadir when she craved Tarkesh. *Stop it,* she ordered herself. She should treasure the memories she had and be grateful for ever having known something so wonderful. Sucking in a deep breath, she grinned down at the shorter woman. "You must be Adriyana."

She looked startled, her large, dark eyes widening. "How did you know that?"

"Lord Baleel told me of you."

A hiss erupted from her throat, and she bared her teeth. "I'll wager he did. I hope you didn't take a word he said to heart."

How was Ketryn to respond to that? She had grown fond of Baleel during their long days of travel. She opened her mouth to redirect the conversation, when Adriyana tucked her arm through Ketryn's and tugged her toward a large entrance in the face of the canyon wall. Her mouth snapped shut as she tried to take in her surroundings. The capital city was stunning, beautiful, and entirely different from anything she had ever seen before. The canyon was a cool retreat from the scorching heat of the desert above, but the interior of the manor wrapped her in almost chilly air. She twisted around to try to take it all in at once. Everything was made of the same stone of the canyons, only polished to a high gleam. Here and there lay exquisite glass and metal sculptures. The home exuded ostentatious wealth. Ketryn felt grubby in the beautiful surroundings, the layer of grime a heavy weight on her scales.

She turned to Adriyana. "I'd like to bathe, if that's possible."

"Well, you need to meet Matriarch Yola first. And you'll have to do the ceremonial bathing before your mating anyway, so it's probably best to wait."

"Ceremonial bathing?"

"Yes, the ritual cleansing before entering into a new phase in your lifeline?" Her eyebrows arched as though she was waiting for Ketryn to understand her meaning.

"I—I don't know anything about dragon rituals. My father was a very busy man, and there were no other dragons on Vesperi, so..."

"Nothing?" an older woman with silver streaked through her raven hair questioned sharply. Adriyana went rigid next to her, and Ketryn could feel the power and authority rolling off the woman. This would be Matriarch Yola, she was certain of it.

"No, my lady. Nothing." Ketryn swept a deep, respectful curtsy.

Yola snorted in derision. "We will have to instruct you in your shortcomings. This will not do. Your father was derelict in his duties, and you'll have to make up for it now."

Ketryn's back straightened. The woman's voice implied it was somehow Ketryn's fault that her father had told her nothing. And she fought the urge to defend her sire. He had spent Turns working for the advancement of Harena trade—that was hardly dereliction of duty. If he was a poor father, that was no one's business except Ketryn's. She fought the wave of dislike for Yola that washed over her. Ketryn was simply tired. The woman's personality would be less grating after she'd bathed and had some sleep.

Yola spun on a heel and walked back out the main door. "Come along."

"Is she serious?" Ketryn looked to Adriyana for confirmation.

Adriyana scurried ahead, following behind Yola. "You will find that my mother is always serious. Don't cross her. Ever. Now, come on."

Exhaustion from the past days of travel and stress slammed into Ketryn. She wanted sleep. Her eyes did not want to remain open. Couldn't they wait until tomorrow to show her whatever they wanted? What was so important that she had to wander around her new home feeling like a filthy beggar woman? A hiss slid from her throat, but she picked up her cloak and hurried to catch up with the other two women.

She saw the flash of Adriyana's red scales disappear into a building to the right of the manor. It was even more ornately carved into the canyon wall. Delicate dragons wrapped around columns that bracketed the massive double doors. She tugged open the heavy, hammered metal doors and stepped inside. Matching doors directly across from her swooshed closed, so she jogged over to pass through them as well. Where were they going? Impatience raced through her as weariness dragged at her bones.

"There you are. Try to keep up. I don't have time to waste on you." Yola stood in the middle of a wide courtyard.

Ketryn's teeth ground together, and she bit back a tart response. She would dearly love to vent her temper on this rude woman. This was no way to treat a newcomer. Fisting her hands tight, she strove for a politic answer. "I am sorry to keep you waiting. The capital is so beautiful—I simply wanted to savor it."

"No doubt Vesperi has nothing to offer in comparison."

"Vesperi is quite beautiful as well." The stiff words jerked from her. Thus far, she preferred the manners of Vesperi over those of Harena.

"I doubt it." Yola turned away to gesture toward two smaller doors across the courtyard. A peaceful garden took up the center of the area, a small, gurgling fountain in the middle. Yola pointed to the door on the left and then the one on the right. "You will prepare yourself for the bonding ceremony there. Your two mates will prepare themselves there. You will enter the temple together. My daughter will serve as your attendant and witness. Are there any questions? Good. Adriyana will show you to your chambers in the manor. I am expected at a council meeting now."

Ketryn blinked and watched her aunt stomp away. She glanced at Adriyana out of the corner of her eye, but her cousin didn't seem to think her mother's behavior was odd. A sigh slid from her lungs. "Can I bathe and eat before the next lesson to overcome my ignorance?"

Adriyana blushed at the acid in her tone, a wry grin formed on her lips, and laughter danced in her wide eyes. "I suppose you're not *so* deficient that we should deny you those. After all, you'll need to keep up your strength. We're a demanding lot."

She rolled her eyes at the red dragon. "After you?"

"No. *With* me." She tucked her arm through Ketryn's and escorted her back through the two sets of double doors. Stopping outside, she gestured to each of the buildings that made up a square. She pointed right. "That is the council building. The matriarchs meet there to govern Harena." She pointed left. "That is our matriarchal manor." She pointed straight ahead. "That is the statue of Kelyn, our ancestor. Beyond that is the capital, which you've already seen."

Ketryn gestured behind them. "And that was the temple?"

"Yes. The Goddess's temple. You'll be mated there tomorrow morning. Any questions?"

"None just yet, but I'll let you know." Her mind was too tired to think at this point. She just wanted sleep. Days of sleep.

"Good." Adriyana led her through the manor again, introducing her to anyone they came upon. Ketryn gave up trying to remember who was who after the tenth person. She was usually very good at names, but there were too many, and she was too tired to care.

They wound through long, stone hallways, passing dozens of doors and smaller hallways that led off in every imaginable direction. She would have to explore them all later.

Adriyana pushed open a set of doors that revealed an enormous suite of rooms. Plush cushions were strewn about the floor, and a wide bed dominated the main room. Sheer silk hangings framed it. It was easily twice the size of her apartments on Vesperi. She shook her head. "It's too large for just me."

Her cousin frowned and looked around. "Well, after tomorrow it won't be just you. Your mates will be here, too. I'm certain with two men in one place, this will soon seem too small."

"They'll be moving in here?" She arched an eyebrow. No man would move into his mate's home on Vesperi. A woman went to her husband's family after she was mated. Then Ketryn's discussions with Tarkesh came back to her. "Ah, yes. Family is based on the female line here. Any child I have will be a member of this matriarchy, so it doesn't matter who fathers the babe."

"See? Not so deficient after all." Adriyana's laugh tinkled out like music, and Ketryn couldn't help but smile in response. Her aunt might be difficult to understand, but she very much liked her cousin. She walked forward to look into the sitting room and then wandered out to a bright terrace. One glance upward told her they used the same light shafts covered in ancient Earthan glass to light the canyons that were used in the palace of Vesperi. Moonlight shone through the glass, and the area would be both cool and sunny during the daytime. She smiled and reentered the bedroom to run her palm along the soft coverlet, noticing as she did so that her nails were caked with sand and dirt. Drawing back, she curled her hand into a ball.

"Where is the bathing room?" She had just realized what was missing. On Vesperi, she'd had her own pool to bathe in.

"Water is scarce on Harena. We have community bathing rooms. Most dragons have to use the public ones, but our manor has its own."

"Well...at least I won't have to walk far then."

Adriyana smiled and tilted her head. "You're funny, Ketryn. And your accent is unusual."

"Not on Vesperi. I sound like everyone else. Werebears and merpeople are the ones who have odd accents."

"There is an ambassador for the merpeople at the landing site, but I've never been allowed to go there and meet her."

"Why?"

"Men are the ones who travel. It's a woman's duty to help see to the governing of her property and ensure the future of our people. Children are precious and rare here."

"I see." Only, she didn't. How would traveling hurt the future of the people? Tarkesh had said there were renegade bands and other dangers inherent in desert travel, but only the men were expendable enough for travel? Her head throbbed, and her heart ached, remembering Tarkesh. Where was he now? Was he thinking about her? He'd looked upset when she'd been pulled away by her family. Why? Because she was mating to another? Because he cared? Her pulse jumped. Goddess, she wanted him with her. Her thighs tingled at the memory of his touch, her pussy dampening as she recalled the thrust of his hard cock within her. She shuddered, her heart pounding. Her nipples puckered into tight crests, and she folded her arms over them to hide them from her cousin's sight.

Following in Adriyana's wake, she bit her tongue to keep from asking about Tarkesh. No one should know she had any interest in a man who wasn't to be her mate. That was her secret to keep.

They entered a wide room with a huge pool in the middle. A small waterfall came out of the stone wall and fell into the pool, and then a stream led away from the other side of the pool. Adriyana pointed to the stream. "That leads to the other bathing pools in the capital. The running water keeps them clean and fresh."

Ketryn nodded and wandered over to the pool to look in. It was deep and crystal clear all the way to the stone bottom. Small grooves were carved into the ledge of the pool, and bags of sweet-scented bathing sand rested in them. She hadn't had a full bath since she'd left Vesperi. The ship had allowed only for short showers every other day. Sitting down, she tugged off her boots and dragged the scarves from around her neck. She stood up and stripped quickly to dive into the water. Goddess, it felt wonderful to be engulfed in the warm liquid. Spinning in the water, she swam to the far end and back again before she surfaced, laughing at the sheer joy of the sensation. She ran her fingers through her tangled hair.

Paddling to the side of the pool, she scooped up a handful of sweet sand and scrubbed it into her hair and over her body. She was too tired to linger, but she promised herself she would come back and enjoy herself some other time. The foaming bubbles of the sand slipped down her face, and she submerged herself to rinse before it stung her eyes. Bobbing back to the surface, she noticed her cousin had knelt beside the pool and settled so her legs were curled up next to her.

"You're going to watch?" Ketryn had no problem with nudity in front of others, but she'd never known a woman to watch another bathe unless they were in a sexual relationship together. Odd. The whole planet and its culture made little sense.

"I am your witness." Adriyana grinned. "All right, for the ritual to be complete, you need to dunk your head beneath the water three times."

"Should I even ask why?"

Her cousin's mouth opened and closed again. "You know, I don't know why. That's just how the ritual works."

"Then I shouldn't ask."

She chuckled. "No, I suppose you shouldn't."

Ketryn ducked under the water and resurfaced three times, feeling ridiculous the whole while. Why did she need to be clean to be mated? What stain was so hideous that she needed to wash it away? Strange, all of it. So foreign. Would she ever feel as though she was part of it, or would she always question why things were the way they were? She sighed and climbed out of the pool, shoving her hair out of her face.

Her cousin handed her a towel and a clean robe. "You can wear this until we get your things unpacked. And tomorrow you'll wear your mating gown."

"Mating gown?"

"Yes, you have to see it. I should have thought to show you as soon as we reached your chambers." She led the way back to Ketryn's rooms, where the low table was set with steaming dishes of food. Ketryn's stomach rumbled as the smell reached her nose.

Laughing, her cousin waved her to the fat pillows placed around the table. "Sit. Eat. I will get the gown."

She swirled back into the room holding a lavender gown a shade lighter than Ketryn's purple scales. It was sleeveless and would show off her arm scaling. Lacing up the sides tied the gown into one piece. It would show off all her scales, she realized. The floor-length skirt was slit up each side all the way to the lacings that ended at the waist. "How did you know where my scaling is?"

Adriyana took the gown back to the closet she had retrieved it from. "You were born here. Yola knew where you were marked."

"Oh. Yes. I forgot." Reaching the capital had made the experience so surreal she lost track of the fact she could ever have been here before. She spooned up some of the delicious soup before her. She suspected the meat was Gila beast, but she was too hungry to stop and ask. She and her cousin ate in companionable silence, but she began to droop halfway through the last dish, her head nodding forward. Jerking awake, she saw Adriyana rise from the table to scoop the dishes onto the tray.

"Get some sleep. I will see you in the morning."

She reached out to catch the other woman's arm. "Thank you, Adriyana."

"That's what family is for, cousin." She bent and kissed her forehead. "Pleasant dreams."

Ketryn curled up onto the wide bed, pulling the soft saltwater silk coverlet to her chin. Her body relaxed into the mattress. A wave of exhaustion rolled over her, dragged her under into deep, dreamless slumber. She felt as if no time had passed at all when Adriyana shook her awake the next morning.

"Mmm. Just a few more moments." She burrowed deeper into the covers.

"I've already let you sleep longer than I should have. Time to rise, cousin."

"Oh, very well." Ketryn sighed and flopped over onto her back to grin at Adriyana.

"Put on your robe, and we'll go to the temple. Your gown is already there. We wouldn't want it to get dusty in the street."

"No, it's much too pretty for that." She sat up and reached for the robe she didn't even remember taking off the night before. Throwing her legs over the edge of the bed, she stood. Dread knotted in her gut. Time to face Nadir and his mate, soon to be her mates. Oh, Goddess. This was a nightmare. She desperately wanted to see Tarkesh but feared how she would react if she did.

"We have time for a quick meal before we go."

Her belly roiled in protest, and she shook her head. "No...no, thank you."

Slipping her feet into a pair of waiting slippers, she fell into step with her cousin and wound back through the manor. She nodded to the smiling faces they passed. She couldn't remember which ones she'd already been introduced to. Most likely, some simply knew who she was.

Relief raced through her at one familiar face she saw when they stepped into the square. The golden dragon, Baleel. A wide smile formed on her lips. He grinned back. *Felicitations, Lady Ketryn.*

She wished it were a moment for felicity, but she nodded in acknowledgment as they walked past. Adriyana hissed low in her throat, glaring at Baleel. He arched an eyebrow, let his smile widen as he looked her over thoroughly, and swept her a bow.

They entered the temple and walked through to the empty courtyard beyond. "Lord Baleel speaks very highly of you. He seems...quite taken with you."

"That presumptuous son of a Gila beast," Adriyana sneered, her voice rising with indignation. "Do you know what he did? He spoke to Matriarch Yola and tried to negotiate for a mating ceremony with me. He didn't ask me, didn't speak to me about it. After the last time, he should know I..."

"The last time?" Ketryn's hand closed around the latch to the door that led to her preparation room.

"I'm sorry, cousin. I should not—"

"Tell me, please. I would love some distraction from my own affairs." Like the fact that she'd finally managed to fall in love, and now she must mate with two other men. Goddess, help her. Her lips kicked up in a grin. She had picked up Tarkesh's religious turn of phrase in the past days, she realized. "Goddess" seemed to fit here among these people. The weretigers would never settle for just one of anything if they could have many. She wished Tarkesh was here to talk to about the weretigers. He had always been interested in anything she had to tell him about them. She missed him so much, and it hadn't even been an entire day since she'd seen him.

Her cousin picked up the lavender gown while Ketryn shed her robe. "I—I was supposed to mate with another dragon last Turn, but he mated to another in secret three days before the ceremony was to take place. He mated to a woman he *loved*."

"You must have been very angry. Did you love him?" she asked when her face emerged from the top of the gown after Adriyana slipped it over her head.

The red dragon sighed. "I didn't love him, and I wasn't angry. I was...sad for myself. He has what I want. Love. Who doesn't want love? But love is not the way of mating. Mating is for alliance, for the good of the matriarchies. Our families were shamed by his actions, and he and his mate have been cast out as renegades. He was a fool."

"To mate for love?"

Ketryn lifted her arms so her cousin could lace up the sides of her gown. It was a perfect fit. "No. To mate for love *in secret*. To make his mating a shameful act. If he had spoken to me, I would have let him go. I would have convinced Matriarch Yola it was for the best. She is not unfeeling, and I am not unsympathetic."

"And how does this affect Lord Baleel?" Ketryn sat in the chair Adriyana motioned her into. Her cousin ran a brush through her hair and began to braid it in an intricate style.

When she glanced over her shoulder, Adriyana flushed, but Ketryn couldn't tell if it was embarrassment or anger. "My shame was so public, so openly flaunted in my face, Matriarch Yola swore I may choose my own mate, that I may have a love match. Baleel tried to force my hand, to take my choice away. That I cannot forgive. There...you're ready."

Adriyana stepped back, and Ketryn caught her hand. She squeezed tight. "I'm sorry, cousin. I like Lord Baleel, but I'm sorry you were hurt."

"Well, no matter." Her small hands fluttered. "When you mate with Lord Nadir and Lord Tarkesh—"

Ketryn jerked to her feet. She felt all the blood leech from her face, and she felt the top of her head tingle with cold. "Excuse me? I am mating with *Tarkesh?*"

Confusion showed on her cousin's face. "Well, yes...I—I assumed you knew. You've...I could smell him on you last evening. Wait... Where are you going?"

Fury erupted in Ketryn's belly, blinding her. Tarkesh had *lied* to her. She didn't even care why. He had let her suffer and worry by not telling her he was the other third of Nadir's *harim.* Her fists bunched into tight knots. She wanted to pummel him until he felt even a shred of the pain she had in the past day when she'd thought she'd never see him again, never touch him again. Had it been part of a game between him and Nadir to make her love him? Shame twisted tight with bitter fury. She stormed from the room, intent on getting her answers from the only man who could answer them. Now.

CHAPTER 7

Tarkesh paced the small chamber he and Nadir were to occupy until the mating ceremony. "I should speak to her. She will be upset when she finds out."

"Calm yourself, Tark. You know they will never allow you to communicate with her in any way until the ceremony is over. It's tradition." Nadir lounged on a floor pillow, his white mating robes draping around his large form. The constant want Tarkesh felt for his mate kicked him, and his cock stirred. Awareness sparked in Nadir's dark eyes, and Tarkesh smiled to acknowledge the need they couldn't fulfill until that night. With Ketryn. He fought a groan as his cock rose to full attention.

"It is a foolish tradition," Tarkesh barked and turned away from his mate.

Nadir sighed. "True, but that doesn't mean it will change."

"I am simply—"

"Worried. Yes, I know." The big, black dragon chuckled.

"One of us has to be," he snapped back.

A single eyebrow rose in response to that. "I worry when I must. I have you to worry the rest of the time."

"You don't know her—"

"Yet. I think you need some distraction, Tark." Nadir rolled to his feet, a wicked smile on his darkly handsome face, and had taken a step forward when the door burst open.

Ketryn, stunning in a traditional mating gown, came to a stop before Tarkesh, her finger lifting to jab him in the chest. "You knew. You *knew* I was to be mated to you as well, and you kept it from me. How could you? I thought...I thought we were friends."

Goddess, he knew this would happen. He should have found some way to tell her. Fury at himself slammed into his gut. He kept his voice low and soothing. "I wanted to know you before I told you everything. You knew so little about your own people. I—"

She sliced a hand through the air. "And do you know me now? Did I pass your little test? Was sleeping with me part of the test, Tarkesh?"

He flinched. "It was not like that, Ketryn. I tried to tell you before we—before you—"

"Now it's my fault you lied to me?" She deepened her voice to mimic his. "*Trust me, Ketryn. Not all dragons are like your father. Trust me, Ketryn. I'll answer any questions you have.* I did trust you, and you hurt me. At least my father was honest in his neglect. I was just a means to an end—for both of you."

"Please, Ketryn. Don't say that. It's more than a convenience between us now. You have to see that. I'm in love with you." The words exploded from Tarkesh, and he slanted an apologetic glance at his mate.

The black dragon merely lifted a brow. *I already knew. You think I don't know what you're like when you're in love?*

"I'm humiliated." Tears welled in her dark eyes, and the expression on her face ripped into Tarkesh's heart.

Nadir moved to stand beside him and placed a supporting hand on his shoulder. Tarkesh didn't deserve the support. He cursed himself a hundred times over for hurting her. He didn't know what to say to mend the damage.

Nadir spoke first. "Lady Ketryn—"

Her gaze narrowed on the larger man. "Lord Nadir, I presume? No wonder you looked me over yesterday as if you owned me." She snorted. "Well, I hope the two of you are incredibly happy together. You'll need to find some other woman to legitimize your mating. Good-bye."

The door slammed behind her after she'd raced back out of the room. Tarkesh staggered as the pain hit him square in the chest. He had ruined it, hurt someone he loved. It was over. The weight of it crushed down on his chest, and he sank onto the pillow Nadir had just abandoned. Nausea rolled through him, and he fought the need to vomit. Lost. He had lost Ketryn, and with her, he would lose Nadir as well. Tarkesh wouldn't accept another woman in their mating, and he and Nadir couldn't stay together without a female to breed with. Goddess above. He loved them both, and now he would lose everything. Because of his actions, his mate would lose, too. "I'm sorry, Nadir. I failed you both."

"You failed no one. I can fix this." Nadir's hand cupped the back of Tarkesh's head, but he didn't look up. "I will fix this. Meet us outside when the bell chimes."

He angled a glance upward at the black dragon. "She's a stubborn woman. She won't go through with the mating just because you want her to."

"Have some faith in my abilities."

Opening his mouth to respond, he found he was too late. Nadir was gone, and he was alone. He shuddered, hoping it wasn't an omen for his future.

Nadir saw Lady Adriyana hovering around Ketryn as she paced the small room that matched the one he'd just left his mate in. He nodded to Baleel as the golden dragon entered the courtyard but kept walking toward the open door to Ketryn's chamber.

Adriyana wrung her hands. "Ketryn? Are you all right?"

Nadir pushed the door open wide and stepped through. He let a wicked grin show on his face. "I believe Lord Baleel is out in the courtyard waiting for you, Lady Adriyana. He said you had scheduled a rendezvous with him."

Her expressive eyes popped wide with sparking anger. Her fists balled at her sides. Two indignant women closed up in one room were more than Nadir knew what to do with. He stepped out of the way as she started for the door.

"Is he really? I never said I would meet him anywhere. Ever. Well, we'll just see about him presuming to..." Her voice trailed off in a string of muttered curses as she stomped out of the room.

Ketryn spun around to face Nadir, the same anger snapping in her eyes as had shown in her cousin's. Her face was flushed, and her lush breasts lifted with each breath she drew. His fingers itched to cup them, suck them. Words exploded from her full lips, tripping together to get out. "What are you doing here? Is this how you think it would be between us? You and Tarkesh teaming together to make me do whatever you want? Ha. I believe I made my position on this matter extremely clear a moment ago. Go. Away."

"No." He kicked the door shut behind him and locked it before stalking forward.

Her eyes narrowed into angry slits, and a dragon hiss ripped from her. "What do you mean, *no*?"

"And Tark claimed you were an intelligent woman." He tsked. For each step he took toward her, she took one back until the wall behind her stopped her progress. He bracketed his palms on either side of her, caging her where he wanted her. "The word *no* typically means a negative response to a question or demand, but I've heard you have problems with the translation of terms from Vesperi to Harena."

"You should learn the definition yourself. I believe I said no to mating with you, and yet here you still are." She widened her eyes innocently, planted her hands on her hips, and glared up at him.

He chuckled at the direct hit. She didn't retract her claws when she fought. He liked that, respected it in an opponent. His cock grew rigid. She was beautiful when she was angry. Not that he was foolish enough to say so, but her passion made her more than he was willing to resist. He dipped down until his lips almost touched hers. She grew still, and a flush rose in her cheeks. "Yes, here I still am. And what are you going to do about it?"

Her mouth opened and closed, but no sound emerged. She drew a deep breath, and the tips of her breasts rubbed against his chest. He glanced down and saw how her nipples thrust against the front of her bodice. His gaze lifted to meet hers. "Or do you want to do anything about it, *my lady*?"

She hissed at him, and he slammed his lips down over hers, thrusting his tongue into the warm wetness of her mouth. Moaning against his lips, she twisted in his arms, fighting to get away. His arms snapped around her, jerking her tight to his chest. She whimpered, moving with him in a duel of lips and teeth and tongues. His cock pressed against her soft belly. Goddess, he wanted to thrust into her wet pussy. She threw her head back, and he dipped down to bite the base of her throat. Crying out, she lifted one leg to wrap around his hip. His hand slid into the slit in her gown. He hissed in a breath. Her thighs were scaled. He wanted to move his tongue up her scales until he could taste her juices.

Her fingers clenched in his hair, tugging on the short strands. He rubbed his goatee against the soft skin of her neck. She shivered. "Nadir."

"Are you hot for me, Ketryn?" She gasped when he slipped his tongue up her throat to suck her earlobe into his mouth. "Are you wet?"

"Yes. I—I don't... You can't..." Her other leg rose so both of them wrapped around his flanks. One of his hands moved to cup her bottom, lifting her higher against the wall. He pushed his cock against her softness.

"I can. I will. I am." He pushed her gown aside with his free hand to press his fingers into the heat of her pussy. His jaw clenched at how wet she was, how responsive. Goddess, she was perfect. Tarkesh was right. They would enjoy her together for the rest of their lives if he played this right. He tried to rein in his raging need, but his fingers pushed deeper into her damp channel.

He pulled back and lowered her to the floor, stepping away from her. She swayed toward him. Her pupils expanded, and the black of her irises spread from corner to corner when he lifted his hand to lick her juices from his fingers. He hummed low in his throat. She choked, watching him. Panting, she stepped toward him, hot want for him in her dragon eyes.

He chuckled as a bell pealed overhead. "That is the chime to call us to the temple."

"You cannot force me to mate with you." Her dark eyes resumed their human form faster than he would have guessed. He cursed and tried another tack.

"Would you ruin the months of work your aunts have put into negotiating your match? Do you think Yola would appreciate your behavior now?" She blanched at that. Ah. He'd found the sensitive area, and he pressed his advantage, as he did in every negotiation he initiated. "Your irresponsibility would shame them. Stop acting like a petulant child and do your duty."

Every inch of color drained from her face. Guilt slammed into his gut as vulnerable hurt shone in her luminous eyes. Then she blinked, and it was gone, hidden behind the coolly polite expression she had worn when he'd first spied her the day before. The fight drained from her as if he had flipped a switch that killed the fiery light in her gaze. It shook him to the core to realize he missed that, he wanted it. What was happening to him? No one had affected him so deeply, so quickly, except Tarkesh. Certainly no woman had managed it.

She stepped around him, brushing her hand down her saltwater silk gown. It had the traditional cut of a mating robe, heavily embroidered with silver threads. Her slim hand closed around the curved door latch, and she slid open the door. He followed her out into the courtyard just as Tarkesh stepped out of the room opposite them. An anxious expression rode Tarkesh's features, and Nadir nodded to reassure him. His shoulders relaxed, and he hurried to join them at the massive, carved double doors that lead to the temple.

"Adriyana," Ketryn's voice rang softly through the courtyard, and Nadir turned toward the scent of Ketryn's cousin. She was wrapped in Baleel's embrace. The two were locked in an angry kiss. Adriyana shoved Baleel back, and they stared at each other, panting hard. Then she snapped around to look at Ketryn, a blank expression on her face.

Adriyana blinked and then blushed a deep red to match her scales. Scurrying forward, she met them at the door just as Tarkesh joined them. Baleel slipped away to enter a side door into the temple. Nadir cupped a hand around Ketryn's elbow, determined not to give her a chance to change her mind. She jerked her arm out of his grasp. A cold, reptilian hiss issued from her throat. "I'm not going anywhere, Lord Nadir. You needn't try to cage me."

"Yes, my mate. Lady Ketryn does not care to have anyone put their hands on her unless she asks." Tarkesh broke into the tense silence, tilting forward to smile down at Ketryn.

"I am not speaking to you. Let's just do this." She tucked a stray strand of her inky hair behind her ear and faced the doors. "Adriyana. Lead us in."

Adriyana's gaze flicked back and forth between her cousin, Nadir, and Tarkesh. She opened her mouth to address her cousin in a tentative tone. "Ketryn, you don't have to—"

Ketryn cut her off. "I don't wish to speak of this. Let us go. Or we can discuss your love life, cousin."

A wild flush raced up Adriyana's lovely face, and she turned for the temple doors. She pushed them wide and walked to her designated location as the family representative. Nadir noticed Baleel's gaze follow her up the aisle as the rest of the assembly stood to face them. Tarkesh's eyes met Nadir's as they both placed a hand on the small of Ketryn's back. She jolted away from their touch, which conveniently started her down the long aisle. A wicked gleam flashed in Tarkesh's eyes as he fell into step beside Nadir, and they followed a stride behind Ketryn up the aisle.

Yola was a nightmare. She'd spent the entire celebration contradicting anything that came out of Ketryn's mouth. She was worse than Ketryn's father in her dismissive attitude toward Ketryn's thoughts on anything. She didn't care for Ketryn to think at all—that much was obvious. The rest of the members of her matriarchy were no better. Ketryn was considered "less than" simply because she was raised on Vesperi and knew very little about dragon culture. Ketryn shoved an angry hand through her hair and stomped toward her chambers. This was *not* how she had pictured any bonding night in her mind. Two mates she would happily skin alive, and a matriarchal leader she'd as soon see flung over a canyon wall than speak to her. She allowed herself to enjoy that mental image for a moment before she drew up in front of her doors. They were in there—she could smell them. Which meant they could smell her out in the hall, hesitating. Good. Let them worry. They ought to know she was displeased with both of them, and she wasn't going to pretend otherwise.

You can stay out there for an hour, if you want. It won't change what will happen when you come in here. Nadir's deep voice stroked over her mind like rough silk.

A pulse of want went through her, loosening her muscles and dampening her sex. She snorted at her own weakness, at her own attraction to her mates. She groaned at the thought. She was *mated* to two males who dragged reactions from her she couldn't stop. She didn't let herself back down, didn't let herself run. Reaching out, she jerked one door open and stepped inside.

Her breath caught at the sight that greeted her. Both men lounged naked on her bed, waiting for her. And both men's cocks were full and hard. Moisture flooded her pussy, and she squeezed her thighs together to ease the screaming ache between them. Oh, Goddess.

Nadir rose from the bed with reptilian grace. A knowing smile curved his lips. "I can smell your desire, little desert blossom. Your nipples are hard. You can't wait for us to slide our cocks into you. Do you know how many ways we could both take you at once?"

Shock rocked her back on her heels, and the images that flashed through her mind were staggering. She could picture it. Both of them. Inside her. She swallowed the lump in her throat that threatened to squeeze the breath from her. Need so deep she shook with it rocked her to her core. Nadir circled her, and she turned to follow him with her gaze. He stepped toward her, and she scrambled back. She didn't think she could withstand him touching her. The want raging through her body was more than she could bear. If he touched her, if either of them touched her, she would shatter. The backs of her knees hit the low bed.

She stopped and glared at the enormous black dragon. "I'm not happy with you. Either of you."

"Let us make it up to you." Tarkesh's voice purred in her ear, and she jumped when his arms went around her from behind. Nadir pressed to her front. Caught. She was entangled between them, and their embrace encompassed each other as well as her.

Throwing her head back, she fought the need to lose herself in the moment. To belong to her mates. She shouldn't. She had good reason to be angry with both of them. "I don't think—"

"Don't think." Nadir dropped to his knees before her. His hands slid into the side slits of her gown, cupping her thighs—and rubbing over her scales. Sensation shot straight from there to her pussy, and her inner muscles fisted on nothingness.

"Oh, Goddess," she breathed.

She won't save you from us. The black dragon dragged his tongue up the pattern of her scales, kissing, sucking, and caressing her flesh with his mouth. Her body bowed, and she choked on a breath.

"Does it feel good, Ketryn?" Tarkesh brushed his lips over her nape. "Do you want Nadir to slide his tongue inside you? I can tell you from experience, he is very skilled."

Nadir chuckled, and her gaze met his. His showed triumph, possession. Defeat ripped through her. She wouldn't win. She wanted them too much. Betrayed by her own heart and body. "I hate you."

No, desert blossom. You love Tarkesh, and soon you will love me, too. That wicked tongue played over her scales, making the wetness that pooled between her legs slip down her thighs. He caught a drop with his tongue, sucking it with relish from her skin. She had been right. The rasp of his goatee on her scales made her want to scream. It felt so good, so hot, so right. Tingles erupted over her body, and heat built fast within her. Goddess, it wouldn't take much more. She was already close to the edge of orgasm.

"Why?"

Because I want your love. I want all you have to give and more.

Tarkesh dipped his head to kiss her arm, to nip at the scales there. Too much, with both of them touching her sensitive flesh. She couldn't take it all in.

And Nadir always gets what he wants. As do I.

Then they both bit her scales, dragon fangs extended to pierce her. She screamed, the sensation pushing her higher and faster than she'd ever gone before. Her pussy clenched wildly, and a shriek ripped from her throat. She felt her own fangs slide out, and she hissed.

Nadir moved up her thighs, jerked her knees over his shoulders, and thrust his tongue into her moist pussy. One of Tarkesh's arms caught her from behind, held her against his broad chest, and she hung weightless between them. Her body twisted in midair as she bucked against Nadir, fighting to get closer to the hot slide of his tongue. She shuddered, desperate for more. Tarkesh's free hand fondled her breasts, pinching her tight nipples while Nadir's lips closed over her clit and sucked. Her hips arched, and she came apart in their arms, another reptilian scream ripping from her.

Tarkesh kept up a wicked litany in her ear, his words pushing her orgasm farther. "We bring out the dragon in you. And we're not done. We'll make you come again and again and again tonight. You'll have no doubt when we're through about how much we want you in our *harim*. No one else will do."

"Please. I can't—" She couldn't think, couldn't stop, couldn't control any of this. Panting for breath, she watched them both extend their claws and slice through the lacings on her mating gown. Tarkesh tugged what was left of it over her head while Nadir lifted her onto the bed.

"Now you can watch us." Nadir flipped Tarkesh onto his back and came down on top of him. They kissed each other with animalistic ferocity. She could see their cocks rubbing together, exciting each other. Tarkesh's hand slipped between them to stroke down the length of Nadir's dick. They both groaned.

"Oh, Goddess." Flames licked at her veins watching them pleasure each other. Her fingers dropped between her legs, stroking over her slick, swollen flesh. She bit her lip. She closed her eyes, but the image of them was burned into her memory. Flicking a nail over her clit, she jolted at the harsh sensation. Her hips lifted. Orgasm made her blood roar in her ears, made the muscles in her belly tighten.

"Let us do that." Tarkesh laughed and moved her hand away from her pussy. She moaned at the loss, but want throbbed through her when he sucked the juices from her fingers. Slowly.

Nadir's hands bit into her thighs, stroking across her scales as he jerked her into his lap. She gasped as his hard, hot cock slid into her pussy. He was so big it almost hurt, but she loved it. Her eyes slid closed as his length worked inside her. She was so wet. He arched her forward, and Tarkesh's hands slid down her back between the globes of her ass. "I have something for you. Oil that will make this even better for you."

His finger probed the pucker of her anus, slid in easily with the oil. It took only a moment before her eyes flew open. Hot pleasure slammed into her, but with it came a burn that wouldn't ease. She whimpered.

A grin flashed across Nadir's face. "It's almost painful it's so good, isn't it?"

"Yes." Her hips twisted, grinding Nadir deeper into her pussy. Her fingers curled into his shoulders, dug into the scales on his flesh. He groaned, and his cock twitched within her. She moved faster, trying to make the burn stop. Then he froze within her, and she gasped out, "Don't stop. Please, don't stop. I need more."

"You'll have it." He pressed against the small of her back, arching her body. Tarkesh's thick cock pushed against her anus, pressed inside her, stretched her until he was seated to the hilt within her. She was so full, so tight. Her breath dragged into her lungs. Tarkesh drew away, and Nadir ground forward. They started a hard, fast rhythm. She was always filled with one of them. Nadir drew one of her nipples into his mouth, biting it gently.

Tarkesh sucked at the sensitive skin at the back of her neck. Goose bumps exploded down her body. She loved it—she loved the way the two of them could play her so well. The drag of their hard flesh in hers, filling her, made her twist in their embrace. Tarkesh dipped to the side, biting the scales on her arm. Her sex contracted reflexively, and her fingers clenched on Nadir's scales. They all groaned.

"So tight," Tarkesh breathed. "I love the feel of you."

So hot and wet, Nadir echoed in her mind, moving to focus his attention on her other nipple. He rotated his hips on the next thrust, grinding against her clitoris.

Then they both slammed into her at the same time, and she screamed. It was enough to tip her over the edge into orgasm. The muscles in her thighs tensed, and they each kept up a hard, bouncing rhythm that sent her spiraling higher and higher. Nadir froze, his fingers digging into her hips to pull her tight to his cock. He erupted within her as Tarkesh pushed into her from behind. He ground his pelvis against her ass and came inside her. She sobbed as it shoved her over into orgasm again.

Forgive us, both of her mates' voices whispered through her mind. *I love you*, added Tarkesh.

Yes. Don't leave me alone. Her head bent back over Tarkesh's shoulder. *I love you, too.* Tears tracked down her face as her orgasm went on and on. Her body shuddered, twisting under the endless lash of pleasure as aftershocks rocked through her. Her breath dragged out in ragged sobs, her control slipping through her fingers, and then the world went black as unconsciousness dragged her away.

She woke to two males in dragon form curled around her. Their tails lay over her legs, twined together with each other. She didn't wake them but took a moment to mull over the events of the day before. The deep connection she'd experienced last night. Were all dragon matings so intense? Lucky dragon women. Her heart squeezed when both weredragons settled closer to her. Reaching out, she smoothed her palm down their scaled sides.

More, Nadir demanded sleepily, but he heaved a slow sigh and fell back asleep.

She gave a soft giggle. If she'd thought things had progressed quickly with Tarkesh, she was woefully unprepared for Nadir. Where Tarkesh had been a slow burn of sweet need, Nadir was like throwing flames onto dry brush. Explosive, hot, irresistible. Each fed a different need within her. The need to be cherished, the need to be possessed, to belong. Oh, sweet Goddess.

Nadir was right—she would soon lose her heart to him as well. Unlike with Tarkesh, she didn't even try to resist. It was right. It felt good. It was the only thing that had fit since she'd come to Harena. Joy ballooned in her chest, and anticipation of the future spread through her. When was the last time she'd looked forward to the future? Not in a very long time, if ever. Not for as long as she could remember. The future had always been so insecure, so uncertain. She slid her hands down each of their backs, a grin tugging at her lips.

Are you going to remain there all day? Yola's snide tones echoed inside her mind. She jerked upright, an arm crossing over her breasts.

"What are you doing in here?"

Yola's small black eyes narrowed. "Be careful what tone you take with me, dragonling. Get up. You are expected to be in the council chambers today. The matriarchs wish to take the measure of you. Don't disappoint me."

Careful not to disturb her mates, Ketryn stood up on the bed and stepped over the silver dragon. She tugged on her robe over her nakedness. She wasn't ashamed to be nude, but she didn't want to show a scrap of vulnerability to this woman. "On Vesperi, newly mated couples are given several days to enjoy each other before reassuming their duties."

Yola harrumphed. "That is not the way of dragons. You must forget your life among the tigers. They are nothing to you now. You must strive to become a true dragon, Ketryn."

Ketryn clenched her teeth to bite back a sharp retort at that. If being a true dragon meant being like Yola, she was uninterested in the position. Yes, she really disliked the matriarch of her family. That could prove a problem. She smoothed all expression from her face when Yola cast her a sharp glance. It was a game of politics. Everything was. Always negotiating, always uncertain where she stood. She'd played this game her entire life on Vesperi and had excelled at it. She just had to learn the rules on Harena. "I will do my best, Matriarch."

And once she knew the rules, she'd know how to break them and get what she wanted. But curse Yola for stealing even a small part of her bonding night. Her shoulders straightened, but she couldn't help a last glance at the two male dragons curled up on her bed. What she wouldn't give to rejoin them and wake them for more of what she'd experienced last night. Then a wide smile curled her lips. She had the rest of her life to enjoy them.

Chapter 8

"She is unhappy here." It had been nearly two weeks since they had mated, and Ketryn seemed to like it there less and less every time she was called to the council chambers to spend time with her family. It worried Tarkesh a great deal. Their mating had been going so well. Ketryn accepted them more each day, and they loved the sharing of her and each other. She trusted them—he could feel it in his bones. Everything had turned out as he'd hoped. Better. Ketryn completed their union, and he loved her deeply.

"I'd noticed she's having trouble adjusting." Nadir lounged across the end of the bed the three of them shared each night.

"Yola rides her too hard."

"Yola is being very lenient with her compared to others in her matriarchy. Though there is something to be said for being ridden hard." His hand slid down Tarkesh's stomach to grasp his cock. His hand slid up and down the shaft.

"I just—" Tarkesh hissed low and groaned at the conflicting sensation. Anger at Yola, desire at Nadir's touch. "We need to take some action here. I found her crying yesterday."

"Ketryn?" Nadir paused, his hand cupping the sacs at the base of Tarkesh's dick.

Tarkesh's fingers caught Nadir's and worked both their hands up the length of his cock. His hips arched into the hot caress. He gritted his teeth. "No, the other female we're mated to. Of course, Ketryn. I'm telling you she isn't happy here, and she isn't going to adjust. She'll simply learn to be silent in her unhappiness. I have no desire to see her broken."

"No. That is...an unacceptable option. What else do you have in mind?" Nadir bent to run his tongue around the head of Tarkesh's cock.

Tarkesh moved down until he could take his mate's dick into his hand. "I'm not certain."

"That's helpful." Nadir groaned when Tarkesh tightened his grip on the base of his cock, the hard length darkening.

"You find a solution to the problem then." He lost track of the conversation as Nadir's skilled mouth and hands worked his flesh over. Just rough enough to push him right up against the edge of orgasm. The hot wetness of his mate's mouth on him was more than he could take for long. He loved being sucked hard, and Nadir knew it.

"Be silent and put your mouth to better use."

Tarkesh chuckled, flipping so he could take his mate's cock into his mouth, and so Nadir could suck him fully between his lips. He hummed on the length of Nadir's cock, and his mate's hips arched hard to push his dick deeper into his mouth. He groaned, raising himself to tease the head of Nadir's cock while his hand pumped the shaft in hard, fast strokes. Nadir groaned on Tarkesh's cock, and Tarkesh couldn't hold back a hiss at the vibrating sensation. Goddess, but that was good.

Nadir's long finger swirled around Tarkesh's anus, toying with him, taunting him. Tarkesh pushed his hips back, forcing the finger inside his ass. Nadir pushed deep, moving in and out, faster and faster. Tarkesh sucked the black dragon's dick inside his mouth hard, just as he knew his mate liked it, shoving the head against the roof of his mouth. Nadir bucked beneath him, coming in hot spurts down Tarkesh's throat. Tarkesh groaned, his own orgasm slamming into him with the subtle force of a Gila beast. He jetted hard into his mate's mouth, sucking the last of his mate's cum from his softening cock.

He climbed off his mate to lie on the bed. Nadir rolled onto his back, propping one arm behind his head and crossing his ankles. He ran his free hand down his goatee—his usual pose for thinking. "We could take her away, become renegades from society, and never have to deal with any of it again."

Tarkesh snorted and sat up to face him. "And we'd also be hunted until they killed us and our fiery little desert blossom. Not to mention the fact that we would need to rob others in order to survive. Tell me that is an option you find acceptable."

The black dragon waved that away. "Calm yourself, Tark. I was only jesting. I—"

"I am not. I do not like to see her upset." His hands fisted against his thighs.

"Nor do I."

Tarkesh heaved a sigh. "Taking her away would be a good option if it didn't require criminal behavior."

Nadir sat up. "That's it."

"What's it? I just said it wouldn't work. That's no kind of solution to anything." He shrugged, hopeless anger welling up inside him. There had to be an answer to this that they could all live with, but he'd been rolling it around in his mind for days and had come to nothing.

"No, we take her away. To Vesperi. As the new ambassadors."

Tarkesh huffed a breath and flopped back in the bed, propping himself on one elbow. "They've already chosen a new ambassador."

"I can get them to change their minds, to decide we are a more suitable option. Besides, Curind has as much intelligence as the rear end of a Gila beast. He is a political appointment because of his matriarchy, nothing more." He flashed a dark, wicked grin. Tarkesh smiled back. He knew that smile. It was the one Nadir always used before he managed to convince someone to do something that was not in their best interest. He could remember a number of matriarchies in outlying settlements that were left wondering what had happened to them when Nadir set his mind to treating with them.

Would Nadir be happy walking away from a life in which he had found so much success? "Are you certain you are willing to do this? Give up everything you know and go to the tiger world? We could hate it there as much as Ketryn hates it here."

The black dragon lifted an eyebrow at him. "You know my feelings on this, Tarkesh. They have not changed. I will do whatever it takes to keep us together, to protect my mate. That now includes Ketryn, but the sentiment remains the same as it always was with you."

"And you are ruthless about it. Ketryn is correct about that." He grinned.

Nadir's broad shoulder lifted in a negligent shrug. "Whatever it takes."

He laughed outright at that. "So you've said."

"The question, my mate, is whether you are willing to make such an enormous change for her."

Tarkesh plucked at the saltwater silk coverlet for a moment, thinking before he looked up and met Nadir's gaze. "I want what I have always wanted, to see my loved ones happy and near me. I will also do whatever it takes to make that happen. If Ketryn needs to be on Vesperi to be happy, then so be it."

"You're certain? Once I make these arrangements, they cannot be unmade." Nadir lifted a knee and propped his elbow on it.

Tarkesh held his mate's dark gaze. "I've considered this problem for days. I can find no better solution that does not leave us hunted outlaws than the one you've suggested. I would never dishonor myself or either of you by choosing the path of a renegade."

"Nor I. That's settled then." Nadir threw his legs over the side of the bed and rose, reaching for his pants. Tarkesh enjoyed the view of his mate's well-formed ass. He grinned.

"Shall we tell Ketryn?"

Nadir glanced back at him. "Where is she?"

He rose as well and shrugged into a robe. "I'm not sure. She was visiting with Adriyana before the council meeting, but that is soon to convene. Let us meet her there."

"Excellent." Nadir curved his fingers around the back of Tarkesh's neck and drew him forward for an easy kiss.

"I'll negotiate a new treaty with the weretiger clans." Curind, the pompous dragon who would leave with Varad and Mahlia in the next few days to take her father's position as ambassador to Vesperi, spoke in a booming whine that scraped over Ketryn's already frayed nerves. Yola had been her usual obnoxious self all day. That Tarkesh and Nadir had joined Ketryn a few moments before had served only as a marginal help. These sessions were torturous. And she would have to put up with them every day for the rest of her life. Goddess above.

Her eyebrows almost lifted to her hairline at what Curind had said. The man was joking, wasn't he? This was a horrible jest. She looked around to see if anyone was smiling, but no one was. She couldn't keep her tongue still. "*Prides.* The weretigers have prides, the werebears have clans. And you cannot negotiate with the prides individually."

"This is men's business, my lady. Women control the lands, but men go out to serve as emissaries to other matriarchs and ambassadors to other planets. Don't concern yourself with this matter." Curind cut her a dismissive glance.

"I'm afraid I cannot remain silent in this. You cannot negotiate with the prides themselves. All treaties are negotiated with Amir Varad only. To do otherwise will insert weredragons into weretiger politics. This can't be allowed. They are contentious to a degree you cannot even imagine. The only way to solidify yourself as a power among them is to align with the royal family. Let the Amir deal with the infighting of the prides, and worry about outmaneuvering him to get what Harena needs. Nothing else is acceptable—Varad will cut ties with us before he lets any ambassador upset the balance among the prides. Trust me in this, my lord. I have spent my life on Vesperi." During her explanation, the room had grown deathly still, and every dragon's gaze turned to her as if she'd gone mad. She glanced at her mates for support—she was in the right here. Varad was far too intelligent a man, too good a king, to let an ambitious ambassador disrupt the always tenuous political structure of the tigers. But Tarkesh's face was a blank, frozen mask, and a muscle jumped in Nadir's strong jaw.

She turned to meet Yola's gaze. The matriarch's face was mottled with rage, but Ketryn didn't back down, met her stare for stare. Goddess on fire, she was right about this. They just didn't know how it was on Vesperi. She needed to make them understand that the course of action this new ambassador wanted to take could damage a trade relationship that had been centuries in the making. Her stomach churned in unease as the thick silence stretched out.

Yola's voice cut like glass across Ketryn's nerves, and she looked at Ketryn while she spoke to the ambassador. "Forgive my niece. She is new to her home world and untrained in the ways of *dragons*. Her youth is showing the extent of her maturity. She lacks some knowledge about what is important to her *own* people."

Righteous indignation rushed through Ketryn like a tidal wave, and her eyes narrowed to dangerous slits. How *dare* anyone think she was being disloyal? She dug dragon's claws into her temper to hold on and keep from spitting out her words like a challenge. She was an ambassador's daughter, and she knew how to keep a cool head in any situation. "I *do* have my people's interest in mind. If I did not, I would have said nothing and allowed him to go blithely on his way to possibly ruin the alliances we've built that benefit our people."

Yola's fists clenched on the arms of her chair, and the black of her irises spread to the corners of her eyes. Her breath bellowed in and out. Ketryn saw Adriyana half rise from her seat to intercede, but Ketryn wasn't certain on whose behalf. This was a matter of pride now. Yola had all but accused Ketryn of betraying her own kind when she had spent her life on another planet helping her father make every dragon's life better and more prosperous. The wound cut too deeply. She couldn't back down now without losing face, and neither could Yola.

Apologize to her. Do it now, and be sufficiently humble. Nadir's thought cut across her mind. Shock rippled through her, and every muscle in her body went rigid with it. *Do it, Ketryn. You challenged a matriarch in public. You must make amends. Now.*

No! Everything in her rebelled at the mere thought.

Trust me, Nadir demanded.

Tarkesh's thought broke in. Nadir had been communicating with both of them. *Trust us, my love. We can make this right if you let us. Trust us not to fail you.*

Did she? Could she? What they asked was too much, more than she could sacrifice.

But did she trust them to do as they promised? Her hands trembled, and she clenched her fingers tightly. The room remained still as death, waiting to see what she would do. What Yola would do to her. Did she trust her mates in this? To save her? *Yes*, she answered herself and them at the same time.

On your knees.

No, it's too much. I won't. Ketryn's gaze met Nadir's, defiance rolling over her. Every muscle in her body went rigid. Issuing a politically necessary apology was hard but acceptable—to debase herself in public was quite another. Bile rose to choke her, and she swallowed hard.

You already said yes. Will you go back on your word, Ketryn? His midnight eyes narrowed to dangerous slits, demanding obedience and rejecting her position in this. *Do it!*

A sob bubbled up in her throat. No matter what she did, she would lose in this. Her pride, her respect. Agony tore at her. She held his gaze, unflinching. *I will never forgive you for this.*

Nadir winced, but his eyes were hard and unyielding. Tarkesh was pale, his skin stretched taut over his sharp cheekbones. He wouldn't meet her gaze.

"I see," she whispered aloud. "I think I finally see." Cold realization rolled through her. She would never fit here. Weredragons were more foreign to her than weretigers could ever be, their unbending social structure not allowing Ketryn to help in the one area she could be of use. The injustice of it cut her to the core.

Rising, she moved to kneel at Yola's feet. Disgust ripped at her deep inside that she had to do this, that she would even consider it. She despised everything about this woman who shared her blood. Lifting her hand, Ketryn placed it over her heart. Her voice rang clear, and she was proud to note there wasn't even the slightest waver to it. "Matriarch Yola. My humblest apologies for speaking out of turn. Please understand I wished only to be of use to my fellow weredragons. I meant no offense."

She saw Adriyana twitch out of the corner of her eye and imagined telepathic words flew hot and fast between her cousin and aunt. Finally, after an eternity that made her keenly aware of how hard the marble floor was beneath her knees, Yola nodded her acceptance of the apology. Her dark eyes reformed to solid human irises, and a nasty, triumphant smile curled her lips. "I do know that you want the best for Harena, but you have much to learn before you can truly be a dragon."

Wrong. She wanted to scream at them all, wanted for the first time in her life to let loose in public. She *was* a dragon. It was her birthright. Culture didn't make her a dragon. Her physiology did that for her. She wasn't a Harenan, perhaps, but no one could take her dragonness away from her. It was fact. She rose from the floor stiffly, nodded to Adriyana, the only person on this cursed planet she didn't wish trampled by an angry Gila beast, and walked to the doors.

She turned back to her mates before she slipped out, a part of her shattering forever. Her heart. Her eyes were dry and gritty—she was too broken to cry. *I was right, wasn't I? It's always going to be the two of you on one side and me on the other. I am such a fool.*

Chapter 9

"Where is she?" Nadir watched Tarkesh pace in a tight circle around the room.

Nadir breathed deep, trying to scent her. Nothing. She wasn't there. She hadn't been there in many hours, not since that morning. His and Tarkesh's scents overlaid hers, so she hadn't come back after the confrontation at the council meeting. His gut twisted. Where would she have gone? She had no close friends he knew of. Adriyana had remained with them, argued in their favor, helped them secure the ambassadorial position.

"Where might she have gone?" Tarkesh echoed his thoughts. "I don't think she was in the state of mind to make rational decisions when she left. She was upset. *We* upset her."

"It was necessary for her to apologize in order to get what we wanted."

"Do you ever stop to think that perhaps the ends don't justify the means? You make decisions and sacrifice whatever it takes to make them happen. Perhaps some things should not be sacrificed."

"You agreed that we should—"

"I know what I agreed to. I did not agree to her humiliating herself before the matriarchal council." Tarkesh's jaw flexed.

Nadir's shoulders drew into a rigid line at the implication that he had forced Tarkesh. "We would not have gotten the ambassadorship without it, not even if she had gone back and apologized later. It had to be done then, and she was in no mood to listen to our scheme to get her away from her family—especially Yola."

"We took that choice away from her by not telling her."

"You are simply still upset that she was angry the last time you kept something from her. This is not the same thing. You had days to tell her that she was mating to both of us, but we had no time to tell her anything before she started an argument with Curind."

"She wouldn't see it that way."

Nadir drew a deep breath through his nose, trying to calm his temper. How had this conversation gotten so out of his control? "It. Is. Not. The. Same. Tarkesh."

"She was not in a rational frame of mind, and I doubt she is now. You're thinking rationally, and that's not likely to convince her of anything."

"What would you suggest?"

Tarkesh crossed his arms in front of him, anguish mixed with anger on his face. "I would suggest that you consider the sacrifices you expect of us—the people you love the most—before you make decisions for us. Ketryn is not one to sacrifice her pride and honor without a moment's thought."

"I didn't force her." The blood rushed out of Nadir's face, and his hands fisted at his sides.

"You pushed her into it." Tarkesh jabbed a finger at him.

He stared at his mate for a long moment before he spoke. "How long have you felt this way? This isn't solely about Ketryn, is it? It's about you and me. Is this what you meant when you were afraid things would change—that she would come between us?"

The silver dragon's eyes widened. "That's ridiculous."

"Is it?"

"I love you."

"But do you like me right now?"

A long moment of silence stretched between them. "No. Not very much, anyway."

"I thought not. Before you become too angry about this and blame me for what happened, remember no matter what, that she would have had to apologize anyway. If it had waited, she would have been humiliated with no reward. And you knew my nature before you mated with me. Remember that when you claim to be displeased with what your decisions have left you." Nadir whipped around, stalking toward the door. His fingers clenched and unclenched, and his shoulders drew into a taut line.

"Where are you going?" A thread of panic wound through Tarkesh's tone.

"Away. I need to go away."

"Wh—when will you return? What about Ketryn? We still don't know where she is."

"You claim to know her needs better than I do. I am certain you will have no difficulty finding her by yourself."

"Nadir—"

"Leave it be, Tark. Just...leave me be." Nadir turned back for a moment before he walked out the door. "Do you honestly think you're the only one who loves her, Tark? I would never do anything I thought would hurt her. The worst part about all this is you don't trust me with her. Or with yourself, obviously."

Anger pumped through Nadir's system as he thrust through the door that led out to the street. Hadn't he given his mates everything they needed? Wasn't he willing to give up everything he had ever known to ensure their happiness? What more could he do? What more could he offer? And yet neither was pleased right now. Perhaps he had gone over the line this time, but it was never with the intent to hurt them. Pain sliced through him at even the thought that he had injured his mates. *Goddess.* Were they right about him? Did his very nature make his mates unhappy? Doubts rolled through him. Everything had become so confused in a matter of hours. Hadn't they lain sated together just that morning? Hadn't he and Tarkesh agreed that taking Ketryn away was the right thing to do?

He stopped and looked around, becoming aware of his surroundings. How long had he been walking the streets of the city? He stood in the capital square, the Goddess's temple before him. Sighing, he scrubbed a tired hand down his face. Reaching for the massive double doors, he pulled one open and slipped inside. Opposite him were the matching doors that led to the temple courtyard. Had it been only two weeks since he had walked through them to bond with both his mates? It felt like Turns.

Inside, the temple was cool and damp, a direct contrast to the outside world of Harena. He shuddered in the cold. The temple hummed with an otherworldly reverence. Stepping forward to the halfway point between the doors, he turned up the long aisle that led to the Goddess's fountain. Pools of fire danced around the edge of the sacred water. Mist so thick it looked like smoke curled over the ground and up the aisle. Dragon's breath, it was called. He dragged in a deep lungful of moist air, struggling to calm the thoughts that plagued him.

A familiar scent filled his nostrils. Ketryn. Narrowing his eyes to scan through the smoke, he caught sight of her slim figure kneeling in silence before the fountain. Her head was bowed. He sighed, steeling himself for her disappointment, her anger. He knew the reasons for what he had done, and he regretted that she had suffered for it, but it had been for her. Would she understand? Uncertainty fisted in his gut.

He approached the front of the temple on silent feet to kneel beside her. "Blossom."

"Nadir." She didn't stir, didn't look at him.

He drew a breath. "I have my reasons for what I did today."

"I know. Adriyana found me. She and Baleel went to find you and Tarkesh."

"Why?"

"I did not ask."

"I never meant to hurt you, Ketryn."

He heard her soft sigh, and he tensed, waiting for her reply. Her reaction now would dictate much of how their *harim* bond would be in the future.

"You push too hard sometimes, Nadir."

"Only with your best interests in mind. If I hadn't pushed you to apologize today—"

"We wouldn't be the new ambassadors to Vesperi. Yes, I know. I understand that painful choices have to be made for politics, for duty. No one would understand that better than I."

"But?"

She shifted and met his eyes. "Sometimes you push so hard you risk pushing us away. Let us make the choices that are best for us. *Talk* to us before you push us to the breaking point. It's only because we love you that we let you push us at all."

"I know." A small, tight smile curved his lips. "Tark says you think I am ruthless."

"You are. That will serve you well when dealing with tigers. Consult with us before you unleash that ruthless core on the politics of other planets. Adriyana said you used my experience with the tigers as an argument to get this new position. Will you ask my opinion before you make decisions on trade matters?"

"Yes."

"Truly?"

"I can change, blossom. For you and Tarkesh. But if you're looking for a man who consults you about everything, then we may have a larger problem than politics. I'm not that man, and I never will be. I can change, but I cannot become someone else. I wouldn't ask that of you, which is why Tark and I decided to leave Harena in the first place."

Her small hand slipped into his. "I love you as you are, Nadir. As does Tarkesh. Never doubt that, no matter how much we may want to kick you for being a Gila beast's fouler cousin."

He chuckled and raised her fingers to his lips. "I love you."

"I know."

"Do you? What you said...before you left..."

"I do know. I was angry and hurt, Nadir. I said things I wish I hadn't. You aren't the only one with regrets, my love."

He closed his eyes, relief rushing through him. Something essential loosened within his chest. "So, then, you can forgive me someday?"

"No."

"Ketryn—"

"I forgive you now. I know you wouldn't hurt me on purpose. I know you and Tarkesh won't join forces against me. We are a *harim*. Together. Always. I *know* that."

"Good. No one could replace you, Ketryn. We need you. You belong to us. I think...we were incomplete without you, and neither of us knew it. You balance us."

Tears welled in her wide, dark eyes. "Nadir—"

"What? What did I say now?" How had he failed her? Panic gripped his gut. He cupped both of his hands around her smaller one. "Ketryn? Tell me, and I will fix it, I swear."

A watery laugh rippled from her. She sniffled and wiped a single tear from her cheek. "You already did."

"I don't understand."

"Do you know how long I've needed that? To belong? My whole life, I've been looking for that. I knew it was a fundamental part of me that was missing. I just didn't know how to get it. And with my family here...I've been so miserable. I'll never belong here."

"Your home is with us. You belong to us. It matters not what planet we are on."

A brilliant smile crossed her face, and her beautiful eyes shone bright with unshed tears. "I know. Isn't it wonderful?"

"Yes, my desert blossom." He lifted his fingers to stroke along the skin of her silken jaw. "You are exactly what we needed. We will do anything to make sure you're happy. Anything."

"I love you."

"Both of us?" Nadir turned to see Tarkesh approaching from the entrance. His mate's dark eyes were stormy and troubled. His gaze flicked between Nadir and Ketryn.

They stood and turned to face him. He curved his arm around Ketryn's waist, pulling her soft curves against his side. She laid her cheek on his chest, and they waited for Tarkesh to reach them.

Tarkesh stopped just before them and met his gaze. "Nadir. I was wrong to—"

Nadir snapped a hand out to catch the back of his neck and haul his mate forward. Dipping down, he settled his mouth over the other man's and thrust his tongue between his lips. Tarkesh's arm banded around his waist. *Do not apologize, my mate. I was just as much in the wrong. We will do better in the future.*

I can handle any change but losing the two of you. Don't ever walk away from me again, Nadir. Ever. Tarkesh's words echoed fiercely in Nadir's mind while his fingers bit into his back, hauling both Ketryn and him closer.

Ketryn's hand slipped inside the waist of Nadir's pants to cup his sex. He groaned into Tarkesh's mouth, their tongues twining together. His hips jerked when she wrapped her slim fingers around his cock and stroked up the shaft. Her thumb rubbed over the head of his dick. Tarkesh ran a nail down the scales that bisected Nadir's chest. He shuddered under the hot flash of pleasure that exploded within him. Ketryn turned her head and sank her dragon fangs into the scales on his shoulder. He threw back his head and roared, his own fangs extending.

I love you, both of them said. He closed his eyes tight, dragging them to him. He wanted to savor this moment with them. Perfect. A band of hot emotion wrapped around his chest. "I love you, too," he whispered.

"Ahem."

Ketryn slid her hand out of Nadir's pants, and he groaned at the loss of contact. His eyes snapped open. She rose on tiptoes to kiss his throat before turning to Baleel with a small smile. He saw Adriyana follow Baleel inside the room. Nadir fought a growl and the urge to order them out of the temple so he and his mates could finish what they'd started. Both wore secretive, slightly smug grins, and he narrowed his eyes at them.

Ketryn lifted her eyebrows. "Yes?"

"I'm going with you to take you to the ship," Adriyana burst out, her smile nearly eclipsing her pretty face.

Baleel cocked an eyebrow at her. "You should stay here and let me take them."

Adriyana folded her slim arms. "You need a fifth person to take all their things, too. And you can't stop me. I'm going, too. I want to meet the mermaid ambassador and the weretiger monarchs before they leave."

"Be it on your head, then, when Yola finds out." Baleel rolled his eyes and turned back to them. "I've arranged to take dune-racers to get to the ship before it takes off. Have you very many things?"

"All of it is still packed from the move into the matriarchy. I wasn't ready to call it home yet, so..." Ketryn shrugged. "We are ready."

Adriyana smiled at her. "You're going home, cousin."

Ketryn looked up at Nadir and then at Tarkesh. Her face softened, and she leaned deeper into Nadir's embrace. Contentment wound through his chest. This was exactly how it should be. The three of them, for the rest of their days. Together. He knew it to his very bones. Then Ketryn spoke the words that summed it up for all three of them.

"I'm already home."

In Mist

WEREPLANETS
BOOK 4

CRYSTAL JORDAN

CJ BOOKS

Chapter 1

S he loved wild, animalistic sex. Sera stood with her hands braced on the wall before her, fingers scrabbling for purchase on the cool expanse of metal as her body rocked to the hot, hard rhythm Bretton set behind her. His long cock stretched her so wide the sensation bordered on pain. The perfect expression of their relationship. Agony and ecstasy twisting together until she couldn't tell one from the other. She craved it. She wanted more.

Each slamming push drove her to the very edge of orgasm but didn't allow her to go over. Frustration screamed through her, sweat sliding in slow beads down her temples and between her breasts.

"Please, Bretton. *Please.*" Her breath rushed out in harsh pants. How long would he make her wait to come? Hours, if he wanted to. She whimpered.

One of his hands drew back and slapped hard against her ass. She jolted, dark pleasure whipping through her as tingles raced over her stinging flesh. His chuckle rumbled up from his broad chest. "Have patience."

"I can't—I need...more." She choked when he ground his hips against her. Her muscles shook in anticipation. She threw her head back so it rested against his shoulder. He licked her throat, sucking kisses up her neck to nip at her earlobe. She moaned low in her throat. "Please, I need *more.*"

"You'll have more. I swear it." He withdrew until only the very tip of his dick was within her pussy. She reached back to grab the flexing muscles of his backside. Her nails dug in, trying to force him to hurry.

"Now." Squeezing her pussy tight around him, she moved with each pounding thrust. He groaned. *Anything* to make him go faster. Desperation ripped into her with jagged claws. She would die if it didn't stop soon. She leaned forward and arched her body to try to *move*.

"Shh." His hand splayed across her lower belly, pressing her back into him. "You're so wet for me, fire fin. So sleek."

His smooth voice caressed her ear, his panting breath blowing the tiny hairs at the base of her neck. She shivered in response. Long strands of his waist-length ebony hair slipped over her shoulder to caress her breasts as he dipped in to kiss her nape.

A sob caught in her throat, and she twisted in his arms. Hot desire whipped through her. "I want you. Just you. Only you."

He shuddered against her, the only outward sign that her words had any effect. And maybe they didn't. Pain lanced through her, and she swallowed. Unexpected tears welled in her eyes, and she was grateful he fucked her from behind this time. So much had happened between them, yet she knew no more of his heart than she had the day they'd met. She pulled in a steadying breath and blinked away the moisture that misted her vision.

"Sera?" He buried his cock deep within her and stilled his movements. She throbbed around him, her body sure of her needs...even if her emotions remained conflicted. He lifted his hands to cup her breasts, and a moan ripped from her when he flicked his nails over her beaded nipples. Fire roared through her veins, and goose bumps rippled down her arms and legs.

"Bretton," she breathed. "Don't stop."

One hand lifted to bracket her chin and nudge her face around so he could look at her. The fingers of his other hand continued to play over her breast. His brilliant turquoise gaze burned with the heated edge of lust, the irises bleeding out until the color spread from corner to corner. "You're certain, fire fin?"

She wasn't sure of anything, just that she wanted him more than her next breath. Tipping her head, she brushed her lips over his. Their mouths moved together, teasing slowly. His fingers stroked over her jaw and down to the pounding pulse at the base of her throat. She smiled and nipped his lower lip. His tongue swept into her mouth as he took control of the kiss. She gasped when his fingers pinched her nipple, twisting the tip. The hot, masculine scent of him filled her nose. It mingled with the smell of sex in the room. God, she loved that. Loved his heavy cock nestled inside her, loved that he could still hold back when she knew he burned for her.

He trailed his fingers down her torso, around her navel, over the swell of her belly, and between her thighs. She sighed against his lips. He played with the hard nub of her clit, rolling his thumb over it. She pushed her ass back, nudging his dick within her. His breath rushed out. She didn't have a lot of room to move, but even the slight friction was enough to send shivers down her spine.

She tossed her long red hair back so she could meet his eyes, so he could see how much she loved what he did to her. What only he had ever done for her.

"You are so lovely." His gaze swept her face.

A flush washed up her cheeks. She'd been the smart one her entire life. Only Bretton had ever claimed she was pretty to look at. She smiled, clinging to this sweetness that she only saw when they were in bed together. This warmth and connection that felt so right, so much like she knew it should be between them always. She shrugged and cleared her throat. Her hips faltered in their movements. "Thank you, Bretton."

He arched an eyebrow, grinding his pelvis against her backside. "You're thanking me for the truth, fire fin?"

Flashing a little smile at him over her shoulder, she nodded. "I'll thank you for a whole lot more if you'll move your ass."

He chuckled. Thrusting, he pressed deeper into her wet sex. She moaned, arching with him. His fingers played over her slick folds, rubbing the stretched lips alongside his stroking cock. Heat unfurled in her belly, rocketing through her system.

His hips bucked hard, picking up speed to a punishing rhythm. She burned hotter and hotter. He pressed down directly on her clit, the force of his thrusts moving her against his finger. A scream burst from her throat, tingles exploding down her legs. He leaned forward and bit the back of her neck. Hard. She jolted, her pussy fisting tight on his cock, milking the hard length. Sensation rolled over her in a suffocating wave, dragging her under until there was nothing except Bretton and his cock driving into her and the rush of orgasm crashing through her body. "I love you," she whispered.

A long groan from him vibrated against her back and drowned out her words so he didn't hear them. Slamming into her one, two, three more times, he froze. He jetted into her, coming hot and deep within her. He nipped the back of her neck again. His free hand raked up the front of her thigh, and she shivered, her pussy clenching in the aftermath of orgasm.

Always it was this way with him. Wicked control of her pleasure before he unleashed the wild side of himself. The side she loved the most because it was just for her—no one else ever saw it.

She collapsed against the cold metal wall, her sweat slicking the surface as her knees buckled and she slid down. Bretton caught her in his arms, lifted her to his chest, and carried her to her bed. She rested her cheek on his shoulder, closing her eyes to savor the moment with him.

Would he stay with her or leave her? She never knew with him. Two steps forward, two steps back. He was unpredictable, a variable in an experiment she didn't understand yet. She turned on her side to face the wall. She didn't want to watch him walk away if he decided to go. A small smile curled her mouth as he crawled in behind her, his front pressed to her back. He brushed his lips over her nape, and she shivered in response.

His arms encircled her in a light embrace, and she sighed at the soft pleasure of his skin against hers. She loved it when he was relaxed and casual. Not the formal diplomat he normally was, but the considerate lover.

She felt the mattress shift as he propped himself up on his elbow behind her. It usually meant he had something on his mind he wanted to talk about. Politics, religion, sex, business. She never knew what he might say, but she often said something that shut him down again, so she tried not to interrupt too much when he was in a rare, open mood.

"The trade ship arrives tomorrow." His fingers drew lazy patterns on her shoulder.

Pulling in a deep breath, she wondered again at the twist of fate that had landed her in this man's arms. She wasn't born in this time or place, yet here she was.

Earth.

Here it was a myth, a legend, a part of history that had died centuries ago. When *she* would have died if her ship hadn't been lost in space. She'd been coming to Aquatilis to help found a new colony. As a scientist with doctorates in mechanical and biological engineering, she'd been recruited to help with the gene-splicing that had created the new species of Homo sapiens that inhabited the colonized planets. In her time, they'd created only merpeople—Bretton's ancestors—and had been considering experiments with large cats such as lions and tigers. Now, in addition to the merpeople on the water world of Aquatilis, weretigers, werebears, and weredragons lived on three other planets. So much change, so much she had missed.

There had been a malfunction with the spaceship she'd taken, but the life-support systems had maintained the passengers and crew in stasis. They'd drifted in space until they were caught in another planet's orbit. They'd crash-landed. She fisted her hands in the bedcovers, vivid memories of that day flashing through her mind—the terror that had coursed through her, the heat of the fire, the disorientation of waking.

Along with one other woman—Jain Roberts—Sera had survived the crash onto the icy, mountainous planet of Alysius. The werebear world. She shivered, remembering the reception of her barbaric saviors. If Bretton hadn't found her... Well, she didn't care to contemplate what would have happened to her without the merman ambassador's intervention.

Jain had been rescued by a different clan of bears and had fallen in love with their leader. Unlike Sera, she'd chosen to remain on the planet. If not for Sera's relationship with Bretton, Sera wouldn't understand the other woman's choice. But there wasn't much Sera wouldn't do to stay with Bretton. She wished he felt the same. She winced at the thought, shying away from what that meant for her. A full year had gone by, and she was no closer to his heart than she had been when he'd taken her from Alysius.

She swallowed and closed her eyes. She loved him. Even the parts of him that drove her insane. His kindness, respect for others, and sense of responsibility. His sweetness when they were alone. His snobbery and aloofness when they were in the company of others. All of it intrigued her, attracted her. She bit back a smile—or maybe it just made her the worst kind of masochist.

He shifted, and the tips of his hair tickled over her skin. "Their transmission said they'd dock at midday."

They no longer had the technology to send long-range communications as they had when she was born, but the weretiger ship had sent a short-wave burst transmission that Jain and her husband, Lord Kesuk, were aboard the ship. Why they ventured to Aquatilis when people from the two planets viewed each other with mutual disdain, Sera didn't know. Unease twisted her stomach. "Jain will be here."

"You've missed her." His lips feathered over her skin, and she shivered, a slow coil of desire winding through her.

She curled her arm under her cheek. "Yes and no."

"Explain." He bit her shoulder lightly. Her nipples peaked tight, and she had to press her thighs together to still the sudden ache between them.

Swallowing, she tried to focus on the conversation. "I've worried about her on that planet. She is, after all, the only one like me—the only one alive who knew what it was like before now, who has seen Earth. That binds us somehow, but we were never close. Her brother and I knew each other well."

"He was your lover." It wasn't a question, and his voice came out a flat monotone. He froze behind her before his hand lifted away from her arm.

She eased around to look at him. "Sometimes, yes. He wasn't why I came here, in case you were wondering."

"I wasn't." He pulled back, rolling to his feet.

Sitting up, she reached for her discarded jumpsuit. "Hang on, I'll come with you."

He shook his head, his black hair slipping over his shoulder as he reached for his clothing. "No."

Frustration punched through her, and she blew out a breath. "You always do this. Pull away. It's like I'm only good enough when you're hard up."

"You're speaking in Earthan euphemisms again." He slid his soft-sided boots over his pants and jerked his shirt over his head. With an efficient movement, he secured his hair in a long queue down his back.

She folded her arms across her breasts, and his turquoise eyes flashed as his gaze dropped to her bare skin. "Then let me say it plainly: are you ashamed to have people know we're sleeping together?"

A muscle in his square jaw ticked, and his nostrils flared in annoyance. She knew he didn't care to talk about their unwieldy relationship. At the moment, she didn't care. She tried not to push, but sometimes she had to. What did she mean to him? Where was this going? Anywhere? Was she wasting her love on a man who could never return her feelings? The questions plagued her more and more often.

It hurt, how he could disregard her in public. Part of her knew it was the nature of the culture that had developed on this world. But the woman in her needed to be acknowledged. Needed some indication that she wasn't so...alone.

"If I were ashamed to sleep with you, I wouldn't be sleeping with you." With that he spun and strode out of the room.

She sighed and pushed to her feet. Reaching again for her jumpsuit, she stepped into it and sealed the front closed. Once she had her boots on, she was ready to get back to the workday Bretton had so pleasurably interrupted.

One of the machines in her lab was giving her inaccurate readings and needed recalibrating. Stepping through the hatchway that separated her private quarters from her lab, she picked up the tools she'd discarded. Forcing herself to put away the emotions Bretton had pulled from her, she ran through the tests she'd already run and considered those she still needed to conduct.

A sad grin tugged at the side of her mouth. As much as Bretton ran from her, he'd probably spend the night in her bed. What a mess. But it was her mess, and she couldn't *not* want him.

"**B**retton."

He froze at the sound of his father's voice behind him. Neptune preserve him, he had no desire to see the older man after a passionate session with Sera. It always left him confused and angry with himself for losing control. He shouldn't want her, shouldn't touch her. And yet he'd been unable to resist since the very first. A full Turn had gone by, and he'd been unable to slake his lust for the curvaceous scientist.

Clasping his hands behind his back, he waited for his father to draw abreast of him. Cuthbert Hahn looked every inch the senior counselor he was. He advised the Senate on all manner of political and social agendas. The Hahn family had always participated in the ruling of Aquatilis. Bretton followed in that proud tradition in his position as the chief ambassador to the other colonized planets. It was an important path before him, one he needed to perfect. He pulled in a deep breath and faced his father.

Cuthbert's nostrils flared. He had the slightly wide and flat nose of a merpeople—all mammals on the planet had been genetically engineered to have their breathing passages lined with gills. His turquoise gaze slid over Bretton's shoulder in the direction of Sera's quarters. He narrowed his eyes and jerked his chin, indicating that Bretton should follow. "I worry you're getting too close to the human, son."

"I'm not sure I understand what you're trying to say." Bretton's jaw flexed. He had no desire to speak of Sera. He knew he should cease his relations with her, but what he *should* do and what he *did* were two very different things with her. He'd worked hard to perfect himself—as did all merpeople—but with her... He cursed himself for his weakness and her for twisting him into knots.

Cuthbert grunted, working hard to keep pace with Bretton's longer stride. "You have a duty to your people. You don't have time to become entangled with someone like her."

"Like her?" The question ground out between Bretton's clenched teeth. While he knew he shouldn't be involved with Sera, it angered him to hear others speak poorly of her. She wasn't a mermaid, so why did so many try to force her to act like one? But he could never vent his frustrations. In public, he had to act as though he was constantly improving himself. Before Sera, he hadn't had to *act*, he had simply *been* what he should be. And anger and frustration—involvement with an imperfect woman—would cause scrutiny he didn't want. He was a political figure, constantly under surveillance for any slip in demeanor.

"Emotional. Volatile. She'd make a poor mate for an ambassador. Especially the chief ambassador. You have an example to set. The ambassadorial corps must be cool, logical, and socially adept—she is none of those things. She's the kind of woman who expects *love* in a mating."

Bretton rolled his eyes. "Neptune forbid."

"This is no jest, Bretton. I'm deadly serious." His father caught his arm. Rabid intensity shone in his gaze.

Bretton snapped to attention and nodded. He knew what his father said was true. His hands balled into fists at his sides, but he kept his tone respectful. "I understand, sir."

"Do not confuse physical compatibility with the makings of a suitable mate." Cuthbert's voice took on the lecturing tone he'd used when Bretton was a child. It grated to hear it now when he was a grown man.

"Sera is not Mother." No, his mother had disgraced their family and left his father to live on a sea cow ranch at the very outskirts of merpeople civilization near the lost city of Pacifica. In doing so, she'd exposed them all to scorn for straying from the path of vigilant self-improvement. It had ruined his father's career. He'd never be elected a senator or make the chancellorship as so many Hahns had before him. Now his father expected Bretton to fill the breach, to be everything Cuthbert could not.

His father gave a derisive snort. "Every woman is like your mother. I refuse to see you make the same mistakes I did."

Bretton pinched the bridge of his nose. He *knew* his father was correct. Mating with the wrong woman had all but ended Cuthbert's political aspirations—and Bretton had no right to dishonor his family like his mother had. He smiled, but it held no amusement. It had taken the Senate very little time to realize that Sera didn't respond well to authority—and the only one who had any luck garnering her cooperation was Bretton. So she'd become his responsibility. Regardless of his official duties, he had to stop seeing her in a personal manner. Had to stop touching her, lusting after her, dreaming of her.

Starting now.

He heaved a weary sigh and ran a hand across his forehead. The trade ship was the most important function of his position each Turn, and letting Sera distract him was an error he couldn't allow himself.

Chapter 2

"Doctor Gibbons?"

Sera grabbed the ledge of the counter above her and pulled herself out from under it to see who was talking to her. She frowned, unhappy with the interruption. She was close to being finished recalibrating this contraption. "Yes?"

An enormous young man with a blond topknot stood quietly inside her doorway. She'd guess his age at late teens, perhaps early twenties. His gaze swept the room once before settling on her. Interesting. Most people couldn't wait to peek at her lab. His dark green irises were rimmed in brilliant, glowing gold, and they never left her face. "The weretiger ship has docked on the landing platform. They bring the Arctic Bear Clan leader and his mate to see you."

She arched an eyebrow. "I know that."

"Yes, Doctor." The young man didn't shift or fidget. He was the *stillest* person she'd ever seen. And he also showed no indication of leaving.

Sighing, she sat up. "What's your name, kid?"

"Oeric Fane."

She tossed aside her tools and wiped her hands on a rag. Grime smeared the front of her jumpsuit. "Whatever they sent you to say, get it said."

"Ambassador Hahn would like you to meet them when they arrive in Atlantis." He hesitated briefly before snapping his mouth shut.

"What else?" A feeling of foreboding crept through her. Bretton hadn't come to her the night before, and she could guess it had something to do with his career, his father, his duty...or some combination thereof. Damn it.

"He asked that you make yourself...presentable." Oeric winced and focused on a spot over her shoulder, not meeting her eyes.

"He did, did he?" Her eyes narrowed to slits. The too familiar frustration boiled into hot anger. Who was Bretton to dictate what she wore? As everyone here pointed out so often, she wasn't a mermaid, and she didn't behave like one. Why should she dress like one? Her work was often dirty, and that helped the citizens of Atlantis more than they'd like to admit.

Bare minutes later, Oeric trailed after her as she stomped into the docking bay wearing her filthy jumpsuit. They wanted to demand her presence? Then they could deal with her less than perfect apparel.

"Doctor Gibbons."

"Counselor Hahn." Cuthbert was a shorter, portly version of Bretton. He should have been jolly looking, but he wasn't. His upper lip curled in disgust as he looked over her attire. She narrowed her eyes and lifted her chin, daring him to say anything.

The one thing she'd never come to understand about these people was why they were so fixated on what others thought. They held themselves in icy reserve, always striving to be perfect. It was especially true for the political families like Bretton's. So much pressure to be the very best. The oddest thing was, it wasn't to be more perfect than each other, but to be the best they could be. The ideal was taken too much to the extreme. No person could be flawless, but anyone less than perfect was looked down upon.

So as much as she was prized for what she could do, the upper classes looked down on her for not striving for the perfection they valued so highly. Her hair was always a mess, clothes always stained with grease. She never said or did the right thing.

Cuthbert arched a brow at her, not backing down. "May I remind you that you are a guest on this planet?"

Clenching her jaw, she held on to the frayed edges of her temper. "I don't need a reminder to know you'll never accept me as I am, Cuthbert."

His nostrils flared at her use of his given name. He hated that, the informality...which was why she did it. The skin around his turquoise eyes, so like Bretton's, tightened. "Perhaps you could consider changing."

She deliberately misunderstood him and brushed at her jumpsuit. "But I'm already here, Cuthbert. I don't have time to change before your guests arrive."

He glowered and glanced at someone over her shoulder. "You deal with her."

"Must you be so difficult?" Bretton's heavy sigh sounded behind her. Tingles shivered down her spine as the warmth of his big body embraced her.

She stiffened and forced herself to step away, turning to face him. She lifted a brow. "I'm sorry, have we met? Hi, I'm Sera."

"I am not amused." His shoulders drew into a rigid line.

A nasty smile curved her lips. "That's too bad. I am."

He folded his arms and stared down at her. "And you're the only one that matters."

"Why do you care so much what other people think?" Her fingers clenched into fists, and her temper slipped. "Isn't it better to be happy with yourself than for everyone else to be happy with you?"

"You assume it's either one or the other. It is possible to be content with yourself and have others feel the same."

She huffed. "Is it? Or is that just what you tell yourself?"

"Selfish." His voice cooled to subarctic temperatures.

Resisting the childish urge to stick her tongue out at him, she retorted, "Sacrificial lamb."

"This isn't the time or place for this discussion."

"You brought it up." Moving backward, she put some distance between them. Physical distance, at least. Her emotions were always in chaos around Bretton. He'd possessed her, body and soul, from the very first moment she saw him. She'd never been able to distance herself from him, and until recently she hadn't even tried. A year of back and forth had exhausted her.

Sera stood with the mermen in a semicircle around a round hatch. A rumbling precipitated the green light flashing beside the door to indicate the hatch had been engaged. The cargo skimmer had ferried their guests from the landing platform to the docking bay at Atlantis. It would make multiple trips to bring all the trade goods down from the other worlds. After a few weeks of haggling and negotiation with vendors here, Aquatilian goods would go back to the ship, and the route would begin again.

Her heart rate picked up, and anticipation whipped through her. Jain would be on this skimmer. As the only person like her, she would understand a lot about the adjustment to a whole new culture. Sera's lips curled in a bittersweet smile. Of course, Jain had had a new husband to help her transition.

The hatch popped open with a whoosh, and the small amount of water trapped between the skimmer and the door rushed down into the grated flooring where it would be pumped back out into the sea. It was just one of the systems Sera had had to repair and improve when she'd arrived.

A composed woman with hair so orange-red it would have been unnatural on Earth stepped through the still dripping water. Mermaid. They were the only species to have such intense hair colors. Often the hair shade matched the tail color when the merperson shifted. But not always. Cuthbert had a black tail to match his hair, whereas Bretton's was turquoise like his eyes. This mermaid must be the Aquatilian ambassador to Harena—the weredragon world. Her name was Elia...something.

"Ambassador Iden." Bretton reached a hand out to her, and he smiled as they touched. Fierce jealousy ripped through Sera. He'd never shown that much pleasure in seeing her. Especially not in public. Bitterness coated her tongue, and she glanced away. Oeric looked at Elia with something akin to worship in his eyes. Sera's eyebrows lifted. The woman was at least ten years his senior. Perhaps more.

The young man bowed to the mermaid and offered his arm. "After a Turn on a desert planet, I imagine you wish to swim."

Intense longing flashed across her face, and she snapped her fingers around Oeric's forearm to allow him to lead her away. Sera turned to see if Jain would exit the skimmer.

But next came a dark, exotic beauty flanked by two large, equally dark men. Their scales marked them as weredragons. One of the men was tall and broad with silver scales, the other was absolutely enormous with black scales. She'd seen only one dragon in the time she'd been here, an older ambassador who had kept to himself.

The woman's purple scales formed a crown on her forehead, and she radiated a calm assurance that Sera would never be able to master. Her gaze slid over the crowd before settling on Bretton. She smiled and swept him a small curtsy. "Ambassador Hahn...so nice to see you again."

He bowed in return. "Lady Ketryn. I must say it is a surprise to see you. I'd heard you returned to your home world of Harena to mate."

"I did." A small, secret grin curved her lips. She gestured to the two men beside her. "May I introduce my mates, Tarkesh and Nadir? The three of us have taken up my father's old post among the weretigers as ambassadors to Vesperi."

Mates? Plural? A million questions ricocheted through Sera's mind. She wanted to ask them all, to know more about the hidden dragon culture. It was her curse, always wanting to know more. With Bretton, it was just plain always wanting *more*.

"Congratulations on your new position." Bretton bowed and spoke to the weredragons but cut Sera a sideways glance—a warning not to say anything, not to embarrass him, not to upset his perfect life. Her polite smile broke, and she looked away to meet Jain's gaze as Kesuk escorted her off the spaceship. Her appearance jolted through Sera. Contentment shone in the woman's leaf-green eyes, and her tiny body was swollen with the advanced stages of pregnancy. Sera felt her eyes widen at the sight. How could someone as petite as Jain carry a child from a *polar bear* shifter? Kesuk was easily the biggest man Sera had ever seen, and every single werebear was huge.

"Jain." With the exception of Bretton, Sera didn't touch very many people. She hadn't been a comfortable child to be around, and her parents had never known what to do with her constant need to learn. They'd sent her away to school as a toddler. Visits home had been awkward for everyone—no hugs were exchanged, very few *words* were exchanged—but she reached for Jain now.

Some quiet fear exploded in her belly. If Jain were to die in childbirth, that would leave Sera alone in the universe. The last of her kind. Even if they lived on different planets, she had always known Jain was out there somewhere. She existed, and that was enough for Sera to take some odd comfort in.

She wrapped the smaller woman in an embrace for long moments. A little laugh bubbled out of Jain as she pulled back, tears sparkling in her eyes. "It's so wonderful to see you again, Sera."

"It is." The first genuine smile of the day bloomed across her face. Here was a woman who had known her before she was a token human, the last of a dying breed of technologically advanced people.

The unhappy shriek of a child pulled Sera's gaze to the hatch again. Amir Varad stepped out with a baby in his arms. The child grabbed two handfuls of the weretiger king's auburn-and-black-striped hair and pulled. He winced and gently disentangled himself from the pudgy little fingers. Stress drew lines around his eyes, but even he looked more content than he had the last time Sera had seen him.

Had everyone suddenly gotten their lives together except her? She snorted at her own self-pitying thoughts. Why was she so *restless* lately? So discontent? It wasn't like her. She used to claim that if she had a laboratory, she would be blissfully happy. She now knew that for the lie it was.

"Varad." A grin curved her mouth.

"Sera Gibbons. Your beauty has only enhanced in the time since I've seen you. Aquatilis treats you well." The thick gold loop flashed in his ear as he inclined his head. The weretiger king was a charming man who'd given her transport to Aquatilis after his trading party had discovered her. Bretton had been with that party—and had been the one who'd convinced the Grizzly Bear Clan to give her to him. What he'd said to them, she'd never know, but she was eternally grateful not to be living as a Grizzly slave.

The Alysians' archaic culture demanded that she serve as a slave because they'd rescued her. Fortunately "slave" was a generic term for any non-clan member who lived in the Den as a servant. She'd made certain the Grizzlies hadn't enjoyed her time there. They'd all felt a mutual and instantaneous antagonism. She doubted Bretton had had to work very hard for them to allow her to leave with him.

A matching baby's scream echoed behind Varad, and he turned to offer his free hand to a woman with the most perfect skin Sera had ever seen. It was the color of pure cream, and the natural kohl lining that surrounded her crystalline blue tiger eyes made them seem enormous. Her hair had blond and brunette stripes. A snow tiger? Sera reviewed what she knew about the genetic anomaly of white tigers. Very little. She made a mental note to look it up in the data archives and then she offered the woman a polite smile. "Hello."

Curiosity lit the woman's gaze. "You're the other human. The non-shifter human?"

"Yes." Sera braced herself for the probing look so common to those who wanted to see the freak of nature who couldn't shift into an animal form. It happened less and less often as the merpeople got used to seeing her, though they still goggled when she put on a rebreather, wet suit, and flippers and went swimming. More often than not, she was checking the integrity of the dome structures that made up Atlantis.

"Ahem." Cuthbert's throat clearing sounded pompous. Everything about him was pompous—from his heavily embroidered saltwater silk robes to his slicked-back hair to the way he carried himself. In so many ways, he was the antithesis of Bretton. Yet Bretton felt the need to act like his father in public. Aquatilis was all about the public appearance of self-improvement and perfection. It drove her insane. She wanted to rip off her clothes and run naked through the botanical gardens screaming at the top of her lungs, just to break the *perfect* bubble they all lived in.

On one hand, she respected anyone who would seek to improve themselves throughout their life, but they were in denial about their ability to reach a state of perfection. In her time, people knew it was a good goal, but no one actually thought they'd achieve it.

Cuthbert bowed low to the new arrivals. "May I introduce myself? I am Senior Counselor Cuthbert Hahn, adviser to the Aquatilian Senate. It appears you all know my son, and I look forward to getting better acquainted in the coming weeks."

She fought the need to roll her eyes. Everyone else took the merman's ingratiating formality in stride. The tigress managed a graceful curtsy even with a baby in her arms. "I am Mahlia, Amira of Vesperi. These are my children, Crown Prince Razak and Princess Varana."

"Charming." Cuthbert smiled at them, and each baby gave a matching wail.

Bretton stepped forward and offered a bow. "I'm sure you've all had a long voyage and would like to rest. My assistants will escort you to your quarters."

Mahlia and Ketryn both returned looks of gratitude before moving off with the young mermen Bretton had motioned forward. Their mates followed behind them, leaving Jain and Kesuk standing with Sera. Tilting her head toward the city proper, she led them out of the docking bay.

She glanced down at Jain's belly, unease rippling through her again at how life-threatening this pregnancy could be for someone as delicately built as Jain. "You came for the medics to give you a cesarean section."

"Yes. I will not risk my mate." Kesuk's deep voice rumbled behind them. Jain stopped walking to reach for him, and he wrapped her hand in his big one. Quiet terror shone in the werebear's gaze, and Sera didn't even want to imagine the kind of hell it would be for a strong man to know his child might kill his wife. What a nightmare for them both.

Jain lifted her palm to Kesuk's jaw. "I'll be all right. This was a standard procedure on Earth."

Naked adoration flashed across their faces, and Sera looked away, feeling as though she'd interrupted a private moment. She cleared her throat. "Um, you'll be staying in the Undine sector."

Jain nodded. "The western leg of Atlantis, if I recall correctly."

"How did you remember that?" Cuthbert puffed up beside them, Bretton trailing behind.

"You forget Aquatilis was my original destination, Counselor." Jain smiled. "I studied the layout before I left Earth."

His thick black eyebrows arched. "But that was five hundred Turns ago."

Sera shook her head at Cuthbert. She started walking again, and the group moved forward. "Not for us. It's been only a year. Remember, we were in stasis the entire time." They'd awoken one day and found the whole universe had changed and passed them by.

"Is that where you live?" Jain pressed a hand to the small of her back, and Sera checked her stride so the other woman wouldn't have to struggle to keep up.

"No, Bretton lives there. I'm in the Titan sector."

"With the laboratories and the medical facilities." Jain pushed her hair out of her eyes.

The dark locks had grown to the middle of her back in the past year. Sera didn't remember a time when Jain hadn't worn her hair short.

Sera shrugged. "You know me, I can't be separated from my passions for too long."

A quiet smile curled the smaller woman's mouth. "I remember you used to get up in the middle of the night to tinker with my father's inventions when you stayed with us."

"I miss him." Sera closed her eyes as a pang hit her chest.

Jain tucked her hand into Sera's. "I'm sorry."

"He was an ass to you." Sera barked out a laugh. Doctor Roberts had been more of a father to her than her own ever had, but she wasn't ignorant of his flaws.

The other woman blinked and squinted up at her. "I never thought anyone noticed. I was the only non-scientist of the family."

"I knew what it was like." Sera tilted her chin down. "My parents would have killed for someone normal like you. Not a freak of nature like me."

"Fate's a bitch, isn't it? My parents always hoped you'd marry my brother so they could have a genius daughter."

Sera wrinkled her nose. "Never would have happened. He was kind of a priggish ass."

A giggle burst forth. "He was."

"But he was brilliant and a good friend." Sera angled a glance at Jain. "I miss him, too."

Her slim hand squeezed Sera's tight. "Me, too."

A rush of noise filtered down the corridor from the entry to the main dome of Aquatilis. It held many shops and restaurants, the botanical gardens, and the Senate chambers. Sera glanced at Kesuk in time to see his eyes goggle at the sight before a mask of indifference slid over his face. The man wasn't about to allow himself to be impressed by a culture he disliked so much, but as far as Sera knew, this was the werebear's first trip off Alysius. She wished it were for a happier reason than dangers to Jain's health. Her stomach twisted at the thought. "Would you like to see the hospital or your quarters first?"

"The hospital," they chorused.

Trying to ignore Cuthbert's grating personality and the lightning strike of attraction every time Bretton leaned in to make a comment, she showed them the birthing pool merpeople used and the surgical ward where Jain would have her C-section. They all ignored how Kesuk's face paled when he saw the operating-room laser. An hour later, Sera left an exhausted Jain in her temporary home and sought refuge in her lab.

Bretton found Sera bent over one of her enormous machines the next morning. He paused for a moment inside the door to her lab to enjoy the tantalizing wriggle of her backside. His cock stiffened in his pants, reminding him that it had been over a day since he'd sunk himself into the hot, wet depths of her pussy. He choked on a groan, and her head popped up and whipped around to look at him. A streak of grease smudged the creamy skin over her high cheekbone. "I wanted to thank you for escorting our Alysian guests around."

She wrinkled her nose. "You'll have to show them the more cultured areas of the city. I'm afraid my specialty is more scientific."

As he groped for a gentle way to discuss why he'd come, he executed a slight bow. "Again, my thanks, Doctor."

The use of her title was deliberate whether she realized it or not. His body ached for wanting her, and he needed the reminder that she was a duty and nothing more. She shouldn't mean any more than, say, Elia Iden. His hands fisted at his sides to keep himself from reaching for her.

Her shoulder hunched in an uncomfortable shrug as she turned around and pulled herself up to sit on her machine. "It's good to have Jain around again."

The wistful note in her voice made his gut clench. What must it be like to be separated from everything and everyone she'd ever known? The questions he'd never allowed himself to ask her bubbled out, and then he kicked himself for giving voice to his curiosity. "Why did you come with me last Turn? Why didn't you stay with Jain? Or go with Varad?"

Wariness and vulnerability flashed in the pretty gray depths of her eyes before a mask settled over her features. He missed the open expression. She looked down at her hands and spoke softly. "When I saw you, I felt less...alone. Not so lost."

"Why?" And why was he asking her this? It would only encourage familiarity. But he always craved more with her than he could allow himself to have.

A low chuckle escaped her, irony glinting in her gaze. "Because I knew you were mine. And I was yours."

His eyebrow arched, surprise sparking in his chest. "So you believe in destiny? How very *un*scientific, Doctor."

"Not destiny exactly. But I believe in the logic of the universe." Absolute certainty sounded in her tone. "Everything is in its place for a reason, and there's a logic to it even if we can't see it. It's a puzzle we haven't figured out yet. So when I saw you I knew this is where I was meant to be."

"I don't understand you." But he wanted to, and he shouldn't. He propped a forearm against the doorframe, cocked a hip, and sighed.

"Me neither." She giggled.

He laughed with her, reluctant affection twisting inside him. If only it were just desire, but as much as she drove him mad, she was also good company.

Pure wickedness twinkled in her eyes. It was his only warning before she hopped down from her perch and approached him. He tensed, fighting the urge to run from a woman half his size. Sweet Neptune, she made him want. His cock throbbed, and sweat made his shirt stick to his back. Her hand slid down the front of his pants, cupping his dick through the fabric. His breath hissed between his teeth, and he forced himself not to grab her, push her up against the wall, and rip that ugly jumpsuit away from the lush curves of her body. "You should not—"

She flashed a siren's grin. "Do you want to say no?"

Yes. No. Damn her for bringing him to this confusing place where nothing was as it should be.

"Do you want me to beg?" Her breath brushed over his ear, and he suppressed a shudder. Heat rolled like molten fire through his body. He wanted her. He shouldn't touch her. He couldn't make himself stop her from touching him. She tugged at the seal on his pants and slipped her hand inside.

Closing his eyes, he groaned. Her palm slid up and down the length of his cock, and then she rolled his balls between her fingers.

His control snapped along with the last vestiges of his sanity. He stepped forward, wrapped his hands around her shoulders, and spun her up against her workbench. He ripped open the tabs on her jumpsuit and shoved it down her arms. Dipping forward, he sucked one of her sweet nipples into his mouth. She mewed and arched her back to press closer. Her fingers still worked up and down his hard dick, and he damn near came in her hand.

A man cleared his throat from just outside the open door. Bretton froze. The Fane boy. Oeric. The real reason for his visit flooded his mind. Bretton pinched his eyes closed and eased away from Sera. His muscles locked in protest, his cock burning for surcease. Both of them straightened and resealed their clothing.

"Come in, Oeric," Bretton called out, and the big merman poked his head in the door. His expression bore its usual impassivity.

Sera's brows arched nearly to her hairline, and she pinned Bretton with a look. "What's going on?"

"I came here today to tell you I found you an assistant."

Her face flushed a dark red, and anger flashed in her eyes. She gave Oeric a sweet smile, and it sent a chill down Bretton's spine. "I'm sorry, Oeric. I don't know what the ambassador told you, but I'm not looking for a lab assistant. Would you excuse us, please?"

The young man nodded and withdrew. Sera waited for his footsteps to fade before she rounded on Bretton. Her voice went deadly soft. "You came to force an assistant on me?"

He couldn't contain a wince at the hurt in her voice. His weakness at touching her had caused this. He could not allow it to happen again. "You need one."

"We've had this discussion before." She pulled in a breath, and her expression flattened. "I don't like having people in my lab. They touch things and ask annoying questions and get in my way."

"That's part of learning, Sera." Exasperation filled him. Yes, they'd had this argument before. Many times.

She turned away, plucking up one of her tools.

He rubbed a hand down his hair, reaching for calm. What was it about this woman that always ignited his temper? She ignited *all* his passions, and he shoved them aside to try to convince her he was correct. The Senate was putting pressure on him to force her to take an apprentice. It wouldn't be long before they called her before their assembly to make demands...and he needed to prevent the explosion that would ensue from both parties. Oeric was perfect for this. He was intelligent and, despite his size, managed to be unobtrusive. "Why can't you just show him how to do what you do?"

"I'm not a teacher, Bretton. If you wanted one of those, you should have begged Jain to come here. That's *her* specialty, not mine." She flicked him an angry glance.

Throwing up his hands, he resisted the urge to pace. "She can't do what you do. And when you're gone, we'll still need to know how to repair things, *create* things the way you do."

"Already ready for me to die, are we?" Her lip lifted in a sneer.

He growled back at her, his patience slipping again. "That's not what I meant, and you know it."

"Fine." She folded her arms over her breasts, and he forced his eyes away from them. She smirked.

A sigh escaped his lips. "There are dozens of people of any age who are willing to learn,

Sera. Just pick *one*."

"No." Her jaw took on a stubborn tilt.

"Sera—"

"I can't teach them what I don't know, Bretton. I don't know how I do most of these things." She waved a hand around at all the wires and cables and half-assembled gadgets on her workbenches.

"Because you're a genius." He pinched the bridge of his nose.

"Yes. What I can do with electronics, nanotechnology, and fiber optics...and, well, pretty much anything mechanical borders on a savant skill. It's always been this way. I passed the tests without reading the books. It just comes to me that this is the way things are *supposed* to be." She sighed and looked away. "I'm trying to help as much as I can, but don't ask me to teach people, because that's something I *can't* do."

"I understand." But he wished he didn't. "And you are helping. Damn it." He shoved a hand through his hair and dislodged the thong that held it back, turned on his heel, and walked out.

Frustration bubbled up in his chest, and there was no one to be angry with. It wasn't her fault, it wasn't anyone's fault, but the fact was that without the knowledge she had locked in her head his people would eventually lose the technology they had. Slowly, over several more centuries, but it would happen. And when it did, Aquatilis would be lost. The water had the same chemical compound as that of Earth, but the air *above* the water wasn't breathable for humans, so they couldn't live on the surface. No technology meant no merpeople society. In time, Atlantis's systems would fail, and they wouldn't know how to fix them.

Because Sera couldn't teach them.

And the Senate was desperate to prevent it. Despite their dogmatic political stance, for once he wholeheartedly agreed with them. Jerking off his clothes as he went, he stalked into a small shifting chamber—others like it were located at the end of each sector in the city. He stuffed his garments into a small locker and keyed it to his personal identification code. It would shoot through a system of high-pressure tubes until it reached his apartments, which were keyed to the same code. Another system Sera had improved. She'd left her mark on the whole city. He growled low in his throat at the thought of her. Stubborn woman. Tempting, beautiful woman.

He jabbed at the button to close the hatch to the shifting chamber. It swished shut with a whoosh and a hissing seal. Then the small room began to fill with seawater. The chill of it bit into his overheated flesh, and he shuddered, gooseflesh breaking down his limbs.

The water soon rose above his head, and he took a deep breath, pulling air in through the gill slits that lined his nasal passages. Then he shifted into his merman form. His legs locked together, and scales rippled down his skin, fusing his thighs and calves. His body vibrated with the force of his bones breaking and reforming into a tail. Turquoise fins tipped in black swirled out from his ankles and feet. When it was done, he palmed the panel to the exterior hatch to let himself out into the sea.

Arching his body, he kicked his tail and let the tide sweep him away from Atlantis. Escape. He needed to clear his head. Of Sera. Of his father, his duties, his position. Propelling through the cool water, he let the current take him and tried to let go of everything except this in the sea where he was embraced in a cocoon of silence.

Chapter 3

Sexual frustration still hummed through Sera's body days later. Bretton hadn't come back to finish what he'd started. Not the argument and not the sex. She tried to push thoughts of him out of her mind so she could concentrate on her work. Just the thought of him and what his clever hands could do to her made her body temperature rise, made goose bumps break out over her flesh, made her skin feel too hot and too tight to bear. She bit her lip to stop a whimper.

She shoved a hand through her hair and bent closer to her current invention. *Focus, Sera.* There was nothing she could do about the lust coursing through her body, so she tried to focus her energy on frustrations she could have some effect on—those of her new project. It would help filter the seawater to make it drinkable. The desalinization system they had was serviceable, but Sera didn't care for the taste. This new gadget would strip out all the excess salt and make it taste like clear spring water from Earth.

Thank God. If she had to swallow more chemical-flavored saltwater, she might vomit.

She cauterized a miniscule tube that held the nanobots in a gelatinous solution. When she was done, the seawater would pass through the nanobots for filtration. The tubing was proving difficult. It was either too porous and water flooded in at a rate the nanobots couldn't process, or was not porous enough so she'd be old and gray before a single glass of water processed.

"Damn it." She tossed aside her sproket and sat back in her chair. Her muscles screamed as she straightened. She'd been hunched over for too long. The hum of arousal that hounded her came roaring back with indecent fury. She closed her eyes. She'd never wanted a man the way she wanted Bretton. A year, and she still burned for him as much as she had the first moment she'd seen him.

Pushing to her feet, she wandered around her lab, picking up wires and tools and putting them down again. Each step brushed her thighs together, increasing the agony of desire that flooded her sex. She walked through the door to her room and looked out the huge round window. The lights from Atlantis illuminated the octopus shape of the city. One large glass dome made up the city proper, and long tentacle-like corridors wound out to smaller domes. In the distance, she could see a few mermaids swimming toward one of the shifting chambers in the main dome. She pressed her forehead to the cool window, hoping the sharp bite of chill would break the fever inside her.

No such luck.

She could only feel the cold press of Bretton's flesh against hers when he'd come in after a swim in the ocean. He'd stripped her bare and slid his cock deep inside her, his wet skin sticking to hers as they moved together. She moaned.

This had to stop. She had to do something. *Anything* to make it stop.

Giving in to the need that rode her, she jerked at the tabs that sealed her jumpsuit closed. She slipped her hands inside, palmed her breasts, and tweaked the tight nipples. Her gasp echoed in the empty room, reminding her how alone she was. Pain and pleasure twisted through her. She focused on the pleasure. Her fingers drifted down her ribs, over the swell of her stomach, and into the soft hair between her legs.

Juices slipped over her hand as she pressed into the slick depths of her pussy. She choked at how good it felt. Her breath panted out, and she leaned against the cool glass. It contrasted with the fire building high and hot within her body. She flicked her fingertips over her swollen clit.

Her thighs jerked, and her knees went weak. Stumbling back, she kicked off her jumpsuit before she sat on her mattress. Her breath shuddered out, and passion wound tight through her. With shaking hands, she punched in the code to open the compartment over her bed. She pulled out her vibrating dildo. It was a smooth metal tube that flexed to conform to the walls of her pussy in ways most alloys couldn't. Lying back in her bed, she spread her legs and flicked on the controls. The vibrator hummed to life, and she teased her clit and lips with it.

Her pussy clenched hard, and moisture slipped from her core. She needed to come so badly her body screamed with it. Goose bumps broke out down her arms and legs. She drew the long shaft of the dildo up and down her wet sex. The vibrations only increased the want she couldn't contain. Sweat beaded on her upper lip and between her breasts.

Instead of pushing the dildo into her pussy, she laid it flush against her clit and let the hum of it shove her fast and hard to the very edge of orgasm. Her heels pressed to the mattress, and her hips lifted into the vibrations.

"Oh, my God."

She whimpered, and her eyes drifted shut as she focused on the sweetness that spun deep inside her. More. Just a little more. God, she was so close.

Look at me, Bretton's voice demanded in her mind.

Her eyes snapped open to see Bretton in merman form floating outside her window with his palms pressed to the glass. She gasped, her body arching. "Bretton."

She froze, and silence fell over her room. Only the sound of the buzzing sex toy broke through. Her breath stopped, and the moment stretched to a fine breaking point. Juices gushed between her thighs as the thought of him watching her masturbate registered in her mind. Yes.

Stroke yourself, Sera. Show me what you like. His deep, sensuous voice filled her thoughts, and his pure turquoise eyes burned with the same suppressed need that had built inside her unrequited since before the trade ship had landed.

A moan dragged from her throat. The muscles in her stomach and legs shook as she moved the dildo over her flesh again. She shivered, met Bretton's gaze, and let a slow, wicked smile cross her face.

"Bretton, I—" She stopped when she realized he couldn't hear her. She licked her lips, and played the toy over her pussy. Teasing them both. His groan echoed in her mind. It made her burn hotter, and moisture gathered thick in her sex. She didn't think she'd ever been so wet in her life. It was shocking how intimate it was to have him watch her pleasure herself.

Plunging the dildo deep inside her, she twisted on the covers as the deep hum rippled through her body.

Yes, fire fin. Move for me.

Her hips arched, and she worked the toy deep inside her. Angling the metal, she stroked it inside herself just as he'd demanded.

His fingers slipped down the glass as if to slide over her naked skin. She shuddered. Yes. She loved his hands on her flesh. She craved it. Him. Always. Every moment of every day. She couldn't get enough.

She felt his gaze almost as if it were a physical touch as it swept over her naked form. He smiled when he met her eyes again. *You know what I would do if I was there? I'd fill my hands with your pretty breasts and suck your nipples until you screamed.*

"Oh, God," she breathed. One hand cupped her breast, and she pinched her nipple hard, twisted the tight tip. Her other hand still pushed the dildo into her pussy. Her sex clenched hard, throbbing with need.

Good, fire fin. I love it. His voice was a low rumble in her mind, a rough silken caress that enflamed her as much as the touch of her own fingers. *Now place your hand between your legs and play with your clit. You're hot for me, aren't you? Hot and wet.*

At the first stroke of her finger over her pulsing clitoris, she cried out. Without even touching her, he controlled her pleasure. She loved it. Flicking a nail against her clit, the muscles in her legs jerked. She moaned, the sound loud in the small room.

His hands bunched into fists against the glass, the turquoise filling his eyes from corner to corner. His long hair formed an inky cloud that flowed around his broad shoulders as he flicked his tail to keep the currents from pulling him away from her window.

Her breath bellowed out, and she couldn't look away. Heat boiled through her like molten lava, and she hovered right at the edge of orgasm. A few more moments, and she'd fly. Desperation swamped her, and her hips rotated on the saltwater silk bedcovers. The slick feel of it against her skin was one more sensation that spurred her on.

His wicked chuckle filled her mind. *Come for me.*

"Yes!" As with everything, she couldn't deny him. She screamed, her body bowing hard off the mattress as her pussy fisted around the vibrator again and again. Too many feelings ripped through her, overwhelmed her, and she sobbed out a breath before she went limp. Tingles raced over her skin as she shuddered in the hot aftermath of orgasm.

"Sera? Are you all right? We heard you yelling." Kesuk's voice sounded loud through the door. "Hurry up and open it, dragon."

Her door snapped wide, and three men filled the space. Nadir froze, and Kesuk and Varad plowed into his back, shoving him forward into her room. She gasped and rolled into a ball, shut off the vibrator that still hummed deep inside her pussy, and dragged her blankets up to shield her body from view. Blood pounded into her face, and she knew her cheeks were fluorescent red.

Glancing at the window, she saw Bretton had disappeared in a cloud of bubbles. Tears smarted her eyes, and she couldn't force herself to meet the gazes of her visitors. "Um...could you wait for me in my lab?"

"Ah...of course." Varad grabbed the back of the other men's shirts and hauled them toward the doorway on the opposite side of the room.

Dumping the vibrator into a small sterilizer she kept by her bed for just that purpose, she scrambled for her jumpsuit and stuffed herself into it.

Her hands shook so it took twice as long as normal to seal the front of her suit. Patting down her hair, she stepped into her lab where the three big men seemed to crowd the space. She only hoped they all had the diplomacy not to mention what they'd walked in on.

"What was that…thing? That buzzed?" Kesuk made a buzzing noise to demonstrate his point.

Sera closed her eyes and tried not to blush harder, humiliation crawling through her. "It's called a vibrator."

"Where can one of these vi-bra-tors be purchased? Is there a shop in Atlantis?" Nadir propped his elbow on her worktable and leaned forward, avid curiosity shining in his dark eyes. She didn't even want to think about which of his two mates he intended to purchase the vibrator for.

"Uh…no." The idea of proper merpeople having a sex-toy shop was enough to make her want to giggle hysterically.

Varad forked a hand through his tiger-striped hair. "It is an invention of yours?"

"Yes. No. They were quite common on Earth, but that particular vibrator was my invention." She closed her eyes, disbelief coursing through her that she was having this conversation. God help her.

"Ingenious." The weretiger smiled.

Kesuk smacked a hand down on the table. "I want one."

"Two for me. Always." Nadir's eyebrow arched as he shared a wicked glance with the other men.

Varad chuckled. "I foresee a very interesting trade agreement coming of this. Tigers are very sensuous creatures."

"Oh, God." She clasped her hands to beg. She wasn't above it at this point. "Please don't mention this to Bretton."

"My dear, he has already seen it. And you." Varad spread his hands and shrugged.

She pinched the bridge of her nose and turned away. This day couldn't get any worse. What filled her mouth with a bitter taste was how eager these men were to be with their mates, how much the adoration shone on their faces. Had Bretton ever wanted her that way? Ever cared about her at all? Or was she merely a sexual convenience? She *had* made herself as convenient as possible. She wanted him, she'd made that clear, and she'd always pursued what she wanted with single-minded determination until she got it. That was how science worked. Try, fail, reassess, try again.

"He's a fool." The weretiger's voice sounded quietly behind her.

She glanced over her shoulder to see he'd approached while she wasn't paying attention. "Excuse me?"

He gestured to her bedroom window. "He's a fool for not mating with you."

A bitter little laugh spilled from her lips. "There's not a merman in his right mind who would. And Bretton is the sanest man I know."

"Sanity and intelligence apparently do not walk hand in hand." He arched a dark brow. "I expected better of Bretton."

Holding her hands up in surrender, she grimaced. "Amir, please."

He sketched a slight bow. "I will speak of it no more."

"Thank you." She thrust a hand through her tangled hair, forced a smile to her face, and sat down at her worktable. "So...what brings you to my sector of the city?"

After her little peep show, Sera did her best to avoid Bretton for a few days. She spent every evening with Jain and the other people from the trading party and threw herself into work during the day. Stepping into one of the most exclusive textile shops in Atlantis, she let herself be led to the back room to meet the proprietress and see the equipment that needed repair.

"Oh, can you fix it, Sera? It's been in my family since settlement." The tiny shop owner wrung her hands, anxious lines creasing her wizened face.

Sera lifted her eyebrows at the mammoth saltwater silk loom that dominated the store's workshop. This was going to be *such* fun. In her time, she would have had a large team of workers to help with something like this. Of course, in her time, she would have been inventing new machines, not serving as a maintenance repairwoman for shopkeepers.

She offered a more confident smile than she felt. "I'll do my best, Ebba."

Stooping down, she set her bag of tools on the floor and stepped over to remove one of the service panels that ran along the base of the loom. She dropped to her knees, slid halfway into the opening, and rolled over on her back to work. She immersed herself in it, and time became fluid and slid away.

"Now, where did my sprocket go?" She sighed, patting the ground beside her hip.

Cool metal slipped into her fingers. "I believe this is it, Doctor."

Ducking down, she saw the light outline of a huge man with his blond hair up in knot.

Narrowing her eyes, she tried to bring him into focus. "Oeric, isn't it?"

"Yes."

"Bretton sent you." It wasn't a question. It was so like the man to avoid her but keep tabs on everything she did.

Oeric nodded. "He thought you might like a hand with the heavy lifting."

"I can manage." Her fingers clenched on the metal of her tool as anger swelled in her chest. Why couldn't Bretton just accept her, accept that she couldn't do what he wanted?

Again, the large merman's chin dipped in a nod. "I'm sure you can."

He didn't sound sarcastic, but the whole situation set her teeth on edge. "Then why are you still here?"

"I have some experience with repairing this loom." He shrugged.

Her eyebrows lifted. "Oh?"

"Ebba's my grandmother."

Well, that explained why he'd claim to know about *this* machine. "Oh."

The flash of white teeth as he grinned made him look less like a statue. "It's a status symbol that she can afford to pay you to fix this for her."

Sera snorted, turning her attention back to her work. "I feel so beloved and glamorous."

His chuckle sounded like a rumble of thunder. Her spanner slid into her hand just as she needed it.

"That blue wire in the back burns out a lot."

"I noticed." It had been one of the first things she'd replaced when she arrived, but it hadn't fixed the problem.

He persisted. "I found that it helped to have someone in the next panel to hold the wires and tubes out of the way."

She rolled her eyes. The kid was right, but she didn't have to give in graciously. "Fine. You can help, but this doesn't mean you're my apprentice. And don't mention this to Bretton."

"Of course." There was no gloating in his voice, so her shoulders relaxed a little. A small metallic *pop* sounded as he opened the panel next to her, and she could see him through the tubing as he wriggled in on his back. It had to be uncomfortable for him. It was a tight fit for her, and she was a third his size.

Well, he was determined but not annoying about it. And he hadn't been exaggerating his knowledge of mechanics. He anticipated problems before they happened, moved wires into her reach just when she needed them, and didn't natter on at her like most merpeople. In fact, most of the next few hours were spent in a companionable silence.

She squinted at the tubing over her head. "I have a theory."

"Oh?" She heard him shift to look at her through the wires.

Using her sproket, she removed a tiny panel. "One sec."

"Sec?"

"One second...one moment...whatever." Impatience laced her voice. An idea was coming to her, and she stared at the loom interior until it formed.

"I see. Your theory?" he prompted.

"Right." She jolted from her reverie and shrugged. "If we adjust the setting on the nanoparticles that run the—"

Before she finished the sentence, she heard him fiddling with controls on his side of the loom. The panels around her lit in arrays of lights and flashes. "Excellent theory, Doctor. I hadn't even thought to touch the nanoparticles."

"Are you messing with me?"

"Merpeople do not like messes." The priggish tone in the deep rumble of his voice made her laugh. "However, I truly hadn't thought of it."

"Fair enough. Let me check if that worked." She crawled out to run diagnostic tests on the holodisplay while he stayed squeezed into the panel to bring the systems back online manually. "Everything checks out."

"We've finished?" Quiet disappointment rang in his tone, but he said nothing more as he hauled himself out.

She watched him as he replaced the panels they'd removed and straightened to face her. His mouth opened and then closed again. He gave a sharp nod and stepped past her toward the door.

"Be in my lab at morning bell tomorrow. Don't touch anything. You only get to watch."

A smile quivered on the corner of his mouth before he controlled it. "Yes, Doctor."

He hurried for the door before she could change her mind. She gathered her tools and cleaned them before placing them back in her kit. Bretton was going to be pleased. Smug, even. She clenched her fingers around her spanner, wishing she could whack Bretton over the head with it. She doubted it would make much of a dent in his thick skull.

But she was angrier with herself than him because she *wanted* to make him happy. She sighed and shoved a hand through her hair. Nothing she did seemed to please him. Not personally and not professionally.

Ebba's voice came from the workroom doorway. "My grandson said you'd finished."

"Yes, he's very helpful." Sera straightened and hefted her tool kit in one hand. "He has a gift with mechanics."

"As long as he constantly improves, of course." The older woman smiled fondly.

Sera fought the urge to roll her eyes at the standard Aquatilian sentiment. "Of course."

"I'll have credits transferred to your account, Sera. My thanks for your assistance." Ebba stepped aside to allow Sera to pass.

A professional smile stretched her lips. "Not a problem."

Ebba's grin was more genuine. "And please take something you like from the shop. Without my loom, I would lose my business."

"Oh, that's all right. The credits will be fine." She shook her head and felt her hair fly wild around her shoulders. One saltwater silk dress hung in her quarters. That was enough because she was bound to get it dirty within minutes of wearing it. She backed toward the shop's entrance.

"Nonsense. I insist." Ebba's wrinkled face set into stubborn lines.

"Then it is an offer she cannot refuse. None make such fine saltwater silk as you, Ebba." The warmth of Bretton's body surrounded Sera, but he didn't touch her. Glancing over her shoulder, she sent him the glare he deserved for shoving an assistant on her.

Ebba flushed under his turquoise gaze. "I—I have spent my life improving on my craft."

"And have done a fine job." He smiled down at her. A far warmer smile than Sera had ever received from him in public. Sera brushed at her mussed clothing. She was out of place in the display room of Ebba's shop. Usually she didn't let it bother her, but it did today.

Perhaps it was seeing how comfortable Jain seemed in her own skin. She should be as much of a misfit as Sera, but she wasn't. It was obvious from the contentment oozing from the woman's pores that she loved her new life and the man she'd found to share it with. Sera had the man she wanted, he just...didn't love her. Pain stabbed at her heart, but she forced herself to see the truth in that statement. He wanted her body and nothing more. And it was obvious he didn't *want* to want her.

Jain had always been searching for a place to be needed, and Sera had never questioned who she was or where she was going. Her path had always been straight ahead. But now it twisted and turned in directions she'd never thought she'd go. Was this what love was supposed to be like? She didn't know. She'd never seen how real love worked. Her parents had sent her away so young. Jain's family had been closer to her than anyone else. But Jain's family had worshipped science and logic. Even then, Sera could see how much that isolated someone like Jain. Now Jain had what Sera wanted most. Belonging. Acceptance. Love.

She doubted she would find those things on Aquatilis.

She hefted her tool kit higher and stepped around the elegant merpeople to walk toward the door. Her skin felt grubby, and she needed to bathe before she met Jain and Kesuk for the evening meal.

"You're right, the silver is the perfect color for you." Bretton's hand closed over her elbow, and he steered her to a display just to the left of the door as if she'd walked toward it instead of the exit. She fought the urge to jerk away from his touch. Even the lightest stroke of his fingers was enough to send shivers streaking over her skin. It was madness what he could do to her. And she loved it. She just...wanted him to love it, too.

She sent a longing glance toward the door. All doors and windows on Aquatilis were round. The perfect shape, they said. A circle had no beginning or end. It had achieved the perfect balance. She wondered what the original architect would think of the symbolism the merpeople had afforded his work. He'd probably love it. What man wouldn't want his work to go down in history as flawless?

Bretton's hand reached out to slide down the sheer silver saltwater silk cloth. It was embroidered with sparkly matching silk thread in a rounded pattern of scales. "A gown in this fabric would make you look like you had a mermaid's tail."

"I'll never be a mermaid, Bretton. No matter how you might prefer it." Her voice dropped to a hiss only he could hear.

His jaw clenched. "Do not insult Ebba."

"It's not Ebba I would wish to insult." Her voice went sweeter than sugar.

A booming laugh spilled from his mouth, and she wanted to kick him. "You'll have to work harder to insult me, Sera. I've had a full Turn to become accustomed to the sharp edge of your tongue."

"Then allow me to remove the irritant." She pivoted to face Ebba. "This is lovely."

The woman beamed. "Shall I wrap a length of it for you?"

"No," Bretton replied. "Send it to the Mermaid's Purse and tell them it is for Doctor Gibbons. They will know what style to cut it into."

Sera ground her teeth, baring them into the semblance of a smile. "Thank you, Ebba. Ambassador Hahn."

"My pleasure," they chorused.

She spun on her heel and rushed out the door, colliding with Oeric. Bretton caught her from behind before she fell, and Oeric snatched her tool kit midair.

"Thank you." She ignored Bretton and smiled at the blond merman when he gave her the tools back.

Bretton swallowed past the tightness in his throat and wrapped his arm around Sera's stomach, pulling her back until the soft curves of her ass pressed against his cock. He fought a tortured groan as his dick swelled in his pants.

Sera stepped away from him, ignoring him as she continued to smile at Oeric. "Tomorrow morning, then."

"Yes, Doctor." Oeric looked at Sera with something close to reverence in his gaze. He had no right to look at her that way. Not *his* Sera.

"You've taken Fane as your apprentice." Bretton should have felt triumphant, jubilant at his success. Instead he favored the younger man with a glare. The tadpole wouldn't even know Sera without Bretton. Something ugly and painful twisted deep inside him. "I am needed elsewhere."

She raised her fingers to flick them in a little wave. "Okay. See ya."

"Good afternoon, Ambassador." Oeric nodded, but neither of them looked up to see him go. They bent together to discuss some mechanical thing. A feeling of inadequacy flooded Bretton. He wanted to stay and participate, but he could not.

Oeric's hand settled on Sera's shoulder, and jealousy sank claws deep into Bretton's gut. His fists clenched at his sides as he fought the intense urge to pummel the big merman. It was irrational, foolish, *imperfect*. He whipped around and stomped away.

The other merman could touch her in front of others if he wanted to. His political views were well known to be a little off-color—enough so that he wouldn't care how imperfect Sera was, wouldn't care that she didn't share his path to self-improvement, wouldn't care what others thought of her potential as a mate.

Mate. Neptune's blood, the thought of her with another man shredded Bretton.

But Oeric worked with mechanics. Unlike Bretton, who worked in politics, who was constantly in the view of the public...and the Senate.

Bretton tightened the thong that held his hair back. What was he going to do with her? What would he do without her? He didn't know. He didn't know anything anymore.

His feet carried him in the direction of peace—the botanical gardens that made up the innermost section of the city.

Many of the plants had been brought to Aquatilis from Earth and had grown in wild abandon under the carefully maintained conditions of Atlantis. He pulled in a deep breath of lush air, willing the tension from his muscles. He had meetings with both Elia and the full Senate today, and they would all notice if he showed signs of distraction. The spiral paths through the gardens were meant to inspire meditative introspection as they wound to a central pool filled with freshwater fish.

Forcing himself to slow his stride, he folded his hands behind his back and attempted to focus on the problem at hand, the same problem he'd had for the past Turn: Sera Gibbons. The mere thought of her was enough to send lust coiling through his belly and to swell his cock to the point of pain. He rubbed a hand over his forehead.

What was he going to do about her? The Senate had left handling her up to him. He'd tried to make it clear in public that she meant nothing to him, and he doubted many knew they were lovers—his father being an unfortunate exception.

As far as Bretton could tell, the woman had only two passions. Technology...and him. He almost tripped over his own feet as the thought shot longing straight to his groin. He'd been inclined to ignore the intense attraction between them when they'd first met. She had not. At first he'd thought her pursuit of him flattering, but when she'd shown up in his chambers nude, his control had snapped, and he'd taken her with a wild abandon he'd never allowed himself with his own kind. Sera had delighted in it. He knew the less control he had in bed, the more she enjoyed it. She was so unlike anyone he had ever met before and so completely unsuitable for anything except a physical relationship. He closed his eyes as a sharp pain stabbed his chest. He didn't *want* more than the carnal relations they shared. He could *not* want more. Sighing, he opened his eyes to continue down the path.

Something had changed recently. Sera seemed...restless. Discontent. His fists clenched. He didn't want her to be unhappy, but there was little he could do to help her. He disliked the conflicting emotions that whipped through him whenever she crossed his mind. He wanted to pull her close, he needed to push her away.

He'd already decided the best course of action was to cut off any personal contact with her, but he hadn't been able to make himself do so.

"You look upset, Ambassador." The soft, feminine voice sounded from a bench hidden beneath the hanging branches of a willow tree.

He stepped off the path and pushed the branches out of the way. "Lady Jain."

A chuckle bubbled out of her while she pressed both hands to her burgeoning belly. "Just Jain, please. I don't feel like much of a lady today."

"Then you must call me Bretton." He knew just what she meant. He never felt like a politician after an encounter with Sera. "Are you in need of assistance, Jain?"

"Oh, I imagine Kesuk will be along soon."

"He doesn't know you're gone?" He winced at the picture of a marauding werebear bellowing for his errant mate as he barreled along the thoroughfares. Sera would enjoy the spectacle, and Bretton would have to fight a laugh as he often did when she was around to make observations about anything.

"I'm sure he does by now." Her green eyes twinkled as she gestured to the bench. "I didn't get very far before I had to sit down, but I needed to escape the coddling for a while. He'll be annoyed and scold me, but he'll understand."

What would it be like to be so comfortable with another? To know that differences were surmountable, no matter how you disagreed? His parents had never had that sort of relationship. For the first time, Bretton wondered if his father had stifled his mother the way he tried to stifle Sera. It had been so many years since he'd seen his mother that he barely remembered her face—she'd died over a decade ago while living on his aunt and uncle's ranch.

Jain put her hand on the back of the bench and pushed herself to a standing position, one palm pressed to the small of her back. His fingers shot out to grasp her elbow and steady her. She sighed. "I've been sitting too long. I need to walk again."

Shifting his grip on her elbow, he wondered how someone so fragile in build could carry a werebear child. Jain was a much smaller woman than Sera. "Would you like me to carry you?"

"I think Kesuk would rip you limb from limb if he saw you holding me." She spoke in such a mild voice he blinked down at her as the sentence processed through his mind.

He snorted but didn't doubt she spoke the truth. Matching her tone, he answered, "Lord Kesuk could certainly *try*."

Her eyebrows lifted, and a wicked grin spread over her face. "Perhaps it wouldn't be so easy for him, but I would lay odds on my mate's victory, of course."

"Of course." He offered his arm, and she tucked her fingers into the crook of his elbow. Moving slowly, he guided her back to the main path.

A laugh gurgled out of her. "It might distress Sera to see you killed. And that would upset me. Kesuk would take that into consideration."

"Good of him." Ignoring the sting to his pride and the urge to laugh, he kept watch on where Jain placed her feet. His muscles bunched as he waited to see if he needed to catch her if she stumbled.

She nodded. "He's always good to me."

"I am glad to hear that."

"And what about you and Sera?" She angled a piercing glance up at him.

His chest squeezed. How much could she know about him and Sera? What would it mean to his career if people knew? He'd no longer be able to protect her from the Senate. Cold sweat made his shirt cling to his back. "Excuse me?"

"Are you always good to Sera?" A quiet knowing filled Jain's gaze when she glanced up at him. "That was what sent you running for the gardens, wasn't it?"

"Did Doctor Gibbons say something to you?" He swallowed.

Shaking her head, she stepped carefully along the path. "Only that when she irritates you, you tend to walk here."

He cleared his throat. "Yes, well. I came here to think long before I had Sera to plague me."

"I'm sorry to hear that." She didn't look up at him.

"That I come here to think? Or that I think at all?" He grinned. "You may have listened to the werebears too much on that count."

"I meant that you believe Sera is here to plague you. I had hoped the two of you would come to a more...amicable relationship once you left Alysius. Especially considering how taken with you she was—*is*."

In love with him, she meant. He froze mid-step as the realization hit him. He'd always known Sera desired him—she'd made no qualms about that—but *love*? He pulled in a deep, steadying breath.

Jain had paused beside him and scrutinized his face. "The two of you haven't slept together since we arrived."

He choked on the breath he'd just taken. "How would you know that?"

"Three reasons." She lifted three fingers. "One: you both ooze sexual frustration. Two: I've heard there was an interesting episode between you that was interrupted. Three: Kesuk can't smell her on you anymore. He could when we landed. Fresh, too. You naughty man."

A deep flush burned his neck. His tongue—usually so smooth in offering political platitudes—twisted into slippery knots. "Ah. I do try to impress the natives."

"Natives, as in primitive, right? Snob."

He arched a brow in mock condescension. "I am a merman. We do have that reputation among the werebears, do we not?"

She lifted her hand to cough into her fist. Her eyes twinkled as she offered him a smile. "You know, when we first met, I pitied Sera for her attraction to you. I had no idea what she saw in you. But I think I do now."

He swallowed and continued on as if she hadn't spoken. Dangerous territory, speaking about Sera's desire for him. Whatever they felt for each other changed nothing about their circumstances. "Aquatilians and Alysians have long had a mutually poor reputation. They claim to have called for aid, but we did not answer. That much is true, but it is also true that we *could* not answer."

"Why? You mentioned something about life-support failing when we met on Alysius, but Atlantis seems to have thrived." She flicked her fingers to indicate the lovely botanical gardens.

"When Earth's sun died, anyone who survived came here. There were several spaceships, military cruisers, space yachts, and the like that had the ability to make the jump to light speed and get here. They flooded this city and a smaller one, Pacifica, to the point that our life-support systems could no longer sustain us. Pacifica flooded, and many died."

"I'm so sorry." Both of Jain's hands squeezed his wrist.

"I think the dislike between merpeople and werebears is likely to continue indefinitely." He huffed a laugh. "We are too different. Merpeople value perfection, and werebears..."

"Do not." She gave a negligent shrug. "Sera is not perfect."

"Sera claims perfection is impossible." Often, and to anyone who wished to speak to her on the matter.

"Yet she's very accepting of people's flaws. My family's, for example."

And Bretton's. And his father's. As much as Cuthbert harassed and annoyed her, Sera never expected him to change. She accepted him as he was. It was one of the qualities Bretton treasured in her. One of the many things he missed now that he didn't spend his nights with her. She didn't expect the merpeople to change either—she simply disagreed with them, and it meant he could never claim her as a mate. Pain twisted through him at the knowledge. He forced a smile to his lips. "What was she like...on Earth?"

"Different. The same." Her slim shoulder lifted in a shrug. "She was Sera. Nothing much could alter that—she's always been sure of who she is, but she's grown in the past year."

"Grown?"

They resumed walking. "Softer, I suppose Kesuk would call it. Fewer sharp angles, and yet she doesn't have the community of scientists to understand her genius as she did on Earth. That has to be difficult for her."

"Less difficult than it would be for her on Alysius." His voice came out stiffer than it should have, more defensive.

"True." Jain let the implied insult slide. "We're very different that way."

"Aquatilis is the right place for you at this time as well." He pointed it out because he'd made certain the Senate asked for nothing in return for helping the werebear lord and his mate.

She smiled, her fingers tightening on his sleeve. "Yes, my daughter will be born soon."

"The medics haven't been able to confirm the gender of your child—only that it will be born a werebear like Kesuk." He blinked down at her bent head.

She tilted her chin, and her dark hair slid forward over her shoulder. "It doesn't matter. I know I'm having a girl."

"Then I bow to the greater wisdom of women in this area." As though he'd be foolish enough to argue with a woman in the advanced stages of pregnancy.

A mischievous grin twitched the sides of her mouth. "My stepson, Nukilik, has requested a new sister. And Kesuk deserves another daughter to coddle."

"And what of Miki?" Kesuk's daughter was playful and sweet, if Bretton remembered correctly. "Does she also desire a sister?"

"Miki is so enthusiastic about not being the youngest anymore, she'd be happy if we brought home a merchild."

He chuckled at the thought of a fish changeling growing up among the rough-and-tumble Arctic Bears. "It is fortunate you carry only one child. I've heard Arctics often conceive twins—like Miki and Nukilik."

She sighed and rubbed a palm across her swollen belly. "If I were having twins, I doubt I would have survived."

He blinked at the bald statement. It was true, but he hadn't expected her to be so matter-of-fact about her mortality.

"I've surprised you." She angled a glance up at him.

"Yes."

Her chin dipped in a nod. "Kesuk and I have spoken to the medics, and they'll tie my tubes when they go in for the C-section."

"Tie your—"

"It's an Earthan saying. It means they'll ensure I can't conceive again. Ever." A wistful note blunted the edge of practicality in her voice. Her fingers danced over her stomach again. "This will be the only child I have, but Kesuk already has an heir, so all will be well."

"Of course," Bretton responded, inserting as much quiet enthusiasm into his voice as he could.

She sighed. "The medics also confirmed that Mahlia's twins don't suffer from the same genetic defect that killed their first son."

"I'd heard that." Varad had told him. The two of them had traveled together the Turn after the weretiger's son had died. Bretton had seen how that grief had weighed upon his friend. He couldn't even begin to imagine the kind of toll that would take upon a woman. What would Sera do to cope in such a situation? He hoped she never had to find out. "It is a blessing for them."

"Yes." With each step, Jain leaned more heavily on his arm. The color had leeched from her face while they walked until her dark hair shone in stark contrast against her pale skin. Relief flooded him when he glanced up and saw the end of the path that opened into the city proper.

"Little bear, you should not be out here." Kesuk stepped out of the bushes to their left. His white-blond hair stood in furrows as though he'd run his fingers through it repeatedly. Worry and annoyance warred in his midnight gaze. A muscle in his jaw ticked as he stooped to lift his mate into his arms. He held her as though she was the most precious thing in his life. And she just might be.

She curled her arms around his neck. "I needed to—"

"I know, little bear." Dipping his chin in Bretton's direction, the Arctic Bear lord turned in the direction of the Undine sector.

"Wait, Kesuk." She patted his giant shoulder, and he stopped in his tracks. She glanced back at Bretton. "You'll dine with us this evening, won't you?"

Bretton's eyebrows arched that the huge man listened to his woman. Bretton's experience with werebears was one of primitive, barely evolved humans. Perhaps he should learn some acceptance from Sera. He bowed to the dark-haired woman. "It would be my honor, Lady Jain."

CHAPTER 4

B ut Bretton never managed to dine with Jain and Kesuk. She'd gone into early labor and been rushed to the medical facilities for surgery. A harrowing night in the hospital led to the birth of a baby daughter—Sakari—for Jain and her werebear lord. Relief filled Bretton's chest because she'd survived and was recovering well.

Knowing Sera would be there and frightened for her friend, he'd forced himself to stay away. He'd want to hold her, and he could not. Comforting her would too easily lead to more. He was already a man at war with himself, his deepest wants battling for supremacy. Leading himself into the temptation to touch her would be foolish. He sighed and leaned his forehead against the cool, bowed glass window in his quarters. He could only pray that it became easier to avoid her in the future.

Light sparkled and flashed just below his window. One glance revealed it was Sera. He sighed again. Her red hair flowed around her as she swam in a tight silver suit. Bubbles rose from her face as she breathed in and out through a small apparatus she held in her mouth—something she had invented to adapt to his world. It was unfortunate that her adaptation was limited to the physical realm and not to the social structure of Aquatilis.

The two bottle-nosed dolphins she'd adopted when she'd come to his world swam in circles around her along with a young sea dragon. Its green scales gleamed in the light from the city. With a rusty chuckle, he wondered if it was related to any of the three weredragons that had come with Varad and Mahlia. Sea dragons had been gene-spliced with humans to create the weredragons that inhabited Harena.

Sera moved along the base of the corridor, and Bretton could only assume she was checking for something. He had no idea what. Technology wasn't something he knew a great deal about. He knew how to operate machinery as well as the next person, but he had no idea *why* it worked. Sera did.

He watched her, and the band of emotion that gripped him whenever he thought of her tightened.

One of the dolphins nudged her side, and she flipped, a rush of bubbles erupting from her nose. If he concentrated he could hear the playful clicks and chirps as the dolphins chattered back and forth. As a merman he had enhanced hearing and sight, especially underwater. He grinned. Sera righted herself and gave a hand signal to the dolphin, who swam away and left her with the other dolphin and the sea dragon.

She continued with her work until the dragon's tail wrapped around her legs, pinning her in place. Her arms pinwheeled in the water as she struggled to get away. The sea dragon whipped her around the way it would while playing with another dragon. Bretton's heart slammed against his ribs when he saw her lose her breathing apparatus. Her hand shot out to grab it. And missed.

Not pausing to see what else happened, he sprinted for the corridor. The muscles in his arms and legs screamed as he pushed himself to the limit to get to the emergency exit. Terror like he'd never known before fisted in his gut. He slammed his palm against the control panel, and the exit spun open. Grabbing the bar above the chute, he lifted his legs and swung himself in feet first. The tube snapped shut behind him, and with a rush of air and water, it ejected him out into the ocean.

Please, Neptune, let her be all right. Please, Neptune, don't let her inhale water. Please.

His hands clawed through the water as he swam. He shifted mid-stroke, and his pants ripped away as his legs snapped together to fuse into a tail. He kicked hard, slicing through the water faster than he'd ever thought possible. Where was she? His gaze caught on the flash of green scales. The sea dragon.

Relief ballooned inside him when he saw Sera still struggling against the grip of its tail. He darted forward, wrapped his arm around her waist, and slammed the flat of his own tail into the dragon's snout. It reared back, stunned. It loosened its hold just enough for Bretton to wrench Sera free.

Her terrified silver gaze met his as they pushed away from the sea dragon. He pulled a breath in through the gills in his nose, sealed his mouth over hers and pushed the air into her lungs. She sucked in a desperate breath, burying her fingers in his hair to hold him to her. Her legs snapped around his waist in a vice grip.

Flicking his tail, he sped them toward the nearest shifting chamber in the main dome. His heart hammered in his ears, fear still pumping adrenaline through his system. He'd almost lost her. Neptune's blood, he'd almost lost her. He slapped his hand against the palm panel so the iris door spun open and then closed behind them. Pushing another breath past her lips, he grunted when she licked her way into his mouth. Fire exploded in his body as the stark terror twisted into molten lust.

Their tongues twined, fighting for control of the kiss. He shifted into his human form, his cock a rigid arc that pressed between her legs. The chamber drained of water quickly and left them shrouded in mist. He shoved her up against the wall, ripping open the seam of her wet suit. He jerked the top of the silver fabric down to her waist. Breaking the kiss, he sucked her nipple into his mouth and bit at the tight crest. She cried out, her hips rotating against his.

"Let go," he ordered, his fingers wrapping around her bent knees.

She whimpered and eased her grip on him. He pushed her legs down and peeled the wet suit off of her and threw it aside. He thrust his fingers into the hot depths of her pussy, working her hard.

"Bretton, I—"

He dragged her to the cold metal floor of the chamber and shoved her thighs wide, pushing himself between them. He had to have her. Now. Their mouths fused together, and he tasted blood when she bit him. It spurred him on, made him wilder than he'd ever been before. He buried his cock deep in her pussy.

She moaned into his mouth, her feet pressing down on the back of his thighs to push him closer. His hips bucked as he thrust into her tight, wet sex. The sleekness of her gripped his cock and made him feel as if his head would explode. He'd never wanted anything as desperately as he wanted her now. He was too rough with her, fucked her as hard and as fast as he could. He ground his pelvis against hers, needed to burn off the terror he'd experienced when he'd seen her attacked by the sea dragon. Her body arched to meet him, demanding he give her everything. Her fingers jerked the thong from his hair and twisted in the dark strands as they spilled down around them.

He broke the kiss, wanting to see her face flushed with passion. Her gray eyes glittered with the same harsh need that ripped through his body. Her fingers fisted in his hair, and her eyes squeezed closed, a tear leaking from the corner. She writhed beneath him, her sex milking his cock in long contractions as orgasm shook through her. Her body bowed so hard she lifted him with her. "Bretton!"

Hammering his hips against her, he felt the thin thread of control he had left snap. Her wetness coated his cock with every shove into her pussy. Fire rushed through his veins until everything but the feel of her silky flesh was burned from his mind. His body locked in a hard line as he came deep into her.

He collapsed against her, his face buried in the smooth curve of her neck. She smelled of the sea and of the signature sweetness that was uniquely Sera. His muscles shook in the aftermath, his breath bellowing out in harsh pants.

"Are you all right, fire fin?" he rasped. He leveraged himself up on his hands over her. Her gray eyes were smoky with spent passion. She nodded, stretched her arms over her head, and yawned.

Her lip was split, and she licked at the small cut. A cut he'd caused. Cold rushed through him. What had he done? He'd fucked her like a madman after she'd nearly drowned. What was *wrong* with him? He'd clearly taken leave of his senses—as he always seemed to when she was involved. Anger at himself mingled with the residual fear for her. He shuddered when he pulled his cock from her body, but he forced himself to push to his feet. He needed to get out of here. His father was right—he'd lost all perspective around Sera. He became someone he shouldn't be. It was lunacy.

Wrapping his fingers around her biceps, Bretton drew her to her feet and turned away while she dressed. He tried to shut out the sounds of her movements, tried not to imagine her soft curves and how much he still wanted her. Approaching the locking panel to the interior door, he stared at it as if he'd never seen one before.

"Is it punishment?"

"What?" He barely heard her as he attempted to gather the unraveling ends of his composure before they stepped out of the shifting chamber and into the main dome of the city.

"The way you avoid seeing me now, even in private. Is it punishment for something I've done?" Hurt softened the edge of her voice, and her voice caught.

His gaze snapped to her face, and his gut twisted tight. Sweet Neptune, don't let her cry. He didn't think he could bear it. It was hard enough to maintain any distance between them without the screaming need to comfort and hold her coursing through him. He snorted a laugh. Oh, he'd had such luck maintaining his distance so far. He opened the door, and both of them stepped through it.

She obviously misinterpreted his laugh, because her chin came up, and her eyes narrowed. "You had to know I'd want you there last night with Jain in surgery."

"I am not at your beck and call, Doctor Gibbons," he grated out, nearly choking on the words that would wound her.

Wincing, she glanced away, and the light faded from her lovely gray eyes. "I never thought you were. I didn't force any of this on you, Bretton."

"I know." His jaw clenched tight. He did know. He'd wanted everything she had to give and more. It just wasn't meant to be.

A deep breath lifted her breasts, and he made his gaze stay locked on her face. "Then...thank you for saving me. I'm sorry to have troubled you."

Turning, she faded into the crowd. It took every shred of his strength not to call her back, to apologize for hurting her, to apologize for being the man he was. They were just so different. Too different. He curled his fingers into tight balls. If he didn't have the fortitude to stay away from her, then this might make her keep away from him. Cursing himself for being a bastard, he slammed his fist against the nearest wall. He welcomed the pain he so richly deserved as it reverberated up his arm.

Several people turned to stare at him, and he knew word of this would get back to his father and the Senate. For once, he didn't care.

S era curled into a ball in her bed and buried her head under the covers. After she'd run from Bretton, she'd wanted to put as much distance between them as possible. How clearer could he have made himself? He wasn't interested. Sex was all she was good for. It hurt, but she had to accept it. Really, finally accept it. She still ached with the soul-deep pain of it after a night's sleep. Forcing herself to crawl out of bed, she dressed, ate, and walked into her laboratory.

Oeric reported to her lab at the time she'd instructed. She'd canceled the day before because she'd spent a long night in the hospital with Kesuk and the weretigers and weredragons while they waited for news about Jain. The young merman knocked once, stepped through the door, and stood at almost military attention. He didn't touch anything, kept his hands folded behind his back.

She sighed, scrubbing a hand over her forehead. What was she going to do with this man? All her problems lately seemed to revolve around males. She suppressed a growl and pushed to her feet from the stool she sat on.

"Have you ever done any underwater repairs?" She needed out of the city today, needed to *not* see Bretton. Reaching for her wet suit, she tucked it under her arm. Then she grabbed her flippers and her small rebreather from their compartments in the wall. The breathing apparatus had arrived this morning in the tubes that connected the shifting chambers with everyone's personal quarters. Bretton must have gone back for it. She closed her eyes over the pang that clenched her heart.

Oeric blinked at the abrupt question. "Ah, no. But I promise not to get in the way."

A chuckle bubbled up from her throat. "That was the right answer."

"I thought as much."

She nodded and led the way down the corridor to the small dome at the end of the Titan sector. Her two sea skimmers were docked in the dome. One was a single-person skimmer, and the other could hold four. She punched in her authorization code to the second docking hatch. It parted in the middle to reveal the cockpit of the larger skimmer.

Stuffing her gear into the tiny shifting chamber at the rear of the skimmer, she performed the mandatory checks before they could get under way. Oeric sealed the door behind him and then stood to the side and watched her work. She shrugged and ignored him. She'd expected it to feel more...uncomfortable to have him here. The man was enormous, nearly the same size as Kesuk and Nadir—the two largest men she'd ever seen. But Oeric was just calm and silent. After a few moments, she forgot he was there and lost herself in the familiar process.

When she turned, he strapped himself into the copilot's chair. She plopped into the pilot's seat and finished the last of the checks. They both put on the headsets that would allow them to hear over the cold fusion engine—the same power source that fueled everything on Aquatilis. Reaching under the dash, she pulled out a holosheet and handed it to Oeric. His eyes narrowed as he read it. He nodded. "The checklist you just ran through."

"Yep."

"Thank you." He tucked the sheet into the front pocket of his jumpsuit. She waited a beat, expecting him to ask where they were going. He didn't.

She grinned. "We're headed for the sea cow ranches on the rim."

"Manatees and dugongs both prefer the warmer waters that erupt from volcanic vents on the rim. *Sea cow,* or sea cattle, is a misnomer."

"Head of the class."

He leaned against his straps to get a look out the bubble-shaped glass that made up the cockpit of the skimmer. Her personal skimmer was simply a ball of glass with controls and sea-floor sensors on the anchor legs, but this one had a large metal body attached to the rear of the glass that made it look like an underwater version of an Earth hovercopter.

The skimmer propelled them at a speed no merman could match, so she imagined this was the fastest Oeric had ever gone. A boyish look of delight crossed his normally impassive face. It made him look his age, which, after she'd read his personnel file, she now knew to be twenty-two. She smiled in response.

She cued the comm. "Atlantis Skimmer Two to Ariel Ranch, come in please."

The line crackled for a moment before a woman's voice came back. "Sera! It's so good to hear from you again."

"Hi, Nara. I'm just going to run some quick external tests on your systems."

"You can't stay for a meal?"

"I want to check the rest of the ranches. If I hurry, I can get to everyone today."

"Next time, then. And please do stop by on your way back to Atlantis if you have time."

"Will do." As they swooped around the ranch, Sera could make out the large herds of slow swimming sea cow.

Flicking several switches over her head, she powered up the scanners that would sweep the ranch and give her readings on the life-support and biological systems. She cleared her throat and quickly explained to Oeric what she was doing. He nodded but didn't comment. She sighed. Good, he wasn't going to ask a hundred questions. Because it was a standard operation, it was easier to explain than when she was working on an invention or fixing anything.

Her dolphins, Aveta and Sulis, darted around the skimmer in wide arcs. She grinned. "Looks like we have company."

"I'd heard of your pet dolphins." He craned his neck to follow the path of Sulis. "Will they stay with us the entire time?"

"Unlikely, but they have once or twice before. I usually go too fast for them to keep up between ranches, and they get bored and go back to Atlantis by the time they catch up to me at the third or fourth ranch."

"I see." He nodded.

The holoscreen on the skimmer flashed the test results. She flicked the comm controls again. "Atlantis Skimmer Two to Ariel Ranch. All systems are green."

Nara's voice came back immediately. "Thank you, Sera. It's such a relief to have you here to do this now."

"You're welcome. Have a good day, and I'll be back in a few weeks to check again. Send me a burst transmission if you have any problems."

"I will." A cheerful lilt sounded in Nara's voice. "And you'll overnight with us next time."

"I promise." Sera often escaped out to the rim when Atlantis got a bit too constricting for her. They were warm and had a hard-nosed practicality that people who lived in the city had never needed to develop.

Four hours later, she let Oeric run the last scan. The kid was bright and willing to learn. Easy to work with, which was not something she could say of many of the uptight merpeople.

Her comm device crackled, and a soft female voice came through. "Hahn Ranch to Atlantis Skimmer Two. Come in, please."

Sera frowned and cued her headset. "This is Atlantis Skimmer Two. Go ahead, Hahn Ranch."

The woman's tone remained neutral. "I have Ambassador Hahn here. He's asked for permission to come aboard and ride back to Atlantis with you."

Her heart slammed in her chest. Bretton. There was no way to say no, which meant spending time with him in the tight quarters of the skimmer. She was more grateful than ever that she'd brought Oeric with her today. What was Bretton doing out on the rim? "Tell the ambassador we'd be happy to give him a lift. We'll set down a kilometer east of your herds. Have him swim out to meet us."

"Acknowledged. Hahn Ranch, out."

Circling the border of the ranch farthest from Atlantis, Sera looked for a good landing site. Spotting a flat area, she brought the skimmer to a slow halt outside a massive dome on the edge of the rim.

Oeric almost pressed his nose to the glass. "Pacifica," he breathed. "The lost city. After Earth's sun died, the life-support systems were lost, and the scientists couldn't save it. So it was abandoned."

She focused on him, desperate to think of anything but Bretton and the fact that she was going to be confined in this skimmer with him. "Ever been this far out to see it?"

"Once as a boy—I was only able to look in the windows. A child can make the swim in a day, but most of us don't leave the city region very often." His eyes twinkled with excitement.

Keying the landing gear, she set them down just outside the city. "Well, you're in luck. Let's see if I can't get us inside."

"Are you serious?" A huge grin lit his face and made his gold and green eyes dance.

"Of course." Anything, *anything* to keep from being locked in this glass jar with Bretton. But Oeric didn't need to know that.

His forehead wrinkled. "This area is supposed to have had some recent wild sea dragon attacks."

"There's a trident in the back as well as a small harpoon gun. Let me change, and then we can go." She unbuckled the straps, hopped up to walk back to the shifting chamber, and shut the door. A year of practice made it a quick change to shed her jumpsuit and stuff herself into the silver wet suit. She hit the panel to open the door as she sealed the seam on the front of her diving outfit.

Oeric stepped naked into the tiny chamber with her. His clothes lay folded in a neat pile on one of the passenger seats. After a year of being around shifters, she'd grown used to the nudity, but she'd never really enjoyed flashing her ass in public.

"As an unaltered human, I have no way of communicating underwater. Keep any questions limited to those that have a yes or no answer."

"There's a kind of infopad sold at a shop near my grandmother's that could be used to remedy that problem. You'd have to input the answers, but it's an idea."

She nodded. "I'll look into it. Perhaps it can be modified."

It was strange to speak of later dates of taking the young merman with her. Intellectually, she knew that was what having an apprentice meant, but she was so used to doing everything on her own.

Placing her rebreather in her mouth, she took a few deep breaths to get used to breathing in through her mouth and blowing out through her nose. Oeric punched in the code to allow water to fill the small shifting chamber while she strapped on her flippers.

The rush of seawater didn't quite manage to cover the sickening suction and pop of bones as Oeric shifted into his merman form. The tips of his fins brushed against her hand while he grabbed the bars overhead to hold himself up while the last quarter of the chamber filled with water.

He went a horrible shade of pasty white. Her eyebrows arched, and she made a gesture to ask if he was all right. The big man nodded and closed his eyes. *I will be fine. I don't care for confined spaces.*

She shuddered as the water level went over her head and she had to use the rebreather. Yes, she could see how even a mild case of claustrophobia would be a problem in this chamber.

Punching in the release code, she grabbed the harpoon gun and handed Oeric the trident before they exited the skimmer. The rear hatch opened wide, and Oeric snapped his tail to get out first. She wedged herself against the wall to give him room before she followed him out.

He jerked to a stop and lifted the trident, but she snapped a hand around his wrist before he let the weapon loose. Her dolphins had followed them out to Pacifica. The man's muscles relaxed under her grip, and he nodded.

Sera. Oeric. Bretton's smooth voice filled her mind and slid like rough velvet down her nerves just before he rounded the end of the skimmer. She shivered and closed her eyes for a moment.

Oeric bowed at the waist, his tail whipping to keep him at a steady level in the water. *Ambassador. Doctor Gibbons has decided to explore Pacifica.*

Before Bretton could respond, Sera flashed a hand signal to Sulis, wrapped her free arm around his dorsal fin, and let him swim her out to the dome. She held her harpoon gun at the ready while the mermen kept pace beside her. They all pressed their noses to the glass when they reached the central dome. She half feared to see ancient corpses floating in the water inside, but it looked empty. The windowpanes were crusted with purple algae.

Pacifica was roughly half the size of Atlantis. It had been incomplete when she'd left Earth, and she hadn't looked into why it had malfunctioned, because there were so many issues in the populated areas of Aquatilis for her to deal with that Pacifica hadn't been a priority.

As if in answer to her question, Oeric spoke to her telepathically. *The backup systems had never been adequately tested before the survivors from Earth arrived and overflowed Atlantis. Pacifica was overloaded, and when the main system failed, there was nothing else. The unaltered humans drowned in the flood that filled the city.*

Bretton nodded. *It was a sad time for mankind.*

I've always wanted to see the inside. What if the damage was reversible? A quiet yearning filled the young man's telepathic voice. Then he grinned, embarrassment in his eyes that he'd revealed so much.

So he had a fascination for the lost city, did he? Interesting. His excitement was contagious. What if Pacifica could be restored?

Intense longing flooded Sera at the thought. What if she could escape some of the overachieving perfectionists of Atlantis? She'd considered moving to one of the rim ranches before, but they didn't have the lab equipment she needed to work.

And Bretton wouldn't be there.

She squashed that thought. Bretton didn't want her. He'd made it clear in more ways than she could count. She'd just refused to pay attention to it. Until now.

A flash of red light caught her eye. She squinted to see if she could find the source. Nothing. Was it a reflection of some kind? Glancing over at the two men, she didn't see anything red. Bretton was all turquoise and black, while Oeric's tail was green tipped with gold that matched his eyes. And nothing she wore flashed. The utility belt built into her wet suit held several instruments, but none with red lights and none of it should have been powered on.

She tapped Oeric on the shoulder and pointed down to indicate she was going to the base of the dome. He nodded and executed a neat flip in the water. Bretton frowned and followed suit. Compared to a merperson, Sera's own movements were slow and ungainly, but she pushed away any impatience.

If Pacifica had the same architectural plan as Atlantis, there were ducts where the base of the dome met the corridors that spiked out. They were used to fill and drain the shifting chambers. There. The red light emanated from one of the duct's control panels. She pulled from her belt a tool that would help her pry the cover from the duct and let her into the shifting chamber. Brushing more of the purple algae away from the control panel, she blinked when she saw the holoscreen light up at her touch. If the systems had failed at Pacifica, why would it have any power at all? The cold fusion that powered everything on Aquatilis was limitless, but if it had failed, there should be nothing left to generate this panel.

Pacifica should no longer have the capacity to generate this system. Oeric's voice took on the intense curiosity she was used to from other scientists. She would have smiled if her mouth hadn't been full of the rebreather.

She lifted her shoulders in an exaggerated shrug. She had no idea what was going on either. Punching in the disengage code that worked at Atlantis, she hoped it worked here, too. A series of lights blipped on the display and then went black. Damn. She was going to have to manually override the system.

The entire panel lit in blue and orange before the duct cover popped open. She glanced over at Oeric and Bretton, motioning for them to stay put.

No. Bretton sliced a hand through the water.

Oeric shook his head. *There may be sea dragons in there, Doctor.*

She doubted that. The dome looked as though it had been sealed after the initial life-support had failed. Because she had no way of arguing with them, she measured the width of the duct opening and compared it to the width of Bretton's shoulders. He *might* fit, but she doubted it. Oeric wouldn't have a chance.

Oeric's jaw clenched, and she would bet he was thinking about what it would be like to get trapped in that tunnel. She patted his arm and used the side of the duct to pull herself into it. Tucking the harpoon gun close to her chest, she made sure it was ready to use just in case she was wrong about the sea dragons. Her last experience with a tame one was more than enough to make her wary.

Her sex clenched at the memory of what had happened *after* the sea dragon incident. Heat lashed through her body, made her muscles shake so hard she had to stop swimming for a moment. God, the man was a menace to her mental well-being even when he was nowhere near her. It was unfair, because she doubted very much that he had the same difficulties. Her jaw tightened, and she forced herself to push forward and shove Bretton firmly from her mind.

The water inside the duct was dark and cloudy, so she flicked on the lights she'd built into the rebreather. Her heart jolted when something moved ahead. Just a few dangling optic cables. Her pulse still raced as she pushed them out of her way. The end of the tunnel lay ahead. This panel should exit into the shifting chamber where she could let the mermen in. Bracing her free hand on the side of the tunnel, she wriggled in the tight space until she lay on her back. Another control panel flickered above her. This time when she punched in the right code, it responded immediately, and the cover flipped open. She clutched the harpoon gun and kept her finger on the trigger, hoping nothing with sharp teeth awaited her inside.

Nothing moved. She blew a breath out of her nose, and a flurry of bubbles rose. Kicking with her flippers, she entered the wider shifting chamber. Within seconds, she had it open for the waiting Oeric and Bretton. They went through a series of what used to be air locks before they reached the main dome. All of it was filled with water, and all of it still appeared completely functional. Lights automatically flickered to life as they moved through the corridors. The dome would have the central control room that might give her a clue about what had really happened at Pacifica.

Because the systems had *not* completely failed.

The control room door stuck a quarter of the way open after she keyed the holodisplay. She wrapped her hand around the edge to push but couldn't budge it.

Oeric's fingers closed over hers. *If I may?*

Gesturing him forward and deliberately avoiding looking at Bretton, she moved back. Might as well let the young merman's massive size and brute strength count for something. After a few minutes of struggle, his tail gave a hard kick, the muscles in his arms and neck stood out in sharp relief, and the door squeaked open.

Oeric and Bretton crowded into the small room with her. Oeric explored the holo-screens while Bretton stayed in the middle of the room, looking irritated. Because he couldn't do anything to help, or because he didn't want to be here? She couldn't tell...and she refused to care. Damn it.

She started from one end of the room and worked her way to the main controls, running diagnostics on every system in the city. Except for the water inside, everything was operational. She shook her head. It made no sense at all.

Oeric wrapped a hand around her elbow and tugged her over to a panel. He tapped his finger against the screen. *The backup systems are reading incorrectly. To borrow your phrase, I have a theory. What if the backup systems did not fail? What if they never worked properly in the first place?*

She nodded. Either the original systems never worked and someone had screwed up, or they'd been installed incorrectly...and someone had screwed up. Both situations could be remedied. Excitement kicked her hard in the gut. Pacifica might be saved. There should be labs and equipment here she could use. Pointing to a holoscreen, she showed Oeric that she proposed to start pumping the water out of the city. It would start in the main dome and work its way outward to the four quadrants. She pointed to Bretton and let Oeric explain her intentions to him.

Again, she didn't meet that piercing turquoise gaze, but she felt it burn into her back as she swam to the front of the room. She keyed in the command that would push the water out of the city. A deep rumbling vibrated through the walls as the pumps kicked on. The initial drain should take a little over an hour. If the backups were working, she could make it happen in a fraction of that time, but she didn't want to tax the mainframe. And she wanted to look at the backup systems before she left.

Glancing back, she made sure the men understood what they needed to do to prepare for the draining. Oeric closed his eyes for a moment as he shifted back into his human form. His legs kicked to keep him afloat. Fortunately his gill passages worked no matter what form he was in. Bretton's eyes narrowed at her before he shifted as well.

She glanced away, pulled the city schematic up on the large screen in the control room, and pinpointed the location of the systems room. North quadrant dome. Turning, she led the way. The men could probably still swim faster than her, but she had no desire to stare at Oeric's naked backside—among other things—the whole way there. And looking at Bretton's nudity would just heat her to the point where she would be unsurprised if the water around her boiled.

It took them almost no time to assess the problem once they reached the systems room. Oeric's eyebrows arched. *Some fool installed this backwards.*

She cut power to the backup systems so they could safely work with it. Everything on Aquatilis was specifically designed to survive water. She should know—she'd helped design it. If it was used properly. She shook her head at the mistake that had cost so many their lives. Whether the mistake was made out of laziness or sheer idiocy, there was no excuse for it. These people had been desperate after the sun had failed, but cutting corners with safety meant people died.

At her nod, Oeric reached in and reinstalled the system while Sera ran a battery of diagnostic tests. Everything checked out perfectly when Oeric was done. Damn, the kid knew his stuff when it came to working with the domes. The water level finally dropped low enough that she could stand and have her head above it. She sucked an experimental breath through her nose. O2 levels read as normal on the holodisplays, and she couldn't smell any gases. Nothing read as odd either. Oeric met her eyes, and their faces stretched into triumphant grins. "Pacifica lives."

Sera groaned, tugged off her flippers, and strapped them to her utility belt. "You realize this means I have to make a report to the Senate."

"Yes, *we* will." Bretton's voice took on a silken, dangerous edge as he spoke into her ear. She shuddered, lust rushing through her with a force that should no longer surprise her but did. Her nipples beaded tight in her wet suit.

Oeric reached out to pat her back in consolation. "I'll come with you. If nothing else, I'm so big I scare Senator Laddon. He turns and scurries away whenever I approach."

"You're joking." Senator Laddon was one of Bretton's father's closest friends. Some would claim the senator was Cuthbert's puppet.

Oeric gave a negligent shrug. "It might have something to do with a slight accident I had when I was younger. The senator felt the brunt of my fist."

Bretton chuckled, his turquoise eyes dancing. Obviously everyone knew the story except Sera. She grinned. "A slight accident? Do tell."

The young merman rubbed the back of his neck, and a flush raced up his face. "I'd rather not."

She laughed out loud, adrenaline and triumph fizzing in her veins. "Okay then. The water should be completely drained soon, so let's explore a little, check the control room one more time, and get back to the skimmer. We're running late."

Oeric met Bretton's eyes, and some silent communication went on between them. The younger man nodded, turned, and slogged through the waist-high water down the corridor. She angled a glare at Bretton. "You ordered *my* apprentice to leave?"

"He knew it was the healthiest choice for him. I gave no orders."

She rolled her eyes at that sideways logic and pushed through the chilly ocean water to open the first door in the corridor. There was nothing in the room but a few metal crates. It looked like a storage area. The water was dropping rapidly now, wrapping around her calves as she walked to the next door. Bretton passed her to look in the rooms on the opposite side of the corridor.

"Sera." She looked up when Bretton spoke. He motioned her forward. "This room was untouched. No water got inside."

Wading through the ankle-deep water, she approached to see that he was right. Everything inside was dry except the floor where he'd let the water in. She nodded. "Hermetically sealed. We'll probably find a few rooms like this in the city."

Her shoulder brushed his chest as she leaned in, and desire raced over her skin. She swallowed and pressed her thighs together. She felt her sex dampen.

Every time she was near him, he pulled reactions from her whether she was willing or not. She choked on a laugh. When wasn't she willing? She had no resistance when it came to him. Her nipples tightened and chafed against her wet suit. She sped past him, trying to get some physical distance, even if her ability to maintain emotional distance was nonexistent.

Chapter 5

Bretton watched Sera step over the threshold into the sealed room he'd found. Curiosity lit her gray eyes, made them sparkle. His hands fisted at his sides as she slid past him. The smell of her and saltwater caressed his nose. He pulled in a deep breath to capture the sweet scent. She'd not spared him so much as a glance the past hour—had hardly spoken to him.

"What were you doing with Oeric at the rim ranches today?" He bit back a groan when she bent over to examine something, her tight silver suit pulling taut across her lush backside. His nudity would do nothing to hide the effect she had on his cock.

"Maintenance checks."

He waited a beat for her to say more, but she didn't. She seemed to have no problem ignoring him. He spoke through clenched teeth. "I was visiting my aunt and uncle at their ranch."

She made a small humming noise in her throat. "That sounds nice."

Anger whipped through him. He couldn't bear this distance between them. It was intolerable that she would pull away from him. It was irrational, this rage bubbling through him. Imperfect. But he couldn't stop it. And that angered him still more. He had no control—her mere presence stripped it from him.

She seemed so unaffected by him now. It challenged him, made him want to bring her down to this raw, wild level where he'd found himself. He ran his hand over his hair, a slow smile tugging at his lips.

He stepped into the bathing chamber, picked up a tiny tray full of some kind of slippery substance, and dipped his fingers into it. "What is this?"

"Gel soap." She flicked a dismissive glance at his hand.

His brows arched. "*Gel* soap?"

She sighed. "It's similar to the cleansing sand some of the shops in Atlantis sell. Except it doesn't start out rough and then lather. It's slick. Gel."

"Ah." A wicked smile pulled at his lips as he set the tray on a small table near the door. "Interesting things can be done with slick substances."

Her eyebrows lifted, and she finally looked at him, at the erection that curved his cock up to his navel, at the lust he knew was reflected in his eyes. She flushed under his gaze, and he saw her nipples bead tight against the thin fabric of her suit. She released a shaky breath. Relief filled him when he saw the heat and passion he was used to seeing stamped on her features. "We shouldn't. You don't really want this."

"You don't think so?" His hand dropped to stroke the soap over his cock, up and down until it was coated in the slippery gel.

She nodded, her gray gaze following every movement of his fingers as they played over his overheated flesh. "Here?"

"Oh, yes. Here." His free hand shot out, and he keyed the panel to shut and lock the door. "Undress. Now."

Her fingers slid down the seam of her suit. "For once, Ambassador, I'm overdressed for the occasion."

His chuckle rumbled in his chest. "Come here."

"I'll come anywhere you want me to." She wriggled her hips to ease the tight wet suit down her legs.

His gaze swept down her in an appreciative glance. She shivered in response. Her nipples tightened further.

He crooked a finger, and she stepped forward to press her breasts to his chest. She shifted her torso to drag the hard tips over his flesh. He groaned.

His mouth swooped down to kiss her, running his tongue along the seam of her lips until she opened for him. He plunged into her mouth, making her moan when he scraped his teeth over her lower lip. He loved the sounds she made, loved to make her cry out with need for him.

His palm rose to cup her heavy breast. She whimpered when he flicked his nail over the nipple and then pinched it. Her thigh lifted to wrap around his hip. The satin feel of her skin on his, the friction as her soft belly rubbed over his cock, made him groan. He gripped her leg and pushed it down to the floor again.

She broke the kiss, panting. Her pupils were dilated with passion. "I thought I was supposed to come."

"You will, fire fin. I promise." He spun her around and pushed her forward over the table. He pulled her arms behind her back and gripped both her wrists in his hands. He'd explode if she touched him, and he wanted to savor her. Show her how much he craved her, even if he could never allow himself to claim her publicly. A hot band of emotion tightened around his chest.

Tossing her wet hair out of the way, she glanced over her shoulder at him. "What are you doing?"

"Turn around." He slapped her ass. She jerked, her silver eyes widening. Oh, yes. He wanted to savor every moment with her. He slipped his fingers between her legs, dipping into the hot wetness there. She gasped, pushing herself into his touch. Neptune's blood, she was so responsive. He loved that, but he wanted more from her. "Turn around, fire fin."

He pulled his hand away until she obeyed. Her hips wriggled back, trying to get closer to him. "Please, Bretton."

"I always give you pleasure, don't I, fire fin?" His palm cracked across her backside again.

"*Yes.*"

He dipped his fingers inside her again. She'd grown hotter, wetter. He grinned and pulled back to spank her harder. His palm heated with each smack, as did the soft cheek of her ass. Her hips danced with each strike until she screamed and wriggled against the hold he had on her wrists. "Oh, yes, Bretton. Please, please, please," she chanted.

He scooped some of the gel soap into his hand and moved to stroke between the smooth globes of her ass. She froze, her breath shuddering out when he pressed the soap into her tight anus.

"I'm going to fuck you here, slide in deep, and you'll still beg for more, won't you?" He gritted his teeth over a groan. His cock throbbed painfully. He needed to be inside her. Now.

She nodded, sobbing in gulps of air. Her muscles shook beneath his hands. "Please, Bretton. I need more."

Working the soap in deep, he made sure she was slick enough to take him easily. He had no desire to harm her. He rubbed the remaining soap up and down his hard cock before he stepped forward to push the head inside her ass. His jaw clenched at the hot feel of her closing around his flesh. He waited for a moment, letting her adjust. When her hips gave an impatient wiggle, he grinned and shoved deeper in small thrusts until he was embedded to the hilt in her backside. The muscles gripped his dick so tight he groaned at the ecstasy of it. Fire burned through his veins, robbing him of coherent thought. Only Sera had ever been able to do this to him. Strip him of control. He shuddered, fighting the need to come hot and hard inside her.

"Bretton. More," she breathed.

"Yes." Releasing her wrists, he placed her hands against the table and covered them with his. Pinned her in place. Perfect. Just where he wanted to be, over her, inside her, inseparable. It was so right and so wrong. He shoved away the thought and focused on her. He wanted her to scream for him.

Withdrawing, he slid back into her ass slowly. She whimpered and lifted her hips to meet him. The silk of her skin pressed to his chest, and he loved the feel of it as they moved together.

Her fingers laced with his, and she squeezed tight. "Harder. Faster. *Now.*"

His cock slammed forward inside her, the slickness of the gel making him slide smoothly in and out. The drag of flesh as her muscles gripped him made him groan low in his throat. He wanted to move slower, but his body demanded he listen to Sera. Harder. Faster. Heat spiraled tighter and tighter in his belly. His hips slapped against the curve of her backside, and their breathing panted out in harsh gasps. Sweat dampened their skin until their bodies sealed together. "We fit so perfectly, fire fin. I crave you."

"Bretton." Sera sobbed beneath him, twisting her body as they moved. Her muscles locked tight around him as she came. "I love you. Oh, God. I love you."

"Sera," he breathed. He kissed her shoulder. Sweet Neptune, how he treasured her. Her words sliced straight to his heart, clouding his mind. He had no choice, no control—his hips bucked as he buried himself inside her again and again until he froze, shuddering as orgasm dragged him under.

Perfect. Nothing had ever been this perfect. They lay there for long moments, nothing breaking the silence in the small room except their heaving breaths. The sweat dried on their skin, and he closed his eyes to hold on to this moment with her. She shifted beneath him, so he levered himself up and pulled his still semi-hard cock from her ass. They groaned together.

He lifted her up and swung her into the shower. Pressing the panel, he started the hot spray. She wriggled away from him to wash herself off. He watched her intently, but she wouldn't meet his gaze, wouldn't look at him. Was this how it felt for her when he had sex with her and then walked away? It hit him like a fist to the gut. Guilt slid down his spine. Sweet Neptune, he'd hurt her. He'd just never understood how much.

He couldn't stand the distance between them, but as painful as he found it, he knew he deserved it. She dressed in tense silence, neither of them willing to talk about what had happened between them. The unspoken arrangement that had carried them through the past Turn was broken, but he had no idea what they would become in the future. *Nothing* was the right answer, the one that ensured the life and career he'd always imagined for himself. *Everything* was the answer his soul demanded. He swallowed, dragged a hand through his hair, and tightened the thong that held it back.

When they exited the room and rounded a corner in the corridor, they ran into Oeric. Sera smiled at him, and ugly jealousy twisted through Bretton. He'd just had her in his arms, and bitter envy ate at him. Other than the slight arch of a brow, Oeric pretended not to notice their disheveled appearance, turned around to precede them, and started opening doors along the corridor back to the main dome. "We must be in the laboratory quadrant, Doctor. This one is an exact replica of your current quarters."

They peeked around him to see he was correct. That meant Pacifica had a layout opposite of Atlantis, where the lab corridor was in the southern sector. Interesting.

The water had dropped to almost nothing, so it was easier to move as they went. Oeric opened another door and then slapped a hand to the holoscreen to shut it again. His face went ghostly pale.

"What's wrong?" Sera surged ahead to look.

He shook his head, his big body blocking her when she tried to reach for the panel. She paused and tilted her head up at his. "They missed a body, huh?"

A sharp nod was her only answer.

"You look a little green around the gills, Oeric." A sassy grin flashed across her face.

He rolled his eyes, his shoulders relaxing when he saw she wasn't going to insist on looking, and kept going. By the time they reached the main dome, there was no water left, but the ceiling dripped in steady streams, and clumps of purple algae dropped onto their heads. They did their best to dodge it, but the stuff covered every surface, so there wasn't much they could do to avoid it.

Bretton lagged behind to try to get a grip on himself. This was the first time Sera had turned away from him after sex. It had left him shaken. He'd never doubted she was *his*, and now his arrogance mocked him. She'd chosen him, but nothing said she couldn't make a different choice. Hadn't he done everything he could to break her of her need for him? Tried to convince her all he'd ever wanted from her was sex? Now he stopped to consider that perhaps she wasn't the only one emotionally invested in their relationship. Not just as a friend or lover but as more. It wasn't sex with a compatible personality. It was...more.

And where did that leave him with his career? Would she continue to accept that he couldn't claim her publicly? He doubted it. Breaking her heart as often as he had just might have killed all that sweet love she'd once showered on him. And he'd been so unworthy of it. Of her.

She laughed when a large clump of algae splattered down Oeric's face and chest. He swiped it away and flung it at her.

"Hey!" She ran for the main control center, narrowly missing his next throw. "You're supposed to be respectful of your elders."

He followed her in. "Have a care, or you'll begin to sound like Counselor Hahn."

"Ha. See? I'm not the only one who thinks he's absurd." Bretton rolled his eyes and fought a smile at the sentiment but froze outside the door at Oeric's next words.

"Hardly. There's a serious break between the old guard who run the Senate and the younger generation who want more independence and free thought."

It was true, but how would Sera respond to such a bald statement? Bretton tried to balance himself between the two extremes. Unless he played by the current regime's rules, he'd never get the power to make changes for the younger citizens of Aquatilis. It was only recently that he'd come to understand just how much that limited his ability to grow as a person. Even if he couldn't gain perfection—as Sera claimed—he believed in the importance of constant self-improvement. And he was no longer certain he'd chosen the right path to better himself.

Sera's voice dropped until he had to strain to hear her. "My coming along to question everything the Senate says didn't help much, did it?"

Oeric grunted. "It depends entirely on which side of the argument you're on."

"Does Bretton know your political views?"

"I don't hold them close, but I'm nowhere near the most vocal opponents of Hahn."

"*Cuthbert* Hahn."

"Perhaps. Thus far, the younger Hahn dances to the Senate's tune."

"Bretton is no one's puppet." Bretton had told Sera some rather biting things about the Senate when they were in private. If it wasn't for him, the Senate would have vacillated with the perfect path to follow when Varad had shown up on his maiden trading voyage.

Bretton's actions made him the only choice for the new ambassadorial corps, even though he was significantly younger than anyone else allowed in a position of power.

Oeric continued on as if she hadn't spoken. "We need to stop perfecting the old and start progressing toward the new. We've stagnated too long."

Bretton doubted she could agree more, but she had to know they were on dangerous political ground, and for once she kept her mouth shut. The irony didn't escape him that now that she wanted to put some distance between them, his cautionary message had sunk in. He heard her sigh. "Well, let's do some final checks and go dance for the Senate."

Oeric lapsed back into his customary silence. Bretton swept a last glance around the algae-encrusted main dome before he stepped around the corner to enter the control room. It would take a substantial amount of work to make Pacifica a viable settlement, but if Sera said it was possible, then it was. Now they just had to convince the Senate.

B retton clenched his jaw when they entered the Senate chambers a few hours later. A flurry of whispers erupted throughout the room. Sera rounded the corner to come in behind Oeric and Bretton. She'd insisted they stop in their quarters to change into their best clothing for this meeting because she didn't want something as foolish as their manner of dress to dissuade the Senate from listening to them.

His breath had seized and his heart had stopped when he'd seen her. She'd put on the gown he'd commissioned from the Mermaid's Purse. He'd been right. She looked phenomenal. The dress cupped her soft curves with the kind of intimacy reserved for a lover. For *him*. It made the deep red of her hair gleam like the fire fin he called her. Her eyes glowed as if they'd been made of silver as she took the podium before the Senate. Her giant assistant stood just behind and to the right of her.

"Doctor Sera Gibbons," the Senate secretary intoned. Every political official on the planet was in this room, from the chancellor of the Senate to Elia and his father. They all leaned forward to see what kind of commotion Sera would cause this time.

She took a deep breath that lifted her breasts. He suppressed a groan—she needed to stop doing that. "Counselors. Senators. Chancellor Pell. On a routine check of the rim ranches, Oeric Fane, Ambassador Bretton Hahn, and I decided to explore the lost city of Pacifica. We found it was not quite as lost as history claims. The city can be restored and house citizens of Aquatilis."

A few murmurs went through the room, and Chancellor Pell raised her hand for silence. Senator Laddon broke in. "Who gave you permission to initiate such an exploration?"

Sera's eyes flashed, and Bretton braced himself for the sarcasm that such a look usually preceded. It didn't come. "No one, Senator. There are no restrictions on exploring any part of the planet. Nor is there a law that says I can't use my skills as a mechanical engineer to restore any equipment that belongs to the citizens of Aquatilis." Her gaze swept the group of political officials, pinning each of them in place. "I realize you may be wary of such a change. Pacifica failed once, and people died, so many tests would need to be run before the city could be repopulated. However, even with the careful measures you've taken to control population size, the people of Aquatilis will someday overcrowd Atlantis. With any luck, the four planets will have recovered enough technology by the time Pacifica reaches capacity to be able to build new cities."

The rumble of negative comments that erupted drowned out whatever Sera tried to say.

Bretton folded his hands behind his back and stepped forward to capture the room's attention. "The point is we will need Pacifica. Perhaps not now, but in the future. While we have the expertise of Doctor Gibbons to recover the city, we should take advantage. She will not live forever, Senators. It is something to consider."

"Thanks so much for the reminder," Sera muttered as he passed her. She lifted a glass of water to her lips to cover her words.

He fought a grin. Neptune's blood, the woman kept him on his toes. *Someone needs to help them come to a decision before you expire of old age.*

She choked on the sip of water she'd taken. Oeric reached over to pat her on the back. Jealousy whipped through Bretton that the other man was allowed to touch her so nonchalantly.

He turned back to the Senate, tamping down the envy. Chancellor Pell brushed her silver hair away from her cheek and spoke up. "I agree with you, Ambassador Hahn. My question is this: who will settle Pacifica? Many fear the stories about the lost city. I won't force our citizens to relocate there."

"There are those of us in the younger generation who might appreciate the hard work and adventure of a settler's life." Oeric's deep voice filled the wide room, and every single person froze to stare at him.

The young man made an excellent point. Many senators would find it advantageous to rid their sectors of political dissidents by sending them to a new province. Make them someone else's problem. And whoever took leadership responsibilities of Pacifica certainly had his or her work cut out for them. Bretton didn't envy them.

Chancellor Pell drew a breath. "The Senate will form a subcommittee to discuss this matter more fully. In the meantime, Doctor Gibbons and her assistant will continue restoring the city to working order. The Senate will require weekly reports on this matter."

Sera winced, and Bretton knew she dreaded the idea of speaking before the Senate so often. He may not be able to claim her as his own, but he could help her with this. He cleared his throat. "I'm certain Doctor Gibbons will provide detailed *written* reports as often as the Senate would like."

The chancellor's lips twitched, but she inclined her head and turned to speak to a counselor on her left. The session broke, and everyone stood to leave.

S era pushed back her hair and watched Oeric's eyes follow the ambassador who'd just returned from Harena. What was her name? After a moment it came to her. Elia Iden. Her orange and red hair was distinctive. When she shifted, she'd probably look like a fancy goldfish from Earth. Very pretty.

Folding her arms, Sera cocked a hip against the railing that separated the audience from the senators. "So, you have a jones for Elia."

"A jones?"

"A hankering. A longing. An addiction."

Fierce intensity filled his gaze. "Addiction. Yes. That's an excellent word to describe it."

"I understand."

He nodded. "With Ambassador Hahn."

"Yeah." She sighed, and they both watched the objects of their affection schmooze with the senators. Jealousy squeezed her heart when Bretton put a casual arm around Elia's shoulder. "A damn shame, isn't it?"

A rough chuckle was her answer before he offered her his arm and gave her a formal bow. He was surprisingly graceful for such a big man. "Shall we, Doctor Gibbons? Pacifica's restoration awaits."

She looped her arm through his. "We have plans to make. Let's get on with it."

Exiting the main chamber, they were accosted by several young mermen. The news of Pacifica had spread like wildfire and, as Oeric had predicted, many younger merpeople were interested in settling the lost city.

She wished Bretton were here to talk to them because, no matter how opinionated they might be, neither she nor Oeric were much in the way of orators. She'd used up every molecule of her diplomacy with her little speech to the Senate. And Bretton still had to step in and save her. Both she and Oeric heaved a sigh of relief when the men left.

"This way. It will take us directly to the Titan sector." Oeric lead her into a narrow side corridor.

She fought a groan when Bretton and Elia stepped into the hallway as well. Bretton's eyes dropped to Oeric and Sera's linked arms. She lifted her chin and stared him down. He didn't want her for anything other than a quick bout of sex, so he could stuff it about who she spent time with. Something flashed in his gaze before he looked away.

Elia smiled brightly, her red, orange, and gold hair catching the light as she moved. "Ambassador Hahn and I were just discussing our interest in relocating to Pacifica."

Sera's heart tripped hard against her ribs. Oh, God. Pacifica looked less and less like a refuge. It had never occurred to her that Bretton might want to live there as well. He was a politician, and political movers and shakers should be in Atlantis. But Oeric said Pacifica wasn't that far to swim. She bit back a whimper. She couldn't do it. She *could not* watch Bretton find a more suitable mate. Someone as unlike Sera as possible. Pacifica just wasn't far enough to escape that, and she wasn't strong enough to endure that kind of pain.

For Oeric's sake, she hoped Bretton didn't choose Elia, but for Sera, it didn't matter who he picked. He wouldn't pick her, and that was the only thing she needed to know.

She had to leave. Not just Atlantis but Aquatilis. It might be cowardly to run, but she knew herself well enough to know what she could handle and what she couldn't. She needed to talk to Varad. He'd once offered her a place in the Vesperi palace, and they were the second-most technologically advanced people. Maybe she would be happy there. Or less tormented by the daily spectacle of Bretton with another woman.

"I'd be happy to discuss it with you, Ambassador." Oeric stepped away from Sera to offer his arm to the other woman.

"Call me Elia." She smiled, placed her hand in the crook of his elbow, and the two moved off down the corridor.

Bretton and Sera watched the other couple until they disappeared at the other end of the hallway. He straightened his tunic and put on his coolest diplomatic demeanor. "Well, that went well."

Her nostrils flared at his sudden formality when he'd just bent her over a table in an abandoned city. "Why do you insist on being such a *cold fish*?"

Anger sent sparks shooting through his turquoise gaze. "Cold, am I? You didn't think so just hours ago. I believe you screamed and begged for more."

Her jaw clenched. "That's just sex. We're in private, Bretton. That's the only time I see the side of you that thinks I'm *slightly* better than pond scum. The rest of the time... Well, I'm good enough to fuck but not for anything else, isn't that right?"

"Sera, you know my position—"

"Right. Of course." Tears filled her eyes. "Why do I even bother? It's hopeless."

"Fire fin, please. Try to understand."

"I understand. That doesn't make it hurt any less." She swallowed. "Will it even matter to you when I give up and try to find someone else? Someone who *likes* me."

"I like you."

"Not enough."

"Will you turn to Oeric?"

Her eyes popped wide, and pure rage flashed through her. "Oeric?"

His chin dipped in a sharp nod. "You seem to be growing very close."

"You *insisted* that I work with him."

"*I know that.* You think I don't know?"

She shook her head, tears slipping down her cheeks. "You don't want me to love you, but you don't want me to love anyone else either. You can't have it both ways, Bretton. How did you put it? *I'm not at your beck and call.*"

"Damn you to Hades."

"I'm already there. You don't want me, Bretton. So leave me in peace."

"Not want you?" Molten anger exploded in his gaze. "I can't stop wanting you no matter what I do."

He backed her up against the wall and didn't stop until her breasts crushed against his chest. They both groaned. "Wh-what are you doing?"

"You're a genius, Sera. What do you think I'm doing?" His fingers gathered her dress until it bunched around her waist. She shivered at the sensuous slide of saltwater silk on her bare skin.

"We're in *public.*" Shifters didn't bother with underwear, so she wore nothing under the gown. She'd stripped out of her wet clothing and grabbed the first proper thing she could find. The Mermaid's Purse had delivered the dress the day before, so it had still hung from a high shelf, and she'd thrown it on before she'd run for the Senate chambers.

His fingertips danced over her thighs, making her sex flood with moisture. He chuckled. "Since when has that been a problem for you?"

This was madness and completely unlike him. A bitter little laugh spilled from her mouth. "Anyone could walk out here and see this. That kind of scandal would end your precious career."

"Unlikely. The Senate session is over. No one is coming out. No one except us." His hand slipped between her legs to stroke her pussy. She knew he'd find her wet and more than ready for whatever his pleasure was. "Ah, not as resistant as you sound, are you?"

"When have I ever resisted? You're the one who—"

His lips slammed down over hers, his tongue shoving past her teeth and into her mouth. She moaned, her nipples going rock hard.

They moved together in an angry rush of passion and pain, lips, tongues, and teeth sucking and nipping at each other's flesh. She broke away and threw her head back, gasping for breath and holding on for dear life to the crumbling edges of her control.

She should resist, should push him away and run as fast as her shaky legs would carry her, but she couldn't. Time enough to go without him when she was gone. One last time, she needed it, and she was going to take it. When this moment of insanity passed and she told him she was leaving, he'd never touch her again. The mere thought ripped at her heart, but she shoved it away to focus on this moment with him. She'd enjoy while they lasted the sensations only he could wrench from her.

One more wild ride in his arms.

Slipping her hand between them, she jerked open the front of his pants, and reached in to stroke his hard cock. He grunted and spanned her hips with his big hands, lifting her against the wall until their sexes aligned. She wrapped her thighs around his flanks and pulled him as close as she could. Her eyes pinched closed, and she focused on the heat rushing through her veins while her heart pounded in her chest.

"Look at me, Sera. I want those pretty gray eyes on me when I fuck you."

She choked, pure fire burning through her when she opened her eyes to obey him. "Please, Bretton."

The head of his cock nudged her slick pussy lips. She whimpered, tightening her legs around his waist. His breath feathered over her ear, making her shiver in response. "Tell me how you want me, fire fin."

"You want me to beg?" Anger shot through her. He didn't want her, but he wanted her to beg for him. She narrowed her eyes at him.

"I want to hear it." He swallowed, a shudder running through him. "Tell me."

She arched her hips, rolling the bulbous tip of his dick in her wetness. "Doesn't my body tell you everything you want to hear, Bretton? Can't you feel it?"

His breath hissed out. "Fire fin."

"Fuck me now, Bretton." She held his gaze with hers and twisted her hips against him. The hot press of his flesh to hers made her want to scream. "Hard and fast. *Now.*"

He slammed deep into her pussy, and she almost came. She was so wet, so ready. His palms curved over her buttocks, lifting her into his pounding thrusts. His movements bordered on rough. Oh, God, she loved it when he went wild.

Burying his face against her neck, he slammed inside her again and again while she shuddered from the impact. He licked her flesh, sucking kisses along her throat and collarbone. The scent of sex and *him* filled her nose, and it made her burn hotter, pushed her higher. She buried her fingers in his hair and clenched them in the long ebony strands. She pulled hard enough to feel him wince against her throat. He bit her neck in response. Hard. Just the way she liked it.

"*Bretton*!" she cried. Her sex fisted tight around his thrusting cock. Tears welled in her eyes to slide down her cheeks.

He panted, and the turquoise began to spread from his irises. "I love my name on your lips, fire fin."

"Bretton." It was so good with him, so amazing. Why couldn't he see it? Why couldn't he love her the way she loved him, needed him, craved him? Lust and despair twisted inside her until she sobbed for breath.

"Sera?"

She shook her head wildly, clenching her walls around his dick hard enough to make him groan. She moved her hips with his, faster and faster, deeper and deeper until they both panted. Sweat rolled down her temples, and her muscles shook.

"Make me come, Bretton. I want you. I want you so much." *I love you.* But she couldn't make herself say it out loud again. Her body could have him, but her heart never would.

His hand dropped between them until his fingers rolled over her clit. She froze, her back bowing before her hips snapped in hard thrusts on his cock. Tingles raced over her skin, and molten heat followed in its wake. She came in a rush so hot it left her weak and shaking in his arms.

He ground his pelvis against hers, and she moaned, the after effects of orgasm making her pussy clench again. His eyes bled to pure turquoise before they slid shut. A muscle twitched in his cheek, and he froze, his hot cum filling her. He groaned. "Sweet Neptune.

Fire fin."

She arched her head back against the wall, tears leaking from the corners of her eyes. Swallowing, she waited for her breathing to slow, for her heart to stop pounding, for her muscles to stop shaking. For the world to stop spinning. God, this was it. It was over. If she stayed, it would hurt her to a point she couldn't recover from. For his sake, for her own sake, she had to leave. They both knew she wasn't what he wanted, who he needed. And the only way to stop it was to go.

Forever.

Chapter 6

Something was wrong. He knew it. Sera had been too quiet the last two days. Avoiding him. And he hadn't been able to speak to her, because he'd spent much of his days closeted with his father and the Senate, negotiating final details of trade treaties with the other planets and deciding how best to settle Pacifica. He loved the bartering, the challenge of politics, but it now left him unfulfilled. He missed Sera. He wanted her, but from what he could gather, she'd been visiting extensively with the Alysians and Vesperi. He didn't want to interrupt her last few days with Jain, so he reined in his impatience. Barely.

Still, it worried him. It wasn't like her to be so willing to stay away from him. The last time he'd had her, against the wall outside the Senate chamber, burned into his mind, haunted his dreams at night, made his cock twitch in his pants.

He approached her quarters, tapped his knuckles against her laboratory door, and waited for her to call out, "Come in."

Her lab was in more than its usual chaos. Every shelf and cubbyhole seemed to have been emptied onto her worktable. "Going to Pacifica?"

"No." She stuffed several mechanical devices into a bag.

"Oh." His eyebrows arched when she said nothing more. "Then, where—"

"I spoke to Varad." Her gray eyes were shadowed, her vibrant red hair pulled back in a tight plait. With no pause, she met his gaze and announced, "I'm leaving."

The news hit him like a blow to the chest, and for a moment he couldn't breathe. No. No, no, no, *no*. He opened his mouth and shut it again. A muscle ticked in his jaw, and pain lanced through his chest. He tried desperately to reason with himself and not to give in to the need to bury himself inside her until she knew she could never part from him. But that was wrong, irrational, imperfect. Selfish. She was not happy here. It was best that she go. She was a temptation he didn't need. She confused things, confused his purpose. What he should want and what he actually wanted twisted whenever she was nearby. But losing her would be bad for Aquatilis. Any personal feelings he had in the matter shouldn't factor in. He knew he lied to himself, but what else could he do? She was leaving, leaving Aquatilis, leaving *him*. He swallowed and tried to come up with a suitable response.

A dry chuckle rippled from him. He'd had a great deal of trouble coming up with "suitable responses" since she'd crash-landed in his life. "The Senate will be upset to see you go."

"The Senate." All lingering traces of hope vanished from her eyes, a light that had been just for him winking out. She gave a slight nod. "I see. I think I finally see."

"No. You don't." But he couldn't allow her to see either. If she knew how desperately he craved her, he would never be rid of her. This was the first sign she'd ever shown of not pressing the relationship between them. If it caused him pain to see her love turn cold, he had no one to blame except himself. "What about Pacifica?"

"Oeric can handle it. He's more than capable of restoring and maintaining the domes. Inventing might be a problem, but he can do what you need." Her shoulder lifted in a shrug.

He balled his fists. "He's a child."

"I was fifteen when I received my doctorates, Bretton." She arched a brow. "You can understand how my perspective is different than yours."

He swallowed. What more could he say? "I hope you enjoy Vesperi. Or Harena. Or Alysius. Or wherever you're going."

"I'm going to try to reestablish as much of the technology as possible on all the planets." She pulled in a deep breath, and his gaze again dropped to the lush curve of her breasts. "Metals to build with are going to be scarce soon, so mining operations are vital. That means a solution to Alysius's predator problem needs to be reached."

"I am certain Lord Kesuk will be grateful for the assistance."

She laughed, but there was no humor in the sound. "No, he won't. He'll be glad to get rid of the threat to his people, but I doubt I'll fit well on any planet. If I can't make it on Aquatilis..."

Her shoulder lifted in a small shrug, and she turned away to continue packing her tools and gadgets. The rooms would be as empty of clutter as they had been before she came. He regretted complaining about the mess now. The whole city would feel deserted without her. He'd taken it so for granted that she would always be there that he couldn't even imagine a time when she wasn't.

Stumbling back, he fled her quarters. He walked down the winding corridors of the city, blind to everything but the turmoil of his thoughts. Leaving. She was leaving. It ricocheted through his mind, taunting him with the finality, with the lack of all hope. No more Sera. Not ever. Gone.

Neptune help him.

Word of Sera's imminent departure spread through the city, and the chancellor herself insisted on speaking to Sera to convince her to stay. The meeting was a failure—probably the first in the older woman's entire political career. A week crawled by, and Bretton forced himself to stay away, to complete his duties as head ambassador, but his heart was no longer in it.

His father noticed and came to his quarters the day of Sera's departure. Bretton had assigned Elia to see the trading party off. He couldn't do it. If Sera wanted to go, he wouldn't make her stay...so he removed himself from the temptation to beg her not to leave. Misery dragged at his very bones, and a weight had settled on his chest that would not let him breathe through the agony of it.

Cuthbert folded his hands behind his back and paced the length of Bretton's quarters. "Son, I've been thinking about your difficulties with the human lately, and I think I've found a solution."

Bretton's eyebrows arched. There must be some mistake. His father suddenly wished to help him with Sera? "Oh?"

"You need a mate."

"Do I?"

"Yes, a nice mermaid to take your mind off of one so unsuitable as Doctor Gibbons."

A bark of laughter wrenched from Bretton's chest. Of course. Not help keeping Sera, help getting rid of her. He doubted it was possible. She'd found her way into his heart, and he'd never be free of her. He didn't want to be. He pressed his fingers to his eyes, and his hair slid forward to cover his face. He hadn't been able to bring himself to tie it back this morning. Sera liked it loose.

What was he going to do without her? The estrangement of the past seven days—knowing it would be the last she ever spent on his world—had ripped at his soul. What if he never saw her again, held her again, fucked her again?

For perhaps the first time he saw what his life would be without her. He'd become his father. Bitter, entrenched in his beliefs, sacrificing for his career the one woman who'd ever mattered. What hollow alternative was that? Why had he never recognized this before?

He'd been so focused on preserving the life he had, never straying from the path before him, that he'd missed how fundamental a change she'd wrought inside him. What life would he have now with no Sera to brighten it? One that would be empty of joy, one that would eventually wear away to nothing more than a bleak existence. No Sera meant no more wild passion, no more days of anticipating the night with her soft body wrapped around his. She challenged him, infuriated him, made him think, made him laugh. He needed her. He loved her.

Neptune save him, he loved her so much it strangled the breath from him. And he was letting her walk away from him forever. He knew if she boarded that ship, it was over. Done. Whether he saw her again or not, she would never be his.

No. A thousand times no. He couldn't do it. He wouldn't lose her. He knew what he risked by going to her now. He'd lose everything else. His position of influence, his career in politics. Unlike his father, he couldn't imagine it making him bitter and cold. Cold was life without Sera—everything else was a pale substitute for the real moments of sheer perfection he found in her embrace.

"Father, I want you to know that I'm mating with Sera." Bretton shoved himself to his feet. No more waiting, no more hesitating. He'd already hurt her so much with his inability to let go of his dogged need to follow in his father's footsteps. Could she forgive him? His heart clutched tight. Whatever it took, he would keep her.

Cuthbert's face mottled to a dark, ugly red. "That is a mistake."

"Then it's my mistake to make." Bretton shrugged, grabbed a satchel, stuffed a few changes of clothes in it along with a sheaf of Vesperi monetary units, and raced for the door.

His father blocked his path. "Bretton—"

Bretton fisted his fingers in Cuthbert's tunic and hauled him up until they stood nose to nose. "I love her, Father. That's the end of the discussion. I understand if you don't approve."

He set his father aside, slipped out the door, and ran for the dock.

"Bretton!"

"**S**era, wait!"

Sera turned to watch Bretton race around the last bend in the corridor that led to the docking bay. His hair danced in wild disarray around his shoulders, hanging loose to his waist. Her eyebrows arched. He never wore his hair down, he never ran, he never shouted.

Alarm streaked through her. Had someone died? What could possibly have happened? She'd never seen him look so out of control in public. After handing Oeric a small crate full of her equipment, she stepped away from the group loading the last shipment onto the cargo skimmer.

"It's about damn time," Nadir growled, taking the crate from Oeric.

"What are you talking about?" Sera's gaze darted from Bretton to the rest of the group. Jain, Mahlia, Ketryn, and even Elia looked unsurprised by Bretton's arrival. Sera wished she could share their nonchalance. She willed numbness into her body. She didn't want to deal with this, didn't want to see him again. The last week had been miserable, but she'd survived. She'd keep on surviving. Without him. Agony tore through her soul, and she gritted her teeth to keep from crying out.

Why, *why* did he have to come now? She closed her eyes tight. Couldn't he just let her leave in peace? Wasn't he the one who liked things perfect and cordial in public? They couldn't get much more *public* than a loading dock full of merpeople and an off-world trading party.

When she opened her eyes, Bretton stood before her panting. God, he was so beautiful. She would miss him so much.

Tarkesh snorted, drawing Sera's gaze as he flicked invisible dust from his sleeve. "We were running out of ways to stall, Hahn."

"My servants were considering mutiny, I'm certain. I would have held you accountable, of course." A small, satisfied smile played over Varad's face.

Kesuk just rolled his eyes and grunted, "Mermen." Then he easily slung the carton he'd been struggling with into the skimmer's loading bay. Or perhaps he'd been *pretending* to struggle.

"Sera."

Her gaze swung back to Bretton. Her genius intellect was having difficulty processing what was going on. Everyone seemed to know something she couldn't quite grasp. "Why are you here?"

He looked dumbfounded for a moment before he dropped the pack he was carrying to the floor. "Can't you guess?"

"No. I'm tired of playing games, Bretton. Just say what you have to say so I can go."

"Fire fin." His fingers lifted to stroke her cheek, and she flinched away. God, he couldn't touch her. She would lose control, and all the pain and grief and heartache he'd caused her would come pouring out. In public. Where it would embarrass him. His hand wilted back to his side. "I made a mistake, fire fin. Many, many mistakes. I was a fool, and I hurt you, and I don't want to lose you, and I'm so very sorry."

A harsh laugh bubbled up, and tears welled in her eyes. "Exactly which part of the last year has been your biggest mistake, Bretton? It's *always* a mistake. You fuck me when you're scared, you fuck me when you're angry. You fuck me when you're imperfect."

He winced. "That's unnecessarily crude, Sera."

"But true." She sniffed, wiped the tears from her cheeks, and set her chin. "I'm not going to be your excuse. Like I said, I can't play these games anymore. You want me, you don't want me. I'm good enough for sex, but God forbid I even *speak* to you in public if it's not directly related to your job."

"I love you." The words tumbled from his mouth, and instead of the intense joy she'd always anticipated in hearing those words from a man she was in love with, she felt only anger. Bitter rage that he would wait until she'd given up to change his mind. It was just more of the same. He liked her one minute and brushed her off the next.

She couldn't do it anymore. Her heart wasn't strong enough. "I can't be who you want. We both know that. I'm rude and opinionated and imperfect."

"And I love you for it."

"Stop." She held up a hand. "Just...stop."

"I can't. You know better than anyone how much I tried to stop, how much I didn't want to love you, need you, *crave* you. But I do. *I love you.*"

A tear streaked down her cheek. "And that's a mistake, too, I'm sure."

His palms came up to cup her cheeks, his thumb stroking away her tear. "Don't say that. Don't ever say that. Loving you is the wisest thing I've ever done. *Denying* it was the mistake."

"I don't know how to believe you. You've always been so sure we were wrong for each other." Her fingers curled into the fabric of his shirt, holding him close when she should pull away. Another tear leaked from the corner of her eye. "And now that I'm literally moments away from getting on a ship to leave, you have an inexplicable change of heart."

"Not inexplicable. And not a change of heart. The thought of losing you forever was what it took to make me admit what I've felt all along. It's why I could never stop myself from touching you, kissing you." His lips brushed hers, and she shuddered in reaction. The heat of his mouth burned her flesh, lit a slow fire that spread to her belly, dampened her sex. His fingers wrapped around her wrists, holding her to him. Despair cinched around her heart. Would she ever not respond to him? She hoped the bone-deep addiction eased once they were apart.

Turning her face aside, she broke the kiss. "I'm leaving, Bretton. This changes nothing. Please let me go."

She tugged at her hands, but he wouldn't release them. "I'm coming with you."

"No. You should stay here. This is where you belong. And I never will." Shaking her head, she tried to pull away again. It was hopeless, useless. Whether he loved her or not didn't fix anything. She ignored the dart of pure, sheer joy that he might love her as desperately as she loved him.

His jaw clenched. "I belong with you, so I'm coming with you. You can't stop me any more than I could stop you."

"Why? We both know you want to be chancellor someday. Mating with me would kill that for you. You'll end up bitter and stifled like your father. All because you loved me. I can't be responsible for that, Bretton."

"I'm a grown man, fire fin. You aren't responsible for my decisions. Or their consequences."

"But I have to live with them. The last year I've lived with your decisions and their consequences, and if we mate—if we did something about your feelings—I'd still live with those consequences to some extent."

"If we *mated*, yes. You would. That is the way of matings, I believe. Two lives, two people, a shared existence." His turquoise gaze focused intently on her face. "I'm sorry the consequences of my decisions have hurt you. It was thoughtless, careless. I won't let it happen again."

"Promise?" The question fell from her mouth before she could stop it, but she didn't want to take it back. God, she wanted to believe him. She wanted him. Had always wanted him.

"Yes." His fingers stroked over her wrists, and tingles of awareness slithered over her flesh. She was pressed against the length of him, and only her hands on his chest separated their bodies. "I don't care where we live, Sera, as long as we live together. Mate with me. Today. Now."

"Are you sure? Really sure?" It would kill her if he changed his mind after they were mated. There would be an open wound where her heart had been that would never heal. She knew herself well enough to know she'd never get over that. Never. "You know there's no un-mating for Aquatilians. There's just estrangement like your parents had."

He pulled back a little so only their interlinked fingers connected them, dragged in a deep breath, and spoke in a voice that was just for her but would carry to the rest of the people in the docking bay. "I take you, Sera Gibbons, as my mate that we may walk together as partners on the journey toward perfection."

Her ears buzzed for a moment, and she swayed on her feet. His fingers tightened their grip, holding her steady. She had to concentrate to remember to breathe. "I guess you're sure."

He just smiled, hope and uncertainty warring for dominance in his gaze. She'd never seen such an open look on his face, not even when they were in bed together. Soft and adoring. Loving. That more than anything else convinced her. Her heart hammered in her chest. Before she could get the words out she had to draw a shaky breath. Two.

"I—I take you, Bretton Hahn, as my mate that we may walk together as partners on the journey toward perfection." She glanced down at their joined hands and back up at him. "I don't know if I can be perfect, Bretton. You know me. I won't give up myself for you."

"I wouldn't ask that of you, fire fin. We walk together, hold each other up when we stumble, love each other despite missteps and flaws. If we never reach perfection, then we can enjoy the journey. Together."

She nodded. "I love you, Bretton."

His gaze snapped to Oeric. "You witness this mating?"

"I do, Ambassador."

"My thanks."

"It was my honor." The big merman bowed to them.

Mahlia sniffled, and Varad handed her a saltwater silk kerchief. She flushed, grinned, and dabbed at her eyes. "I love mating ceremonies, though the merpeople have a very brief one compared to those on Vesperi."

Jain grimaced. "The werebear ceremony involves bloodletting for blessings in fertility."

"At least it's interesting." Ketryn tossed her long hair over her shoulder. "The were-dragons' carries on so long, you merely *wish* to stab something for sheer entertainment. Believe me, Mahlia, Vesperi has nothing to Harena."

"Well, your mate would not allow me to come to the ceremony to judge for myself, so I may refuse to believe." Mahlia lifted a cool brow at the slimmer of Ketryn's mates.

Tarkesh chuckled. "Humblest apologies, your majesty. It is the way of our people."

Mahlia's nose wrinkled.

Bretton ignored them, hauled Sera up against him, and kissed her for the first time in public. No shame, no avoidance, just pure, unadulterated passion.

A man cleared his throat loudly. They looked up to see Senator Laddon puffing up from the main dome. Cuthbert followed in his wake, a look of angry determination on his face.

"Ambassador Hahn."

Bretton inclined his head at the two older men. "Senator. Father. Should I even bother to ask what's taken you away from your duties?"

"Counselor Hahn informs me of your intention to mate with—"

"Not intention. It is done."

Cuthbert's turquoise eyes bulged. "She's not a citizen. It can't be legal."

"I challenge anyone to question my mating." His gaze swept the two men and then the gathered men and women who helped the weretigers load the skimmer.

None answered. Silence reigned on the docking bay.

The senator raised his hands in a placating manner. "Ambassador Hahn. Please do not upset yourself. It's unseemly. This...mating of yours seems to be influencing your sense of judgment and decorum. Perhaps your father is right to question how this will affect your position as the chief ambassador."

Bretton's eyes narrowed at the senator. "If you're asking me to choose between my mate and my job, I'll give you my resignation immediately."

Cuthbert choked on the shocked breath he sucked in through his gaping mouth.

The senator sputtered for a moment. "That—this is a most unexpected turn of events. I'm not certain the council will be able to see how she can help you on your journey to perfection."

Bretton focused on Sera's eyes and stroked a thumb down her cheek. "None could aid me in my life's journey as well as Doctor Gibbons—*Hahn*."

Tears welled up in her eyes again, love squeezing her heart.

Senator Laddon's face flushed, and he looked around at the people watching the exchange before he answered. "Very well. You leave me no choice. I accept your resignation."

"*Cynric*," Cuthbert wheezed. "You can't do this to my son. He's not in his right—"

"Done." Bretton nodded to the two men and turned back to Sera. "Shall we leave for Vesperi then, my mate?"

Shock slid like icy fingers down her spine. "Bretton, what are you doing? You're not even going to try to keep your job? This is what you *do*. I don't want you to give that up without a fight."

A laugh straggled out of Bretton. "You were right, Sera. I'll never be perfect. I'm not even sure I want to be if it makes me a bitter, unsatisfied man like my father."

"Bretton—"

He cupped her face in his palms. "Being with you, loving you, is as close to perfection as I've ever been. What wouldn't I give to hold on to that?"

She slid her hands up his back, embracing him. In her wildest dreams, she'd never imagined him walking away from his career for her.

A smile softened his aristocratic features. "I *need* you as I've never needed anyone or anything before. My life is so much better for having you in it."

"I love you."

He laid his forehead against hers. "I love you, too."

Cuthbert broke in again. "Who will be the new head of the ambassadorial corps? No one is as qualified as my son."

"Elia Iden would serve quite well in the ambassador's stead. She has recently returned from a successful expedition." Oeric's voice was deceptively casual.

"I agree." Bretton nodded, straightening.

"The Harenans were quite pleased with her performance." Tarkesh grinned. "And you all know how difficult weredragons are to please."

"I don't want to go to Vesperi." Sera pulled in a breath, drawing Bretton's attention back to her. "With Oeric's help, there's a lot I can do for the other planets from here, but I want to move to Pacifica and help settle it."

Bretton tilted his head, considering. "I think a break from Atlantis is an excellent idea."

"It is wonderful to hear you say that." Chancellor Pell swept into the docking bay in a swirl of sapphire saltwater silk that matched her eyes. "It so happens that our new province at Pacifica will need a governor. I take it you'd like the position."

Senator Laddon folded his arms. "I do not think—"

"That's nothing new for you, Cynric." She snorted back. "You haven't done much in the way of thinking in the last half century. If you started now, you might hurt yourself."

Cynric's eyes bulged. Sera choked on an inappropriate laugh.

The whole room sucked in a breath at the blunt speaking, so rare among the faultlessly polite merpeople. The woman's eyebrow arched. Her wrinkled brow furrowed as she angled Bretton a glance. "When you reach my age, spawn, you'll find that you say what you will and none can gainsay one who has striven for perfection so long and strayed from the path so little."

"My thanks." He inclined his head in respect.

Her arms folded over her chest. "Are you interested in the position or not?"

He blinked, and Sera felt a radiant smile cross her face. His gaze softened when he looked down at her, and he stroked his thumb across her cheekbone. "I'll have to discuss it with my mate before I can—"

"He's interested." Sera turned to the chancellor. "Set up a meeting to confirm it with the Senate the day after tomorrow."

"Why not tomorrow?" The older woman's eyes narrowed in suspicion.

"We've just been mated." A wicked grin curled the corners of Sera's mouth. "We have plans."

"Then I'll leave you to it. Governor Hahn. Doctor Hahn." Her silver head bowed to them, not quite hiding her smile. She spun on her tiny feet and jerked her chin at the two older mermen to precede her down the corridor to the city proper. "Cuthbert. Cynric. We have business matters to discuss. Let the young be."

Bretton's hand curved under Sera's chin, forcing her to meet his gaze. "And the young will be happy, won't they?"

Tears glutted her eyes, but she blinked them away. "*Perfectly* happy."

He huffed out a laugh. "You're certain you don't mind me remaining in politics? I'd give it—"

"I know you would." He *had* given it up. For her. So they could be together. After a year of coming in second to his career, the wonder of that overwhelmed her. Contentment bloomed in her chest, and she closed her eyes for a moment to savor it. When she opened them again, it was to see the same quiet peace reflected in his beautiful eyes. "You need to be involved. There are going to be some serious changes here with the Pacifica settlement. More than the Senate is willing to admit. I don't think anyone could make that happen as well as you."

"Only with you beside me to remind me when I'm being a *cold fish*." He arched his brow and tightened his arms around her waist.

She slid her fingers through the loose strands of his hair. She loved seeing it down.

"Count on me."

"I do, fire fin. I do." He winked at her, and her laugh was smothered by his kiss.

This was real perfection. Not striving constantly, but savoring this moment, this breath, this heartbeat. With him. He was right about that. The journey was the most important part, and they'd travel it together. And that, for her, was perfect.

THE END

Want to read bonus short stories in the Wereplanets series?
Join Crystal's mailing list for FREE copies:
https://www.crystaljordan.com/bonus-content

About Crystal Jordan

Crystal Jordan is originally from the San Francisco Bay Area but has lived and worked all over the United States as an academic librarian. After many years of wandering, she returned to her home state and now resides in southern California with her husband. An award-winning author, Crystal has published paranormal and futuristic romance independently and with publishers such as Harlequin, Kensington Books, and Entangled Publishing.

Also by Crystal Jordan

On the Prowl series

Claim Me

Take Me

Need Me

The Between series

Between Lovers

Taken Between

Between the Sheets anthology

Twilight of the Gods series

Reclaimed by the Immortal Viking Wolf

Reclaimed by the Immortal Viking Bear

Reclaimed by the Immortal Viking Shifter anthology

In the Heat of the Night series

Total Eclipse of the Heart

Big Girls Don't Die

It's Raining Men

Crazy Little Thing Called Love

Wereplanets series

In Ice

In Heat

In Smoke

In Mist

Excerpt from Claim Me

Antonio watched the men circle his mate from atop a building far above the alley they'd cornered her in. A few nimble leaps brought him to the end of the shadowed corridor. He jerked his clothes off and dropped them as he ran, shifted into his Panther form to let his black fur blend into the night, and stalked the men as they had stalked her.

The predators became the prey.

He ran his tongue down a long fang, anticipation and rage boiling hot in his veins. They would pay for scaring her. God and all the saints couldn't save them if they harmed her.

It had taken two days to track her scent after he'd sensed her in the city. And now he'd found her. Nothing compared to the ice that froze the blood in his veins when he heard her first scream, the terror of seeing men hunt her. Yes, these men would beg for his mercy before the night was through. A growl rumbled from his chest as he moved down the alley, his claws clicking on the pavement.

When one of the men grabbed for her, a roar ripped from his throat. Everyone froze, turning in slow motion to stare at the newcomer. A Panther. He bared his teeth and watched the man closest to him turn ghostly pale. He could smell their fear, taste the tang of it on his tongue, and he took a small amount of satisfaction in that.

This close, even his rage couldn't cloud the fact that the men weren't human. They were Panthers, like him. Worse, they were from his Pride. The Ruiz brothers—Javier, Felipe, and Roberto. His own people, under his rule. Why would they hunt a Panther female? If she belonged to another Pride and was visiting his territory, then her Pride leader would hold him responsible for any harm his people caused her. Not to mention she was his mate and he would shred them alive for hunting her in the first place.

She screamed, and the frozen tableau broke into chaos. Antonio lunged forward, slicing his claws into Roberto's calf. He went down with a spray of blood and saliva, squealing and clutching his leg.

Antonio leaped over the fallen man to sprint forward, intent on reaching his mate. Felipe shifted to Panther form, hissing a warning, but it meant nothing to Antonio. They were past the point of warnings. A single leap forward and the two of them clashed midair, claws and fangs tearing into each other. Antonio slashed across the young Panther's face and he rolled away with a whimper, his black fur matted with dark crimson blood.

Antonio's tail whipped around as he sprang for Javier. The man—barely more than a teen—tried to climb the wall, but he had no more chance of escape than Antonio's mate had. Antonio dragged him down to the ground, his fangs digging into the man's jeans. Both front paws planted on the younger man's chest, making him wheeze, and Antonio shoved his face into Javier's. A growl vibrated his vocal cords, and what little blood was left in the man's face fled. His bloodshot eyes went wide with horror.

His mate's soft cry reached Antonio's ears, jerking him back from the edge of feral. He shuddered, fighting the instincts of his Panther nature. He turned toward her, wanting to comfort her and soothe her fear.

But she wasn't looking at him—she snarled at Felipe, bracing her back against the wall as she hissed deep in her throat. A purr rumbled his chest at her courage.

Javier took the opportunity to speak. "Please, sir. Listen to me. She doesn't deserve protection. She's a—"

A roar ripped free from Antonio's throat as he transformed into his human form. He hoisted the shorter man up by his T-shirt until they were nose to nose. *"Silence!* The three of you will be in my study when I return to the mansion. Is that clear?"

"But how long until—"

"Obey me. You won't enjoy the consequences if you don't. But I will." He dropped Javier to his feet. The younger man scrambled away and ran. His brothers had already disappeared.

He turned back to his mate. "Are you all right?"

"Yes. You?" She shoved her dark hair out of her face, her fingers sifting through the streaks of blond that shot through the long strands. He soaked in the details of her, taking in every curve of her face and body. Her chocolate-brown eyes searched him and they went wide when she saw the straining erection jutting between his thighs. Shifting back had left him naked. A wry smile pulled at his lips. He was going to have to figure out where he'd dropped his clothes and hope some vagrant didn't steal them before he got there. For the moment, he focused on his mate.

She sucked in a quick breath when he took a step toward her. Swaying on her feet, she stared at him for long moments. The silence stretched to a fine breaking point. She shook her head, pressing the heel of her hand to her forehead. "It can't be."

She'd finally sensed it—that they were mates.

"Oh, but it can be. It is." Stalking forward, he backed her up against the brick wall. His nostrils flared to catch her sweet scent, the one he would become addicted to. He had no doubt she had the same adrenaline humming through her as he did, and it morphed into something hotter, more carnal. Anger and fear still pumped through his system. His shaking fingers fisted at his sides. His eyes narrowed at her and a dart of excitement flashed through her gaze. The delicate smell of her wetness filled his nostrils. It was heady. She swallowed, her lids dropping to half-mast.

She released a breathy laugh, and naked want shone in her gaze. "I don't believe it. We can't be mates."